THE RUINS

ROBERT CRUISE

Table of Contents

ONE:

A DEFEATED GERMANY

On 10 May 1945, the morning light filtered weakly through a veil of ashen clouds, casting a pallid glow over the ruins of Hamburg. Klaus Engelhardt stood before what remained of his home, the once-sturdy brick façade now a jagged skeleton against the grey sky. The air was thick with the lingering scent of smoke and the faint tang of salt from the nearby harbour. He clutched the tarnished handle of his walking stick, his knuckles white, as he surveyed the devastation that stretched as far as the eye could see.

"*Vater, sollen wir hineingehen?* (Father, should we go inside?)" Frieda's voice broke the heavy silence. She stood beside him, her eyes reflecting both determination and sorrow. At 22, her youthful face bore the lines of weariness beyond her years. Klaus glanced at his daughter, nodding curtly. Words felt cumbersome, inadequate to bridge the chasm of despair that separated them.

Marta moved past them, her footsteps crunching over shattered glass and splintered wood. "We must see what's left," she murmured, her voice steady but laced with an undercurrent of urgency. She tightly pulled back her greying hair, with strands escaping to frame a face etched with resilience. She navigated the debris with practised ease, as if the act of moving forward could ward off the paralysis of hopelessness.

Hans lingered at the edge of the rubble-strewn path; his hands shoved deep into the pockets of his threadbare coat. At 17, his eyes held a storm of defiance and confusion. He kicked a loose stone, watching it skitter into the gutter where rainwater mingled with soot. The distant wail of a siren echoed through the streets, a haunting reminder of the omnipresent turmoil.

Klaus took a tentative step towards the gaping doorway of their apartment building. The entrance hall was a cavern of shadows, the familiar marble floor obscured by layers of dust and debris. Memories flickered at the edges of his mind—the echo of laughter, the warmth of gatherings now lost to time. He felt a surge of bitterness rise within him, a bile that tasted of defeat and betrayal.

"Careful, there might be loose beams," Marta cautioned, her gaze fixed on the precarious ceiling. She reached out to steady a fallen picture frame, its glass cracked but the photograph intact—a sepia-toned image of their family in happier times. She brushed the dust away with a gentle hand, her eyes glistening.

Frieda moved purposefully towards what had been the sitting room. Once the centrepiece of countless evenings, the grand piano lay in ruin—its polished wood marred by deep gouges, strings snapped and twisted. She pressed a key out of habit; a discordant note rang out, hanging in the air like a lament.

"*Es ist alles zerstört* (It's all destroyed)," Hans muttered from the doorway, his tone a mix of anger and resignation. He kicked at a broken chair, the clatter echoing sharply. "What's the point?"

Marta shot him a stern look. "We salvage what we can. We start again."

"Start again?" Hans scoffed. "In this?" He gestured broadly at the devastation surrounding them. "The Allies have left us with nothing."

"Enough," Klaus barked, his voice harsher than intended. The weight of his son's words pressed upon him, igniting a familiar shame. The uniform he wore felt like a mockery—a relic of a cause that had led them to ruin. He turned away, unable to meet Hans' gaze.

Outside, the sound of footsteps approached. Neighbours emerged from the shadows, faces gaunt and eyes hollow. *Frau Müller*, a woman of Marta's age, clutched a bundle of belongings tied in a faded cloth. *"Guten Morgen,"* she offered weakly.

"Frau Müller," Marta acknowledged, forcing a semblance of a smile. "How are you managing?"

"As well as any of us can, I suppose." *Frau Müller's* gaze drifted to the Engelhardts' home. "If you need anything, we're all trying to help one another."

"Thank you," Marta replied softly. "We'll manage."

Klaus stepped back into the daylight, the sky overhead now threatening rain. He watched as an Allied jeep rolled by, the soldiers inside casting indifferent glances at the Germans picking through the remnants of their lives. He felt a flush of anger, his fists clenching involuntarily.

Frieda joined him, her eyes following his line of sight. "They are not all our enemies, *Vater*," she said quietly.

He grunted in response. "They occupy our city. They treat us like beggars in our own land."

She sighed. "The war is over. We must live in this new reality."

Klaus turned to face her, his eyes hard. "A reality they have forced upon us. Do not be so quick to forget what they have done."

"And what of what we have done?" Frieda's voice was barely above a whisper, yet it cut through the air sharply. "We cannot ignore our own actions, our own…" She hesitated, searching for the words.

"Enough." His tone brooked no argument. He strode away, the conversation leaving a bitter taste in his mouth.

Marta watched the exchange from a distance, her heart heavy. She approached Frieda, placing a comforting hand on her shoulder. "Give him time," she murmured.

"Time won't change the past," Frieda replied, her gaze fixed on her father's retreating figure.

Hans sifted through the remaining items in his room inside the remnants of their home. He picked up a scorched photograph of himself and his friends, all smiles and youthful arrogance. The edges crumbled between his fingers. With a frustrated sigh, he tossed it aside.

"Finding anything?" Marta asked gently as she entered.

"Just rubbish," he replied tersely.

She knelt beside him, sifting through the debris. "We can rebuild. We'll make this place liveable again."

Hans shook his head. "What's the point, Mutter? The world we knew was gone. There's nothing left here for us."

She paused, weighing her words. "Home is not just a building, Hans. It's where we are together."

He met her eyes briefly before looking away. "Maybe for you."

Outside, the first drops of rain began to fall, tapping softly against the rubble. Klaus stood under the fractured archway of the doorway, allowing the rain to dampen his face. It was a cold, cleansing sensation that momentarily washed away the grime, but not the weight he carried within.

He recalled the date—10 May 1945. Just days earlier, on 7 May, Germany had surrendered unconditionally. The news had spread like wildfire, igniting a mixture of relief and despair. For Klaus, it signified the collapse of everything he had believed in, misguided as it may have been.

A distant church bell tolled a sombre melody that resonated through the empty streets. Klaus closed his eyes, the sound stirring memories of Sundays long past, of family gatherings unmarred by conflict. He longed for the simplicity of those times before the fervour of nationalism had consumed them all.

Frieda approached cautiously. "Vater, come inside. You'll catch a cold."

He opened his eyes, regarding her thoughtfully. "Perhaps that would be a mercy," he muttered.

She frowned. "Don't say such things."

He sighed heavily. "What would you have me say? That I see hope in this desolation? That I believe we can simply pick up the pieces and carry on?"

"We must try," she insisted. "For all our sakes."

He studied her earnest expression, a flicker of something akin to pride stirring within him. "You are strong, Frieda. Stronger than I."

"It's not about strength," she replied softly. "It's about necessity."

He nodded absently, his gaze drifting once more to the horizon where the skeletal remains of buildings pierced the skyline. "Tell me, do you think they will ever forgive us?"

She followed his gaze. "Who?"

"The world. For what we've done."

She hesitated. "Forgiveness begins with ourselves. We must acknowledge our part before we can hope for absolution."

He gave a bitter laugh. "Spoken like someone who believes in redemption."

"Don't you?" she challenged gently.

He didn't answer, instead turning away to re-enter the building.

As evening approached, the family gathered in what remained of the kitchen. Marta had managed to scavenge some canned goods, and a small fire flickered in the hearth, providing a modicum of warmth. They ate in silence, the crackling of the fire the only sound.

Hans broke the silence abruptly. "I heard the Americans are setting up food stations."

Marta looked up. "We can see about getting supplies tomorrow."

Klaus grunted. "Accepting handouts from them now, are we?"

Marta's eyes flashed. "We have little choice, Klaus. Pride won't fill our stomachs."

He glared at her but said nothing further.

Frieda pushed her bowl aside. "I can go in the morning. Perhaps I can find out about any work opportunities as well."

Hans snorted. "Work? Doing what? Cleaning up their mess?"

"Rebuilding, Hans," she replied patiently. "We need to rebuild our city, our lives."

He shook his head. "You're deluding yourself."

"Enough," Marta interjected firmly. "We cannot afford to fight amongst ourselves."

The room fell silent once more.

Later that night, Klaus stood alone on what had been their balcony, now a precarious ledge overlooking the darkened streets. The rain had ceased, leaving the air crisp and cool. He lit a cigarette with shaky hands, inhaling deeply. The glow of the embers cast fleeting shadows across his worn features.

He thought of the men he had served with, many of whom would not be returning to scenes such as this. He wondered if their fate was kinder than his own. Survivor's guilt gnawed at him, a relentless ache that no amount of rationalisation could soothe.

"Vater?" Hans's voice startled him. He hadn't heard his son approach.

"What is it?" he asked without turning.

Hans hesitated. "I… I wanted to ask you something."

Klaus exhaled slowly. "Go on."

"Do you regret it? Any of it?"

Klaus felt a surge of irritation. "What kind of question is that?"

"A fair one," Hans replied, his tone steady. "Do you regret the war? Fighting for what we did?"

Klaus turned to face him, the flicker of the cigarette illuminating his stern expression. "You wouldn't understand."

"Try me."

He considered his son for a long moment. "We believed we were fighting for our country's future."

"And now?"

"Now…" He paused, searching for words. He paused, searching for words, and said, "Now I see perhaps we were misled."

Hans pressed on. "Did you know about… the camps? What they were doing to people?"

Klaus's jaw tightened. "Where is this coming from?"

"Answer the question."

"That's enough, Hans."

"No, it's not!" Hans's voice rose. "People are saying terrible things about what was done. Things I can't believe we'd be part of."

Klaus's gaze hardened. "War is terrible. Atrocities happen on all sides."

"That's not an answer."

"It's the only one I have," Klaus snapped. "Go to bed."

Hans stared at him, a mix of disappointment and disgust clear in his eyes. "Perhaps you're right. Maybe I don't understand you at all." With that, he turned and retreated inside.

Klaus stood alone once more, the weight of the conversation settling heavily upon him. He crushed the cigarette underfoot; the ember extinguished against the cold stone.

In the days that followed, the Engelhardt family settled into a grim routine. Frieda ventured into the city centre, joining queues for food rations and seeking information about reconstruction efforts. She returned each day with meagre supplies and news of the changing landscape—Allied directives, emerging local councils, whispers of trials for war criminals.

Marta focused on making their home habitable, patching holes and salvaging materials. She traded with neighbours, bartering for essentials in a makeshift economy born of necessity.

Hans wandered the city, being drawn to gatherings where people made impassioned speeches about Germany's future. He listened to voices calling for socialism, for a new order that rejected the old ways. The ideas ignited something within him—a sense of purpose, a way to channel his anger.

Klaus remained withdrawn, and his interactions with his family were strained and infrequent. He avoided the Allied patrols, harbouring a simmering resentment that threatened to consume him. The date weighed on him—15 May 1945—another day in a world he scarcely recognised.

One evening, Frieda returned home with a stack of newspapers. "There are reports coming in from all over," she announced. "They're uncovering more about what happened during the war."

Marta looked up from her sewing. "What do you mean?"

"Atrocities. Authorities imprisoned and killed people in camps. The Allies are publishing everything."

Hans entered the room, drawn by the conversation. "I've heard about this too."

Klaus shifted uncomfortably. "Propaganda," he muttered. "They seek to demonise us further."

Frieda shook her head. "These are facts, *Vater.* We can't ignore them."

"We don't know the full story," he insisted.

"Maybe we should find out," Hans interjected. "Maybe we need to face the truth."

Klaus's eyes flashed with anger. "You would take their word over your own countrymen?"

"Our countrymen may have lied to us," Frieda said softly.

Marta intervened. "This isn't helping. Arguing won't change what's happened."

"She's right," Frieda agreed. "But we mustn't hide from the truth. If we are to rebuild, we need to acknowledge our past."

Klaus stood abruptly. "I will not sit here and listen to this." He left the room, the echo of his footsteps fading down the corridor.

The remaining family members exchanged weary glances.

"He can't avoid this forever," Hans remarked.

"Give him time," Marta urged. "He's struggling, just as we all are."

Frieda sighed. "Time may not be enough."

That night, Klaus wandered the deserted streets. The moon cast a pale glow over the ruins, shadows stretching like spectres. He passed the remnants of shops and cafes, their signs hanging askew, windows shattered. The silence was oppressive, broken only by the distant bark of a dog or the rustle of debris underfoot.

He reached the harbour, where the charred skeletons of ships jutted from the water like broken teeth. The smell of brine mingled with the lingering scent of smoke. He stood at the pier's edge, gazing out over the dark expanse. The weight of his memories pressed upon him—the camaraderie of soldiers, the adrenaline of battle, the justifications that now rang hollow.

"15 May 1945," he whispered to himself, as if anchoring his existence to the date could provide clarity. "What have we become?"

The question lingered unanswered in the night air.

As dawn approached, Klaus made his way back home. The first rays of sunlight pierced the horizon, casting a fragile light over the devastated city. He entered the apartment quietly, careful not to disturb his sleeping family.

In the small hours of the morning, he sat at the worn kitchen table, a cup of cold water cradled in his hands. The enormity of their situation settled upon him—a defeated nation, a fractured family, a future shrouded in uncertainty.

He resolved then to try, if only for the sake of those he held dear. To find a path forward, to navigate the rubble of their lives with whatever strength he could muster. It was a tiny spark of determination in the vast darkness, but it was something.

The rest of the Engelhardt family slept upstairs, unaware of the quiet shift within their patriarch. Outside, Hamburg stirred, its inhabitants rising to face another day amidst the ruins.

ooo

The first day of June arrived with a sullen sky, the sun obscured by a thick haze that clung to the ruins of Hamburg like a shroud. Klaus Engelhardt stood at the window of their partially restored apartment, gazing out at the skeletal remains of the neighbouring buildings. The distant hum of Allied vehicles patrolling the streets was a constant reminder of the new reality they faced. He tightened his grip on the windowsill, the rough wood biting into his palms.

"*Die Amerikaner sind wieder unterwegs* (The Americans are on the move again)," Hans remarked, entering the room with a sullen expression. At seventeen, his youthful features were hardened by lines of frustration and restlessness. He slouched against the wall, arms crossed tightly over his chest.

Klaus glanced at his son, noting the smudge of dirt across his cheek and the defiance in his eyes. "They are everywhere," he replied curtly, his voice heavy with disdain. "Our city crawls with them."

Hans shrugged. "Perhaps they will bring food. People are saying they have supplies."

"At what price?" Klaus snapped. "Our dignity? Our freedom?"

Before Hans could retort, Marta appeared in the doorway, wiping her hands on a faded apron. "Breakfast is ready," she announced softly. "Come and eat before it gets cold."

In the small kitchen, the family gathered around a worn table. The meal was meagre—a thin broth made from scraps and a loaf of dense, coarse bread. Frieda entered last, her hair neatly braided, a determined set to her jaw.

"Good morning," she greeted, placing a small jar of jam on the table. "I traded for this at the market."

Marta offered a faint smile. "That's wonderful, *Liebchen.*"

They ate in near silence, the clatter of spoons against bowls the only sound. Klaus's gaze drifted to the newspaper folded beside his plate, the headlines proclaiming new directives from the occupying forces. He pushed it aside with a grunt.

Frieda noticed. "You should read it, *Vater.* There is information we need to know."

"I have no interest in their propaganda," he replied tersely.

"It's not propaganda," she insisted. "They're establishing order, setting up systems to help us rebuild."

Klaus slammed his hand on the table, the sudden movement causing the dishes to rattle. "Rebuild under their terms! Do you not see how they seek to control us?"

Marta placed a calming hand on his arm. "Please, Klaus. This won't help."

Hans leaned forward, his eyes flashing. "Maybe Frieda is right. Maybe we need to accept things as they are."

Klaus glared at him. "You would so readily bow to them?"

"I'm tired of fighting," Hans retorted. "What good has it done to us?"

Frieda intervened. "We all want the same thing—a chance to move forward."

Klaus pushed back from the table, rising abruptly. "You may do as you wish. I will not surrender what little pride we have left." He stormed out of the room, leaving a heavy silence in his wake.

Marta sighed, her shoulders slumping. "He just needs time."

"Time won't change the situation," Hans muttered. "We have to adapt."

Frieda reached across the table to squeeze his hand. "We'll find a way."

Navigating the complexities of life under occupation, the Engelhardts found the days stretched on, with each one blending into the next. Amidst the rubble filling the streets, struggling civilians filled the buzzing atmosphere created by the patchwork of Allied patrols. The occupying forces, carrying identification papers, imposed curfews, became mandatory for everyone. The sound of foreign languages—English, French, Russian—mingled uneasily with the German spoken by the locals.

On 7 June 1945, Frieda ventured into the city centre, a basket hooked over her arm. She weaved through the crowded streets, avoiding the gaze of the American soldiers who loomed in every corner. The marketplace was a shadow of its former self, stalls sparsely filled and vendors wary.

"Fräulein Engelhardt!" a voice called out. She turned to see *Herr Becker*, a portly man with a kind face, beckoning her from his stall.

"Guten Tag, Herr Becker," she greeted him warmly.

He offered a small sack. "Potatoes. Not many, but better than nothing."

She smiled gratefully. "Thank you. What do you ask in return?"

He waved a dismissive hand. "Consider it a favour. Your family has always been good to me."

"That's very generous."

He leaned in conspiratorially. "Be careful, *ja?* The soldiers are watching everything. There are rumours of arrests."

Her brow furrowed. "Arrests? For what?"

"Anything, it seems. They are looking for anyone associated with the Party or the military."

Frieda felt a chill run down her spine. "I understand. Thank you for the warning."

As she made her way home, her mind raced. She thought of her father and his service in the Wehrmacht. Though he had never been an ardent supporter of the Party, his role could draw unwanted attention. She quickened her pace, and the weight of the potatoes suddenly felt much heavier.

At home, she found Klaus seated in the parlour, staring blankly at a photograph in his hands. It was a picture of him in uniform, standing proudly beside his fellow officers.

"Vater," she began cautiously. "We need to talk."

He looked up, his eyes distant. "What is it?"

She sat beside him. "There are reports that the Allies are conducting investigations. Looking for those connected to the military."

He sighed wearily. "They will find many. The war involved us all."

"Perhaps we should prepare in case they come here."

He met her gaze. "What would you have me do? Deny who I am? Hide like a criminal?"

"I'm asking you to be cautious. For our family's sake."

He considered her words before nodding slowly. "Very well. I will be discreet."

On 15 June 1945, their fears materialised. A sharp knock echoed through the apartment. Marta answered the door to find two American soldiers flanked by a German interpreter.

"Good afternoon," the interpreter began. "We are conducting routine inspections. May we come in?"

Marta hesitated, but stepped aside. "Of course."

The soldiers entered, their eyes scanning the room with practised efficiency. "We need to see identification for all residents," the interpreter stated.

Klaus appeared, his face a mask of controlled emotion. He presented his papers silently. The soldiers scrutinised them before moving on to the others. Once satisfied, they began a systematic search of the apartment.

Hans watched them with a mixture of curiosity and resentment. "Is this necessary?" he asked.

The interpreter responded coolly. "These are standard procedures."

Frieda felt a surge of indignation as the soldiers rifled through drawers and cupboards. She clenched her fists, willing herself to remain calm. Marta stood beside her, a hand resting lightly on her arm.

One soldier emerged from Klaus' study, holding a small box. He opened it to reveal medals and insignia from Klaus's military service.

"These are to be confiscated," the interpreter declared.

Klaus stepped forward. "Those are my belongings."

"All military paraphernalia is to be surrendered."

Klaus's jaw tightened. "They are symbols of honour."

"Symbols of a regime that no longer exists," the interpreter replied sharply.

Before Klaus could protest further, Marta intervened. "Please, take them if you must."

He turned to her, betrayal flickering in his eyes. "Marta—"

She held his gaze steadily. "It's for the best."

The soldiers completed their search, taking with them any items they deemed significant. As they departed, the interpreter offered a curt nod. "Thank you for your cooperation."

Once they were alone, the tension in the room erupted.

"How could you let them do that?" Klaus demanded, his voice shaking with anger.

Marta faced him calmly. "We had no choice. Resisting would have only made matters worse."

He threw up his hands in frustration. "They strip us of everything! Our possessions, our dignity—"

Hans interjected. "Perhaps we don't need such relics anymore. Maybe it's time to let go."

Klaus turned to him. "You speak of letting go? Those medals represent my life's work!"

"An outdated legacy," Hans shot back. "Look where it has led us."

"Enough!" Frieda shouted, her voice ringing through the room. "We are tearing ourselves apart while the world moves on without us."

Silence fell as the weight of her words settled over them.

Marta sighed heavily. "We must live in this new world. Fighting amongst ourselves will solve nothing."

Klaus sank into a chair, the fight draining from him. "I don't know how," he admitted quietly.

Frieda approached him, her expression softening. "We can help each other, but we have to be willing."

He nodded absently, his gaze fixed on a spot on the floor. "Perhaps you're right."

The days that followed were a study in contrasts. The Engelhardts attempted to resume some semblance of normal life, even as the occupiers' presence grew more pronounced. Curfews tightened, and resources became scarcer. Yet amidst the hardship, small acts of kindness emerged—a neighbour sharing extra rations, children playing amidst the rubble with makeshift toys.

On 22 June 1945, Frieda attended a meeting organised by local community leaders. Held in the remains of the town hall, the gathering aimed to discuss rebuilding efforts and the formation of citizen committees.

"Thank you all for coming," began Herr Schneider, a respected teacher. "We face immense challenges, but together we can begin the process of recovery."

Frieda listened intently as they outlined plans for clearing debris, establishing food cooperatives, and liaising with the Allied authorities. The atmosphere was one of cautious optimism, a stark contrast to the pervasive despair.

After the meeting, she approached Herr Schneider. "I would like to volunteer," she said. "Anything I can do to help."

He smiled warmly. "Your enthusiasm is most welcome, Fräulein Engelhardt. We need young people like you."

As she walked home, Frieda felt a glimmer of hope. Perhaps there was a path forward, a way to contribute positively amidst the turmoil.

Back at the apartment, she shared her experiences with her family over a simple dinner.

"That's admirable," Marta praised. "We should all do our part."

Hans looked sceptical. "Working with the Allies? You're just playing into their hands."

"It's about rebuilding our community," Frieda countered. "Not about allegiance."

Klaus remained silent, pushing food around his plate.

Marta glanced at him. "What do you think, Klaus?"

He met Frieda's eyes briefly before looking away. "If it helps, then perhaps it's worth considering."

Frieda felt a surge of encouragement. "We can make a difference, *Vater.*"

He nodded slowly. "Yes, perhaps."

On 30 June 1945, the city posted a notice announcing mandatory registration for all former military personnel. Failure to comply would cause severe penalties.

Klaus read the notice with a sinking feeling. "They are tightening the noose," he remarked bitterly.

"We should prepare," Marta advised. "Gather any documents they might require."

He shook his head and uttered, "They will not be satisfied until they have completely stripped us bare."

"Defiance will only bring trouble," Frieda cautioned. "We need to be prudent."

Hans observed his father thoughtfully. "Maybe this is an opportunity."

Klaus raised an eyebrow. "An opportunity for what?"

"To show them we have nothing to hide. That we can be part of the solution."

Klaus considered his son's words. "You are suggesting cooperation?"

"Yes," Hans affirmed. "A new beginning."

Klaus recognised the irony. His children were encouraging him to follow a path of compliance he had vehemently opposed. Yet perhaps they saw possibilities he could not.

"Very well," he conceded. "We will do as required."

That evening, as the family gathered their papers, a quiet determination settled among them. The act of organising documents became a metaphor for assembling the fractured pieces of their lives.

Frieda carefully arranged certificates and letters, her fingers lingering over a photograph of the family from years past. She handed it to Klaus. "We should keep this safe."

He gazed at the image—a moment frozen when the future had seemed inevitable. "Thank you," he whispered.

Marta placed a gentle hand on his shoulder. "We will get through this."

He covered her hand with his own. "Together."

As June drew to a close, the Engelhardts stood on the precipice of an uncertain future. The Allied occupation had imposed a new order that challenged their identities and beliefs. Yet amidst the adversity, there were signs of resilience—a willingness to adapt, a glimmer of hope for reconciliation.

The city of Hamburg remained scarred, and its once-grand architecture was reduced to rubble. But within its streets, life persisted. Neighbours forged new connections, children laughed despite the ruins, and the scent of fresh bread occasionally wafted from makeshift bakeries, mingling with the lingering aroma of smoke.

On the night of 30 June 1945, Klaus stood once more at the window, the moon casting a silvery light over the landscape. He watched as a group of American soldiers passed by, their voices carrying softly in the stillness.

"*Es ist eine neue Welt* (It is a new world)," he murmured to himself. A new world indeed—one he did not fully understand, but one he was accepting.

Behind him, the soft sounds of his family preparing for bed echoed through the apartment. The familiar creaks of the floorboards and the murmur of hushed conversations were all reminders that some things remained constant amidst the chaos.

He turned away from the window, extinguishing the lamp. As he made his way to his room, he paused outside Hans' door. Faintly, he could hear his son humming a tune—a melody Klaus recognised from his own youth.

A small smile touched his lips. Perhaps there was hope, after all.

ooo

Early autumn leaves rustled softly along the cobblestone streets of Hamburg, their golden hues starkly contrasting with the grey rubble still dominating the cityscape. On 15 September 1945, a chill wind swept through the broken windowpanes of the Engelhardt residence, carrying the distant sound of church bells tolling—a reminder of time passing, of seasons changing even amidst the devastation.

Frieda sat hunched over the kitchen table, the dim light of a single lamp casting elongated shadows across scattered newspapers. Her fingers traced the bold headlines: reports of camps, of unspeakable horrors emerging from the ashes of the Third Reich. Each word was a dagger, piercing the fragile cocoon of denial she had unconsciously woven around herself.

"*Mutti,* have you seen this?" she called out, her voice trembling slightly. Marta appeared in the doorway, wiping her hands on a faded dishcloth.

"What is it, *Liebchen?*" Marta asked, concern etching lines deeper into her already weary face.

Frieda handed her mother the newspaper, her eyes searching Marta's for a glimmer of understanding. As Marta scanned the article, her expression shifted from curiosity to shock and then to profound sorrow.

"Mein Gott," Marta whispered. "I had heard whispers, but I didn't… I couldn't have imagined,"

Frieda nodded slowly. "How could we not have known? How could anyone not have known?"

Marta sank into a chair beside her daughter, the weight of the revelation pressing down upon her. "Perhaps we didn't want to see," she admitted softly.

The air grew heavy between them, laden with unspoken questions and the suffocating guilt that now seeped into every corner of their consciousness.

In the days that followed, Frieda became a voracious consumer of information. She sought every newspaper and every radio broadcast that offered details about the unfolding truths. On 20 September 1945, she attended a gathering at the local community centre, where a British officer presented a slideshow of photographs taken at the liberated camps.

The emaciated figures stared blankly at the camera, the mass graves hastily covered, and the belongings piled high like macabre monuments seared into her memory. The room was silent save for the occasional gasp or muffled sob. When the presentation ended, Frieda remained seated, her hands clasped tightly in her lap.

"Fräulein Engelhardt?" A gentle voice interrupted her thoughts. She looked up to see Greta Schmidt, a journalist she recognised from previous meetings.

"Yes?" Frieda replied, her voice barely above a whisper.

"I've seen you at several of these events," Greta said, offering a small, sympathetic smile. "It's heartening to see others seeking the truth."

Frieda managed a weak smile in return. "It's overwhelming," she confessed. "I feel as though I've been living in a fog."

Greta nodded. "Many of us do. But acknowledging the past is the first step towards rebuilding our future."

They walked together into the crisp evening air, the scent of burning wood mingling with the pervasive odour of damp stone. "Have you considered getting involved more actively?" Greta asked. "Groups are forming, advocating for transparency and justice."

Frieda considered the proposal. "I want to help," she said earnestly. "But I don't know where to start."

"Come to our next meeting," Greta suggested. "We could use passionate voices like yours."

"Thank you," Frieda replied. "I will."

At home, however, Frieda faced a different challenge. On 25 September 1945, she attempted to share her experiences with her father. Klaus sat in his armchair, the glow of his pipe casting a warm halo around his stern features. The radio played softly in the background—a soothing classical piece that contrasted with the turmoil within the household.

"*Vater,* may I speak with you?" Frieda ventured cautiously.

Klaus glanced up, his eyes reflecting a guarded curiosity. "Of course."

She took a deep breath. "I've been attending some meetings. Learning more about… about what happened during the war."

He stiffened slightly. "What do you mean?"

"About the camps," she continued. "About the people who suffered, who were killed," she continued.

Klaus shifted uncomfortably. "You shouldn't involve yourself with such things. It's all propaganda meant to vilify us further."

"It's not propaganda," Frieda insisted, her voice rising. "These are facts, documented by witnesses and even our own soldiers."

He frowned deeply. "I was a soldier and saw none of what they claim."

"Perhaps not directly, but can you truly say you did not know?"

Klaus stood abruptly, his pipe clattering onto the side table. "You accuse me of complicity?"

She met his gaze unwaveringly. "I am asking you to acknowledge the possibility that we, as a nation, allowed terrible things to happen."

He turned away, his hands clenched into fists. "I fought for my country, for our survival. War is brutal—atrocities occur on all sides."

"That doesn't excuse our responsibility," she pressed.

He whirled around, anger flashing in his eyes. "Enough, Frieda! I will not have you disrespecting the sacrifices made by honourable men."

Before she could respond, he stormed out of the room, leaving her standing alone amidst the echoes of their confrontation.

Marta found Frieda in the kitchen later that evening, staring blankly at a cup of untouched tea. "I heard raised voices," Marta whispered. "Is everything all right?"

Frieda sighed heavily. "I tried to talk to *Vater* about the reports. He refuses to listen."

Marta placed a comforting hand on her daughter's shoulder. "He's struggling, *Liebchen.*"

"So am I," Frieda replied bitterly. "But ignoring the truth won't change it."

"Give him time," Marta urged. "We all need time to process what's happening."

As October settled in, the atmosphere within the Engelhardt household grew increasingly tense. Hans started spending more time away from home, attending gatherings where they fiercely discussed ideas about socialism and a new Germany.

On 10 October 1945, Hans returned home late, his eyes alight with a fire that Frieda hadn't seen before.

"Where have you been?" she asked, noting the flushed excitement on his face.

"Meeting with some comrades," he replied evasively.

"Comrades?" she echoed. "What are you getting involved in?"

He shrugged. "People who believe in building a better future. Without the shackles of the past."

She regarded him carefully. "And what does that entail?"

"Embracing new ideologies," he explained. "Moving towards equality and away from the corruption that led us here."

Frieda felt a pang of concern. "Be careful, Hans. Aligning yourself with radical groups could be dangerous."

He laughed dismissively. "You're one to talk, attending your own meetings and lectures."

"Seeking truth differs from blindly following a new doctrine," she retorted.

He bristled. "At least I'm taking action, not just wallowing in guilt."

Before she could respond, he brushed past her, disappearing into his room. The realisation left Frieda grappling with the fact that she scarcely understood the world her brother was slipping into.

On 20 October 1945, organisers arranged a public exhibition in the city square, displaying artefacts and testimonies from the concentration camps. Frieda attended, despite the icy drizzle that dampened the event. She overheard snippets of conversations as she wandered among the displays—some expressing disbelief, others denying.

A man beside her shook his head at a photograph. "This must be exaggerated," he muttered. "They wouldn't allow such things."

Frieda turned to him. "But they did. And we must face it."

He eyed her sceptically. "You believe everything they tell you?"

"I believe the evidence before me," she asserted. "We cannot rebuild on a foundation of lies."

He scoffed and walked away, leaving her feeling isolated yet resolute.

Returning home that evening, Frieda found Klaus seated at the dining table; papers spread out before him. He glanced up as she entered. "We need to discuss something," he said solemnly.

She hesitated. "What is it?"

"I've received notice that former officers are being called to account for their actions," he explained. "There are forms to fill out, declarations to make."

"That's a good thing," she replied cautiously. "Transparency is important."

He sighed. "You don't understand. They are looking for scapegoats, people to blame."

"Perhaps they are seeking justice," she countered.

He shook his head. "Justice? Or vengeance? The lines become blurred."

She approached the table, her gaze softening. "*Vater,* if you have nothing to hide, there's nothing to fear."

He met her eyes, a flicker of vulnerability breaking through his stoic façade. "I did what was necessary. I followed orders."

"Sometimes orders are wrong," she said gently.

He looked away. "It's not that simple."

"Maybe not," she conceded. "But acknowledging our mistakes is the first step towards healing."

He remained silent, and she placed a hand on his arm. "We can face this together."

He nodded slowly, though his expression remained distant.

As November arrived, the Engelhardts found themselves increasingly pulled in different directions. On 5 November 1945, Marta attended a church service, seeking solace amidst the turmoil. The pastor spoke of forgiveness and reconciliation, his words echoing through the sparsely filled sanctuary.

After the service, Marta lingered, lighting a candle for those lost—both known and unknown. She whispered a silent prayer for her family, for unity and understanding.

At home, Frieda continued her efforts to engage her father and brother in dialogue. On 15 November 1945, she organised a modest family dinner, hoping to bridge the widening gaps between them.

The meal started awkwardly, with benign comments about the weather and the repairs being made to the building. Finally, Frieda broached the subject that weighed heavily on her mind.

"I've been thinking," she began, "perhaps we could all attend one of the community meetings together."

Hans rolled his eyes. "Not interested."

Klaus raised an eyebrow. "What purpose would that serve?"

"It might help us understand each other's perspectives," she suggested.

Hans scoffed. "You mean you'd like us to adopt your views."

"That's not fair," she protested. "I simply want us to have an open discussion."

Klaus set down his fork. "These meetings—are they not led by those seeking to undermine what little stability we have left?"

"People lead them who want to ensure we don't repeat the mistakes of the past." she clarified.

Hans pushed his chair back. "I've had enough. I won't sit here and allow someone to lecture me."

"Hans, please," Marta implored.

He shook his head. "No, *Mutter.* I'm tired of this constant guilt-tripping. We need to look forward, not dwell on what's done."

With that, he left the table, his footsteps echoing down the hall.

Frieda turned to her father. "*Vater,* will you at least consider it?"

He showed thoughtfulness as he addressed Frieda, saying, "I appreciate your intentions, but I fear our beliefs are too divided."

"Then let's find common ground," she urged.

He sighed heavily. "Perhaps in time."

On 30 November 1945, the tension reached a breaking point. Frieda returned home to find Klaus sitting alone, a nearly empty bottle of schnapps beside him. A glazed look came over his eyes, with a mixture of sorrow and anger simmering beneath the surface.

"*Vater,* have you been drinking?" she asked gently.

He looked up, his expression hardening. "Is that your concern now? My habits?"

She took a seat across from him. "I'm worried about you."

He laughed bitterly. "Worried that I won't conform to your new moral compass?"

"That's not fair," she replied. "I'm trying to help us all come to terms with what's happened."

He slammed his fist on the table, causing the bottle to topple over. "You presume to judge me? To judge all of us who sacrificed everything?"

She recoiled slightly, but held her ground. "I'm not judging. I'm asking you to see the truth."

"Whose truth?" he challenged. "Is that the one written by our enemies? The one that paints us all as monsters?"

She was insistent that the evidence was undeniable. "We cannot hide from it."

He staggered. "I did what I had to do. For our country. For our family."

"At what cost?" she demanded, tears welling in her eyes. "While we turned a blind eye, how many lives did we destroy?" she demanded, tears welling in her eyes.

He shook his head vehemently. "I won't listen to this."

"You can't keep running away," she implored. "We must face this together."

He glared at her, his voice cold. "Perhaps it's you who can't accept reality."

She rose, her composure slipping. "Our nation committed atrocities, and we have a responsibility to acknowledge them."

He pointed a trembling finger at her. "You are naïve, blinded by guilt sown by those who wish to keep us subdued."

"Denial won't absolve us," she retorted. "It only perpetuates the cycle of ignorance."

Their words hung in the air, sharp and unforgiving. Finally, Klaus turned away, his shoulders sagging. "I have nothing more to say."

Frieda watched as he retreated to his room, the door closing with a resounding thud. She sank back into her chair, the weight of helplessness settling upon her.

Marta entered quietly, having overheard the exchange. She placed a comforting hand on Frieda's back. "He needs time," Marta whispered.

Frieda shook her head. "Time won't heal this wound if we don't address it."

"Perhaps," Marta conceded. "But pushing too hard may only drive him further away."

"I don't know what to do," Frieda admitted, her voice barely audible.

"Be patient," her mother advised. "Continue to lead by example. Your intentions are noble, and he may come to see that in time."

As November drew to a close, the Engelhardt family found themselves fragmented, each member grappling with their own inner turmoil. The once warm and inviting home now felt cold, shadows lurking in the corners where light once prevailed.

Outside, the city of Hamburg showed signs of renewal. Reconstruction efforts were underway, and the spirit of resilience flickered among the populace. Yet, for the Engelhardts, the path to healing remained obscured by the lingering ghosts of the past.

On the evening of 30 November 1945, Frieda stood by the window, gazing out at the moonlit streets. Snow had fallen softly, blanketing the ruins in a thin layer of white—a deceptive purity overlying the scars beneath.

She whispered a silent vow to herself: to continue seeking truth, advocate for justice, and hold onto the hope that her family and country could find redemption.

Behind her, the faint strains of a familiar lullaby drifted from Marta's room, a melancholic melody that echoed the unspoken yearning for peace.

In his room, Klaus sat alone, the dim glow of a candle illuminating the worn photograph of his unit. He traced the faces with a calloused finger, memories of camaraderie clashing with the harsh realities he could no longer ignore.

Hans lay awake in his bed, staring at the ceiling. The ideologies he once clung to seemed insufficient now, and questions gnawed at the edges of his conviction.

Like Germany itself, the Engelhardts stood at a crossroads—a precipice between acknowledging the darkness of the past and forging a path towards a brighter, more honest future.

ooo

The first breath of December 1945 settled over Hamburg like a frigid blanket, the air sharp with the promise of a harsh winter. Snowflakes drifted lazily from a leaden sky, settling atop the skeletal remains of bombed-out buildings. Though battered and sparse, the Engelhardt family's apartment offered a semblance of shelter against the encroaching cold.

Marta stood by the frosted windowpane, her breath forming ephemeral clouds on the glass. She watched as neighbours shuffled through the snow-laden streets, their figures hunched against the biting wind. Ration books clutched tightly, they queued in endless lines for meagre portions. The war had ended, but the struggle for survival had only begun.

On 5 December 1945, Marta wrapped a woollen shawl around her shoulders, the fabric thin but comforting. "Frieda, I'm heading to the market," she called out, her voice steady despite the gnawing uncertainty that plagued her.

Frieda appeared from the small bedroom, tucking a loose strand of hair behind her ear. "I'll come with you, Mutti," she offered. "Perhaps we can find extra potatoes this time."

Marta nodded appreciatively. "Every bit helps."

The streets were a patchwork of ice and rubble, the once-vibrant city reduced to shades of grey and white. As they navigated the treacherous paths, the scent of burning coal mingled with the distant strains of a violin— a melancholic melody echoing from a nearby alley.

At the marketplace, a cacophony of voices filled the air. Stalls were sparse, many vendors having nothing left to sell. An old man with a weathered face held up a single jar of jam, his eyes pleading. "*Bitte,* only a few Reichsmarks," he implored.

Frieda's heart ached at the sight. "How much do we have left?" she whispered to Marta.

"Not enough," Marta replied grimly. "We'll have to make do with what we have."

As they moved through the crowd, a group of children darted past, their laughter incongruous amidst the desolation. One of them, a little girl with pigtails and smudged cheeks, offered Frieda a folded piece of paper. "For you," she said shyly before scampering away.

Frieda unfolded it to reveal a hastily drawn dove, a symbol of peace rendered in charcoal. She smiled softly, tucking it into her coat pocket. "Hope persists, even now," she mused.

On 10 December 1945, Hans returned home late, his boots caked with mud and his eyes shadowed. Klaus, seated at the kitchen table, glanced up sharply. "Where have you been?" he demanded.

Hans shrugged off his coat, avoiding his father's gaze. "Out. Just… around."

Klaus's brow furrowed. "These are dangerous times to be wandering. They strictly enforce the curfew."

"Since when do you care about following their rules?" Hans retorted, a hint of defiance colouring his tone.

"Mind your tongue," Klaus warned, his voice low.

Marta intervened, sensing the brewing conflict. "Perhaps we should all sit down to dinner. The stew is still warm."

Hans shook his head. "I'm not hungry." Without another word, he disappeared into his room, the door closing with a muted thud.

Frieda exchanged a worried glance with Marta. "He's been distant lately," she remarked.

Marta sighed. "He's struggling to find his place in all this. We all are."

As the days passed, the Engelhardts settled into a tenuous routine. Marta dedicated herself to stretching their scant resources, often rising before dawn on 20 December 1945 to queue for rations. She bartered and traded, sometimes venturing into the shadows of the black market—a clandestine network that thrived amidst scarcity.

One evening, Marta returned home with a small sack of flour tucked discreetly beneath her coat. Frieda eyed it cautiously. "Is that from the usual vendor?" she asked.

Marta hesitated before replying. "No, but we cannot afford to be selective. This will help us through Christmas."

Frieda nodded slowly. "I worry about the risks."

"Desperate times call for desperate measures," Marta said firmly. "I won't let us starve."

On 24 December 1945, the family gathered around a modest Christmas tree, its branches adorned with handmade ornaments crafted from scraps of fabric and paper. The flickering glow of a single candle cast warm shadows across their faces.

Klaus cleared his throat. "Despite everything, we are together. For that, I am grateful."

"Frohe Weihnachten," they echoed, the sentiment heartfelt even in its simplicity.

Hans presented a small package to Frieda. "It's not much," he admitted.

She unwrapped it carefully to reveal a worn copy of Goethe's poems. "It's wonderful," she said sincerely, her eyes meeting his. "Thank you."

For a fleeting moment, the weight of their struggles lifted, replaced by a sense of unity and hope.

But the respite was short-lived. On 2 January 1946, the chill deepened, temperatures plummeting to record lows. Pipes froze, and electricity became intermittent. The Engelhardts huddled together for warmth, layering every blanket they possessed.

Food became scarcer. Ration portions dwindled, and the queues grew longer. Marta's ventures into the black market became more frequent, her determination unwavering.

On 6 January 1946, Hans approached Marta as she prepared to leave. "Let me go to your place," he offered.

She eyed him sceptically. "It's not safe."

"I'm stronger," he insisted. "I can handle myself."

Marta considered his proposal. "Very well, but be cautious. And avoid the main streets."

Hans nodded, a flicker of resolve in his eyes. "I will."

That evening, Hans returned with a loaf of bread and a tin of preserved meat. "It's not much, but it's something," he said, placing them on the table.

"Thank you," Marta replied, relief clear in her voice.

Frieda watched him closely. "Where did you find these?"

"An acquaintance," Hans replied evasively.

"Be careful," she warned. "The authorities are cracking down on illegal trade."

He shrugged. "We have to survive somehow."

On 12 January 1946, fate caught up with them. Hans was making his way back from a transaction when Allied soldiers emerged from the shadows, their torches illuminating the dark alley.

"Halt!" one of them commanded.

Hans froze, his heart pounding. "I was just—"

"Hands where we can see them," the soldier barked.

They searched him, uncovering the contraband tucked beneath his coat. The interpreter sternly declared that black market trading is prohibited.

Hans swallowed hard. "I was only trying to feed my family."

"Tell it to the magistrate," the soldier replied, hauling him towards their jeep.

The Allied outpost interrogated Hans for hours. The fluorescent lights cast a harsh glare, amplifying his exhaustion. They eventually let him go with a hefty fine and a stern warning.

When Hans stumbled through the door in the early hours of 13 January 1946, his clothes dishevelled and faced ashen; the family rushed to his side.

"What happened?" Marta exclaimed, guiding him to a chair.

He recounted the ordeal, his voice strained. "They took everything. And they imposed a fine of fifty Reichsmarks on us."

Klaus's expression darkened. "This comes from consorting with criminals."

"I was helping us survive!" Hans retorted, his frustration boiling over. "While you sit here doing nothing!"

"Watch your tongue," Klaus snapped, rising to his feet. "You bring shame upon this family."

"Shame?" Hans laughed bitterly. "We lost our honour long ago."

"Enough!" Marta interjected, stepping between them. "This solves nothing."

Klaus's gaze hardened. "Your leniency has led him astray," he accused Marta.

"Don't you dare blame her," Frieda interjected, her eyes flashing. "We're all doing what we can."

Klaus clenched his fists. "In my day, we understood discipline and respect."

Hans met his stare unflinchingly. "Your day is over. Look around you—everything you stood for lies in ruins."

Silence engulfed the room, the weight of Hans's words hanging heavily. Klaus's shoulders slumped, the fight draining from him. Without another word, he retreated to his room, the door closing with a resounding finality.

Marta sank into a chair, her face etched with worry. "This family is tearing apart," she whispered.

Frieda placed a comforting hand on her mother's shoulder. "We'll find a way through."

Over the following days, the atmosphere in the household remained tense. Klaus withdrew further, spending hours staring out of the window or poring over old photographs. On 20 January 1946, Frieda found him sitting alone, a faded picture clutched in his hands.

"Vater," she began softly. "May I join you?"

He glanced up, his eyes distant. "If you wish."

She sat beside him, the silence stretching. "I know things have been difficult," she ventured.

He exhaled. "I feel… powerless."

"We all do, in some ways," she admitted. "But perhaps we can channel that into rebuilding."

He shook his head. "The world I've known is gone. Replaced by uncertainty and humiliation."

Frieda searched for the right words. "Change is inevitable. But we can choose how we respond."

He met her gaze briefly. "You have always been the optimist."

She smiled gently. "And you have always been strong. We need that strength now."

He nodded slowly. "Perhaps you're right."

On 23 January 1946, Frieda attended a meeting at the community centre, where discussions about democratic reconstruction were gaining momentum. Men and women of varying ages filled the room, their faces reflecting determination and hope like a mosaic.

As he took the podium, the speaker declared, "We stand at a crossroads. Our nation has been brought low, but we can build a better future from this devastation."

Frieda felt a stirring within her. The words resonated, igniting a spark of purpose. After the meeting, she approached the organiser. "I'd like to volunteer," she said.

"Welcome," he replied warmly. "We need all the help we can get."

Meanwhile, Hans found solace in the writings of socialist thinkers, intrigued by the promise of equality and a new societal order. On 1 March 1946, he attended a gathering in a dilapidated warehouse, where like-minded youths debated passionately.

"The old systems have failed us," one proclaimed. "It's time to embrace a new ideology—one that serves the people, not the elite."

Hans listened intently, feeling a sense of belonging he hadn't experienced in months.

At home, the divide between the siblings became more pronounced. Frieda's involvement with democratic initiatives clashed with Hans's burgeoning socialist ideals.

On 24 January 1946, they found themselves embroiled in a heated debate.

"Democracy is the path forward," Frieda insisted. "It allows for freedom and representation."

Hans countered, "Democracy under capitalist influence only perpetuates inequality. Socialism offers true fairness."

"You speak of fairness, yet socialism can lead to authoritarianism," she argued.

"Only if corrupted. At its core, it empowers the masses," he retorted.

Marta intervened, her voice weary. "Please, enough. We cannot afford to be divided."

Frieda softened. "You're right, Mutti. We need unity now more than ever."

Hans nodded reluctantly. "Agreed."

On 28 January 1946, someone informed the family that their fine had increased because of late payment. The financial strain became critical.

"We'll have to sell more belongings," Marta concluded grimly.

Klaus stood abruptly. "No. We've sacrificed enough."

"What choice do we have?" Marta challenged gently.

He took a deep breath. "Perhaps it's time I sought employment."

Frieda looked at him with surprise. "Do you think that's possible?"

"I can try," he replied. "There must be work for someone with my experience."

On 1 February 1946, Klaus ventured into the city, seeking opportunities. He encountered rejection at every turn—people often shunned former military officers, considering their pasts a barrier to reintegration.

Returning home, he confessed to his failure. "No one will hire me," he admitted, defeat lacing his words.

Marta placed a reassuring hand on his arm. "We'll find another way."

In the early days of February, the Engelhardt family gathered around their modest table, the remnants of a simple meal before them.

"Next month, the thaw will come," Frieda observed. "Spring brings new beginnings."

Hans offered a small smile. "Perhaps better times are ahead."

Klaus gazed at his children, a mixture of pride and melancholy in his eyes. "You both have grown so much."

Marta reached across the table, her hand covering his. "We'll face whatever comes together."

TWO:

THE HUNGER WINTER

The dawn of 8 February 1946 broke over Hamburg with cruel indifference, the sun a pale disc behind a veil of grey clouds. Snowflakes drifted silently, settling atop the mounds of rubble that once were shops and homes. The city's wounds were raw and aching, much like those of its inhabitants.

In the Engelhardt home, a battered building that only provided the bare necessities of shelter, frost clung stubbornly to the inside of the cracked windowpanes. Klaus sat at the scarred wooden table in the kitchen, his hands wrapped around a chipped porcelain cup of lukewarm water. His breath formed faint wisps in the frigid air, disappearing as quickly as the warmth in his hands.

Marta moved about the cramped kitchen with measured purpose. Her reddened and numb fingers struggled to grip the tarnished spoon as she stirred a thin gruel in a dented pot. The meagre contents barely covered the bottom, a watery mixture of potatoes and wilted cabbage leaves salvaged from yesterday's ration queue.

Frieda stood beside her mother, her eyes fixed on the swirling steam that offered a fleeting illusion of warmth. She reached out to steady the pot as Marta's hand trembled. "Let me, *Mutti,*" she suggested softly.

Marta nodded gratefully, stepping back to rub her hands together. *"Danke, Liebchen,"* she whispered. "The cold has seeped into my bones."

Klaus watched them in silence, a heaviness settling in his chest. The sound of the spoon scraping against metal seemed unnaturally loud in the stillness. He glanced around the kitchen—the peeling wallpaper, the empty shelves, the faded family photograph hanging crookedly on the wall.

Memories of better times flickered at the edges of his mind, taunting him with their unattainable comfort.

"Perhaps we should light the stove," Frieda suggested, her breath visible as she spoke.

Marta shook her head. "We must conserve the coal. There is so little left."

Klaus cleared his throat, his voice rough. "We cannot live like this," he muttered.

Marta turned to him, her eyes weary but resolute. "What choice do we have?"

He looked away, unable to meet her gaze. "There must be a way to improve our situation without resorting to… dishonourable means."

Frieda's jaw tightened. "Dishonourable? *Mutti* is doing everything she can to keep us alive."

"By bartering with thieves and profiteers," Klaus retorted, his tone edged with bitterness.

"Enough," Marta interjected firmly. "This is not the time for arguments. We need to stand together."

A heavy silence descended upon them. Outside, the wind howled, rattling the loose window frames. The chill seemed to penetrate deeper, settling into their very cores.

Over the next few days, the cold intensified. On 14 February 1946, the temperature plunged further, and the city's already fragile infrastructure strained under the weight of the relentless winter. Pipes froze and burst, electricity flickered intermittently, and the ration queues grew longer as supplies dwindled.

Marta ventured out daily, braving the treacherous streets in search of food. She clutched a worn satchel close to her body, its contents a collection of personal items she hoped to trade—a silver locket, her mother's wedding band, a set of porcelain figurines that had miraculously survived the bombings.

One afternoon, as she navigated the icy pathways between collapsed buildings, she encountered *Frau Müller*, a neighbour with whom she occasionally shared resources.

"Grüß dich, Helga," Marta replied, offering a faint smile.

"Any luck today?" Helga inquired, nodding towards Marta's satchel.

"Not yet," Marta admitted. "But I remain hopeful."

Helga sighed. "It's becoming more difficult. The merchants demand more for less."

"Desperation breeds greed," Marta observed quietly.

"Take care, my friend," Helga cautioned. "There are rumours of increased patrols. The Allies are cracking down on black market activities."

"I will be cautious," Marta assured her.

Marta's thoughts drifted to her family as she continued on her way. The weight of responsibility pressed heavily upon her. Each trade felt like a small surrender of their past, fragments of their lives exchanged for the barest necessities. Yet, she pushed forward, driven by an unwavering resolve to see her family through these dark times.

Back at the apartment, Frieda busied herself with mending clothes, her fingers stiff from the cold. The rhythmic motion of needle and thread offered a semblance of normalcy. Hans sat nearby, huddled under a thin blanket, his gaze distant.

"Have you heard from any of your friends?" Frieda asked, attempting to engage him.

Hans shrugged. "Most have left the city. Those who remain keep to themselves."

She hesitated before continuing. "Perhaps we could attend one of the community meetings together. They're discussing ways to improve conditions."

He glanced at her sceptically. "Talking won't fill our stomachs."

"It might lead to solutions," she countered gently.

He shook his head. "I prefer to focus on immediate needs."

Frieda sensed the undercurrents of frustration and restlessness within her brother. "Be careful, Hans," she cautioned. "Desperation can lead to dangerous choices."

He met her gaze briefly before looking away. "I could say the same to you."

Marta returned home later than usual on the evening of 17 February 1946, her cheeks flushed from the cold and exertion. She placed a small bundle on the table—a loaf of coarse bread and a few potatoes.

"Where did you find these?" Klaus demanded, eyeing the items warily.

Marta met his gaze steadily. "I traded."

"With whom?" he pressed.

"Does it matter?" she replied calmly. "We have food for a few more days."

Klaus's expression hardened. "At what cost? Our dignity?"

"Our survival," Marta corrected firmly. "I will not let pride stand in the way of keeping our family alive."

He stood abruptly, the chair scraping against the floor. "I cannot condone this."

"Then offer an alternative," she challenged. "What have you done to improve our circumstances?"

Frieda intervened, her voice soft but insistent. "Please, let's not fight. We need to support each other."

Klaus turned away, his shoulders slumped. "I am going for a walk."

As the door closed behind him, Marta sank into a chair, exhaustion etched into her features. "I don't know how much more of this I can endure," she whispered.

Frieda placed a comforting hand on her mother's arm. "We will get through this, *Mutti.*"

Marta sighed deeply. "Your father is struggling. His pride blinds him to reality."

"He feels helpless," Frieda observed. "Perhaps we can include him."

Marta offered a wan smile. "Your compassion is a gift, Frieda. Never lose it."

Frieda decided on 20 February 1946 as the cold showed no signs of relenting. The family's food supplies were nearly exhausted, and the ration queues yielded little. She approached Marta cautiously.

"*Mutti,* I want to help," she began.

Marta regarded her daughter with a mix of concern and curiosity. "What do you have in mind?"

"I can go to the market district," Frieda proposed. "Perhaps I can trade some of my belongings for food."

Marta hesitated. "It's risky. And your father would not approve."

"I know," Frieda acknowledged. "But we cannot afford to let pride dictate our actions."

Marta considered her words carefully. "Very well. But you must be cautious. Avoid the main thoroughfares and keep a low profile."

"I will," Frieda promised.

That evening, under the cover of darkness, Frieda bundled herself in layers of worn clothing. She tucked a few precious items—a silver bracelet, a silk scarf—into a small satchel. With a determined breath, she slipped out into the night.

The streets were eerily quiet; the snow muffling her footsteps. Shadows stretched long and menacing under the sparse glow of gas lamps. She navigated the labyrinth of alleys, her senses heightened.

Reaching the edge of the market district, she spotted a cluster of figures huddled around a makeshift stall. A man with a thick beard and wary eyes glanced up as she approached.

"I have items to trade," she replied, keeping her voice steady.

He eyed her appraisingly. "Let's see them."

She revealed the bracelet and scarf. "These are valuable," she offered.

He inspected them briefly. "I can give you two loaves of bread and some cured meat."

"That's hardly fair," she protested.

"Take it or leave it," he shrugged. "Times are tough."

Frieda weighed her options. "Fine," she conceded.

As they completed the exchange, a sudden commotion erupted nearby. Allied soldiers emerged, their torches casting stark beams across the market.

"Everyone, halt!" one of them commanded.

Panic spread like wildfire. Traders grabbed their goods, scattering into the night. Frieda clutched her satchel tightly, her heart pounding.

Before she could react, a soldier shone his light directly at her. "You there, stop!"

She froze, her mind racing. "I'm just returning home," she stammered.

He approached cautiously. "What are you carrying?"

"Just some bread for my family," she replied, attempting to sound composed.

He regarded her suspiciously. "It's past curfew. You should not be out."

"I'm sorry," she apologised. "I lost track of time."

After a tense moment, he nodded. "Go straight home. And be careful."

"Thank you," she breathed, relief washing over her.

She hurried away, the adrenaline coursing through her veins. Reaching the safety of their building, she slipped inside quietly.

Upstairs, Marta awaited her anxiously. "Did everything go well?" she whispered.

"Mostly," Frieda admitted. "I had a close call with a patrol."

Marta's eyes widened. "They didn't catch you, did they?"

"No, but it was a reminder of the risks," Frieda said, placing the food on the table.

Marta embraced her tightly. "I'm glad you're safe."

As they prepared for bed, the tension of the evening lingered. Frieda's thoughts churned, a mix of fear and resolve.

The family gathered for breakfast. The meagre spread included the bread and meat Frieda had bought.

Klaus eyed the food suspiciously. "Where did this come from?"

Frieda met his gaze steadily. "I traded for it."

His expression darkened. "You went to the black market?"

"Yes," she replied firmly. "We needed food."

He slammed his fist on the table, causing the dishes to rattle. "I forbade such actions!"

"You forbade us from surviving?" Frieda challenged, her voice rising. "We cannot endure this winter on pride alone."

"You defy me," he accused, his face flushed with anger.

"I act because you will not," she retorted. "Mutti and I are doing what is necessary."

Klaus stood abruptly. "This is unacceptable. You endanger us all."

Marta intervened, her tone measured but firm. "Klaus, sit down."

He glared at her. "You support this disobedience?"

"I support keeping our family alive," she stated calmly. "We cannot afford to let stubbornness dictate our choices."

Hans watched silently, tension clear in his posture.

Klaus's shoulders sagged, the fire in his eyes dimming. "You have no respect for authority," he muttered.

"Authority has failed us," Frieda countered gently. "We must adapt."

He sank back into his chair, the weight of defeat settling upon him. "Perhaps I am no longer needed," he whispered.

Marta reached out to touch his hand. "We need you, Klaus. But we need you to understand our reality."

He withdrew his hand. "I need some air."

As he left the room, the remaining family members exchanged weary glances.

"I didn't mean to upset him," Frieda sighed.

"He must come to terms with our circumstances," Marta reassured her. "In time, he may see reason."

Hans spoke up for the first time. "Perhaps we can find a way to involve *Vater*. Give him a purpose."

Frieda considered his suggestion. "That's a good idea. Maybe he can help with repairs around the neighbourhood or assist others in need."

Marta nodded. "It might restore his sense of worth."

That afternoon, Frieda found Klaus sitting on a bench overlooking the frozen Elbe River. She approached cautiously.

"May I join you?" she asked softly.

He gestured vaguely. "If you wish."

They sat in silence for a moment, the icy wind biting at their faces.

"I'm sorry for defying you," Frieda began.

He sighed. "You were right. I have been holding onto ideals that no longer serve us."

She glanced at him, surprised by his admission. "We are all adjusting."

He turned to face her. "I feel… useless. My family is lacking the provisions. I cannot protect you."

"You can still guide us," she encouraged. "Your experience is valuable."

He gave a faint smile. "Perhaps."

She took a deep breath. "We thought you might help others in the community. There are many who could benefit from your skills."

He considered her words. "What could I offer?"

"Organisation, leadership," she suggested. "Assisting with rebuilding efforts."

He nodded slowly. "I will think about it."

As they made their way back home, the sky began to clear, revealing a hint of pale blue amidst the grey. The air, though still cold, carried a subtle promise of change.

That evening, the family shared a modest meal. The atmosphere was lighter; a tentative peace settled among them.

"Tomorrow is a new day," Marta remarked. "Perhaps it will bring better fortunes."

"Let's hope so," Hans agreed.

Klaus raised his cup of weak tea. "To resilience," he toasted quietly.

"To resilience," they echoed, clinking their cups gently.

The shadows danced softly on the walls, and for a moment, warmth blossomed in the hearth of their hearts. Despite the hardships, they faced the uncertain future together, bound by the unspoken strength of familial love.

As February 1946 drew to a close, the Engelhardt family nestled into their beds, the chill of the night tempered by layers of blankets and the closeness of shared hope. Outside, the city of Hamburg lay shrouded in snow, its ruins bathed in the silvery light of the moon—a silent testament to endurance and the quiet defiance of those who refused to be broken.

ooo

The first of March 1946 dawned with a tentative warmth, the sun casting pale rays over the battered skyline of Hamburg. Patches of snow clung stubbornly to the shadows, but the air carried a hint of spring's promise. Frieda stood at the window of the Engelhardt apartment, watching as droplets of melting ice traced lazy paths down the glass. The city, though still scarred, seemed to breathe a sigh of relief as winter loosened its grip.

"Komm, Frieda," Marta called softly from the kitchen. "Breakfast is ready."

Frieda turned away from the window, the faint smile on her lips fading as she entered the dimly lit room. Someone set the table with care, but the offerings were sparse—a loaf of coarse bread, a small dish of butter, and a pot of weak tea.

"Did you sleep well?" Marta asked, her eyes reflecting concern.

"Well enough," Frieda replied, taking a seat beside her mother. "The sound of the ice melting kept me awake, but it's a welcome change."

Hans shuffled into the kitchen, rubbing sleep from his eyes. "Perhaps the thaw will bring better fortunes," he mumbled, reaching for a slice of bread.

Klaus entered last, his posture rigid, eyes distant. "Spring or not, there's much work to be done," he remarked curtly, seating himself at the head of the table.

Marta poured tea into their mismatched cups. "I've heard there's a meeting at the community centre today," she said, glancing at Frieda. "They are organising efforts to clear the rubble."

Frieda nodded eagerly. "Yes, I plan to attend. It's important that we all contribute to the rebuilding."

Klaus scoffed lightly. "Rebuilding under the watchful eyes of the occupiers. How generous of them to allow us to clean our own streets."

"Klaus, bitte," Marta admonished gently. "This is an opportunity for us to restore our city."

He looked away, his jaw tightening. "Restore it to what? A shell of its former self?"

Frieda's gaze hardened. "We have to start somewhere, Vater. Holding onto the past won't change our circumstances."

An uneasy silence settled over the table, broken only by the sound of Hans tapping his fingers against his cup.

On 5 March 1946, Frieda made her way to the makeshift community centre, a converted school building whose walls bore the scars of bomb blasts. The hall buzzed with activity—men and women of all ages gathered around tables strewn with maps and lists. The air was thick with a mix of determination and uncertainty.

"Frieda!" a familiar voice called out. She turned to see Greta Schmidt approaching, her satchel slung over one shoulder.

"Greta, it's good to see you," Frieda greeted warmly.

"I didn't expect to find you here," Greta admitted. "Are you volunteering?"

"Yes," Frieda affirmed. "I want to help in any way I can."

Greta smiled appreciatively. "That's admirable. I'm covering the reconstruction efforts for the newspaper."

"Then we'll be working side by side," Frieda remarked. "Perhaps we can catch up over coffee later?"

"I'd like that," Greta agreed.

As the meeting began, an American officer stepped forward, his uniform crisp against the backdrop of the dilapidated hall. "Good morning," he began in accented German. "Thank you all for coming. Together, we can rebuild Hamburg into a thriving city once more."

Murmurs rippled through the crowd—some were sceptical, others hopeful. Frieda listened intently as they described plans for debris removal, ration distribution, and the restoration of essential services.

After the meeting, Frieda joined a group assigned to clear rubble from a nearby street. Armed with shovels and wheelbarrows, they worked tirelessly, the physical labour providing a cathartic release from months of pent-up frustration.

On 15 March 1946, as the sun climbed higher in the sky, Frieda wiped sweat from her brow, catching her breath. An elderly man beside her leaned on his shovel. "It's hard work, but it's honest," he remarked.

She nodded. "It feels good to be making a difference."

He extended a calloused hand. "Josef Müller."

"Frieda Engelhardt," she replied, shaking his hand firmly.

"Your family must be proud," Josef observed.

Frieda's smile faltered slightly. "I hope so."

Returning home that evening, Frieda found Klaus sitting alone in the parlour, his gaze fixed on the fading light outside. "You're back late," he noted without turning.

"The days are longer now," she replied, removing her coat. "There's much to be done."

He sighed heavily. "Working for them won't change anything."

"I'm working for us," she countered gently. "For our future."

He shook his head. "Our future is no longer ours to shape."

She approached him cautiously. "*Vater,* I know this is difficult. But we have to move forward."

He finally met her eyes, a flicker of sadness clear. "You are young, Frieda. You believe in possibilities that no longer exist."

"Only if we refuse to see them," she insisted.

He stood abruptly. "I'm tired. Good night."

As he retreated to his room, Frieda felt a pang of sorrow. The chasm between them seemed to widen with each passing day.

On 1 April 1946, Hans began attending meetings with a group of youths exploring new political ideologies. One afternoon, he approached Frieda as she prepared to leave for the community centre.

"Do you have a moment?" he asked hesitantly.

"Of course," she replied, noting the seriousness in his expression.

"I've been thinking," he began, "about the direction our country is taking."

She regarded him thoughtfully. "Go on."

"I believe that socialism offers solutions to the inequalities we've faced," he continued. "I've met people who are passionate about rebuilding Germany based on fairness and shared prosperity."

Frieda considered his words. "I understand the appeal, but we must be cautious. Aligning ourselves too closely with any ideology can be dangerous."

He frowned slightly. "Isn't that what you're doing with the Americans?"

"I'm working to rebuild our city," she clarified. "Politics aside, we need to restore basic living conditions."

He nodded slowly. "Perhaps we can both contribute in our own ways."

"Perhaps," she agreed, offering a small smile. "Just promise me you'll be careful."

"I will," he assured her.

Meanwhile, Marta continued her efforts to secure provisions for the family. On 6 April 1946, she ventured to the market district, where stalls were reappearing amidst the ruins. Fresh produce and lingering smoke permeated the air with their mingled scents.

Approaching a vendor, Marta examined a basket of apples. "Wie viel? (How much?)" She inquired.

"Fünf Reichsmark per kilo (Five Reichsmarks per kilo)," the vendor replied.

She hesitated. "That's quite steep."

He shrugged. "

She negotiated gently, eventually settling on a fair price. As she turned to leave, she spotted Jakob Fischer across the way. His stern demeanour and sharp gaze set him apart from the bustling crowd.

"Jakob," she greeted cautiously as he approached.

"Marta," he acknowledged with a curt nod. "I see you're embracing the new order."

She bristled slightly. "I'm purchasing food for my family."

He glanced disdainfully at the vendors. "Feeding into the hands of profiteers."

"We all must do what we can to survive," she retorted.

He smirked. "Some of us refuse to compromise our principles."

"Principles won't keep us warm at night," she replied evenly.

"Perhaps not," he conceded. "But dignity is worth preserving."

She met his gaze steadily. "Take care, Jakob."

"Give my regards to Klaus," he said as she walked away.

That evening, Marta recounted the encounter to Klaus. "He's as obstinate as ever," she concluded.

Klaus sighed. "Jakob has his convictions."

"And you share them?" she pressed gently.

He hesitated. "I understand his perspective."

She placed a hand on his arm. "We can't live in the past, Klaus. Our children need us to be present."

He looked away. "It's not that simple."

"Maybe it is," she suggested softly. "Perhaps we can bridge the gap."

The family gathered for dinner—a modest meal of potato soup and freshly baked bread. The atmosphere was lighter than it had been in months.

"I heard a wonderful piece of news today," Frieda announced. "They're planning to reopen the library next month."

"That's excellent," Marta responded. "It's been too long since we've had access to books."

Hans perked up. "I'd like to visit when it opens."

"Perhaps we can go together," Frieda suggested.

Klaus offered a faint smile. "It's good to see some normalcy returning."

Marta seized the moment. "Maybe we could all attend the community fair next week. It would be nice to enjoy an outing as a family."

Hans agreed readily. "I'd like that."

Klaus hesitated before nodding. "Very well."

The fair brought a burst of colour and life to the war-torn city. Banners fluttered in the breeze, and the sounds of laughter and music filled the air. The Engelhardts strolled among the stalls, sampling treats and admiring handmade crafts.

Frieda spotted Greta near a carousel. "Greta! Over here!"

Greta joined them, her camera slung around her neck. "Isn't this marvellous?" she exclaimed. "It's like a breath of fresh air."

"It truly is," Marta agreed.

Klaus watched a group of children playing a game of ring toss. Their carefree joy seemed both foreign and familiar. "It's good to see the younger generation finding happiness," he mused.

"Perhaps there's hope after all," Marta said quietly, slipping her hand into his.

As the sun set, casting a warm glow over the fairgrounds, the family found a spot to sit and enjoy the evening. Hans leaned back, gazing at the sky. "I can't remember the last time we did something like this."

"It's been too long," Frieda agreed.

Klaus took a deep breath. "Maybe it's time I joined the efforts to rebuild," he admitted.

Frieda turned to him, her eyes bright. "We could use your help, *Vater.* Your experience would be invaluable."

He nodded thoughtfully. "I can't promise I'll agree with everything, but I can no longer stand idle."

Marta squeezed his hand. "That's all we ask."

Frieda attended another community meeting a few weeks later, featuring a panel of American officials and local leaders. Anticipation filled the room as the panel unveiled plans for rebuilding infrastructure.

A young American engineer stepped forward. "We aim to restore electricity to all districts by the end of the year," he announced. "With your cooperation, we can achieve this goal."

Applause rippled through the audience, and Frieda felt a surge of optimism. After the meeting, she approached the engineer. "Excuse me," she began, "how can I assist with these efforts?"

He smiled warmly. "Volunteers are essential. We need people to help with coordination, translation, and on-the-ground tasks."

Offering her language skills, she said, "I'm fluent in both English and German." "I can help bridge communication gaps."

Handing her a leaflet, he replied with gratitude. "Join us at the site tomorrow morning."

Returning home, Frieda shared the news with her family. "I'll be working directly with the reconstruction teams," she said excitedly.

"That's wonderful," Marta praised.

Hans raised an eyebrow. "Collaborating closely with the Americans, are we?"

Frieda met his gaze steadily. "Yes. It's an opportunity to make a tangible difference."

Klaus regarded her thoughtfully. "If you believe in this, then you have my support."

She smiled gratefully. "Thank you, *Vater.*"

Over the following weeks, the city's transformation became increasingly visible. The Engelhardt family stood on their balcony, observing the bustling streets below. Workers hoisted beams into place, and the sounds of hammers and saws echoed through the air.

"Look at how far we've come," Frieda remarked.

Hans nodded. "It's impressive."

Klaus rested his hands on the railing. "Perhaps there's merit in embracing these changes."

Marta leaned against him. "It's a new beginning for all of us."

As twilight settled over Hamburg, the city glowed with a quiet resilience. The Engelhardts, though still grappling with their individual struggles, found solace in the shared endeavour of rebuilding their home.

"Tomorrow is another day," Frieda said softly.

"And we'll face it together," Klaus affirmed.

The scent of blossoming trees drifted on the evening breeze, mingling with the faint aroma of fresh paint and newly sawn wood. Hope, once a distant notion, took root amidst the Ruins, nurtured by the collective spirit of those determined to rise from the ashes.

ooo

The first light of 1 June 1946 filtered through the tattered curtains of the Engelhardt apartment, casting a pale glow over the modest furnishings. Frieda sat at the small writing desk near the window, her pen poised above a blank page. The distant sounds of hammers and voices rose from the street below, a symphony of reconstruction that had become the soundtrack of their days.

She gazed out at the awakening city. Workers moved amidst the rubble, their figures silhouetted against the morning sun. Banners fluttered from lampposts, bearing messages of hope and renewal: *Gemeinsam Wiederaufbau*—Rebuild Together. The scent of fresh bread from a nearby bakery mingled with the lingering aroma of dust and stone.

"I'll be right there," Frieda replied, setting down her pen. She folded the letter she had been composing—a request to join the local committee discussing the proposed American aid—and slipped it into an envelope.

At the breakfast table, the family gathered in a semblance of normalcy. Klaus stirred his coffee absently, his eyes distant. Hans picked at his bread, lost in thought.

"I heard there's a meeting at the town hall this afternoon," Frieda began cautiously. "They're discussing the potential for economic assistance from the Americans."

Klaus' gaze snapped to hers. "Economic help?" he repeated, a hint of disdain in his voice. "You mean further meddling in our affairs."

Frieda met his eyes steadily. "It could be an opportunity to revitalise our economy, Vater. We need all the help we can get."

He scoffed lightly. "Help that comes with strings attached. They seek to control us, to mould Germany into their puppet."

Marta placed a gentle hand on his arm. "Perhaps we should listen to what they offer."

Klaus pulled away, his expression hardening. "I will not have my family indebted to the very people who brought us to our knees."

An uneasy silence settled over the table. Hans glanced between his parents, his brow furrowed. "Maybe we should consider all perspectives," he ventured. "Nothing is straightforward these days."

Frieda sighed softly. "I believe it's worth exploring. I'll attend the meeting and report back."

Klaus pushed his chair back abruptly. "Do as you wish," he muttered, leaving the room.

That afternoon, Frieda made her way to the town hall, the envelope tucked securely in her handbag. The streets bustled with activity—vendors hawked their wares from improvised stalls, children played amidst the debris, and posters announcing various initiatives adorned the walls. She read one: *Demokratie für ein neues Deutschland*—Democracy for a New Germany.

The town hall stood as a beacon of resilience, its façade scarred but standing proud. Inside, the main chamber buzzed with conversation. Rows of chairs faced a makeshift stage where a banner proclaimed: *Wirtschaftliche Zusammenarbeit für den Wiederaufbau*—Economic Cooperation for Reconstruction.

Frieda found a seat near the front, recognising familiar faces among the crowd. Greta waved from across the aisle, her notebook and pen at the ready.

"Good to see you here," Greta whispered as she slid into the seat beside Frieda.

"And you," Frieda replied with a smile. "Are you covering the meeting?"

"Yes, it's a significant development," Greta confirmed the division in public opinion, but also noted a growing interest.

An American official stepped up to the podium and adjusted the microphone. "Guten Tag, meine Damen und Herren (Good day, ladies and gentlemen)," he began in carefully practised German. "Thank you for coming. We are here to discuss the prospect of financial aid to support Germany's recovery."

He outlined the preliminary plans—funding for infrastructure, support for industry, and resources to stabilise the economy. Murmurs rippled through the audience, a mix of curiosity and scepticism.

Frieda listened intently, her heart quickening with cautious optimism. This could be the catalyst they needed to rebuild, not just physically, but socially and politically.

During the question-and-answer session, she raised her hand. "What conditions does this aid have attached to it?" she asked. "Will we keep autonomy in how it's utilised?"

The official nodded appreciatively. "Our goal is partnership, not control," he assured. "We seek to support your initiatives and work collaboratively."

Satisfied with his response, Frieda felt a glimmer of hope. Perhaps this was a step towards a brighter future.

Later that week, Frieda attended a meeting of the local democratic youth group. In a restored café, the group hosted the gathering, creating an atmosphere filled with the aroma of strong coffee and animated conversation.

"Frieda, over here!" called Ernst, a fellow volunteer. "What did you think of the town hall meeting?"

She joined the circle of young men and women, their faces alight with enthusiasm. "I believe the aid could be transformative," she replied. "But we must ensure it's implemented transparently."

"Agreed," Anna chimed in. "We shape the new Germany into a true democracy."

Hans entered the café hesitantly, spotting Frieda among the group. She beckoned him over. "Hans, come meet my friends."

He offered a shy smile. "Hello."

"This is my brother," Frieda introduced. "He's been exploring different perspectives."

Ernst extended his hand. "Any brother of Frieda's is welcome here."

Hans shook his hand tentatively. "Thank you."

As the evening progressed, discussions ranged from political ideologies to cultural revival. Music played softly in the background—a jazz tune that felt both foreign and invigorating.

"Have you considered joining our efforts?" Anna asked Hans.

He hesitated. "I'm still figuring out where I stand."

"That's understandable," Frieda assured him. "It's important to explore all viewpoints."

Back at the apartment, Klaus sat by the radio, tuning into a broadcast. The announcer spoke of the proposed American aid, analysing its implications.

"Propaganda," Klaus muttered under his breath.

Marta entered the room quietly. "Klaus, perhaps you should give it a chance."

He glanced at her, frustration clear in his eyes. "They're exploiting our vulnerability."

She sighed softly. "Frieda believes it's an opportunity."

"Frieda is naïve," he retorted. "She doesn't understand the complexities."

"She's trying to make a difference," Marta countered gently. "We all are."

He shook his head. "At what cost?"

On 15 June 1946, Frieda returned home late after a day of volunteering. She found Klaus seated at the kitchen table, a half-empty glass of schnapps before him.

"Vater," she greeted cautiously. "You're still up."

He looked up, his gaze penetrating. "Out late again, embracing the American dream?"

She bristled at his tone. "I'm working towards our collective future."

"Our future?" he echoed bitterly. "Or theirs?"

"Why must you see everything as adversarial?" she challenged. "We need to rebuild and can't do it alone."

He stood abruptly. "I won't stand by while you sell our soul to the highest bidder."

"That's not what I'm doing," she insisted. "I'm trying to secure a better life for all of us."

He scoffed. "Their promises blind you."

She met his gaze firmly. "And you're shackled by your pride."

His expression darkened. "Careful, Frieda."

She took a deep breath, willing herself to remain calm. "*Vater*, please. Let's find common ground."

He turned away. "There's nothing more to say."

On 18 June 1946, Hans approached Frieda as she sat reading in the parlour. "May I join you?"

"Of course," she replied, setting aside her book.

He settled into the chair opposite. "I've been thinking about the discussions about the American aid."

She regarded him thoughtfully. "And what are your thoughts?"

"I'm torn," he admitted. "I see the potential benefits but also understand *Vater's* concerns."

"It's a complex issue," she acknowledged. "But we have to weigh the risks against the gains."

He nodded slowly. "I've also been attending meetings with some socialist groups."

She raised an eyebrow. "Oh?"

"They believe that aligning with the Soviets could offer a different path to recovery," he explained.

Frieda considered his words. "Do you believe that's the right direction?"

"I'm not sure," he confessed. "Both sides have their merits and flaws."

She leaned forward. "Hans, whatever path you choose, make sure it aligns with your values."

He offered a small smile. "Thank you. I value your perspective."

On 21 June 1946, the Engelhardt family sat down to dinner. The atmosphere was tense but civil.

"Announcing it cautiously, Frieda revealed that someone had offered her a position on the local committee for economic development."

Marta smiled warmly. "That's wonderful news."

Hans nodded appreciatively. "Congratulations."

Klaus remained silent, his gaze fixed on his plate.

"Vater?" Frieda prompted gently.

He looked up slowly. "Do what you think is best."

She swallowed hard. "I intend to."

That evening, Frieda penned a letter to the committee, accepting the position. She felt a mixture of excitement and trepidation. The responsibility was significant, but she was determined to contribute meaningfully.

On 23 June 1946, Frieda hosted a small gathering of neighbours in the apartment to discuss community initiatives. The room buzzed with conversation and the clink of teacups.

"The aid could revitalise our industries," Frieda explained passionately. "We can rebuild schools, hospitals, and infrastructure."

A neighbour, *Frau Becker,* nodded enthusiastically. "Our children deserve a future."

"Exactly," Frieda agreed. "We create lasting change."

Unbeknownst to her, Klaus stood just outside the doorway, listening intently. His hands clenched into fists as he heard his daughter advocate for what he perceived as capitulation.

Unable to contain himself, he strode into the room. "Is this what we've come to?" he demanded, his voice cutting through the chatter. "Begging for scraps from those who defeated us?"

The room fell silent, all eyes turning to Klaus.

"Vater," Frieda began, her cheeks flushing. "We're discussing constructive solutions."

"Solutions that compromise our sovereignty," he retorted. "You speak of rebuilding, but at what price?"

Frieda stood her ground. "At the price of progress and survival. We can't cling to the past."

He glared at her. "You dishonour our nation by embracing foreign control."

She felt a surge of frustration. "And you dishonour our future by refusing to adapt."

Gasps rippled through the gathering. Marta stepped forward, her eyes pleading. "Please, let's not do this here."

Klaus ignored her, his focus unwavering. "You side with the occupiers against your own people."

"I'm siding with humanity," Frieda countered. "With hope for a better life."

He shook his head in disbelief. "You've lost your way."

She met his gaze, her voice steady. "No, *Vater.* I've found it."

He turned on his heel and left the room, the door slamming behind him.

An awkward silence settled over the guests. Greta approached Frieda, placing a comforting hand on her shoulder. "Are you alright?"

Frieda took a shaky breath. "I'm sorry for the outburst."

Frau Becker offered a sympathetic smile. "We understand. Tensions are high for everyone."

Marta addressed the group. "Perhaps we should adjourn for the evening."

As the neighbours departed, offering words of support, Frieda sank into a chair. Hans lingered nearby; uncertainty etched on his face.

"That was intense," he remarked softly.

She nodded wearily. "I didn't mean for it to escalate."

"He needs time," Hans suggested. "It's hard for him to accept change."

She looked up at him. "What about you? Where do you stand?"

He hesitated. "I see validity in both perspectives. But I think progress is necessary."

She offered a faint smile. "That's something, at least."

Later that night, Frieda found her father in his study, staring out the window at the moonlit streets.

"Vater," she ventured quietly.

He did not turn. "What do you want?"

"I wanted to apologise," she began. "Not for my beliefs, but for the way I spoke to you."

He remained silent for a moment before responding. "You are passionate. I can't fault you for that."

She stepped closer. "I respect your experiences and your wisdom. But I need you to understand why this matters to me."

He sighed heavily. "You believe this is the path forward."

"I do," she affirmed. "But I don't want it to drive a wedge between us."

He finally turned to face her, his expression weary. "The world is changing in ways I barely recognise. It's difficult to find my place in it."

She reached out tentatively. "Perhaps we can navigate it together."

He regarded her outstretched hand before taking it gently. "Perhaps."

The Engelhardt household stirred in the morning with a renewed, albeit fragile, sense of understanding. The rays of sunlight filtered through the curtains, casting a warm glow over the room.

Marta prepared breakfast, the aroma of fresh coffee filling the air. "Let's sit and eat," she suggested softly.

As they gathered around the table, Frieda shared her plans for the day. "I'll be meeting with the committee to complete the proposal."

Hans added, "I have a discussion group this afternoon."

Klaus nodded thoughtfully. "I may attend one of the community forums."

Marta smiled gently. "It's good to see us all engaged."

Frieda glanced at her father. "Thank you for being open-minded."

He met her eyes with a faint smile. "We must all adapt in our own ways."

The clatter of cutlery and the soft murmur of conversation filled the room—a semblance of normalcy returning.

Outside, the city of Hamburg buzzed with the energy of rebuilding. The scent of newly cut timber and the sound of construction echoed through the streets. Bicycles whirred past, their riders calling out greetings to neighbours. Flower boxes adorned windowsills, bright splashes of colour against the stark backdrop.

As the family parted ways for the day, a sense of cautious hope lingered. The path ahead remained uncertain, fraught with challenges and ideological divides. Yet, amidst the ruins, seeds of reconciliation and progress took root.

Frieda stepped into the sunlight, her heart buoyed by the possibilities. She was determined to contribute to a future where unity and prosperity prevailed over discord and despair.

And perhaps, just perhaps, her family would find their way forward together.

ooo

As the crisp air of 1 September 1946 settled over Hamburg, leaves turned shades of amber and crimson, hinting at autumn. The city's ruins were slowly being overshadowed by new scaffolding and the sounds of reconstruction. Hans Engelhardt stood at the crossroads of his own personal rebuild, drawn to whispers of a burgeoning movement promising equality and renewal.

He found himself on a train to Berlin, the rhythmic clatter of the wheels matching the tumult of his thoughts. The Soviet sector beckoned with the allure of socialist ideals. He attended meetings filled with vibrant young minds in dimly lit apartments tucked away in the backstreets of Berlin. Hans sat among them, the glow of a single lamp casting shadows that danced across passionate faces. The room smelled of damp plaster and burning candles, the air thick with smoke and the aroma of strong coffee.

"Comrades," a young man named Viktor proclaimed, his voice steady, "we can build a society free from the chains of oppression and inequality."

Hans felt a stirring within him. The discussions of class struggle and collective welfare resonated deeply, starkly contrasting the disillusionment that had settled in his heart since the war's end.

Back in Hamburg, Frieda immersed herself in the democratic reconstruction efforts. She stood before a crowd at a community centre, advocating for transparency and justice. "We must confront our past honestly," she urged, her voice echoing in the hall. "Only then can we forge a future we can be proud of."

People greeted her words with a mix of applause and scepticism. Some neighbours whispered their doubts, clinging to old prejudices. Frieda remained undeterred, her resolve hardened by the challenges.

Meanwhile, Klaus grew increasingly restless. The crisp mornings of early October found him pacing the length of their modest home, the floorboards creaking underfoot. He noticed Hans's absences, the secretive glances, the worn pamphlets tucked hastily into pockets.

On 15 September 1946, as the family gathered for a tense dinner, Klaus could no longer hold his silence. "Hans," he began, his tone edged with suspicion, "where have you been spending your time?"

Hans met his father's gaze evenly. "In Berlin, attending meetings."

"What meetings?" Klaus pressed, even though he seemed to know the answer already.

"Discussions about socialism," Hans replied calmly. "About rebuilding Germany on principles of equality."

Klaus's fist clenched around his fork. "You consort with those who wish to dismantle our nation's identity?"

Hans's eyes flashed with defiance. "Our nation's identity led us to ruins. Perhaps it's time for a fresh path."

The room fell silent, the air thick with unspoken tensions. Marta glanced between her husband and son, her face pale. "Please, let's not do this."

Klaus stood abruptly, his chair scraping loudly against the floor. "I won't have this under my roof," he declared.

Hans rose as well. "Then perhaps it's time I found my own path."

Frieda watched the exchange with a heavy heart, the familial bonds fraying before her eyes.

As October approached, the chill in the air mirrored the growing coldness within the Engelhardt household. On 5 October 1946, Hans returned from Berlin with a newfound determination. He approached Frieda in the parlour, where she sat reviewing community reports.

"Frieda," he began softly, "I need to talk to you."

She looked up, noting the earnestness in his expression. "Of course."

"I've decided to move to Berlin," he announced. "There's important work to be done there."

She felt a pang of sadness. "What about the family?"

He sighed. "Father will never accept my choices. Perhaps distance will help."

She reached out to touch his arm. "Be careful, Hans. The world is more complicated than ideals."

He offered a faint smile. "I know. But I have to follow my convictions."

On 15 October 1946, Hans packed a small suitcase. Marta stood at the doorway of his room, tears glistening in her eyes. "My boy," she whispered, "must it be this way?"

He embraced her gently. "I need to find my place, *Mutti*. I'll write often."

Klaus remained in his study, the sound of the door closing behind Hans echoing through the silent apartment.

The scent of coal fires hung heavy over Berlin as Hans stepped onto the platform at Ostbahnhof on 16 October 1946. The city's scars were as deep as Hamburg's, but an undercurrent of determination invigorated him.

He made his way to a small flat shared with other comrades. The space was sparse—a mattress on the floor, a shared kitchenette, walls adorned with socialist slogans and posters of Marx and Lenin.

He attended a significant gathering in a cellar beneath a shuttered café. The room overflowed with people, their voices hushed but passionate. A prominent speaker from the Soviet administration addressed them.

"Germany stands at a crossroads," the speaker intoned. "We have the chance to reject the failures of capitalism and embrace a system that values every worker, every citizen equally."

Applause erupted. Hans felt a surge of purpose. Here, he believed, he could contribute to meaningful change.

Back in Hamburg, Frieda received news of the Nuremberg Trials' progression. She gathered with colleagues to listen to the radio broadcasts detailing the prosecutions of high-ranking Nazi officials.

"This is justice," she remarked to Greta, who sat beside her, taking notes for an article. "But it's only the beginning. We ensure that we never repeat such atrocities."

Greta nodded solemnly. "People say that public sentiment is divisive. Many want to forget, to move on without confronting the past."

Frieda's gaze hardened. "We cannot build a future on a foundation of denial."

On 25 October 1946, Klaus ventured into the city, the chill wind biting his cheeks. He wandered aimlessly until he found himself outside a familiar pub. Inside, he spotted Jakob Fischer nursing a drink.

"Klaus!" Jakob called out, waving him over. "Join me."

Klaus hesitated before taking a seat. "It's been a while."

Jakob smirked. "These are strange times. How fares your family?"

Klaus sighed. "Fragmented. Hans has embraced socialist ideals. Frieda has become caught up in the occupiers' agendas."

Jakob scoffed. "Youthful folly. They don't understand the value of tradition and loyalty."

"Perhaps I failed them," Klaus mused quietly.

Jakob shook his head. "External forces have swayed them. We must stand firm."

Klaus stared into his glass. "I'm not sure what I stand for anymore."

Marta organised a modest family gathering as the month drew to a close. She hoped to rekindle a sense of unity despite Hans's absence.

Frieda helped her mother set the table. "It's beautiful, *Mutti.*"

Marta smiled wistfully. "I wish Hans were here."

"Have you heard from him?" Frieda asked gently.

"A letter arrived yesterday," Marta revealed. "He's well. Busy with his work."

Klaus entered the room, his expression unreadable. He surveyed the scene before taking his seat. "Shall we begin?"

As they sat together, the flickering of candlelight and the distant sounds of the city on the street below punctuated the silence.

"Perhaps we can find common ground," Marta ventured hopefully.

Klaus glanced at Frieda. "Your work continues?"

She nodded. "Yes, *Vater.* We're making progress with the housing initiatives."

He considered her response. "That's commendable."

A tentative peace settled over them. Outside, a light snow fell softly, blanketing the city in a hush.

In Berlin, Hans stood by the window of his flat, watching the snowflakes dance under the glow of streetlamps. He felt a mixture of melancholy and resolve. Pulling out a notebook, he wrote,

Dear Mutti,

The work here is challenging, but fulfilling. I believe we are on the cusp of significant change…

He paused, contemplating the distance—both physical and ideological—that separated him from his family.

As he penned his thoughts, the strains of a familiar melody drifted through the walls—a neighbour playing *Stille Nacht* on a worn piano. The music stirred memories of simpler times, of family gatherings before the war had torn their lives apart.

Hans closed his eyes, allowing himself a moment of vulnerability. The path he had chosen was fraught with uncertainty, but he clung to the belief that his efforts would contribute to a better Germany.

Back in Hamburg, Frieda stood on the balcony, the cold seeping through her coat. She gazed up at the night sky, stars obscured by the gentle snowfall.

"Thinking of Hans?" Greta's voice came from behind her.

Frieda turned, surprised. "Greta, I didn't hear you come in."

Greta joined her at the railing. "I thought you might like some company."

They stood in companionable silence before Greta spoke again. "Do you ever doubt your choices?"

Frieda considered the question. "The path forward isn't always clear. But I believe in what we're doing."

Greta nodded. "It's hard when those we care about choose different roads."

"Yes," Frieda agreed softly. "But perhaps our paths will converge again someday."

As November gave way to December, the Engelhardt family faced the encroaching winter with a mixture of hope and trepidation. The ideological divides that had splintered them seemed insurmountable, yet beneath the surface lingered the unspoken bonds of family.

Klaus began attending church services more regularly, seeking solace and perhaps redemption. He lit a candle in the quiet sanctuary, the flickering flame reflecting in his weary eyes.

"Forgive me," he whispered, though whether he sought forgiveness from a higher power or from himself remained unclear.

Marta continued to hold the family together, her quiet strength a steadying presence. She wrote to Hans frequently, cherishing his replies.

Frieda dedicated herself to her work, her conviction unwavering. She believed Germany could heal and emerge stronger through transparency and dedication.

Hans delved deeper into the socialist movement, his days filled with meetings and organising efforts. Yet, in the quiet moments, he grappled with doubts and the longing for familial connection.

The ruins of their lives mirrored the ruins of their nation—a fractured landscape yearning for restoration. As the snow blanketed the cities of Hamburg and Berlin, it covered scars and seeds, concealing the pain while nurturing the potential for fresh growth.

The Engelhardts stood at the crossroads of history, each navigating the complexities of identity, ideology, and the family's enduring ties. The path ahead was uncertain, but as autumn turned to winter, there remained a glimmer of hope that amidst division and discord, reconciliation was still possible.

ooo

The biting chill of 1 December 1946 crept into every corner of the Engelhardt home, seeping through the cracks and settling into their bones. Klaus sat alone in the dimly lit living room, his silhouette etched against the frosted windowpane. Outside, snowflakes drifted silently, blanketing the ruins of Hamburg in a shroud of white. The city lay still, as if holding its breath against the harsh winter.

Klaus fixed his gaze on the street below, where a lone figure trudged through the snow, leaving a trail of footprints that quickly vanished under the relentless fall. His breath fogged the glass, obscuring the desolate scene momentarily before fading away. The faint scent of burning coal from distant chimneys mingled with the cold air, a reminder of warmth that felt just out of reach.

In the kitchen, Marta wrapped her shawl tightly around her shoulders, her fingers numb despite the woollen gloves she wore indoors. She stirred a pot of thin gruel over a meagre flame, the contents barely enough to feed them both. With Hans in Berlin and Frieda often away on her community work, the apartment felt emptier than ever. The clatter of a spoon against the metal pot echoed in the silence.

On 5 December 1946, Frieda returned home, her cheeks flushed from the cold and a day's efforts in the rebuilding initiatives. She shook the snow from her boots at the door; the dampness spreading into a small puddle on the worn floorboards.

"*Mutti,* I've brought some extra bread," she announced softly, placing a loaf on the table.

Marta offered a weary smile. "You're a blessing, Liebchen. We'll make it last."

Frieda glanced towards the living room. "How is *Vater* today?"

Marta's eyes flickered with concern. "The same. He hardly speaks."

Frieda sighed, removing her coat and hanging it by the door. "Perhaps I can try talking to him."

She entered the living room cautiously. *"Vater,"* she greeted, her voice gentle.

Klaus did not turn. "Frieda," he acknowledged flatly.

"I wanted to share some news," she began, approaching the chair where he sat hunched. "We've made significant progress in the housing project. Families are moving into new homes before Christmas."

He remained silent, his gaze distant.

"It's a step forward," she continued, undeterred. "People are finding hope again."

Klaus exhaled slowly. "Hope," he repeated, the word heavy with irony. "What does that mean in a world stripped of honour?"

She knelt beside him, placing a hand on his arm. "*Vater,* holding onto the past won't heal the wounds. We must look ahead."

He pulled away slightly. "You speak like a stranger, Frieda. Embracing the ideals of those who conquered us."

She felt a pang of frustration. "I'm working for our future—for Germany's future."

He finally met her eyes, his own filled with sorrow she could scarcely comprehend. "The Germany I knew is gone."

As days passed, the frost thickened, and the days grew shorter. Marta ventured into the market square, braving the icy streets in search of provisions. Stalls were sparse, and prices had soared. She haggled with a vendor over a sack of potatoes, her breath forming clouds in the frigid air.

"Please, I can offer this," she pleaded, holding out a few coins.

The vendor shook his head. "I'm sorry, *Frau*. Times are hard for all of us."

Defeated, Marta turned away, clutching her purse tightly. As she made her way home, she passed by the church, its bells tolling solemnly. She hesitated before stepping inside, seeking solace from the cold and the weight of her burdens.

The warmth within was a stark contrast to the chill outside. Candles flickered along the altar, their flames dancing shadows across the vaulted ceiling. Marta knelt in a pew, her hands clasped together.

"Give me strength," she whispered, her eyes closing. "For my family— for Klaus."

On 15 December 1946, Marta confronted Klaus. She found him in the bedroom, sitting on the edge of the bed, his shoulders slumped.

"Klaus, we need to talk," she began firmly.

He glanced up, the hollows under his eyes more pronounced. "What is there to say?"

She took a deep breath. "You can't continue like this. Isolating yourself, shutting us out. We are your family."

He looked away. "My family no longer understands me."

"We are trying," she insisted. "But you must meet us halfway."

He shook his head slowly. "I am a relic, Marta. A remnant of a world that no longer exists."

She knelt before him, her hands reaching for his. "That's not true. You are my husband, Frieda's father. We need you."

He withdrew his hands. "You don't need me. Frieda has her causes. Hans has his new ideologies. You manage everything without me."

Her eyes filled with tears. "I can't carry this alone. I miss the man you were."

He closed his eyes, his voice barely above a whisper. "That man is gone."

On 20 December 1946, Frieda attended a community gathering to distribute winter supplies. The hall was bustling with activity—children laughing as they received warm blankets, elders expressing gratitude for the provisions.

"Thank you, Fräulein Engelhardt," an elderly woman said, clutching a parcel of food. "You bring light to these dark times."

Frieda smiled warmly. "We all must help each other."

As she left the hall, she noticed Greta approaching, her notepad in hand.

"Frieda, may I have a moment?" Greta asked.

"Of course," Frieda replied.

"I'm writing an article on the impact of the winter on displaced families," Greta explained. "Your perspective would be invaluable."

Frieda nodded. "Anything to raise awareness."

They walked together through the snow-dusted streets, discussing the challenges faced by the community. The glow of lanterns illuminated their path, casting elongated shadows behind them.

"How is your family?" Greta inquired gently.

Frieda hesitated. "Strained. *Vater* is… struggling."

Greta touched her arm reassuringly. "It's difficult for many. The wounds of the war run deep."

Frieda sighed. "I just wish we could find common ground."

On 24 December 1946, Christmas Eve arrived with a quiet stillness. Marta decorated a small pine branch with handmade ornaments, determined to preserve some semblance of tradition. She prepared a modest meal—roasted vegetables and the last of their preserved meat.

"Frieda, could you set the table?" Marta requested.

"Of course, *Mutti*," Frieda agreed, arranging the mismatched plates and cutlery.

Klaus emerged from his room, his steps slow. He surveyed the scene with a distant expression.

"Frohe Weihnachten, Vater (Merry Christmas, Father)," Frieda offered softly.

He nodded slightly. "Frohe Weihnachten."

They sat together; the silence punctuated by the ticking of the clock on the mantelpiece.

Marta raised her glass. "To our family, near and far. May the new year bring us peace."

They clinked glasses, the sound echoing in the quiet room.

After dinner, they gathered around the small radio to listen to a broadcast of traditional carols. The melodies filled the space, evoking memories of happier times.

Klaus gazed into the flickering candlelight, his mind drifting. Images of the war flashed before him—the roar of artillery, the faces of fallen comrades, the devastation wrought by choices made.

On 28 December 1946, the city's energy grid faltered under the strain of the cold. Power outages became frequent, plunging the apartment into darkness. Klaus sat by the window, a candle casting a weak glow over his features.

Frieda approached cautiously. "*Vater,* would you like some tea?"

He did not respond.

She placed a cup on the table beside him. "I thought it might warm you."

He turned to her, his eyes reflecting the candle's flame. "Do you ever regret your choices?" he asked suddenly.

She was taken aback. "In what way?"

"Aligning yourself with those who occupy us. Abandoning the values we once held dear."

She contemplated her response. "I believe that embracing change is necessary for progress. Holding onto old grudges hinders us."

He sighed heavily. "Perhaps you are right. Or perhaps I am too set in my ways to see clearly."

She reached out to touch his hand. "It's never too late to find a new path."

He withdrew his hand. "For you, maybe. For me, the shadows are too long."

On 31 December 1946, New Year's Eve descended upon the city with an unforgiving chill. Snow piled high against the buildings, muffling the sounds of the outside world. The Engelhardts huddled around the small fireplace, the flames offering scant warmth.

Marta suggested they share their hopes for the coming year. "Perhaps it will lift our spirits," she said, attempting a smile.

Frieda agreed. "I hope for continued progress in our rebuilding efforts, and for our family to find harmony."

Marta nodded. "I hope for health and for Hans to return home safely."

They turned to Klaus expectantly.

He stared into the fire, his expression inscrutable. "I hope," he began, his voice trailing off.

Suddenly, he stood up abruptly, knocking over his chair. "What hope is there?" he exclaimed, his voice cracking. "Our country is in ruins, our family shattered. What is there to celebrate?"

Marta rose quickly. "Klaus, please, calm down."

He paced the room, his agitation growing. "I failed you all. I failed our nation. The weight of it is unbearable."

Frieda stepped forward. "*Vater,* we don't blame you. We're trying to move forward."

He turned on her, his eyes filled with anguish. "Move forward to what? Is everything I believed in condemned in a world where I move forward? Who will move forward with that? Where my own children reject me?"

Marta reached out to him. "We don't reject you. We love you."

He recoiled from her touch. "Love? How can you love a man who is a ghost of himself?"

The room fell silent, the crackling of the fire the only sound.

Klaus sank to his knees, his shoulders shaking. "I can't escape it—the memories, the guilt. It's all-consuming."

Marta knelt beside him, tears streaming down her face. "Let us help you."

He shook his head. "I am beyond help."

Frieda watched helplessly, her own eyes brimming with tears. "Vater, we need you. Please don't shut us out."

He looked up at them, the torment etched deeply into his features. "I'm sorry," he whispered. "For everything."

As the clock struck midnight, heralding 1 January 1947, the family remained huddled together on the floor, the shadows of the past year looming over them.

Outside, distant church bells rang out, their tones muffled by the snow. The new year had begun, but for the Engelhardts, the weight of the old lingered heavily.

In the quiet aftermath of Klaus's breakdown, Marta and Frieda exchanged a glance of mutual understanding. They knew that the road ahead would be fraught with challenges, but they also knew that they had to face it together.

"Happy New Year, *Mutti*," Frieda whispered.

Marta squeezed her hand. "Happy New Year, *Liebchen*."

They turned their attention back to Klaus, who had lapsed into a fitful sleep by the hearth. Marta placed a blanket over him, her gaze softening.

"We'll get through this," she murmured.

Frieda nodded, a flicker of determination igniting within her. "Yes, we will."

As the first light of dawn crept over the horizon, casting a pale glow over the snow-covered city, the Engelhardt women prepared to face the uncertainties of the new year. The cold remained, both outside and within, but amidst the frost, there was a glimmer of resilience—a quiet strength that whispered of the possibility of healing.

THREE:

THE COLD WAR LOOMS

The morning of 15 June 1947 dawned with a tentative warmth, the sun casting a golden hue over the partially cleared streets of Hamburg. Klaus Engelhardt stood at the window of the modest apartment, his gaze fixed on the city slowly stirring below. The distant clang of metal against stone echoed through the air as workers continued the arduous task of rebuilding. He sipped his bitter coffee, the aroma mingling with the faint scent of dust that seemed ever-present.

A knock at the door pulled him from his reverie. Marta entered, a folded newspaper in her hands. "Klaus, have you seen the news?" she asked softly, her eyes searching his face.

He took the paper from her, briskly unfolding it to reveal the bold headline: *Amerikanische Marshallplan angekündigt*—American Marshall Plan Announced.

His jaw tightened as he scanned the article. "So, the Americans wish to bind us with their so-called generosity," he muttered.

Marta sighed. "Perhaps it is an opportunity, a chance to rebuild."

"At what cost?" Klaus retorted, tossing the newspaper onto the table.

Just then, Frieda entered, her cheeks flushed with excitement. "*Vater, Mutti,* have you heard? The Marshall Plan could change everything!"

Klaus eyed his daughter warily. "Change everything, indeed. Bind us further to the whims of foreign powers."

Frieda frowned. "It's not like that. This aid could help us rebuild our homes, our lives."

"At the price of our sovereignty," he snapped.

Marta placed a calming hand on his arm. "Let us discuss this calmly."

Frieda took a deep breath. "I've decided to volunteer with the distribution efforts. They're organising groups to help with rebuilding projects."

Klaus's eyes narrowed. "You would consort with the occupiers?"

"They're here to help, *Vater.* We need to move forward."

He shook his head, turning away. "You are naïve, Frieda."

She stood her ground. "No, *Vater.* I am hopeful."

Over the next few days, Frieda devoted herself to volunteer work. On 20 June 1947, she joined a team clearing rubble from the remains of a school near the harbour. The air was thick with dust, and the sun was beating down as they lifted broken beams and shattered bricks. Sweat mingled with grime on her skin, but she felt invigorated.

"Pass me that shovel, *bitte,*" she called to a fellow volunteer.

A young man handed it to her with a grin. "You're quite the hard worker, *Fräulein.*"

She smiled back. "There's much to be done."

Amidst the labour, she found camaraderie and purpose. They shared stories and laughter, small pockets of joy amid the ruins.

A couple of days later, Frieda attended a meeting at the central square, where American officials discussed implementing the Marshall Plan. Banners emblazoned with slogans in English and German hung from the makeshift stalls: *Wiederaufbau für eine bessere Zukunft*—Rebuilding for a Better Future.

An American officer stepped onto a platform, addressing the crowd in accented German. "We are here to support your efforts to rebuild. Together, we can restore prosperity."

Frieda listened intently, her heart swelling with cautious optimism.

Back at the apartment, Klaus sat alone, the silence oppressive. He fiddled with his worn pocket watch, the ticking of a constant reminder of time slipping away. The walls seemed to close in, the shadows lengthening as the afternoon light faded.

On 28 June 1947, he ventured out, drawn by a restlessness he couldn't quiet. The streets were a hive of activity, people bustling with renewed energy. He passed by the central square, pausing at the edge of the gathering.

He spotted Frieda amidst the crowd, her auburn hair catching the light as she conversed animatedly with an American official. She gestured passionately, her eyes alight with purpose. Klaus felt a pang of something— was it pride or betrayal?

He retreated into the shadows of a nearby alley, watching from a distance. The clang of shovels against stone rang out, the rhythm discordant to his ears. Children laughed as they played among the debris, their innocence jarring against the backdrop of destruction.

A fine layer of dust coated everything, stirred up by the constant movement. It settled on Klaus's coat, mingling with the frayed threads. He ran a hand over the rough fabric, a tangible connection to a past that felt increasingly distant.

On 30 June 1947, Frieda was at the distribution centre early, the morning air crisp with the promise of a clear day. She organised supplies, her hands deftly sorting through crates of canned goods and medical supplies.

"*Fräulein Engelhardt,* could you assist over here?" called out *Herr Müller,* the coordinator.

"*Natürlich* (Of course)," she replied, moving to help unload a shipment.

As she worked, she noticed a familiar figure at the square's periphery. Klaus stood rigid, his posture stiff as he surveyed the scene. Their eyes met briefly, his expression inscrutable.

She approached him hesitantly. "*Vater,* what brings you here?"

He glanced around dismissively. "I was merely passing by."

She gestured to the bustling activity. "It's remarkable, isn't it? So many people coming together."

He grunted noncommittally. "Remarkable, perhaps."

She searched his face. "Why won't you see the good in this?"

He met her gaze, his eyes hardened by years of disillusionment. "Because I see only the chains being forged, not the so-called freedom you speak of."

She sighed. "We can't remain bound to the past. This is our chance to rebuild, to create a better Germany."

He scoffed lightly. "A better Germany under foreign rule?"

"Under cooperation," she insisted. "We need allies, *Vater.*"

He shook his head. "Allies? Or masters?"

Before she could respond, a call came from the distribution centre. "Frieda, we need you!"

She glanced back. "I have to go. Please, consider what I've said."

He watched her return to the fray, her steps purposeful. The clang of metal and the hum of conversation in mixed languages all grated against him. He felt like a relic, a ghost haunting the edges of a world that no longer had a place for him.

As he turned to leave, a gust of wind stirred the dust, swirling it around him. He closed his eyes against the grit, the sensation transporting him back to the Eastern Front—the acrid smoke, the cries of comrades, the weight of a rifle in his hands.

When he opened his eyes to the present, the sounds of rebuilding replaced the echoes of war. Yet the dissonance remained. He wandered through the streets, passing familiar landmarks now reduced to skeletal frames.

Children darted past him, their laughter a stark contrast to his sombre mood. Vendors hawked wares from carts—fresh bread, handmade trinkets, even American cigarettes. The scent of baking mingled with the ever-present dust, creating an unsettling blend of the old and the new.

He paused before a half-collapsed church, the once-grand spire now jagged against the sky. Inside, he could see a makeshift shelter where displaced families huddled together. A woman sang a lullaby to a restless child, the melody hauntingly familiar.

"Schlaf, Kindlein, schlaf... (Sleep, little child, sleep…)," she crooned softly.

Klaus felt a tightness in his chest. Memories of Marta singing the same lullaby to Hans and Frieda flooded his mind. A time when he felt secure in his purpose, his role as protector and provider.

Now he felt adrift. His son was distant, entangled in socialist ideals. His daughter embraced the aid of those he considered adversaries. And he—what was left for him?

On his way back home, he encountered Jakob Fischer emerging from a tavern, the older man's gait unsteady.

"Klaus!" Jakob called out, his voice slurred. "Join me for a drink."

Klaus hesitated. "Not today, Jakob."

Jakob chuckled darkly. "Ah, too proud to share a drink with an old comrade?"

"It's not that," Klaus replied. "I have much on my mind."

Jakob leaned in conspiratorially. "These times are changing too quickly. Can't trust anyone anymore."

Klaus nodded absently. "Indeed."

"Your daughter, she's mixed up with the Americans, *ja?*" Jakob continued.

Klaus's eyes narrowed. "That's none of your concern."

Jakob raised his hands defensively. "Just an observation. Be careful, my friend."

Without another word, Klaus resumed his walk, the encounter leaving a bitter taste.

Upon returning home, he found Marta knitting by the window, her needles clicking softly.

"Did you go out?" she asked gently.

"Yes," he replied curtly.

She looked at him thoughtfully. "It's good to get some fresh air."

He sat heavily in a chair. "Fresh air tainted by the stench of occupation."

She set her knitting aside. "Klaus, please. Not everything is as bleak as you make it out to be."

He met her gaze, frustration simmering beneath the surface. "Our children are slipping away, embracing ideals that erode the very fabric of our identity."

"Our children are finding their own paths," she countered. "We should support them."

"Support them in abandoning their heritage?" he challenged.

She exhaled. "Perhaps it's time we consider that the world has changed, and we must adapt."

He stood abruptly. "I refuse to bend to the will of those who seek to control us."

Marta watched him leave the room, a sadness settling over her features.

That evening, as the sun cast long shadows over the city, Frieda returned home, exhaustion etched into her posture. She found her mother in the kitchen, preparing a simple meal of potatoes and cabbage.

"Let me help," Frieda offered, washing her hands.

"Thank you, *Liebchen,*" Marta smiled warmly.

"How was your day?" Frieda asked.

"Quiet," Marta replied. "Your father is… struggling."

Frieda nodded solemnly. "I saw him today at the square."

"Oh?" Marta prompted.

"He seems so distant, so angry."

"He carries heavy burdens," Marta whispered.

Frieda stirred the pot thoughtfully. "I wish he would let us in."

"Give him time," Marta advised. "He needs to find his own way."

After dinner, Frieda sat by the window, gazing out at the city bathed in twilight. Lights flickered in the distance as generators hummed to life. She could hear faint strains of music—a radio playing a new jazz tune, likely from an American station.

She pulled a notebook from her satchel, jotting down her thoughts.

We are at a crossroads. The old ways are crumbling, and we must choose how to rebuild our cities and hearts.

In his study, Klaus paced restlessly. The shadows danced around him as the lamplight flickered. He reached for a book on the shelf—a volume of Goethe's poems. Thumbing through the pages, he sought solace in the familiar words.

"Wer nie sein Brot mit Tränen aß" he whispered. ('Who never ate his bread with tears").

The lines resonated deeply. He closed the book, the weight of his melancholy pressing down.

On 1 July 1947, the city buzzed with news of further aid shipments arriving. Frieda prepared to head out early, her resolve steadfast.

"Frieda," Klaus's voice stopped her at the door.

She turned, surprised. "Yes, *Vater?*"

He hesitated, the words catching in his throat. "Be careful out there."

A flicker of warmth touched her expression. "I will. Thank you."

He nodded curtly, retreating into the apartment.

As she made her way through the bustling streets, Frieda felt a glimmer of hope. Perhaps, beneath his stern exterior, her father was softening.

But Klaus remained ensnared in his internal conflict. The world around him was changing rapidly, and he grappled with his place within it. The clang of reconstruction, the chatter of mixed languages, and the sight of his daughter embracing a new future deepened his sense of isolation.

He wandered once more through the ruins of familiar neighbourhoods, the echoes of the past mingling with the uncertain present. The scent of fresh mortar and sawdust filled the air, signs of renewal that he struggled to accept.

Standing before the remnants of a grand building—a theatre where he and Marta once attended performances—he closed his eyes, letting the memories wash over him. Laughter, music, and the warmth of shared experiences now faded into whispers.

A voice interrupted his thoughts. *"Herr Engelhardt?"*

He turned to see a young man, a volunteer, holding a clipboard. "Yes?"

"We're cataloguing buildings for potential restoration. Do you have any information about this site?"

Klaus regarded him coolly. "It was a place of culture and art, now reduced to rubble."

The volunteer nodded sympathetically. "We're hoping to preserve what we can."

Klaus's gaze hardened. "We cannot rebuild some things," Klaus said, his gaze hardening.

The young man shifted uncomfortably. "Every effort counts."

Without responding, Klaus walked away, leaving the volunteer perplexed.

As the days continued, the city pressed forward, and each brick laid a testament to resilience. Yet for Klaus, the reconstruction felt hollow, a façade that failed to address the deeper fractures within himself and his family.

The Marshall Plan had ignited a spark of hope for many, but for Klaus, it illuminated the shadows of his discontent. He stood at the crossroads of a nation in flux, uncertain of which path to tread.

And so, the Engelhardts continued their divergent journeys—Frieda embracing the promise of a new Germany, Klaus clinging to the remnants of a past that no longer existed, and Marta striving to bridge the widening gap between them.

The sounds of rebuilding echoed through the streets, a chorus of renewal that Klaus could not bring himself to join. Instead, he remained a solitary figure amidst the Ruins, a man out of time, watching as the world moved on without him.

ooo

The first light of 5 July 1947 filtered through the cracks of the Engelhardt apartment shutters, casting thin beams across the worn wooden floor. Frieda sat at the kitchen table, poring over a leaflet detailing the proposed currency reform. The title read: *Einführung der Deutschen Mark – Ein neuer Anfang*—Introduction of the Deutsche Mark – A New Beginning.

Marta placed a steaming cup of chamomile tea beside her daughter. "You've been up early these days," she observed gently.

Frieda looked up, her eyes bright with determination. "There's so much to be done, *Mutti*. The currency reform could change everything."

Marta smiled softly. "Your father is less enthusiastic."

Frieda's expression clouded. "I know. But we can't let fear hold us back."

In the adjoining room, Klaus sat silently, the muffled voices reaching him like echoes. He gazed at an old Reichsmark note, the paper thin and creased. The familiar portrait of President Hindenburg stared back at him, a symbol of a Germany he once knew. The thought of replacing it with the Deutsche Mark felt like erasing the remnants of his past.

Later that day, Frieda attended a public meeting at the community hall. The room buzzed with energy as locals gathered to learn about the impending currency reform. Posters adorned the walls, proclaiming messages like *Stabilität und Wohlstand für alle*—Stability and Prosperity for all.

A man in a crisp suit took the podium. *"Meine Damen und Herren,"* he began, "the introduction of the Deutsche Mark is not merely a change of currency; it's a step towards economic recovery and a brighter future."

Frieda felt a surge of hope. She glanced around the room, noting the mix of apprehension and anticipation on the faces of her neighbours.

After the presentation, she joined a group of volunteers distributing informational pamphlets. "If you have any questions, please don't hesitate to ask," she encouraged an elderly couple.

"Will this really help?" the woman asked, her eyes weary.

"I believe it will," Frieda replied earnestly. "With a stable currency, we can rebuild our economy and our lives."

As the days passed, Frieda's involvement deepened. On 15 July 1947, she helped organise a forum where citizens could voice their concerns.

Meanwhile, Klaus grew increasingly agitated. He saw the posters plastered across Hamburg; the Deutsche Mark symbol emblazoned boldly. To him, it was a constant reminder of the shifting tides he resisted.

One evening, he confronted Marta. "This currency reform is just another way for the occupiers to control us," he declared.

Marta met his gaze steadily. "Or it's a chance for us to stabilise and move forward."

He shook his head. "You sound like Frieda."

"Perhaps because she makes sense," she countered gently.

As August 1947 approached, Klaus decided to attend a town meeting, intent on voicing his dissent. The hall brimmed with people, the air heavy with summer heat and the murmur of conversation. He spotted Frieda at the front, engaged in animated discussion with a group of young people.

The speaker, an economic advisor, took the stage. "The Reichsmark has become unstable, leading to inflation and hardship. The Deutsche Mark will restore confidence and facilitate trade."

Klaus couldn't contain himself. "At what cost?" he called out.

All eyes turned towards him. The speaker paused. "Pardon me, sir?"

Klaus stood tall. "You're asking us to abandon our heritage, to accept a currency imposed by foreign powers."

Frieda's eyes widened as she recognised her father's voice. "*Vater,* please," she whispered under her breath.

The advisor responded calmly. "The Deutsche Mark is a necessary step towards economic recovery, regardless of its origins."

Klaus scoffed. "Necessary for whom? Those who wish to see us subservient?"

Murmurs rippled through the crowd. Frieda felt a flush rise to her cheeks, torn between her respect for her father and her conviction in the reform.

A man nearby spoke up. "We've suffered enough. If this helps put food on the table, I'm all for it."

Others nodded in agreement.

Klaus felt the weight of their collective gaze. "You're willing to trade your dignity for a handful of coins?"

Frieda stepped forward. "*Vater,* people are hungry. This is about survival."

He looked at her, a mixture of frustration and sorrow in his eyes. "You, of all people, should understand the importance of preserving our identity."

She met his gaze steadily. "A piece of paper doesn't define our identity. It's in how we rebuild and move forward."

The tension was palpable. The advisor cleared his throat. "Perhaps we can continue this discussion respectfully."

Klaus turned abruptly and left the hall, the doors swinging shut behind him.

Outside, the evening air was thick with humidity. He wandered, the sounds of the city fading into a blur. The cobblestone streets showed signs of wear, while the buildings displayed the scars of war. A group of children played nearby, their laughter echoing off the walls. One of them kicked a ball towards him, and it rolled to a stop at his feet.

"Entschuldigung, Herr (Excuse me, sir)," a boy called out.

Klaus picked up the ball, its surface scuffed and patched. He hesitated before tossing it back gently. "Be careful," he said gruffly.

"Vielen Dank! (Thank you very much!)" the boy replied, grinning before rejoining his friends.

Klaus watched them momentarily, a pang of nostalgia piercing his defences. Memories of Hans and Frieda as children flooded back—carefree days before the world became so complicated.

On 2 August 1947, Hans returned home for a brief visit. The family gathered for dinner; the atmosphere strained, yet hopeful.

"Tell us about Berlin," Marta prompted.

Hans shrugged. "The socialist movement is gaining momentum. People are eager for change."

Klaus frowned. "Change seems to be the word of the day."

Hans glanced at his father. "We can't cling to the past forever."

Klaus's eyes hardened. "First, the currency, now this. You're both so eager to discard our heritage."

Frieda interjected. "It's not about discarding, Vater. It's about adapting."

Hans nodded. "We need solutions that work for everyone."

Klaus slammed his fist on the table, the dishes rattling. "Solutions that strip us of who we are!"

Marta reached out a calming hand. "Please, let's not argue."

Silence settled over the room like a heavy fog.

Later that night, Hans found Frieda sitting on the balcony, the city lights flickering in the distance.

"Quite the dinner," he remarked, leaning on the railing beside her.

She sighed. "It's like we're speaking different languages."

He nodded thoughtfully. "*Vater* sees the world changing and feels powerless."

"We all do," she admitted. "But resisting won't stop it."

Hans gazed out over the rooftops. "Sometimes I wonder if any of these ideologies truly have the answers."

She looked at him curiously. "Doubts about socialism?"

He shrugged. "Doubts about everything. The more I see, the more complex it becomes."

Frieda placed a hand on his arm. "We're all trying to find our way."

As days passed, the main square hosted a larger public debate. The summer sun beat down as crowds gathered, a symphony of voices filling the air. Stalls lined the streets, vendors selling everything from fresh pretzels to handcrafted toys.

Klaus stood at the edge of the crowd, listening as a government official extolled the virtues of the Deutsche Mark. "This reform is essential for our nation's recovery," the man declared.

Unable to contain himself, Klaus stepped forward. "And what of those who do not wish to trade their history for hollow promises?"

The official eyed him cautiously. "Sir, the Reichsmark is no longer viable. We must look to the future."

"The future you're offering is one where we have no say," Klaus retorted.

A few people in the crowd murmured in agreement, but many more shook their heads.

A woman called out, "We need stability! My family can't survive on pride alone."

Another added, "Let go of the past. It's time to rebuild."

Klaus felt a surge of isolation. "You're all blind," he muttered, pushing his way through the crowd.

Frieda, who had been distributing flyers nearby, witnessed the exchange. She hurried after him. "*Vater,* wait!"

He spun around, his eyes flashing with anger. "Do not convince me, Frieda. I see now that I am alone in this."

She felt a sting at his words. "You're not alone. We just have different perspectives."

"Different perspectives?" he scoffed. "You side with those who would see our nation moulded into their image."

"That's not fair," she protested. "I'm fighting for a Germany where we can thrive again."

He shook his head wearily. "Perhaps it's I who no longer belongs."

He walked away, leaving her standing amidst the multitude of people.

The following days were heavy with unspoken tension. Marta tried to bridge the gap, but Klaus withdrew further. He spent his time wandering the city, lost in thought.

Looking to get away, Klaus visited an old friend, *Herr Beckmann,* who owned a small bookshop tucked away in a quiet alley. The scent of aged paper and leather greeted him as he stepped inside.

"Klaus! It's been too long," Beckmann exclaimed.

They sat amidst stacks of books, sipping strong coffee. "The world is changing faster than I can comprehend," Klaus admitted.

Beckmann nodded sagely. "Change is inevitable. It's how we adapt that defines us."

"I fear I've become obsolete," Klaus confessed.

"Nonsense," Beckmann replied. "Your experiences are valuable. Share them with the younger generation."

Klaus sighed. "They don't wish to hear it."

"Perhaps they need to," Beckmann suggested gently.

As he left the shop, Klaus pondered his friend's words. The streets were quieter now, the bustle of the day giving way to the stillness of evening. A church bell tolled in the distance, marking the hour.

On 31 August 1947, the day before the official implementation of the Deutsche Mark, Frieda stood before a gathering of volunteers.

"Tomorrow marks a significant step towards our nation's recovery," she began. "We rebuild not just our economy but our sense of community."

Applause rippled through the crowd.

She continued, "Let us approach this change with open hearts and minds, honouring our past while embracing the future."

Back at home, Klaus sat alone. The old Reichsmark notes spread before him like relics. He traced the intricate designs with a finger, each line connecting to memories of a different time.

Marta entered quietly. "The new currency comes into effect tomorrow," she said softly.

He didn't look up. "So I've heard."

She sat beside him. "Holding onto these won't bring back what we've lost."

He clenched his jaw. "It's all I have left."

"You have us," she reminded him gently. "Your family."

He met her eyes, the walls around his heart beginning to crack. "I've pushed you all away, haven't I?"

She took his hand. "We're still here."

He sighed heavily. "I don't know how to move forward."

"One step at a time," she encouraged. "Perhaps start by talking to Frieda and Hans."

He nodded slowly. "Perhaps."

That evening, the family gathered for supper. The atmosphere was tentative but hopeful.

Klaus cleared his throat. "I realise I've been… difficult."

Frieda and Hans exchanged a glance.

"I've struggled to accept the changes happening around us," he continued. "But I don't wish to lose my family over it."

Frieda reached across the table, her eyes softening. "We don't want that either, Vater."

Hans added, "We may have different views, but we're still family."

Marta smiled, relief clear in her expression.

Klaus managed a small smile. "Perhaps we can find common ground."

As night fell, the city braced for the dawn of a new economic era. The Deutsche Mark would soon circulate, bringing hope and uncertainty to it.

Frieda stood by her bedroom window, gazing at the stars that pierced the velvet sky. She whispered a silent prayer for unity and understanding.

In his room, Klaus tucked away the Reichsmark notes, folding them carefully into a drawer—perhaps a farewell to the past and a tentative step towards acceptance.

The Engelhardts faced the future together, their bonds tested but not broken. Amidst the ruins of their world, they rebuilt their surroundings and the bridges between them.

As the first light of 1 September 1947 crept over the horizon, a new chapter unfolded for Germany and the Engelhardt family.

ooo

Autumn wrapped Hamburg in a cloak of damp chill as 1 September 1947 dawned grey and unyielding. The skies wept a constant drizzle, turning the city's scarred streets into a mosaic of puddles reflecting the sombre clouds above. Hans Engelhardt stood on the platform of the Hauptbahnhof, a threadbare rucksack slung over his shoulder. The hiss of steam and the clatter of trains filled the air, mingling with the murmurs of passengers shuffling about with purposeful haste.

He glanced back towards the city centre, where the spires of St. Michael's Church pierced the low-hanging mist. A pang of nostalgia gripped him, but a steely resolve swiftly replaced it. The East called to him with promises of equality and renewal—a chance to be part of something greater than himself. He boarded the train bound for Berlin, the carriage swaying gently as it pulled away from the station.

The journey eastward unfolded through landscapes of stark contrast— fields left fallow, villages slowly rebuilding, and forests bearing the scars of conflict. Hans gazed out the window, his reflection superimposed over the passing scenery. His mind buzzed with anticipation for the months ahead, filled with meetings and the camaraderie of like-minded youths striving for a socialist future.

On 5 September 1947, Hans arrived in Berlin, a city teetering between ruin and resurgence. The Soviet sector bustled with activity; red banners adorned the streets, emblazoned with slogans like *"Proletarier aller Länder, Vereinigte euch!*—"Workers of the world, unite!" The air was thick with the smell of coal smoke and the tang of wet stone.

He made his way to a modest flat shared with other members of the socialist youth movement. The building stood stoically amidst the rubble, its façade pockmarked but resilient. Inside, the atmosphere was one of extreme purpose. Maps, pamphlets, and newspapers cluttered every surface, and discussions spilt from room to room like an endless tide.

"Comrade Engelhardt, welcome back!" greeted Lena, a spirited young woman with keen eyes and a ready smile.

"Hans, please," he corrected with a grin. "How are preparations for the conference coming along?"

"Intense," she replied, leading him to a cramped kitchen where a pot of thin soup simmered on the stove. "But spirits are high. We have delegates arriving from all over the Soviet zone."

Over the following weeks, Hans immersed himself in organising the conference scheduled for 15 October 1947. Late nights blurred into early mornings as they drafted agendas, prepared speeches, and debated the nuances of socialist theory. The shared conviction among the group filled him with a sense of belonging he had not felt in years.

Back in Hamburg, Klaus grew increasingly aware of his son's prolonged absence. On 20 September 1947, a letter arrived—a brief note from Hans explaining that he was working in Berlin and would return home when he could. Klaus read the letter with a mixture of relief and apprehension. The lack of detail gnawed at him.

"He's finding his own way," Marta offered gently, sensing her husband's unease.

"His own way?" Klaus retorted. "In the East? Under Soviet influence?"

Marta placed a reassuring hand on his arm. "He's young and idealistic. Perhaps it's not as dire as you fear."

Klaus turned away, the weight of his doubts pressing heavily upon him. "I should have seen this coming," he muttered.

Meanwhile, Frieda busied herself with her own endeavours, though worry for her brother lingered at the edges of her thoughts. She had not heard from Hans directly, and the whispers of increasing Soviet control in the East unsettled her.

On 10 October 1947, a chill wind swept through Berlin as Hans and his comrades completed preparations for the conference. The venue was a discreet building tucked away in a quiet neighbourhood—a former school repurposed for their cause. Red flags draped the walls, and portraits of Marx and Lenin gazed sternly upon the gathering.

As delegates filtered in from various regions, the air buzzed with animated conversations. Hans felt a surge of pride as he watched Lena confidently greet attendees, her passion mirroring his own.

That evening, they gathered in a dimly lit room, the scent of damp wood and ink permeating the air. A makeshift podium stood at the front, illuminated by a single bulb that cast elongated shadows.

"Comrades," began Viktor Müller, a seasoned organiser with a resonant voice, "we are on the cusp of a new era. The proletariat shall rise, and together, we will forge a Germany free from the shackles of capitalist oppression."

Applause rippled through the crowd.

Hans listened intently as speakers elaborated on plans to nationalise industry, redistribute land, and establish workers' councils. The vision painted before him was one of unity and justice—a stark contrast to the fractured society he had left behind.

On 15 October 1947, the conference begun in earnest. Hans took the stage to deliver a speech on youth involvement in the socialist movement.

"Friends and comrades," he began, his voice steady despite the flutter of nerves, "we are the architects of our nation's future. It falls upon us to dismantle the vestiges of fascism and build a society where equality is not merely a dream but a reality."

He spoke of solidarity, education reform, and their collective power. As he concluded, the room erupted in applause, and a sense of exhilaration washed over him.

That night, as the delegates celebrated with songs and shared stories, Hans felt a profound connection to those around him. Yet, amidst the camaraderie, a sliver of doubt crept in. He wondered how his family would perceive his choices, particularly his father.

Back in Hamburg, Klaus's suspicions intensified. On 20 October 1947, he confronted Marta.

"Have you heard from Hans?" he demanded.

She shook her head. "Only you have."

"I can feel it," Klaus declared. "He has become entangled with the communists."

Marta sighed. "Even if that is so, condemning him will not bring him back."

"We must do something," he insisted. "I cannot stand by while my son betrays his country."

"Perhaps reaching out to him with understanding would be wiser," she suggested gently.

Klaus bristled. "Understanding? Of treachery?"

On 25 October 1947, Frieda received a letter from Hans. He wrote of his involvement in the movement, his belief in a fairer society, and his hope that she might understand. Concerned, she sought Greta Schmidt for advice.

They met at a quaint café nestled amidst a row of linden trees shedding their golden leaves. The air was crisp, carrying the scent of roasted coffee beans.

"Greta, I don't know what to do," Frieda confessed, stirring her tea absently.

Greta considered her words. "Hans is searching for purpose, much like many of us. The allure of socialism is strong, especially for those disillusioned by the past."

"I fear he's becoming entrenched in something dangerous," Frieda admitted.

"Perhaps you can reach out to him," Greta suggested. "Bridge the gap before it's too wide."

As November approached, the chill in the air deepened. On 5 November 1947, Hans returned to Hamburg, hoping to share his newfound convictions with his family. He arrived unannounced, the familiar creak of the front door echoing in the quiet house.

"Hans!" Marta exclaimed, enveloping him in a warm embrace.

"*Mutti,* it's good to be home," he replied, the scent of her lavender soap invoking memories of simpler times.

Klaus emerged from the study, his expression guarded. "So, you've graced us with your presence."

Hans met his father's gaze steadily. "I have much to tell you."

They gathered in the parlour, the atmosphere thick with unspoken tension. Hans recounted his experiences in Berlin, the ideals that fuelled his passion, and his belief that socialism was the path to Germany's redemption.

Klaus listened in stony silence. When Hans finished, he spoke with measured restraint. "You align yourself with those who seek to dismantle our nation from within."

"I seek to rebuild it, *Vater,* so that we never repeat the atrocities of the past," Hans countered.

"You are naïve," Klaus retorted. "The Soviets care nothing for Germany. They will use you and discard you."

Hans's temper flared. "At least they offer a vision of hope, not the stagnation you cling to."

"Enough!" Klaus roared, slamming his fist on the table. "I will not tolerate this insolence under my roof."

Marta interjected softly, "Please, both of you, calm down."

Frieda, who had remained silent, finally spoke. "Hans, perhaps there's a way to pursue change without alienating your own family."

He looked at her imploringly. "Frieda, you see that the West offers nothing but hollow promises."

She shook her head. "I see a Germany that can rebuild through cooperation and democracy, not through the suppression of individual freedoms."

Klaus seized upon her words. "Listen to your sister. She understands the value of our heritage."

Hans stood abruptly. "If valuing our heritage means ignoring the suffering of the masses, then I want no part of it."

On 30 November 1947, tensions reached a boiling point. The family sat down for dinner, the clatter of cutlery the only sound punctuating the heavy silence.

Klaus fixed his gaze on Hans. "I will not have a communist sympathiser under my roof."

Hans met his stare unflinchingly. "And outdated nationalism will not silence me."

Marta's eyes filled with tears. "Please, this is tearing us apart."

Klaus's voice was bitter. "You have a choice, Hans. Renounce this folly or leave."

Hans felt a surge of defiance mingled with heartbreak. "If that's what you wish, *Vater,* then I will go."

Frieda reached out. "Hans, don't do this."

He looked at her sadly. "I cannot stay where I am not accepted."

He packed his belongings swiftly, the weight of his decision pressing upon him. As he stood at the doorway, Marta embraced him tightly. "Take care of yourself," she whispered, her voice thick with emotion.

"I will, *Mutti,*" he assured her, holding on a moment longer.

Frieda hugged him next. "Write to me," she implored.

He nodded. "I will."

Klaus remained seated, his back turned. Hans hesitated, then spoke softly. "Goodbye, *Vater.*"

There was no response.

As Hans stepped out into the frigid night, a light snow fell, dusting the streets in a thin layer of white. Each step away from his childhood home felt heavier than the last, but he steeled himself with the conviction that he was pursuing a just cause.

Inside, Marta confronted Klaus. "How could you let him leave like that?"

Klaus's façade cracked ever so slightly. "He has made his choice."

"That boy is your son!" she cried.

Despite a flicker of doubt shadowing his eyes, Klaus declared, "He is a stranger to me now."

Frieda stood by the window, watching Hans's figure recede into the darkness. A profound sense of loss settled over her. The family was fracturing, mirroring the divide, tearing Germany apart.

Over the following days, the Engelhardt household existed in a state of strained normalcy. Conversations were terse, and the absence of Hans hung like a spectre in every room.

ooo

The first day of December 1947 dawned crisp and clear, a rare gift in the typically grey Hamburg winter. The city stirred with a newfound energy as the sun cast a golden hue over the rebuilding skyline. Frieda Engelhardt stood on the steps of the Rathaus, the ornate city hall, its façade partially restored to its former glory. She clutched a stack of documents to her chest; the chill seeping through her gloves, but her spirit remained undaunted.

"*Frau Engelhardt,* congratulations on your new appointment," called out *Herr Müller,* a senior official she respected.

"*Vielen Dank, Herr Müller* (Thank you very much, Mr Müller)," she replied warmly. "I am eager to begin."

He smiled appreciatively. "Your dedication is precisely what Hamburg needs."

Just that morning, 1 December 1947, Frieda had accepted a position working directly with the city's municipal council. Her efforts in volunteer work and her passionate advocacy for reconstruction had not gone unnoticed. The role promised challenges but also the opportunity to influence meaningful change.

As she walked through the bustling streets, the sounds of hammers striking nails and the hum of machinery filled the air. The scent of fresh timber mingled with the lingering aroma of roasted chestnuts from a nearby vendor. Children laughed as they played amidst the scaffolding, their cheeks flushed pink from the cold.

At a construction site near the harbour, workers hoisted beams into place, rebuilding warehouses essential for the city's economic revival. Frieda observed her breath forming delicate clouds. She felt a swell of pride; the Marshall Plan was no longer just a promise—it was tangible progress.

Back at the Engelhardt apartment, Klaus sat by the window, his gaze fixed on the world outside, yet seeing none of it. The December light cast long shadows across the room, accentuating the lines etched deeply into his face. He turned the worn pages of a book absentmindedly, the words blurring together.

Marta entered quietly, carrying a tray with steaming mugs of herbal tea. "It's colder today," she remarked, setting a mug beside him.

He nodded curtly. "So it seems."

"Frieda has taken a new position with the city council," she ventured cautiously.

"Yes, I heard," he replied, his tone unreadable.

"She's doing remarkable work," Marta continued. "Perhaps you might speak with her about it."

Klaus sighed heavily. "Her world is no longer mine."

"She is your daughter," Marta reminded him gently.

He closed the book with a soft thud. "A daughter who embraces a Germany I scarcely recognise."

Marta rested a hand on his shoulder. "Change is inevitable. We must find our place within it."

He remained silent, his thoughts a labyrinth of regret and disillusionment.

On 10 December 1947, Frieda attended a meeting with the municipal council. The room buzzed with discussion as officials reviewed plans for infrastructure projects funded by the Marshall Plan. Blueprints covered the table, detailing new roads, bridges, and public buildings.

"By improving transportation links, we can stimulate trade and connect communities," Frieda asserted, pointing to a map. "This bridge over the Elbe River is crucial."

An older councillor raised an eyebrow. "Ambitious, but do we have the manpower?"

"With proper organisation and the continued support of our allies, it's workable," she insisted.

Her confidence and clear vision impressed many in the room. After the meeting, *Herr Becker,* a seasoned architect, approached her.

"Your passion is inspiring, *Fräulein Engelhardt,*" he remarked. "Have you considered a career in politics?"

She laughed lightly. "I'm merely focused on rebuilding our city."

"Precisely why you should consider it," he encouraged.

As Frieda immersed herself in her work, Klaus withdrew further. On 15 December 1947, he ventured into the city, seeking familiarity in a landscape that had irrevocably changed. The once-grand avenues were a patchwork of ruins and new construction. He wandered aimlessly, the cacophony of progress a discordant melody.

He passed by a group of American soldiers conversing with locals. Their easy camaraderie stirred a bitterness within him. Nearby, a billboard proclaimed in bold letters: *"Dank der Marshall-Plan-Hilfe—Eine bessere Zukunft für Deutschland*—Thanks to Marshall Plan aid, a better future for Germany."

Klaus scoffed under his breath. "A future dictated by foreign powers," he muttered.

Stopping at a small park, he sat on a bench overlooking a frozen pond. Children skated clumsily, their laughter ringing out across the ice. He recalled bringing Hans and Frieda here when they were young—their faces alight with joy, unburdened by the weight of the world.

A familiar voice pulled him from his reverie. "Klaus?"

He looked up to see Jakob Fischer, his old war comrade, his features hardened by time and unrepentant resolve.

"Jakob," Klaus acknowledged.

They sat in silence for a moment before Jakob spoke. "The city is unrecognisable."

"Indeed," Klaus agreed. "They rebuild over the ashes without a thought for what was lost."

Jakob's eyes flashed with anger. "They betray our sacrifices, embracing the enemy's handouts."

Klaus hesitated. "My daughter is among them."

Jakob sneered. "Then she is blind to the truth, as are so many."

A pang of defensiveness stirred within Klaus. "She believes she is helping."

"Helping whom?" Jakob challenged. "The Americans? The ones who seek to mould Germany in their image?"

Klaus stood abruptly. "I must be going."

"Don't lose yourself, Klaus," Jakob warned. "Remember who you are."

As he walked away, Klaus felt the weight of Jakob's words pressing on him. But doubt gnawed at him—was clinging to the past any better than blind acceptance of the new order?

On 20 December 1947, Frieda returned home late, her cheeks flushed from the cold. She found Marta knitting by the fireplace, the soft glow casting warmth into the room.

"*Mutti,* is *Vater* home?" she asked.

"He's in his study," Marta replied. "I think he would appreciate a visit."

Frieda nodded, making her way to the door left slightly ajar. She knocked softly. *"Vater?"*

"Come in," came the muted response.

She entered to find him hunched over his desk, papers strewn about. "I wanted to share some news with you."

He glanced up, his eyes weary. "Yes?"

"I received an offer for a more prominent role within the council," she began tentatively. She tentatively began, "I thought you might be pleased,"

He regarded her for a long moment. "Your accomplishments are… noteworthy."

She detected a hint of pride beneath his guarded tone. "Thank you."

"But tell me, Frieda," he continued, "do you truly believe this path serves Germany's best interests?"

She met his gaze steadily. "I believe it offers hope for a better future."

"A future dependent on foreign aid?" he pressed.

"A future where we rebuild ourselves, with help," she countered. "We cannot do it alone."

He sighed. "Perhaps I am too old to understand."

She softened. "I value your perspective, *Vater.* Your experiences are important."

He looked away. "My time has passed."

"Not if you choose to be part of the present," she implored gently.

He did not respond, and after a moment, she excused herself, the unspoken distance between them lingering.

Christmas approached, and the city adorned itself in modest decorations. On 24 December 1947, the Engelhardts attended a church service, the sanctuary filled with candlelight and the harmonious strains of a choir singing *"O Tannenbaum."* The familiar rituals brought a semblance of peace.

After the service, they walked home through softly falling snow. Klaus walked slightly apart, his breath visible in the frosty air. Frieda hesitated before reaching out to link her arm with his.

"It's beautiful tonight," she remarked.

He nodded. "It reminds me of winters long ago."

She smiled. "Perhaps we can create new memories."

He glanced at her, a flicker of warmth in his eyes. "Perhaps."

On 31 December 1947, the city held a grand celebration to mark the end of a tumultuous year and the hopeful beginning of the next. The central square teemed with people bundled against the cold, their faces illuminated by strings of lights and the glow of lanterns. Stalls offered warm pastries and mulled wine, the scents mingling invitingly.

Frieda stood on a temporary stage erected for the occasion, the hum of the crowd a steady backdrop. She wore a tailored coat and a crimson scarf, her posture confident yet humble.

"Citizens of Hamburg," she began, her voice carrying through the crisp night air, "we stand here tonight not only to bid farewell to the year behind us but to celebrate the resilience and spirit that has brought us this far."

Applause rippled through the audience.

"Our city has faced unimaginable challenges," she continued. "Yet, through unity and determination, we are rebuilding—not just structures, but the very fabric of our community."

She spoke of the progress made possible by the Marshall Plan. Of the schools reopened, the homes restored, the businesses revived.

"This is just the beginning," she declared. "Together, we will forge a future marked by prosperity and peace."

The crowd erupted in cheers, a palpable sense of optimism surging.

At the edge of the square, Klaus watched from the shadows, his features obscured by the brim of his hat. He observed his daughter commanding the attention of so many, her words stirring hearts. A mixture of pride and alienation churned within him.

"She has a gift," remarked a voice beside him.

Klaus turned to see *Herr Becker*, the architect. "Indeed."

"You must be proud," Becker added.

Klaus hesitated. "She has achieved much."

Becker nodded. "Her vision inspires others. She represents the best of what Germany can become."

Klaus looked back at Frieda, now descending the stage amid congratulations. "Perhaps," he murmured.

As midnight approached, the bells of St. Michael's Church tolled. The crowd counted down in unison, voices mingling in anticipation.

"Drei… Zwei… Eins… Frohes Neues Jahr!"

Fireworks burst overhead, painting the sky with vibrant colours. The collective cheer was a cathartic release, a shedding of past burdens.

Frieda made her way through the throng towards her father. *"Vater!"* she called out, her eyes bright.

He met her halfway, the noise fading into the background. "Happy New Year, Frieda," he offered, his tone softer than she had heard in a long time.

She smiled warmly. "Happy New Year."

They stood together, the fireworks reflecting in their eyes. For a fleeting moment, the chasm between them seemed to narrow.

"Perhaps this year will bring us closer," she ventured.

He considered her words. "Perhaps."

Back at home, Marta had prepared a modest feast, and the table was set with care. They sat together, the clatter of cutlery punctuating the comfortable silence.

"To new beginnings," Marta toasted, raising her glass.

"To hope," Frieda added.

Klaus raised his glass thoughtfully. "To family."

The clink of glasses resonated with unspoken promises.

Later that night, as the city settled into the quiet of the early hours, Klaus retreated to his study. He lit a candle, its flame casting a gentle glow. From a drawer, he retrieved a worn photograph of the family taken years before—a captured moment of unity.

He traced the faces with his finger, lingering on Hans's youthful smile. A pang of regret pierced him. Setting the photo aside, he pulled out a sheet of paper and wrote.

Lieber Hans,

Perhaps it is time we spoke…

The words came haltingly at first, but soon flowed with earnestness. He wrote of memories, of misunderstandings, of a desire to bridge the distance.

As dawn approached on 1 January 1948, Klaus sealed the letter, his resolve firm. The new year stretched out before him—a canvas yet to be filled.

In the months that followed, the Engelhardts continued to navigate the complexities of a nation in flux. Frieda's star rose, and her influence grew. Klaus wrestled with his place in this evolving landscape, torn between the shadows of the past and the possibilities of the future.

But on that first morning of the year, there was a glimmer of reconciliation—a fragile thread connecting them amidst the ruins of what once was and the foundations of what could be.

ooo

Winter tightened its grip on Hamburg as 1 January 1948 dawned under a blanket of grey skies and biting cold. The Elbe River lay stiff and silent, its edges crusted with ice. Frost clung to the windowpanes of the Engelhardt home, etching delicate patterns that blurred the world outside. Klaus sat at the kitchen table, cradling a cup of black coffee that had long since gone cold. The aroma of fresh bread wafted through the room, but his appetite was absent.

Marta watched him from the doorway, concern etched into the lines of her face. *"Guten Morgen,"* she offered softly.

He glanced up briefly. *"Morgen."*

"Did you sleep well?" she inquired, though she knew the answer.

He shrugged. "As well as one can these days."

She sighed, moving to pour herself a cup of tea. The silence between them was heavy, filled with unspoken words and lingering shadows. "There will be a memorial service on 15 January," she mentioned casually. "To honour those lost during the war."

Klaus stiffened. "What purpose is it to dwell on such things?"

"It's important to remember," she replied gently. "For healing."

He scoffed lightly. "Healing. Perhaps some wounds are best left undisturbed."

Marta hesitated. "I think it might be good for you to attend."

He met her gaze sharply. "And why is that?"

"To find peace," she said simply.

He looked away, the set of his jaw tightening. "Peace is a luxury I cannot afford."

The days dragged on, each as bleak as the last. Snow fell intermittently, covering the city in a shroud of white that did little to brighten the mood. On 10 January 1948, Frieda returned home late in the evening, her cheeks flushed from the cold and the invigorating discussions at the council meeting.

"Mutti, Vater," she greeted, shedding her coat and scarf. "There's talk of expanding the memorial to include personal testimonies. Survivors will share their stories."

Marta nodded approvingly. "That's a meaningful addition."

Klaus remained silent, his eyes fixed on the newspaper spread before him.

Frieda continued, undeterred. "I think it's crucial for us to hear these accounts firsthand. It brings a human connection to the history."

Klaus folded the paper deliberately. "Isn't it enough that they have humiliated and occupied us? Must we now subject ourselves to tales of suffering we could not prevent?"

Frieda bristled. "We had a hand in that suffering, *Vater.*"

He stood abruptly. "You will not lecture me in my home," he snapped.

She took a deep breath, steadying herself. "Ignoring the past won't change it."

He glared at her, the air between them crackling with tension. "Some things are better left unspoken."

With that, he retreated to his study; the door closing with a resolute thud.

Marta placed a comforting hand on Frieda's arm. "He carries burdens he cannot yet share."

Frieda sighed. "I just wish he would let us help."

On 15 January 1948, the memorial service took place at St. Nikolai Church, its spire a sombre silhouette against the overcast sky. The partially restored church stood as a testament to resilience amidst ruins. A chilly wind whispered through the streets, carrying the faint scent of incense and melting snow.

Klaus walked towards the church, almost against his will. The cobblestones beneath his feet were slick, and he pulled his coat tighter against the chill. As he approached, the tolling of the bells echoed like a solemn heartbeat. He entered quietly, hoping to remain unnoticed.

Inside, people filled the nave—survivors, families, officials, and ordinary citizens. Candles flickered along the aisles, casting a warm glow that contrasted with the icy world outside. The air was thick with a mixture of grief and reverence.

He slipped into a seat at the back, the wooden pew creaking softly under his weight. Voices hushed as the service began. A choir sang *"Ach, wie flüchtig, ach wie nichtig,"* their harmonies weaving a tapestry of sorrow and hope.

A man stepped up to the lectern, his face etched with lines that spoke of unimaginable hardships. "My name is Samuel Weiss," he began, his voice steady yet heavy with emotion. "I am a survivor of Auschwitz."

Klaus felt his chest tighten.

Samuel recounted his experiences—the loss of his family, the horrors witnessed, the struggle to keep a shred of humanity amidst the inhuman. His words painted vivid images that seared into Klaus's mind. Each detail was a blow, chipping away at the defences Klaus had built around his conscience.

A woman followed, her hands trembling as she spoke of the Kindertransport and the parents she never saw again. Tears glistened on cheeks throughout the congregation.

Klaus's vision blurred. The walls seemed to close in, the air thinning. Memories he had suppressed clawed their way to the surface—villages burned, faces twisted in fear, orders barked without question. The weight of his past pressed down upon him like a vise.

He stood abruptly, stumbling towards the exit. Heads turned, whispers murmured, but he heard nothing beyond the pounding of his heart. Outside, the cold air hit him like a slap. He leaned against the stone wall, gasping for breath.

Marta had seen him leave and followed, concern etched across her face. "Klaus!"

He didn't respond, his gaze fixed on some distant point beyond the harbour.

She placed a hand on his arm. "Please, talk to me."

He shook her off gently. "I can't… I can't breathe."

"Let me help you," she implored.

He turned to face her, eyes wild with a turmoil she hadn't seen before. "How can you? How can anyone? There's no absolution for me."

Tears welled in her eyes. "You don't have to carry this alone."

He looked away. "It's too late."

She stepped closer. "It's never too late to seek forgiveness."

He laughed bitterly. "From whom? God? Those we've wronged? Myself?"

"From those who love you," she whispered.

He met her gaze, the anger draining to reveal a profound sadness. "I am not the man you once knew."

"Perhaps not," she conceded. "But you are still my husband, the father of our children."

He closed his eyes, a single tear escaping down his weathered cheek. "I've failed you all."

She reached up to wipe the tear away. "Failure is not final unless you give up."

He pulled away, and the moment of vulnerability shuttered. "I need to be alone."

Marta watched as he walked away, his figure blending into the monochrome palette of the winter landscape. She wrapped her arms around herself, a chill deeper than the weather settling into her bones.

Over the next few days, Klaus retreated further into himself. He spent hours in his study, the door closed to the world. Marta left meals outside his door, most of which went untouched.

On 20 January 1948, Frieda approached her mother. "I'm worried about him."

"So am I," Marta admitted. "He refuses to speak."

"Perhaps we should call for Dr Schneider," Frieda suggested.

"He won't see a doctor," Marta sighed. "He barely acknowledges me."

"Maybe I can try," Frieda offered.

Marta hesitated. "He hasn't been receptive to you lately."

"All the more reason to try," Frieda insisted.

She knocked softly on the study door. "*Vater?* It's Frieda."

Silence.

"I just want to talk."

After a long pause, she heard a faint, "Come in."

She entered cautiously. The room was dim, the curtains drawn. Papers littered the desk, and the air was thick with the smell of stale tobacco. Klaus sat by the window, staring blankly at the street below.

She took a seat opposite him. "*Mutti* and I are worried."

He didn't respond.

She continued. "We care about you. Whatever you're going through, we want to help."

He finally spoke, his voice barely above a whisper. "You can't help."

"Let us try," she urged.

He turned to look at her, his eyes hollow. "Do you think me a monster?"

She was taken aback. "Of course not."

"Perhaps you should," he said bitterly. "I've done things… followed orders… that haunt me."

Frieda chose her words carefully. "The war compelled many to act against their conscience."

He shook his head. "That's no excuse. I knew. I saw. And I did nothing to stop it."

She reached out to touch his hand. "Acknowledging that is the first step."

He withdrew his hand. "What good does that do now? Those people… their lives,"

"Perhaps you can honour their memory by facing the truth," she suggested gently.

He laughed without mirth. "And how do I do that?"

"By speaking out. By ensuring such atrocities never happen again."

He looked at her with a mixture of despair and disbelief. "You are naïve."

"Maybe," she admitted. "But I believe in redemption."

He stood abruptly. "Redemption is for the innocent."

She rose to face him. "No, it's for those who seek it."

He turned away. "Leave me."

"Vater—"

"Please," he implored, his voice cracking.

She hesitated, then nodded. "I'm here if you need me."

As she left, the weight of his anguish pressed upon her. She found Marta in the kitchen, her hands submerged in soapy water.

"How did it go?" Marta asked, not turning around.

"Not well," Frieda confessed. "He's in so much pain."

Marta sighed heavily. "I fear he's slipping away from us."

"Perhaps we need to give him time," Frieda suggested.

"Time may not be enough," Marta murmured.

On 25 January 1948, a letter arrived from Hans. It was brief, detailing his continued work in the East and his hopes for a reunified Germany under socialist principles. There was no mention of personal matters, no inquiries about their well-being.

Klaus read the letter with a detached air. "He's entrenched himself fully," he remarked.

Frieda sensed an opportunity. "Maybe we can reach out to him and find common ground."

Klaus shook his head. "He has lost himself, just as I have lost myself,"

"Don't say that," she pleaded. "We haven't lost you."

He met her gaze. "Haven't you? Look at me. I am a ghost, lingering where I no longer belong."

"That's not true," she insisted.

He sighed wearily. "You and your mother deserve better."

Marta entered the room, sensing the gravity of the conversation. "We are a family. We face things together."

Klaus looked between them. "I've burdened you both for too long."

Marta stepped forward. "We choose to bear that burden because we love you."

He seemed to shrink before their eyes, the weight of his guilt crushing. "I don't know how to be the man you need me to be."

"Just be here with us," Marta urged. "Let us in."

He hesitated, the walls he'd built showing the slightest cracks. "I don't know if I can."

Frieda reached out. "One step at a time."

He nodded faintly. "Perhaps."

The days that followed were a tentative dance of proximity and distance. Klaus emerged from his study more often, joining them for meals, though he spoke little. Marta and Frieda refrained from pressing him, allowing space for healing.

On 31 January 1948, a rare glimpse of sunlight broke through the clouds. Klaus suggested a walk along the harbour, surprising them both.

As they strolled, the crisp air filled their lungs, and the distant sounds of ships echoed across the water. Seagulls circled overhead, their calls a reminder of life carrying on.

Klaus paused by the railing, gazing out at the horizon where the sea met the sky. "I used to dream of voyages," he mused quietly.

Marta smiled gently. "You always loved the sea."

He turned to them. "Perhaps it's time to set sail on a new journey."

Frieda's eyes lit with hope. "We're with you, whatever course you choose."

He managed a small smile. "Thank you."

They continued along the pier, the sun casting elongated shadows that stretched before them like a path into the future. The chill in the air remained, but a subtle warmth kindled within their hearts.

As January gave way to February, the Engelhardts faced the uncertain days ahead with a renewed, albeit fragile, sense of unity. Klaus's path to reconciliation would be arduous, fraught with the spectres of his past. But for the first time in a long while, he will take that first step, guided by the unwavering support of his family.

During a nation grappling with its identity, the Engelhardts mirrored that struggle within their own home. The ruins they navigated were not just the physical remnants of war, but the emotional landscapes scarred by guilt, loss, and the hope for redemption.

Together, they braced for the thaw of winter, anticipating the possibilities that spring might bring—a season of renewal, both for their family and for a country seeking to heal its deepest wounds.

FOUR:

THE DIVISION OF GERMANY

The sun hung low over Hamburg on 12 June 1948, casting elongated shadows that stretched across the cobblestone streets of the city square. A brisk wind whispered through the alleys, carrying with it the mingled scents of fresh bread from a nearby bakery and the ever-present tang of coal smoke. Klaus Engelhardt stood on the outskirts of the gathering crowd, his collar turned up against the sharp snap of the late spring breeze.

He watched as people converged around the public loudspeaker mounted atop a weathered pole in the centre of the square. The device crackled to life, emitting a high-pitched whine before settling into a steady hum. Faces turned upwards, a mosaic of anticipation and unease etched into each one. Mothers clutched the hands of their children, old men leaned on canes, and young workers wiped soot-streaked hands on their overalls.

Klaus felt a knot tighten in his stomach. He was a man apart, an observer in a world that seemed to move on without him. The murmur of the crowd swelled as the announcer's voice boomed across the square, crisp and authoritative.

"Citizens of Hamburg, we bring urgent news. The Soviet Union has initiated a blockade of all land and rail routes into West Berlin."

A collective gasp rippled through the assembly. Whispers turned to hushed conversations. Klaus's heart pounded in his chest, each beat echoing the heavy toll of a distant bell.

"The blockade is an attempt to force the Western Allies to abandon their post in Berlin," the announcer continued. "But let everyone know, we continue to take actions to counter this aggression," the announcer continued.

Klaus's gaze swept over the crowd. He noted the furrowed brows, the tight lines around mouths, the flicker of fear in eyes that had seen too much already. A young man beside him clenched his fists, knuckles whitening.

"This can't be happening," the youth muttered.

Klaus shifted his weight, the soles of his worn boots scraping against the cobbles. He felt an urge to say something, to offer a word of solace or solidarity, but the words lodged in his throat like stones. Instead, he pulled a crumpled cigarette from his pocket, striking a match against the rough fabric of his trousers. The first inhale did little to calm his nerves.

As the crowd began to disperse, pockets of discussion flared up like small fires. Some spoke of hope, confident that the Allies would prevail. Others whispered in fear, worried that this was the prelude to another conflict.

Klaus turned away, threading his path through the throng. The distant rumble of trucks echoed from the harbour, where goods were being loaded and unloaded in a ceaseless dance of commerce. Yet, even amidst the activity, there was an undercurrent of tension, a palpable sense that the fragile peace was fracturing.

He wandered aimlessly, the city a blur around him. Memories pressed in—images of bombed-out buildings, the acrid smell of smoke, the cacophony of sirens and screams. The war had left indelible marks not just on the landscape, but on the soul of the nation. And now, as Germany stood on the precipice of division, Klaus felt those wounds tearing open anew.

By the time he reached his apartment, the light was fading; the sky painted with streaks of crimson and gold. He climbed the narrow stairwell, each creak of the wooden steps a familiar refrain. Inside, the warmth of the kitchen greeted him, along with the soft clatter of dishes.

Marta looked up from the stove, her eyes searching his face. "You heard the news?" she asked gently.

He nodded, hanging his coat on the peg by the door. "Yes."

She hesitated. "Frieda is organising a meeting tonight. To support the efforts in Berlin."

Klaus felt a flicker of irritation. "Of course she is."

"She's trying to help," Marta whispered.

"Help whom?" he retorted. "The Americans? The British? Those who would carve up our country for their own gains?"

Marta's shoulders sagged. "She's our daughter. She believes in what she's doing."

He waved a hand dismissively. "Belief is a luxury we can ill afford."

She turned back to the stove, stirring a pot of thin soup. The silence between them stretched taut like a wire.

Later that evening, Klaus sat alone in the parlour, the glow of a single lamp casting long shadows. He unfolded the newspaper, eyes skimming over headlines that spoke of political manoeuvres and international tensions. His mind drifted to Hans, his son, now somewhere in the East, embracing the very ideology that threatened to split their nation in two.

A knock at the door startled him. Frieda entered, cheeks flushed from the wind, a satchel slung over her shoulder.

"*Vater,*" she greeted him, breathless. "I didn't expect to find you still up."

He regarded her coolly. "Where else would I be?"

She set her satchel down, extracting a stack of leaflets. "We're mobilising support for the Berlin Airlift. The Allies are organising flights to bring supplies into West Berlin."

He raised an eyebrow. "And you think this is a cause worth championing?"

"People are starving," she implored. "They need food, medicine, coal. We can help."

Klaus leaned back in his chair, fingers steepled. "By aligning yourself with the very forces that seek to dominate us?"

Frieda's eyes flashed with determination. "This isn't about politics, *Vater*. It's about humanity."

He scoffed. "You're naïve if you think the West acts out of altruism."

She stood her ground. "And what of the East? Do you believe their intentions are pure?"

He fixed her with a hard stare. "At least they are Germans, not foreign occupiers."

"The Soviet Union controls the East," she countered. "They've imposed their will just as much as any other."

Klaus felt a surge of anger. "Enough. I won't debate this with you."

Frieda gathered her leaflets, her expression a mixture of frustration and sadness. "I wish you'd see I'm trying to make a difference."

He looked away. "Go on with your efforts, if you must. Just don't expect my approval."

She lingered a moment longer before turning and leaving the room. The door clicked softly behind her, the sound echoing in the quiet space.

Klaus rubbed his temples, a dull ache throbbing at the base of his skull. The world was shifting beneath his feet, and he felt powerless to halt its course. His children were slipping away—Hans to the East, Frieda to the West—and he stood stranded in the middle, a relic of a shattered past.

On 18 June 1948, the city square buzzed with heightened activity. American military trucks rumbled through the streets, laden with crates stamped with foreign lettering. Uniformed officers directed traffic, their voices sharp against the backdrop of hissing brakes and revving engines.

Klaus found himself drawn back to the square, unable to quell his curiosity. He watched as volunteers loaded supplies, their faces set with purpose. Among them, he spotted Frieda, her sleeves rolled up, a smudge of dirt streaked across her cheek. She moved with efficiency, coordinating efforts, her voice clear and commanding.

A sense of pride mingled with his disapproval. She was strong, undeniably so, but he couldn't shake the feeling that she was being pulled into a narrative not of her own making.

A man approached him—a tall American officer with a genial smile. "Good afternoon, sir. Care to lend a hand?"

Klaus bristled. "I have no interest in aiding your endeavours."

The officer raised his hands in a placating gesture. "Just thought I'd ask. Every bit helps."

"Helps whom?" Klaus challenged.

"Helps the people of Berlin," the officer replied evenly. "We're all in this together."

Klaus shook his head. "You are here on foreign soil, meddling in affairs you scarcely understand."

The officer's expression remained neutral. "Perhaps. But we can't stand by while people suffer."

Before Klaus could respond, Frieda appeared at his side. "Is everything alright here?"

"Just a friendly conversation," the officer assured her before moving on.

Frieda turned to her father, concern clear. "*Vater,* please. There's no need for hostility."

He clenched his jaw. "I won't apologise for speaking my mind."

She sighed. "Why do you insist on seeing enemies everywhere?"

"Because they are everywhere," he retorted. "We are pawns in a game played by greater powers."

"Or perhaps we have the chance to rebuild, to create something better," she suggested.

He regarded her with a weary gaze. "Your optimism blinds you."

"And your cynicism chains you," she replied softly.

They stood in silence, the bustle of the square swirling around them. Finally, Frieda placed a hand on his arm. "I have to get back. Please consider joining us. Even in a small way."

He pulled his arm away gently. "This is your path, not mine."

She nodded, a hint of resignation in her eyes. "Take care, *Vater.*"

As she walked away, Klaus felt the distance between them widen. An unbridgeable gulf carved by time and ideology.

On 24 June 1948, news spread that the Berlin Blockade had intensified. The Soviet forces had tightened their grip, cutting off electricity and further restricting access. The airlift became not just a temporary measure but a lifeline.

As supplies were redirected to support the effort, an influx of activity filled Hamburg's port. The skies above the city buzzed with aircraft, their engines droning like distant thunder.

Klaus sat by the window of his apartment, watching as planes soared overhead. The sound reminded him of darker days, of air raids and the relentless onslaught that had reduced much of the city to ruins. He couldn't reconcile the sight of these machines now being hailed as harbingers of hope.

Marta entered the room quietly. "They're saying the airlift is making a real difference."

He didn't respond.

She took a seat beside him. "Frieda is heading to Berlin tomorrow. To assist with distribution."

He turned sharply. "She's going into the midst of this conflict?"

"She believes it's where she can do the most good," Marta explained.

Klaus felt a surge of fear masked by anger. "And you support this?"

"I support our daughter's convictions," she said firmly.

He stood up, pacing the length of the room. "First Hans, now Frieda. Both running towards danger, towards ideals that will only lead to disappointment."

"Or perhaps towards a future they can help shape," Marta suggested.

He stopped, facing her. "You always were the hopeful one."

She offered a small smile. "And you the realist. Maybe we balance each other."

He sighed, the fight draining out of him. "I just want them safe."

"So do I," she agreed. "But we have to trust them."

That evening, Klaus ventured out into the streets. The city was alive with a restless energy. Posters adorned walls, urging solidarity and support for Berlin. Children played amidst piles of rubble, their laughter a stark contrast to the grim surroundings.

He passed a group of men gathered outside a tavern, their voices loud and animated.

"Did you hear? They've flown in over a thousand tonnes of supplies already," one exclaimed.

"At this rate, the Soviets will have to back down," another added.

Klaus moved on, their words ringing hollow in his ears. He turned down a quiet alley, the din of the main streets fading behind him. The walls around him bore scars, with bullet holes marking the bricks, reminding of the battles fought not so long ago.

He came upon a small courtyard where an old man sat playing a melancholic tune on a violin. The notes wafted through the air, intertwining with the soft rustle of leaves. Klaus paused, letting the music wash over him.

The musician opened his eyes, noticing Klaus. "Beautiful evening, isn't it?"

Klaus offered a nod. "The music is… haunting."

The old man smiled wistfully. "A song from before the war. When times were simpler."

"Were they ever truly simple?" Klaus mused.

"Perhaps not," the man conceded. "But memory has a way of smoothing the edges."

Klaus took a seat on a nearby bench. "Do you think we can ever find peace again?"

The violinist considered the question. "Peace is not a destination, but a journey. Each day we move towards or away from it."

"Wise words," Klaus acknowledged.

"Experience has been my teacher," the man replied.

They sat in companionable silence for a while, the music filling the spaces between thoughts.

As night descended, Klaus made his way home. The streets were quieter now, the earlier frenzy subdued. He felt a weariness settle deep within him, a bone-deep fatigue that sleep could not cure.

Back at the apartment, he found Frieda packing a small suitcase. She looked up as he entered.

"You're really going, then," he stated.

She nodded. "I leave at dawn."

He hesitated before speaking. "Be careful."

A flicker of surprise crossed her face. "I will."

He stepped forward. "Frieda, despite our differences, I want you to know that I… respect your commitment."

Her eyes softened. "Thank you, *Vater.* That means a lot."

He reached out awkwardly, patting her shoulder. "Just come back safely."

"I promise," she said earnestly.

As he left her room, Klaus felt a slight easing of the tension that had long existed between them. It was a small step, but perhaps the beginning of a bridge over the chasm that had grown.

The next morning, on 25 June 1948, Klaus stood at the window, watching as Frieda departed. She walked with purpose, her suitcase in hand, determination etched into every line of her posture. Marta joined him, slipping her hand into his.

"She'll make a difference," Marta whispered.

"Maybe she will," he conceded.

They watched until Frieda disappeared from sight, swallowed by the bustling city streets.

Klaus turned away, a heaviness settling over him. The world was changing rapidly, and he felt himself adrift. The divisions within his family mirrored those within the nation—fractures that seemed impossible to mend.

He knew not what the future held, but as the days unfolded, he resolved to find his place within it, to navigate the complexities with as much grace as he could muster.

For now, all he could do was wait and hope—that his children would remain safe, that his country might find a path to unity, and that he might one day reconcile the ghosts of his past with the uncertain promise of tomorrow.

ooo

The summer sun beat down on East Berlin on 1 July 1948, casting sharp shadows across the austere buildings that lined the streets. Hans Engelhardt stood amidst a throng of young people outside a nondescript building on Wilhelmstraße. The air was thick with the scent of warm asphalt and the distant hum of trams clattering along their tracks. A red banner fluttered above the entrance, emblazoned with the hammer and sickle—a beacon calling them to action.

"Comrades, this way," a fellow activist urged, beckoning them inside. Hans followed, his heart pounding with a mixture of excitement and purpose.

The interior was dimly lit, the walls adorned with posters of Marx and Lenin, their stern gazes seeming to appraise each newcomer.

As they settled into the crowded room, the murmur of voices created a low symphony of anticipation. Hans took a seat near the front, eager not to miss a word. The speaker, a charismatic man named Erich Mielke, took the podium. His voice resonated with conviction.

"Today marks a turning point," Mielke proclaimed. "We stand on the precipice of building a new Germany—one founded on equality, justice, and the power of the proletariat!"

Applause erupted, and Hans clapped enthusiastically. The energy was infectious, a stark contrast to the desolation he had felt in the war's aftermath. Here, among like-minded individuals, he sensed the possibility of redemption—not just for himself but for the nation.

Over the following weeks, Hans immersed himself deeper into the socialist movement. On 10 July 1948, he attended clandestine meetings in the back rooms of cafés and in the basements of abandoned buildings. The discussions were intense, fuelled by endless cups of strong coffee and the shared belief that they could reshape society.

"Education is key," insisted Lena, a fiery young woman with piercing blue eyes. "We must enlighten the masses, dispel the capitalist lies."

Hans nodded. "But we also need action. The workers must see tangible changes."

"Agreed," interjected Matthias, a fellow activist. "The formation of collective farms is progressing. We can show the benefits of shared labour and resources."

As they strategised, the warmth of camaraderie enveloped Hans. Each meeting reinforced his commitment, each plan sketched on paper brought them closer to their vision.

In the city of Hamburg, the refreshing cool breezes coming from the Elbe River provided relief from the intense summer heat. Coordinating volunteers for the Berlin Airlift support efforts, Frieda Engelhardt stood on the steps of the Rathaus on 20 July 1948. The plaza was a hub of activity, with trucks being loaded with supplies, pilots busy preparing for their flights, and citizens eagerly contributing to whatever they could. With the firsthand knowledge of the requirements of Berlin, she had returned to Hamburg and was actively assisting in coordinating the efforts.

"Please mark these parcels clearly," she instructed, as she handed a clipboard to a volunteer. "They contain medical supplies and must reach Tempelhof Airport by tomorrow."

The man nodded. "Right away, *Fräulein Engelhardt.*"

Her efficiency and dedication had not gone unnoticed. American officials often sought her input, appreciating her organisational skills and her fluency in English.

"Miss Engelhardt," called out Captain Thompson, an American liaison officer. "A moment, please."

She approached, shielding her eyes from the sun. "Yes, Captain?"

"I wanted to commend you on your outstanding work here," he said with a smile. "Your efforts are making a significant difference."

"Thank you," she replied graciously. "We all have a part to play."

"Indeed," he agreed. "By the way, there's a reception this evening for key personnel. Please attend."

Frieda hesitated briefly. "Of course. I'll be there."

Back at the Engelhardt household, Marta prepared supper, the aroma of simmering stew filling the modest kitchen. Klaus sat at the table, sifting through the day's newspaper. Reports on the Berlin Blockade and the escalating tensions between East and West dominated the headlines.

"Frieda seems quite busy these days," Marta commented, setting plates on the table.

Klaus grunted. "Too busy aligning herself with foreign interests."

"She's working to help people," Marta countered gently. "Is that so wrong?"

He folded the newspaper with a sigh. "It's not that simple. Our country is being torn apart, and she throws her lot in with those who seek to control us."

"Perhaps she's trying to bridge the divide," Marta suggested.

He shook his head. "And Hans? He's disappeared into the East, chasing utopian fantasies."

"Have you heard from him?" she asked softly.

"Not directly," Klaus admitted. "But I've heard rumours."

On 15 August 1948, those rumours solidified when news reached them at a significant socialist conference in East Berlin. Reports described throngs of young activists rallying behind the socialist cause, their zeal likened to that of revolutionaries.

Klaus clenched his jaw as he read the accounts. "Our son is among them," he spat, tossing the newspaper onto the table.

Marta picked it up, scanning the article. "How can you be sure?"

"I know Hans," he replied bitterly. "This is exactly the spectacle he'd involve himself in."

"Maybe he's found something he believes in," she offered.

"Believes in?" Klaus echoed incredulously. "He's turning his back on his heritage, his family."

"Or perhaps he's seeking a way to atone," Marta mused. "We all carry burdens from the past."

He stood abruptly. "I won't have you defending his choices."

She met his gaze steadily. "I'm not defending, Klaus. I'm trying to understand."

He turned away, frustration boiling over. "First Frieda with her Western affiliations, now Hans with his socialist delusions. It's as if our family is intent on tearing itself apart."

Marta reached out to touch his arm, but he pulled away. "We can't control their paths," she said softly. "All we can do is hope they find their way."

In East Berlin, Hans felt invigorated as he stood among thousands in Alexanderplatz. The square was awash with red flags and banners proclaiming solidarity and revolution. The air buzzed with excitement on 15 August 1948 as speakers took to the stage, their voices amplified over loudspeakers.

"Comrades!" the lead speaker shouted. "Today, we unite to forge a new destiny for Germany!"

Cheers erupted, and Hans joined in, his voice hoarse with enthusiasm. The sense of collective purpose was overwhelming.

Beside him, Lena squeezed his hand. "Isn't it incredible?" she exclaimed.

He nodded, eyes shining. "This is what I've been searching for—a chance to be part of something bigger than myself."

As the rally continued, Hans felt a deep connection with those around him. They shared stories of hardship, of loss, and of an unwavering desire to build a just society.

Later that evening, they gathered in a nearby hall for further discussions. The atmosphere was electric, charged with ideas and plans.

"We need to focus on education," Hans proposed during a breakout session. "Rewriting textbooks to reflect the truth, to free minds from the shackles of fascist indoctrination."

"Agreed," Matthias concurred. "And we ensure that workers have a voice in governance."

They mapped out strategies late into the night, the glow of kerosene lamps illuminating their earnest faces. Outside, the city was quiet, but inside, they were alive with possibility.

Back in Hamburg on 20 August 1948, Frieda attended a council meeting to discuss the ongoing support for the Berlin Airlift. The room brimmed with local officials and allied representatives.

"The airlift has been a success thus far," Captain Thompson reported. "But we expect increased pressure from the Soviets."

"We ensure that supply lines remain uninterrupted," Frieda asserted. "Our commitment cannot waver."

Herr Bauer, an older councilman, raised a concern about our stretched-thin resources, asking, "But at what cost? Perhaps we should consider negotiations."

"Negotiations?" Frieda challenged. "With those who seek to starve a city into submission? We cannot capitulate."

Murmurs spread through the room. Captain Thompson interjected. "Miss Engelhardt is correct. Maintaining a firm stance is crucial."

After the meeting, Frieda walked along the Alster Lake, the water reflecting the pastel hues of the setting sun. She contemplated the weight of the responsibilities she had shouldered. The path she had chosen was fraught with challenges, but she remained steadfast.

As she reached a bench, she noticed Greta Schmidt, her old friend and a journalist, sitting and scribbling in a notebook.

"Greta!" Frieda called out.

Greta looked up, a smile spreading across her face. "Frieda! Sit, please."

They embraced before settling side by side.

"What brings you here?" Frieda asked.

"I'm covering the Airlift efforts," Greta explained. "There's so much happening, and the world needs to know."

"How have you been?" Frieda inquired. "It's been too long."

Greta sighed. "Challenging. Many prefer to forget the past rather than confront it. People have not responded well to my articles on war crimes."

"I'm sorry," Frieda said sincerely. "But your work is important."

"Thank you," Greta replied. "And you? Making waves in local government, I hear."

Frieda chuckled lightly. "Just trying to do my part."

They sat in comfortable silence for a moment, the gentle lapping of the water a soothing backdrop.

"Have you heard from Hans?" Greta ventured cautiously.

Frieda shook her head. "Not directly. I know he's involved with socialist groups in the East."

"Do you worry about him?" Greta asked.

"Every day," Frieda admitted. "But he's always been headstrong."

Greta nodded. "These are turbulent times. Families are torn between ideologies."

Frieda gazed out over the lake. "I just hope he stays safe."

On 25 August 1948, a letter bearing the East German postmark arrived at the Engelhardt home. Marta's hands trembled slightly as she opened it, recognising Hans's familiar handwriting.

Dear Mutter,

I hope this finds you well. I wanted to share with you the incredible progress we're making here. The movement grows stronger each day, and I feel I'm truly contributing to the future of Germany.

Marta read aloud to Klaus, who sat stoically across from her.

"He writes with such enthusiasm," she remarked.

Klaus snorted derisively. "Brainwashed by propaganda."

"He's passionate," Marta countered. "Perhaps we should be proud that he's found purpose."

"Proud?" Klaus echoed. "He's aligning himself with those who would see our nation subjugated under Soviet control."

"Is that so different from the influence the West wields here?" she challenged gently.

He narrowed his eyes. "At least the West doesn't pretend to be our comrades while plotting to consume us."

She sighed. "Klaus, holding onto bitterness will only drive our children further away."

He stood, pacing the room. "What would you have me do? Embrace their choices blindly?"

"Not blind," she replied. "But with understanding."

He paused, rubbing his temples. "Perhaps it's too late for that."

In East Berlin, Hans folded the duplicate letter he'd penned to Frieda, sealing it carefully. He hoped that reaching out might bridge the gap that had grown between them. On 28 August 1948, he posted the letter, watching as it disappeared into the postbox—a missive sent across the ideological divide.

Returning to his shared flat, he found Lena poring over pamphlets.

"Another propaganda piece from the West," she scoffed, tossing it aside. "They think they can sway us with promises of capitalism's freedoms."

Hans picked it up, skimming the contents. "They underestimate our resolve."

"Exactly," she agreed. "We must counteract their influence."

"Education," he reiterated. "We need to reach people at the grassroots level."

She smiled warmly. "Your dedication is inspiring, Hans."

He felt a flush rise to his cheeks. "We're in this together."

As August drew to a close, the tension between East and West showed no signs of abating. On 31 August 1948, reports circulated of increased Soviet restrictions and Western countermeasures. The air was thick with uncertainty, and whispers of a potential escalation stirred unease.

In Hamburg, Frieda received Hans's letter. She read it eagerly, a mixture of relief and concern washing over her.

"At least he's well," she told Marta.

"Will you write back?" her mother asked.

"Yes," Frieda affirmed. "I want him to know that despite our differences, he's still my brother."

That evening, she penned her response.

Dear Hans,

I'm glad to hear you're safe and that you've found purpose. Here in Hamburg, we're working tirelessly to support those affected by the blockade. Though our paths diverge, I hope we can remain connected.

She hesitated before adding,

Perhaps one day, we'll find common ground.

As Frieda sealed the envelope, a pang of longing for the simpler times of their childhood, when ideological lines hadn't yet drawn between them, washed over her.

In the quiet of their respective rooms, both Hans and Frieda gazed out at the night sky, the same stars spanning the distance between East and West. Each harboured hopes for reconciliation, even as the world around them threatened to solidify the barriers.

At the Engelhardt home, Klaus sat alone, the weight of his thoughts pressing heavily upon him. The faces of his children lingered in his mind, reminders of a future he struggled to comprehend.

Marta found him there, placing a gentle hand on his shoulder. "They're still our children," she whispered.

He nodded slowly. "I fear losing them."

"Then don't let pride keep you apart," she counselled.

He sighed deeply. "Perhaps it's time I tried to understand."

As summer waned, the Engelhardt family stood at a crossroads, each member grappling with their convictions and the ties that bound them. The ruins of their past loomed large, but amidst the uncertainty, glimmers of hope persisted—a testament to the resilience of family and the enduring quest for unity in a divided world.

ooo

The first chill of autumn settled over Hamburg on 1 September 1948, creeping into the corners of the Engelhardt home like an unwelcome guest. The air carried a crispness that hinted at the colder months ahead, rustling the leaves that clung stubbornly to the branches outside. Klaus Engelhardt sat by the window, his gaze fixed on the grey skies that mirrored the heaviness in his heart. The distant hum of the city's bustle felt muted, as though a veil separated him from the world beyond.

Marta moved quietly through the house, her footsteps soft against the worn wooden floors. She paused in the parlour's doorway, observing her husband's rigid silhouette against the pale light. His once broad shoulders seemed to have narrowed, hunched forward as if bearing an invisible weight. The lines on his face had deepened, etching a permanent expression of resignation.

"Klaus," she called gently. "Would you like some tea?"

He did not turn. "No, thank you."

She hesitated before retreating to the kitchen, the warmth of the stove offering little comfort against the growing coldness between them. The kettle whistled, releasing a plume of steam that fogged the windowpane. Marta wiped it away with the corner of her apron, revealing a view of the small garden where the last of the summer flowers wilted.

On 10 September 1948, Frieda arrived home earlier than usual, her cheeks flushed from the brisk walk and the excitement of the day's events. She shrugged off her coat and entered the kitchen, where Marta was kneading dough for the evening's bread.

"*Mutter,* you won't believe it," Frieda exclaimed, her eyes bright. "They have invited me to attend a conference in Bonn next month. They're gathering young politicians from across West Germany to discuss the future of our nation."

Marta smiled warmly. "That's wonderful news, *Liebling.* You've worked so hard for this."

Frieda washed her hands at the sink, the cool water soothing against her skin. "It's an incredible opportunity. We'll be meeting with Chancellor Adenauer himself."

At the mention of the Chancellor, Klaus appeared in the doorway, his expression unreadable. "So, you're off to consort with the architects of our division," he remarked.

Frieda turned to face him, her smile fading. "*Vater,* this conference is about rebuilding. We shape policies that will benefit everyone."

"Everyone in the West, you mean," he retorted. "While we cast aside the East," he retorted.

She took a deep breath. "We can't change the past, but can influence the future."

Klaus shook his head. "Naïve idealism. You're blind to the reality."

Marta interjected softly. "Perhaps we could discuss this over dinner?"

"There's nothing to discuss," Klaus muttered, retreating to his study.

The tension lingered in the air, settling like dust on the surrounding surfaces. Frieda sighed, her shoulders sagging. "I don't know how to reach him."

Marta placed a comforting hand on her daughter's arm. "Give him time. He struggles to let go."

As the days shortened, the shadows in the Engelhardt home seemed to lengthen. On 20 September 1948, a letter arrived from Hans, bearing the postmark of East Berlin. Marta retrieved it from the postman, her fingers trembling slightly as she recognised her son's handwriting.

"Frieda! A letter from Hans," she called out.

They gathered around the kitchen table, unfolding the crisp paper carefully.

Liebe Mutter und Schwester,

I hope this letter finds you well. My work here is progressing. We are making strides in education reform and youth engagement. They have entrusted me with the leadership of a committee on cultural programs.

Frieda read aloud, her voice steady but tinged with a hint of melancholy. "He sounds fulfilled."

Marta nodded. "It seems he's found his place."

Klaus's footsteps approached, and he paused at the threshold upon seeing the letter. "From Hans?"

"Yes," Frieda replied, looking up hopefully. "Would you like to hear it?"

He hesitated before stepping into the room. "Go on."

She continued reading,

I believe that through socialism, we can build a fair and just society. I know our views differ, but I hope you can understand my intentions.

Klaus's jaw tightened. "He's deluded."

"Vater, he's passionate about his cause," Frieda implored. "Just as I am about mine."

He met her gaze. "And what about loyalty to family? To one's heritage?"

"Perhaps loyalty means supporting each other, despite our differences," she suggested gently.

He scoffed. "Idealistic nonsense."

With that, he turned and left, leaving Frieda and Marta exchanging weary glances.

On 1 October 1948, the leaves had turned to shades of amber and crimson, blanketing the streets in a tapestry of autumnal hues. Hans stood on a podium in a crowded square in East Berlin, the crisp air invigorating as he addressed the assembled youth.

"Comrades," he proclaimed, his voice carrying over the murmurs of the crowd. "We are the architects of our future. Through unity and dedication, we can forge a society that values equality and justice above all."

Applause erupted, and Hans felt a swell of pride. Among the faces, he saw Lena, her eyes shining with admiration. After the rally, they walked together along the cobbled streets, their breath visible in the cool air.

"You were inspiring," she said, linking her arm with his.

He smiled modestly. "I only speak from the heart."

She gazed at him thoughtfully. "Do you ever think of your family?"

"Of course," he admitted. "I wonder how they are, especially Frieda. We were always close."

"Have you considered visiting them?"

He shook his head. "It's complicated. Our paths have diverged so much."

"Perhaps reaching out could help bridge the gap," she suggested.

Hans looked up at the sky, where the setting sun cast a golden glow. "Maybe. But I'm not sure they'd welcome it."

Back in Hamburg, on 15 October 1948, Marta prepared a simple supper of potato soup and fresh bread. The aroma filled the kitchen, a nostalgic reminder of better times. Klaus sat at the table, absently stirring his spoon, his thoughts distant.

"Klaus," Marta began carefully. "We need to talk."

He glanced up warily. "About what?"

"About us. Concerning this family." She took a seat opposite him, folding her hands neatly. "I'm worried about you."

"There's no need," he replied curtly.

"But there is," she insisted. "You've withdrawn from us. From Frieda. You barely speak to her, and when you do, it ends in conflict."

He sighed heavily. "The path she has chosen is not something I can support."

Marta insisted, "She is your daughter. She seeks your approval, your guidance."

With bitterness in his voice, he made a remark about how she didn't need him.

Marta's eyes flashed with a rare intensity. "That's unfair. She's working tirelessly to rebuild this country, to make it a better place for all of us."

"By aligning with those who occupy us?"

"By embracing change," she countered. "Something you refuse to do."

He pushed back his chair, his legs scraping loudly against the floor. He declared, "I won't tolerate being lectured in my home."

She stood her ground. "This isn't a lecture, Klaus. It's a plea. I'm asking you to let go of this bitterness. It's poisoning you. It's tearing this family apart."

He turned away, his shoulders stiff. "You wouldn't understand."

"Then help me understand," she implored, her voice softening. "Tell me what haunts you so."

Silence stretched between them, heavy and oppressive. Finally, he spoke, his tone strained. "I carry burdens you cannot imagine. Regrets that cannot be undone."

"We all have regrets," she whispered. "But shutting us out won't heal anything."

He faced her, the lines on his face deepening. "What do you want from me?"

"I want my husband back," she said simply. "I want our children to have their father."

Emotion flickered in his eyes, fleeting but unmistakable. "I don't know if that's possible."

"It is," she insisted. "If you're willing to try."

He sighed, the weight of his defences beginning to crumble. "Perhaps… perhaps I've been too harsh."

Marta reached out, covering his hand with hers. "It's not too late, Klaus."

On 20 October 1948, Frieda returned home to find Klaus seated in the parlour, a book resting unopened in his lap. He looked up as she entered, an unreadable expression on his face.

"Vater," she greeted cautiously.

"Frieda," he acknowledged. "I hear you're heading to Bonn soon."

She nodded, surprised. "Yes, for the conference."

He shifted slightly. "That's quite an accomplishment."

A faint smile touched her lips. "Thank you."

An awkward silence settled before he continued. "I… I wanted to say that I recognise your dedication."

Her eyes widened. "Really?"

He cleared his throat. "We may not agree on everything, but I can see that you're committed to your cause."

Emotion welled within her. "It means a lot to hear you say that."

He offered a slight nod. "I suppose I've been… distant."

She took a tentative step forward. "Perhaps we could discuss our perspectives. Find some common ground."

He hesitated. "I'm not sure where to begin."

"Maybe by simply talking," she suggested gently. "Over tea?"

A hint of a smile appeared at the corner of his mouth. "Very well."

As they settled into conversation, the barriers between them eased, if only slightly. They spoke cautiously, navigating the sensitive topics with care. It was a start—a fragile bridge over a deep chasm.

Meanwhile, Hans continued to rise within the ranks of the socialist youth movement. On 1 November 1948, they appointed Hans to a regional leadership position, expanding his responsibilities to include organising educational programs and political rallies.

During a meeting that evening, Comrade Müller, an older party official, pulled him aside. "Your dedication is impressive, Hans. You have a bright future ahead."

"Thank you," Hans replied earnestly. "I believe in our mission wholeheartedly."

"Good," Müller affirmed. "We need strong leaders like you to guide the youth."

As Hans left the building, the streets of East Berlin glowed under the streetlamps, the chill of the night air biting at his cheeks. He contemplated Lena's earlier words about reconnecting with his family. Despite his accomplishments, a lingering emptiness gnawed at him.

On 10 November 1948, he penned a letter to his father.

Lieber Vater,

> *It has been some time since we last spoke. I wanted to share
> with you my recent achievements and to express my hope that
> we might understand each other. Our ideologies may differ, but
> you are still my father, and I wish for reconciliation.*

He sealed the letter with a sense of apprehension, uncertain of the reception it would receive.

Back in Hamburg, the days grew shorter, darkness falling earlier with each passing evening. On 15 November 1948, Marta found Klaus in his study, the letter from Hans unopened on the desk before him.

"A letter from our son," she observed.

He stared at it, conflicted. "I'm not sure I want to read it."

"Why not?" she asked softly.

"Because I fear it will only deepen the divide," he admitted.

"Or perhaps it could begin to mend it," she suggested.

He looked at her, the vulnerability in his eyes startling. "What if I've lost him?"

"You haven't," she assured him. "But you might if you don't try."

With a heavy sigh, he picked up the letter, breaking the seal carefully. As he read, his expression shifted from guarded to contemplative.

"He wishes for reconciliation," Klaus murmured.

Marta smiled gently. "That's a good sign."

He folded the letter thoughtfully. "Maybe… maybe I've been too rigid."

She placed a hand on his shoulder. "It takes strength to change."

On 20 November 1948, Klaus ventured out to the local church, the stone edifice standing resolute against the autumn sky. Inside, the air was cool, the scent of candle wax and polished wood enveloping him. He took a seat in a pew near the back, his hands clasped tightly.

The priest approached quietly. "*Herr Engelhardt,* it's been a while since we've seen you here."

Klaus nodded absently. "I've been… preoccupied."

"Is there something on your mind?" the priest inquired gently.

He hesitated before speaking. "I feel as though I'm adrift. My family is slipping away, and I don't know how to anchor myself."

"Faith can provide guidance," the priest offered. "But so can humility and openness."

"I've been holding onto the past," Klaus confessed. "Perhaps at the expense of the present."

"Recognising that is the first step towards healing," the priest said kindly.

As Klaus left the church, a lightness touched his spirit, a tentative hope that he might find a way forward.

On 25 November 1948, the Engelhardt family gathered around the dinner table for the first time in months. The meal was modest but prepared with care—roast chicken, potatoes, and Marta's homemade apple strudel.

"To family," Marta toasted, raising her glass.

"To family," they echoed.

Conversation flowed more easily than before, with anecdotes and shared memories bridging the gaps. Klaus listened as Frieda recounted her experiences in Bonn, her enthusiasm infectious.

"And Hans?" Klaus ventured cautiously. "Have you heard from him?"

Frieda exchanged a glance with Marta. "I received a letter yesterday. He's doing well. He mentioned he was hoping to visit soon."

Klaus nodded slowly. "That would be… acceptable."

Marta beamed. "It would be wonderful to have us all together again."

As the evening drew to a close, Klaus felt a warmth he hadn't experienced in a long time—a sense of belonging and the faint stirrings of peace.

On 30 November 1948, the first snowflakes of the season drifted down, dusting the city in a pristine white. Klaus stood at the window, watching as children laughed and played in the street below, their joyful voices rising like a melody.

Marta joined him, slipping her arm through his. "Beautiful, isn't it?"

He smiled softly. "Yes, it is."

She rested her head on his shoulder. "Winter brings its own kind of renewal."

He pondered her words. "Perhaps it does."

In that moment, Klaus allowed himself to hope—that the fractures within his family could heal, that he might find redemption, and that amidst the ruins of the past, they could build something enduring.

The Engelhardt home, once shadowed by silence and estrangement, echoed again with the sounds of life—laughter, conversation, the clatter of dishes, and the soft strains of Marta's humming. The path ahead remained uncertain, but together, they were taking the first steps towards reconciliation.

As November gave way to December, the family prepared to face the challenges of a divided Germany with renewed strength. They embraced the possibility that even in the darkest of times, they could find light, bound by love and a shared history.

ooo

The biting chill of 10 December 1948 settled over Hamburg like a heavy blanket. Snowflakes danced lazily from a slate-grey sky, dusting the rubble-strewn streets and the newly constructed buildings alike. Frieda Engelhardt pulled her woollen scarf tighter around her neck, her breath forming delicate clouds that dissipated into the frosty air. The scent of burning coal mingled with the crispness of winter, a stark reminder of the city's struggle to keep warm amidst lingering shortages.

She navigated the bustling corridors of the aid centre, a converted warehouse near the docks. Stacks of canned goods, blankets, and medical supplies towered around her, a testament to the relentless efforts to support those affected by the Berlin Blockade. The distant hum of lorries loading and unloading supplies provided a constant backdrop to the flurry of activity.

"Frieda, we've just received a shipment of powdered milk," called out *Herr Müller,* a fellow volunteer. As he entered the room, his glasses fogged from the sudden change in temperature.

"Excellent," she replied, her eyes scanning the inventory list. "Make sure it's prioritised for families with young children."

He nodded, disappearing amidst the maze of crates. Frieda sighed softly, her fingers tracing the edges of the clipboard. The blockade had been ongoing since June, and the strain was palpable. Yet, die Luftbrücke—the airlift—had become a beacon of hope. Planes soared overhead daily, their cargoes vital lifelines to the isolated sectors of Berlin.

On 24 December 1948, Christmas Eve brought a semblance of normalcy. The Engelhardt household was modestly adorned with sprigs of pine and handmade ornaments. The aroma of roasting goose filled the air, mingling with the sweet scent of freshly baked *stollen.* Marta hummed softly as she set the table, her movements graceful and measured.

"Frieda, could you fetch your father?" she asked, adjusting the candles that cast a warm glow over the room.

"Of course, *Mutti,*" Frieda replied, stepping into the dimly lit study.

Klaus sat in his worn leather armchair, gazing into the crackling fireplace. Shadows danced across his lined face, etched deeper by the weight of memories. An untouched glass of Schnapps rested on the small table beside him.

"*Vater,* dinner is ready," Frieda announced gently.

He glanced up, his eyes reflecting the flicker of the flames. "Thank you, *mein Kind,*" he murmured, slowly rising to his feet.

As they gathered around the table, an empty chair poignantly reminded them of Hans's absence. The silence stretched, filled only by the soft clinking of silverware and the distant tolling of church bells.

"Has there been any word from Hans?" Klaus inquired, his gaze fixed on his plate.

Frieda exchanged a glance with Marta before answering. "Not recently. The postal service is unreliable these days."

"He's busy with his studies," Marta added, a note of forced optimism in her voice.

Klaus grunted, taking a deliberate sip of wine. "Or he's too consumed by his new comrades."

"Let's not spoil the evening," Frieda interjected softly. "It's Christmas."

The days that followed were a blur of activity—on 1 January 1949, the New Year dawned with a fragile sense of hope. Fireworks burst over the cityscape, their brilliant colours reflected in the icy waters of the Elbe River. Frieda stood on the rooftop of the aid centre, watching the spectacle alongside other volunteers.

"To a year of progress," toasted *Herr Müller,* raising a steaming mug of *Glühwein.*

"Prost! (Cheers!)" they chorused, the warmth of the spiced wine seeping through them.

Yet, beneath the surface, tensions simmered. The division of Germany loomed like an approaching storm, and conversations often circled back to the political uncertainties.

On 15 January 1949, Frieda attended a meeting at the Rathaus, where local leaders discussed the implications of the potential formation of a separate West German state. The grand hall echoed with fiery debates, the ornate tapestries and chandeliers starkly contrasted with the turmoil outside.

"Establishing the Federal Republic is essential for our autonomy and alignment with democratic ideals," asserted *Herr Becker,* a prominent politician, his voice carrying over the murmurs.

"Agreed," Frieda added, standing to address the assembly. "We must ensure that our future is not dictated by external forces but shaped by our commitment to rebuilding a just society."

Applause rippled through the room, though not all faces reflected agreement. The fractures within the nation mirrored those within families, hers included.

Meanwhile, in the Soviet zone, Hans immersed himself deeper into communist circles. On 30 January 1949, he stood amidst a crowd in Berlin, listening intently as speakers extolled the virtues of socialism and the protection against capitalist exploitation.

"The workers must unite to build a society free from oppression," declared Comrade Schmidt, his fist raised emphatically. "The blockade is a necessary defence against imperialist aggression."

Hans felt a surge of conviction. The energy was palpable, a collective determination that resonated with his own disillusionment of the past. Yet, a sliver of doubt lingered, unacknowledged.

Letters between Hans and his family became infrequent. On 14 February 1949, Frieda received a terse note on paper that was creased and smudged.

Liebe Schwester,

I trust this finds you well. I am engaged in important work here. Our ideals are for the betterment of all Germans. I hope you will understand one day.

Mit besten Grüßen (With best regards),

Hans

She traced the familiar handwriting, a knot forming in her stomach. The distance between them extended beyond mere kilometres; it was a chasm carved by diverging beliefs.

On 1 March 1949, the airlift intensified as the blockade showed no signs of abating. Frieda organised a fundraiser to support the pilots and crews undertaking the perilous flights. The event was held in a refurbished concert hall, the echoes of music replaced by impassioned speeches and the clatter of donation boxes filling.

"These brave individuals risk their lives daily to sustain our brethren in Berlin," Frieda addressed the attendees, her voice steady. "Their actions exemplify the solidarity and courage that we must all strive for."

As she stepped down from the podium, Greta Schmidt, a journalist and close friend, approached her.

"Powerful words as always," Greta commended, her eyes sharp behind wire-rimmed glasses. "I plan to feature this in my next article."

"Thank you, Greta," Frieda replied, a hint of weariness creeping in. "Visibility is crucial."

"Have you considered the possibility that Germany may not reunite?" Greta asked cautiously.

Frieda sighed, glancing around the bustling hall. "I try to remain hopeful, but the reality grows bleaker each day."

Back at home on 10 March 1949, tensions surfaced during a rare family dinner. The gramophone played softly in the background, the melody of a Beethoven symphony filling the spaces between words.

"Klaus, you hardly touched your meal," Marta observed, concern etched on her features.

He pushed the plate aside. "Food tastes different when the nation is tearing itself apart."

Frieda set down her fork. "We're working tirelessly to prevent that. The establishment of a democratic West Germany is a step towards stability."

"At the cost of our unity," Klaus retorted. "We are Germans first. These political manoeuvres only serve foreign interests."

"Father, aligning with democratic nations is crucial for our recovery," Frieda argued gently. "We cannot revert to old ways."

He rose abruptly from the table. "Old ways? You speak as if our history is something to discard."

"Klaus, please," Marta implored.

He shook his head, retreating to his study without another word. The echo of the closing door resonated like a final note in a discordant composition.

The following weeks saw Frieda engrossed in preparations for the upcoming elections. On 3 April 1949, she met with fellow organisers in a quaint café adorned with faded floral wallpaper and the aroma of freshly brewed coffee.

"We need to ensure that voter turnout is high," she emphasised, spreading maps and pamphlets across the table. "Every voice matters in shaping our future."

"There's concern about apathy," remarked Stefan, a young activist. "Many feel disillusioned."

"Then we must reignite their belief," Frieda asserted. "Show them that their participation is essential."

Amidst the flurry of activity, news from the East grew increasingly troubling. On 20 April 1949, reports surfaced of crackdowns on dissent and the tightening grip of Soviet influence.

Greta shared the latest articles with Frieda over tea. "Freedom of speech is being stifled," she noted grimly. "It's becoming more difficult to get accurate information."

Frieda's thoughts drifted to Hans. "I worry about my brother," she confessed. "He's blinded by ideology."

Greta reached across the table, squeezing her hand. "You're doing all you can. Sometimes, people must find their own way."

On 1 May 1949, International Workers' Day, demonstrations erupted across both East and West. In Hamburg, crowds marched peacefully, banners proclaiming solidarity and progress. Frieda joined the procession, the rhythmic chants echoing through the streets lined with budding trees and storefronts displaying spring fashions.

In contrast, Hans found himself amidst a more burning gathering in Berlin. The atmosphere was charged, speeches laced with rhetoric against the West. As flags bearing the hammer and sickle waved, he felt a pang of uncertainty. The intensity that had once inspired him now felt oppressive.

That evening, he penned a letter but hesitated to send it.

Liebe Frieda,

Today was... different. I question certain aspects of our movement. Perhaps I was naïve. I hope we can talk soon.

He folded the letter carefully, sealing it with a wax stamp. Whether it would reach her remained uncertain.

On 12 May 1949, the news broke: the Berlin Blockade was lifted. Cheers erupted throughout Hamburg, church bells rang, and people embraced in the streets. The air was electric with relief and triumph.

Frieda stood during the celebration, a smile breaking across her face. "This is a victory for freedom," she declared to those around her.

At home, she shared the news with Marta. "It's a significant step forward," she beamed.

Marta nodded, though her eyes held a hint of sadness. "I pray it brings us closer to peace."

Klaus remained sceptical. "One blockade ends, but the division remains," he remarked, staring out the window at the festivities.

"Father, we must take heart in progress," Frieda urged.

He sighed heavily. "Perhaps."

As 20 May 1949 approached, preparations intensified for formally establishing the Federal Republic of Germany. Frieda was invited to attend the inaugural ceremonies in Bonn, a recognition of her contributions to the aid efforts and political activism.

On 18 May 1949, she packed her suitcase, carefully folding her best dresses and placing a worn photograph of her family atop the neatly arranged items. The image captured a moment from years past—smiles unburdened by the weight of current divisions.

Before departing, she sat with Marta in the garden, the fragrance of blooming roses enveloping them.

"Do you think Hans will ever return?" Frieda mused aloud, watching a butterfly alight on a nearby blossom.

Marta reached over, tucking a stray strand of hair behind Frieda's ear. "Hold on to hope, my dear. Hearts can change."

"I wish Father shared that sentiment," she sighed.

"He struggles in his own way," Marta acknowledged. "Be patient with him."

Frieda nodded, standing as the car horn signalled her driver's arrival. "I'll send word when I arrive."

"Travel safely," Marta called after her, waving until the car disappeared from view.

The journey to Bonn took her through the rolling countryside, fields of golden rapeseed stretching towards the horizon under a clear blue sky. As the landscape unfolded, Frieda allowed herself a moment of reflection. The road ahead—both literal and metaphorical—was uncertain, yet she was determined to forge a path towards unity and healing.

Upon arriving on 20 May 1949, the city buzzed with anticipation. Delegates and dignitaries from across the Western zones gathered, their conversations a mosaic of languages and dialects. The weight of history hung in the air, palpable yet invigorating.

Frieda stood amidst the grandeur of the assembly hall, chandeliers casting a warm glow over the assembled faces. As speeches began, she listened intently, the words resonating with her own convictions.

"The formation of the Federal Republic marks not just a political milestone but a commitment to the principles of democracy and human rights," proclaimed Chancellor Adenauer, his voice steady and unwavering.

Applause filled the room. Frieda joined in, her hands coming together with a sense of purpose. Yet, a whisper of melancholy lingered—an awareness of those absent, of the divide that still cleaved her nation and family.

That evening, as twilight painted the sky in shades of lavender and gold, she penned a letter to Hans.

Lieber Bruder,

Today was significant. I wish you could have been here. Despite our differences, I hold onto the hope that we can find common ground. Please write when you can.

In solidarity and love,

Frieda

Sealing the envelope, she felt a mix of determination and wistfulness. The path ahead would not be easy, but she was steadfast in her resolve to bridge the divides that time and turmoil had wrought.

Back in Hamburg, Klaus sat alone in the dim light of his study. The soft ticking of the clock marked the passing moments as he contemplated the shifting landscape of his world. The walls seemed to close in, adorned with relics of a bygone era—medals tarnished, photographs faded.

He lifted his gaze to the window, where the faint glow of the city lights shimmered against the night sky. "Perhaps it's time," he murmured to himself, though the nature of that resolution remained unspoken.

FIVE:

GERMANY OFFICIALLY DIVIDES

In Hamburg, on the dawn of May 23, 1949, a hesitant glow crept in as the sun cast pale rays over the remnants of a city striving to rebuild. The Engelhardt household stirred slowly. The scent of freshly brewed coffee wafted through the modest flat, mingling with the faint aroma of plaster and paint—a testament to ongoing repairs. Frieda Engelhardt stood by the kitchen window, her fingers wrapped around a warm cup. She gazed out at the streets below, where cobblestones gleamed with morning dew, and the chatter of neighbours hinted at a day of significance.

Today marked the official founding of the Federal Republic of Germany. Frieda felt a flutter of excitement coursing through her. The date, 23 May 1949, would etch itself into history—a new beginning for a nation scarred by war and divided by ideology. She sipped her coffee; the bitterness grounding her amidst her swirling thoughts.

In the living room, sunlight filtered through sheer curtains, casting delicate patterns on the worn rug. Frieda meticulously organised documents, speeches, and leaflets and spread them across the table to prepare for her involvement in the day's events. A small vase held a handful of daisies she had picked the day before, their simple beauty brightening the room.

Klaus Engelhardt sat in his armchair near the corner, shadows playing across his stern features. His once robust frame had thinned, and his grey hair seemed more silver in the morning light. He stared at the radio on the side table, the soft hum of static preceding the expected broadcast. His hands rested heavily on his lap, fingers interlaced tightly, as if holding onto something unseen.

Marta entered quietly, carrying a tray with a plate of rye bread and cheese. "Would you like some breakfast, Klaus?" she asked gently.

He shook his head without looking up. "Not hungry."

She sighed softly, setting the tray on the table. "You should eat something."

Frieda glanced over, concern flickering in her eyes. "*Vater,* it's an important day. Perhaps we could listen to the announcement together."

He met her gaze briefly, a flicker of something unreadable passing over his face. "You go ahead. Celebrate your new Germany."

She pressed her lips together, choosing her words carefully. "It's our Germany. A chance to rebuild, to move forward."

He scoffed lightly. "Forward into the arms of the West, under the watchful eye of the Allies. This is not the Germany I knew."

Before she could respond, the radio crackled to life. The announcer's voice filled the room, solemn yet hopeful. *"Heute, am 23. Mai 1949, wird die Bundesrepublik Deutschland offiziell gegründet* (Today, on May 23, 1949, the Federal Republic of Germany is officially founded)."

Frieda turned up the volume, her attention fully captured. The announcer detailed the adoption of the Basic Law, the appointment of Konrad Adenauer as Chancellor, and establishing Bonn as the provisional capital. Each word resonated with promise.

Klaus rose abruptly, the chair creaking under the sudden movement. "I've heard enough," he muttered, striding towards the door.

"*Vater,* please," Frieda called after him. "Stay. This is a pivotal moment."

He paused in the doorway, his back to her. "Pivotal indeed. A nation divided is no nation at all." With that, he disappeared down the hallway, the echo of his footsteps lingering.

Marta placed a comforting hand on Frieda's shoulder. "Give him time," she whispered.

Frieda sighed, her shoulders sagging slightly. "Time seems to widen the gap between us."

She straightened, steeling herself. There was much to do. She gathered her papers, slipping them into a leather satchel. "I need to head to the community centre. The ceremony starts soon."

"Be careful," Marta urged. "And remember, we're proud of you."

Frieda offered a grateful smile. *"Danke, Mutter."*

Stepping out into the street, a city alive with activity greeted Frieda. Bicycles whirred past, their bells chiming merrily. Shopkeepers opened their doors, arranging displays with a touch of optimism. The German tricolour—black, red, and gold—fluttered from windows and lampposts, a visual chorus of unity.

As she made her way towards the community centre, she passed the ruins of buildings yet to be restored, their skeletal frames a stark reminder of the past. Children played amidst the rubble, their laughter a poignant contrast to the devastation.

"Frieda!" a voice called out. She turned to see Greta Schmidt hurrying towards her, a notebook tucked under her arm.

"Greta, guten morgen," Frieda greeted warmly.

"Exciting day, isn't it?" Greta's eyes sparkled with enthusiasm. "I am assigned to cover the ceremony for the newspaper."

"That's wonderful news," Frieda replied. "We could use your eloquence to capture the spirit of the moment."

They walked together, the conversation flowing easily. "Do you think people truly believe in this new beginning?" Greta asked thoughtfully.

"I hope so," Frieda answered. "We need to believe in something better. The Federal Republic offers us a framework to rebuild our infrastructure and our values."

Greta nodded. "And yet, there are those who feel left behind."

Frieda knew she referred to people like her father. "Change is difficult," she acknowledged. "But clinging to the past won't heal our wounds."

They arrived at the community centre, a modest building adorned with banners proclaiming, *"Demokratie und Freiheit* (Democracy and Freedom)." Inside, the atmosphere was electric. Volunteers bustled about, arranging chairs and setting up a podium draped with the national colours.

"Frieda, over here!" called *Herr Müller,* a local official with whom she had been coordinating.

She excused herself from Greta and joined him. "Everything is almost ready," he informed her. "We're expecting a good turnout."

"Excellent," she replied. "I'll ensure I prepare the speakers."

As the hall filled, Frieda took a moment to survey the crowd. Faces reflected a mixture of anticipation and apprehension. Among them were war veterans, young families, students—all brought together by the promise of renewal.

The ceremony began at precisely 11:00. *Herr Müller* stepped up to the podium, his voice carrying through the hall. "*Meine Damen und Herren,* today we stand at the threshold of a new era. The Federal Republic of Germany is born, offering us the chance to shape our destiny."

Applause rippled through the audience. Frieda felt a surge of pride. When it was her turn to speak, she approached the podium with confidence.

"Friends," she began, her voice clear. "We have endured much—loss, hardship, division. But today, we embrace the opportunity to rebuild not just our nation but the very principles that define us. Democracy, justice, and unity must be our guiding stars."

She spoke of the importance of participation, of holding their leaders accountable, and of fostering a society where every voice mattered. As she concluded, the applause was robust, affirming her belief in the path ahead.

After the ceremony, Frieda mingled with attendees, engaging in earnest discussions about policies and community initiatives. Greta approached her, a grin on her face. "You were inspiring up there," she praised.

"Thank you," Frieda replied modestly. "I only hope my words resonate beyond today."

Greta tapped her notebook. "They will. I'll make sure of it."

As the afternoon wore on, Frieda felt a deep sense of fulfilment. Yet, beneath the surface, a pang of sadness lingered—her father's absence a silent void.

Meanwhile, back at the Engelhardt home, Klaus sat alone in the dim light of his bedroom. The heavy curtains drawn created a perpetual twilight in the room. He held a photograph in his hands—an image of himself in uniform, flanked by a younger Frieda and Hans. Their smiles were bright, untainted by the shadows of war.

A soft knock interrupted his reverie. "Klaus?" Marta's voice sounded muffled through the door. "May I come in?"

He hesitated before responding. "Yes."

She entered quietly, carrying a tray with a steaming bowl of soup. "I thought you might be hungry."

He set the photograph aside. *"Danke."*

She placed the tray on the bedside table, her gaze lingering on his weary face. "It's a big day for Germany," she ventured.

He grunted noncommittally.

She sat on the edge of the bed. "Frieda did well today. Her actions are making a difference.

"She aligns herself with those who would see our traditions erased," he retorted.

"She's working towards a better future," Marta countered gently. "Isn't that what we all want?"

He looked away. "The future they're building has no place for men like me."

"That's not true," she insisted. "There's always a place for those willing to adapt."

He shook his head. "Adaptation means surrender. I cannot embrace a Germany dictated by foreign powers."

She reached out, covering his hand with hers. "Klaus, holding onto the past won't bring it back. We have to move forward together."

He withdrew his hand. "You and Frieda seem content to forget. I cannot."

Marta sighed, a heaviness settling in her chest. "It's not about forgetting. It's about learning and growing."

He remained silent, the distance between them palpable.

As evening fell on 23 May 1949, Frieda returned home, her steps lighter despite the day's exhaustion. She found Marta in the kitchen, peeling potatoes for supper.

"How did it go?" Marta asked, her eyes reflecting both hope and concern.

"It was wonderful," Frieda replied, washing her hands at the sink. "The turnout was better than expected, and people seemed genuinely engaged."

"I'm so proud of you," Marta said warmly.

"Did *Vater* eat anything?" Frieda inquired, glancing towards the hallway.

"A little," Marta admitted. "He's struggling."

Frieda's expression softened. "I wish he could see that this is an opportunity, not a threat."

"He needs time," Marta repeated.

"Time may not be enough," Frieda murmured.

After supper, Frieda sat at the small desk in her room, writing letters to colleagues and organising notes from the day's discussions. The lamp's glow cast a circle of light, illuminating her determined features.

A soft knock drew her attention. "Come in," she called.

Klaus stood in the doorway, his posture stiff. "May I have a word?"

"Of course," she replied, surprised.

He entered slowly, his gaze wandering around the room, which still held remnants of her childhood—a faded tapestry and a shelf of well-worn books.

"I wanted to… acknowledge your efforts today," he began awkwardly.

"Thank you," she said cautiously.

He cleared his throat. "I may not agree with everything, but I recognise your commitment."

She offered a tentative smile. "That's all I ask—that we can respect each other's perspectives."

He nodded slowly. "Perhaps."

An uncomfortable silence settled before he spoke again. "Do you hear from Hans?"

"Not recently," she admitted. "Communication across the zones is difficult."

He sighed. "I worry about him."

"So do I," she confessed. "I hope he's found what he's looking for."

Klaus seemed to age before her eyes. "I fear we've lost him to ideals as well."

"Maybe one day we'll be reunited," she suggested.

"Perhaps," he echoed, though his tone lacked conviction.

He turned to leave. "Goodnight, Frieda."

"Goodnight, *Vater.*"

As he closed the door behind him, Frieda felt a mixture of hope and despair. The gap between them remained, but perhaps a bridge was forming.

In the night's quiet, Klaus returned to his bedroom. The house was still the only sound was the distant hum of traffic and the occasional bark of a dog. He settled into his armchair; the cushions moulding to his familiar shape.

He reached for the radio, tuning it until the soft strains of classical music filled the room. The melody of Beethoven's "Moonlight Sonata" enveloped him, stirring memories of a time long past. He closed his eyes, allowing the music to wash over him.

Images flashed through his mind—marching under crisp banners, the camaraderie of soldiers, the pride he once felt in serving his country. But interwoven were darker recollections—the horrors of war, the faces of the fallen, the weight of actions he could not undo.

A tear traced a path down his cheek. On this day, 23 May 1949, a significant change occurred in Germany, the country he had known. He felt adrift, untethered from the moorings of his identity.

Yet, amid the sorrow, a small voice whispered of the possibility of redemption. Perhaps, in embracing the new, he could atone for the past.

The music swelled, reaching a poignant crescendo. Klaus opened his eyes, gazing into the dimly lit room. The shadows seemed less oppressive, the air lighter.

He stood, moving to the window. Pulling back the curtain, he looked out at the city. Lights twinkled in the distance, a constellation of lives. He watched as a couple strolled down the street, their laughter faint but discernible.

At that moment, Klaus made a decision. He would try—to understand, to reconnect, to find his place in this redefined Germany.

The night enveloped Hamburg, but dawn was inevitable. As 23 May 1949 drew to a close, the Engelhardt family stood at the cusp of transformation—personal and national. The path ahead was uncertain, fraught with challenges, but perhaps also with hope.

ooo

The morning of 7 October 1949 crept into Hamburg under a shroud of grey clouds, the autumn chill seeping into the cracks of the Engelhardt household. Klaus Engelhardt sat on the edge of his bed, the mattress sagging beneath his weight. The faint light filtering through the tattered curtains cast long shadows across the room, accentuating the lines etched deeply into his face. The floorboards groaned softly as he shifted, a cold draft whispering through the ill-fitted window panes.

Klaus held an envelope bearing the East Berlin postmark in his trembling hands. The paper was thin, edges worn from the journey. He recognised Hans's neat handwriting, each letter meticulously formed—a reflection of the discipline he had instilled in his son. Klaus hesitated the weight of the unopened letter heavy in his grasp. The distant hum of the city filtered in—a murmur of life moving forward without him.

Downstairs, the clatter of dishes and the muted conversation between Frieda and Marta drifted upwards. The aroma of freshly brewed coffee mingled with the faint scent of coal smoke from the hearth. Klaus drew a deep breath, the air cool in his lungs. He traced a finger over the return address, his heart tightening. Steeling himself, he carefully broke the seal.

"Lieber Vater," the letter began. Klaus's eyes scanned the words, his grip tightening as he read. Hans wrote of the dawn of a new era, of the German Democratic Republic's official founding on this very day, 7 October 1949. He spoke of hope, of rebuilding a nation rooted in equality and socialist ideals. Each sentence enthusiastically echoed, a conviction that impressed and unsettled Klaus.

> *…I believe, Vater, that this path will lead us to true prosperity, free from the shackles of past failures. I wish you could see what I see—a future where all Germans stand united under a just system.*

Klaus exhaled slowly, the letter trembling in his grasp. A surge of conflicting emotions coursed through him—pride in his son's passion, anger at his naïveté, and a deep-seated fear of the widening chasm between them. The walls of the room seemed to close in, the shadows elongating as the light shifted.

He folded the letter meticulously along its original creases and placed it back into the envelope. Rising unsteadily, Klaus moved to the small writing desk by the window. Remnants of his past—military commendations, faded photographs, a tarnished pocket watch—cluttered the surface of the small writing desk by the window. He picked up the watch. It's once-bright silver now dulled. Opening it, he observed the stopped hands, frozen at a moment long passed.

A sudden knock at the door jolted him. "Klaus?" Marta's voice was soft, tentative. "May I come in?"

He cleared his throat. "Yes, come in."

The door creaked open, and Marta entered, her eyes immediately drawn to his ashen face. "Breakfast is ready," she said gently. "We thought you might like to join us."

He avoided her gaze. "I'm not hungry."

She stepped closer, noticing the envelope on the desk. "Is that from Hans?"

"Yes," he replied curtly.

"What does he say?" she ventured, her hands clasped tightly before her.

Klaus hesitated. "He writes of the establishment of the German Democratic Republic. He's stayed there."

Marta's shoulders sagged slightly. "I see."

"He believes socialism will rebuild Germany," Klaus continued bitterly. "Thinks it will bring prosperity."

She placed a hand on his arm. "He's young, Klaus. Full of ideals."

"Ideals that will lead him astray," he snapped, pulling away. "He's aligning himself with those who would see our nation divided permanently."

"Perhaps he simply wants to make a difference," she offered softly.

Klaus turned sharply towards the window. "At what cost? He's abandoning his family, his heritage."

Marta sighed, her gaze resting on his rigid back. "We haven't lost him yet."

He remained silent. The tension in the room was palpable. Outside, the faint strains of a street musician's accordion drifted up, the melancholic tune underscoring the moment's heaviness.

"I'll leave you be," Marta whispered, retreating from the room.

As the door closed, Klaus sank back into the chair. He rubbed his temples, the beginnings of a headache throbbing at his temples. The reality of the day's significance pressed upon him—the official division of Germany, his son's unwavering commitment to a cause he could not support, and the erosion of the life he once knew.

He glanced around the room, his eyes settling on a framed photograph atop a bookshelf. Years ago, someone took a portrait of the family. Frieda and Hans stood on either side of him and Marta, their smiles bright, the future full of promise. He reached for the frame, his fingers brushing against the glass. A pang of longing struck him—a yearning for the simplicity of the past before war and ideology tore them apart.

Downstairs, Frieda set the table with care, the clink of porcelain cups punctuating the silence. She sensed the heaviness in the house, an undercurrent of unspoken tension. Marta entered the kitchen, her expression weary.

"He's not coming down, is he?" Frieda asked quietly.

Marta shook her head. "No. He's… struggling."

Frieda sighed. "I wish he wouldn't shut us out."

"He feels betrayed," Marta explained. "By the world, by the times, perhaps even by us."

Frieda poured coffee into the cups. "I received news today as well."

Marta looked up. "From whom?"

"From the party office. They've assigned me to a new committee on economic development."

"That's wonderful," Marta said, a small smile lifting the corners of her mouth.

"Yes, but," Frieda hesitated. "I fear telling *Vater* will only widen the gap."

Marta reached across the table, squeezing her daughter's hand. "He may not show it, but he is proud of you."

"I'm not so sure," Frieda murmured.

The doorbell rang abruptly, startling them both. Frieda rose to answer it, the wooden floors creaking beneath her feet. She opened the door to find Greta Schmidt, her cheeks flushed from the crisp air.

"Frieda! I hope I'm not intruding," Greta said, her breath visible in the chilly air.

"Not at all," Frieda replied warmly. "Come in."

Greta stepped inside, removing her gloves. "I thought you'd want to see this." She handed over a copy of the morning newspaper.

Frieda unfolded it, her eyes scanning the bold headline: "German Democratic Republic Established—East Germany Solidifies under Socialist Unity Party."

She bit her lip, absorbing the weight of the news. "So it's official," she said softly.

Greta nodded. "Indeed. It's a significant moment."

"Significant and troubling," Frieda remarked.

Marta joined them, offering Greta a cup of coffee. "It's hard to believe, isn't it?" she said.

Greta accepted the cup gratefully. "The world is changing so rapidly. It's difficult to keep pace."

Frieda folded the newspaper carefully. "I worry about Hans."

"Have you heard from him?" Greta inquired.

"He wrote to *Vater,*" Frieda explained. "But I doubt he'll share much."

Greta placed a reassuring hand on her friend's arm. "Perhaps I can help. I have contacts in the East. I might find out how he's doing."

"Would you?" Frieda asked, hope flickering in her eyes.

"Of course," Greta affirmed. "Anything for you."

As they settled into conversation, Klaus descended the stairs silently. He paused at the kitchen's threshold, observing the scene—Frieda and Greta engaged in earnest discussion, Marta bustling about. The warmth of their interaction contrasted starkly with the coldness he felt within.

"Good morning," he announced, his voice gruff.

All eyes turned to him, surprise clear on their faces.

"Vater," Frieda greeted cautiously. "Would you like some coffee?"

He nodded stiffly and took a seat at the table. Marta hurried to pour him a cup, the steam curling upwards as she set it before him.

Greta offered a polite smile. "*Herr Engelhardt,* it's good to see you."

He acknowledged her with a curt nod. "Miss Schmidt."

An uneasy silence settled. Frieda cleared her throat. "We were just discussing the news from the East."

Klaus's jaw tightened. "Yes. Hans has informed me of his decision."

"Perhaps it's an opportunity for dialogue," Greta suggested diplomatically.

"Dialogue?" Klaus echoed bitterly. "With those who seek to undermine everything we stand for?"

"*Vater,* please," Frieda implored. "Hans believes he's contributing to Germany's future, just as I do in my way."

"Your ways couldn't be more different," he retorted.

Marta intervened gently. "Let's not turn this into a confrontation. We're family."

Klaus pushed back his chair abruptly. "Family? A family divided by conflicting loyalties is hardly a family at all."

He stormed out of the room, leaving an uncomfortable silence in his wake.

Greta exhaled slowly. "I'm sorry. Perhaps I should go."

"No," Frieda insisted. "It's not your fault."

Marta patted Greta's hand. "He'll come around. He just needs time."

Klaus retreated to his study upstairs—a small room lined with bookshelves and mementoes of his military service. He paced the floor, his mind a tumult of emotions. His children's faces swirled in his thoughts—Frieda, steadfast and principled; Hans, passionate and idealistic. Both were so different, yet both embodied aspects of himself he could no longer reconcile.

He approached the window, gazing out at the street below. A group of children played, their laughter piercing the stillness. Neighbours conversed on doorsteps, their gestures animated. Life continued unabated, indifferent to his inner turmoil.

Klaus sank into the worn leather chair by the desk. He pulled open a drawer, retrieving a bottle of schnapps and a small glass. Pouring a measure, he raised it to his lips, the fiery liquid burning a path down his throat. He closed his eyes, seeking solace in the familiar warmth.

A knock interrupted his solitude. "What is it?" he called out, irritation colouring his tone.

"It's me," Frieda replied softly. "May I come in?"

He hesitated before responding. "Very well."

She entered cautiously, her expression earnest. "*Vater,* we need to talk."

He gestured for her to sit. "What is it you wish to say?"

She took a seat opposite him, folding her hands in her lap. "I understand that you're upset about Hans. I am too."

"Are you?" he challenged.

"Yes," she affirmed. "But alienating him won't bring him back."

"What would you have me do?" he asked wearily.

"Reach out to him. Try to understand his perspective," she suggested.

He shook his head. "His perspective is misguided."

"Perhaps," she conceded. "But dismissing him outright only widens the gap."

He regarded her thoughtfully. "You speak with wisdom beyond your years."

She offered a faint smile. "I've had good teachers."

He sighed deeply. "I fear the world has moved beyond me, Frieda. I no longer recognise it."

"The world is changing," she acknowledged. "But that doesn't mean you can't find your place in it."

He looked away, his gaze falling upon a map of Germany pinned to the wall. The bold line dividing East and West seemed to mock him—a physical manifestation of the divisions tearing his family apart.

"How can I find my place when everything I believed in has crumbled?" he whispered.

"By adapting," she replied gently. "By embracing the opportunity to shape the future."

He met her eyes, vulnerability flickering in his own. "I'm not sure I know how."

She reached across the desk, her hand covering his. "You don't have to do it alone."

For a moment, the distance between them lessened. Klaus felt a glimmer of hope, fragile yet persistent.

"Perhaps you're right," he conceded softly.

"Will you consider writing back to Hans?" she asked.

He hesitated. "I don't know what I would say."

"Start with honesty," she encouraged. "Share your thoughts, your concerns. Let him know that despite everything, you still care."

He nodded slowly. "I will think about it."

"That's all I ask," she said, reassuringly squeezing his hand.

As Frieda left the room, Klaus remained seated, the weight of the conversation settling upon him. He turned his attention back to the desk, pulling out a sheet of paper and a pen. The blank page stared back at him, an invitation and a challenge.

He wrote, the pen scratching hesitantly across the surface.

Lieber Hans,

I received your letter and have read it with a heavy heart

Words flowed haltingly at first, then with increasing clarity. He poured out his thoughts—his fears, disappointments, and lingering affection. He spoke of shared memories, lessons taught, and a desire to bridge the divide.

As the afternoon light waned, Klaus set down the pen and read over the letter. It was imperfect, but it was a start.

The sound of footsteps ascending the stairs drew his attention. Marta appeared in the doorway, her expression cautious.

"How are you?" she asked softly.

He gestured to the letter. "I've written to Hans."

Her eyes lit up with a mixture of surprise and relief. "That's wonderful."

He managed a faint smile. "Perhaps it's not too late to mend what has been broken."

She crossed the room, wrapping her arms around his shoulders. "It's never too late."

They stood together in the fading light, the quiet enveloping them like a protective cloak.

That evening, the Engelhardt family gathered for supper. The atmosphere was tentative but hopeful. Conversations flowed more easily, the shadows of the day's earlier tensions receding.

"Did you know," Greta mentioned, "that traditional harvest festivals are making a resurgence this year? Communities are coming together to celebrate despite the hardships."

"That's good to hear," Marta remarked. "We could use more reasons to unite."

Frieda nodded. "Perhaps we could attend one. It might lift our spirits."

Klaus considered the idea. "It would be… pleasant."

Marta and Frieda exchanged surprised glances.

"Then it's settled," Marta declared with a smile. "We'll go as a family."

As the meal concluded, a sense of camaraderie lingered. The divisions that once seemed insurmountable now appeared, if not bridgeable, at least less daunting.

Later that night, Klaus stepped outside onto the small balcony adjoining his bedroom. The crisp air carried the scent of wood smoke and damp leaves. Above, the stars glittered against the inky sky, distant and unchanging.

He gazed upwards, a quiet peace settling within him. The world was in flux, but perhaps, amidst the ruins of the past, there was room for renewal.

On this day, 7 October 1949, as Germany stood officially divided, Klaus Engelhardt took his first tentative steps towards reconciling with both his family and himself. The path ahead remained uncertain, fraught with challenges he could not yet foresee. But for the first time in a long while, he allowed himself to hope.

In the stillness, he whispered a silent prayer—for Hans, for Frieda, for a future where unity might one day prevail.

ooo

The first day of December 1949 arrived in Hamburg with a bitter chill. Frost latticed the windows of the Engelhardt home, delicate patterns etched by the unforgiving cold. Klaus Engelhardt lay awake in his bed, staring at the intricate designs, his breath forming small clouds that dissipated into the dimness of his room. The thin blanket pulled up to his chin did little to ward off the creeping cold that seeped through the cracks in the window frames. The solitary candle on his bedside table flickered weakly, casting elongated shadows that danced across the bare walls.

He could hear the distant sounds of the city stirring—a tram rattling along its tracks, muffled voices of workers braving the morning frost. But within his room, silence reigned, broken only by the occasional creak of the floorboards as he shifted his weight. Klaus's hands, once steady and strong, trembled as he reached for the glass of water on the table. His fingers closed around it, but a sudden tremor sent the glass slipping, shattering on the wooden floor.

Downstairs, Marta paused her preparations for breakfast, her ears attuned to the slightest disturbance. The clatter from above prompted her to climb the narrow staircase, her footsteps careful. Pushing open the door to their bedroom, she found Klaus sitting on the edge of the bed, shards of glass glinting at his feet.

"Klaus, are you alright?" she asked softly, concern etching lines on her face.

He looked up at her, eyes clouded with fatigue. "Just a clumsy moment," he muttered. "No need to fuss."

Marta sighed, retrieving a dustpan and brush from the corner. As she cleaned the fragments, she cast a worried glance at him. "You should come downstairs. It's warmer by the stove."

"I prefer to stay here," he replied curtly.

"At least let me bring you a proper breakfast," she offered.

He shook his head. "I'm not hungry."

She hesitated before standing up. "Klaus, isolating yourself won't help. The winter is harsh, and you need your strength."

He waved her away. "Please, Marta. Leave me be."

Defeated, she left the room, closing the door gently behind her. In the kitchen, she found Frieda wrapping a woollen scarf around her neck, preparing to leave for the day.

"Is *Vater* joining us?" Frieda asked, noticing her mother's troubled expression.

Marta shook her head. "He's not himself. I'm worried about him."

Frieda frowned. "Perhaps I can speak with him later. The new year approaches, and maybe we can convince him to embrace some change."

"Be gentle with him," Marta advised. "He's… fragile."

"Of course," Frieda agreed, squeezing her mother's hand before heading out into the crisp morning air.

The streets of Hamburg were a flurry of activity despite the cold. Shopkeepers swept snow from their doorsteps, and the aroma of fresh *brötchen* wafted from the bakeries. Children bundled in layers hurried along, their laughter rising in plumes of white. Frieda drew her coat tighter, her breath forming clouds as she made her way to the Rathaus for a council meeting. The city was slowly healing, scars of war giving way to signs of rejuvenation.

At the council chamber, discussions centred around the continued reconstruction efforts and the challenges posed by the harsh winter. Frieda asserted with a clear voice, "We ensure that no family is left without adequate heating. Our resources are strained, but we cannot allow our citizens to suffer."

Her colleagues nodded in agreement. *Herr Bauer,* an older member with a kind demeanour, added, "Perhaps we can allocate funds from the surplus generated by the Marshall Plan aid."

Frieda made notes, her mind already planning plans to assist the most vulnerable. Yet, amid her civic responsibilities, thoughts of her father lingered. His withdrawal since the official division of Germany had deepened, and she feared for his well-being.

Back at the Engelhardt home, the days dragged on in a monotonous rhythm for Klaus. The 10th of December 1949 found him staring out of the frost-covered window, watching as a thin layer of snow blanketed the street below. The cold had seeped into his bones, a persistent ache that he attributed to age and the burdens he carried. Memories haunted him— images of the Eastern Front, the faces of fallen comrades, the weight of commands given and orders followed.

A knock on the door interrupted his reverie. *"Vater?"* Frieda's voice called softly.

"Enter," he said begrudgingly.

She stepped inside, the warmth from the hallway briefly piercing the chill of the room. "I brought you some tea," she said, setting a steaming cup on the table.

He glanced at it but made no move to reach for it. "Thank you."

She sat in the worn armchair opposite his bed. "I've been thinking," she began cautiously. "Perhaps you could join me at the council meeting next week. Your experience could provide valuable insights."

He scoffed lightly. "What use is an old soldier among politicians and bureaucrats?"

"You have a perspective that is important," she insisted. "Germany is rebuilding, and we should hear voices like yours," she insisted.

He turned his gaze back to the window. "This new Germany has no place for me."

"That's not true," she argued gently. "We need unity now more than ever."

He remained silent, the furrow in his brow deepening.

"Vater, isolating yourself won't change the past," she implored. "Please, consider becoming part of the present."

Letting out a deep and heavy sigh, he made it clear that even though he spoke about unity, there was a fracture within their own family. "Hans is lost to us, and you… you embrace a world I barely recognise."

"Hans made his choices," she acknowledged. "But we can still reach out to him. And you can choose to be part of my world, our world, if you allow yourself."

He shook his head. "I am tired, Frieda. Tired of fighting battles, both real and imagined."

She stood, frustration and concern warring within her. "Please, don't give up on us."

As she left the room, the door closing softly behind her, Klaus felt a pang of regret. But the weight of his guilt and disillusionment pressed heavily upon him, anchoring him to his solitude.

Tension filled the Engelhardt household on the evening of 15 December 1949. Marta busied herself in the kitchen, preparing a simple stew of potatoes and carrots. The meagre rations stretched thin, but she infused the meal with herbs to mask the scarcity. Frieda returned home, her cheeks flushed from the biting wind.

"Any luck with you father today?" Marta asked hopefully.

Frieda shook her head. "He refuses to engage. I'm at a loss."

"Perhaps we should try together," Marta suggested. "He can't ignore both of us."

They ascended the creaking staircase, the lantern in Frieda's hand casting a warm glow ahead of them. Knocking softly, they entered Klaus's room. He sat hunched over on the bed, the candle casting shadows that stressed his gaunt features.

"Klaus," Marta began gently. "We need to talk."

He looked up, eyes dull. "About what?"

"Your health," she said firmly. "You're not eating properly, and this cold is too much for you alone in here."

"I manage," he replied tersely.

"No, you don't," Frieda interjected. "We can see you're suffering."

He bristled. "Suffering is a part of life. I've endured worse."

"That doesn't mean you have to now," Marta insisted. "Please, let us help you."

"I don't need help," he snapped, a flicker of anger igniting in his eyes. "What I need is to be left in peace."

"Isolating yourself won't solve anything," Frieda pressed. "You're punishing yourself for things beyond your control."

"You know nothing of what weighs on me," he retorted sharply.

"Then tell us," she challenged. "Let us share the burden."

He stood abruptly, swaying slightly, and said, "Enough! I won't allow myself to be badgered in my home."

As he took a step forward, his legs buckled. His hands grasped at the air before him, seeking support that wasn't there. Frieda and Marta lunged forward, catching him before he hit the floor.

"Klaus!" Marta cried out, fear lacing her voice.

"*Vater,* can you hear me?" Frieda asked urgently.

His face was ashen, beads of sweat forming on his brow despite the cold. His breathing was shallow, each inhale a struggle.

"We need to get you to bed," Marta commanded, her tone leaving no room for argument.

Together, they guided him back to the bed, his body heavy and unresponsive. Marta pulled the blanket over him, tucking it around his thin frame.

"I'm calling for a doctor," Frieda declared, turning towards the door.

"No," Klaus rasped, his hand gripping her wrist weakly. "No doctors."

"You need medical attention," she insisted.

He shook his head feebly. "I won't have it."

"Why?" Marta demanded, tears welling in her eyes. "Why won't you let us help you?"

He closed his eyes, a pained expression crossing his face. "Perhaps this is what I deserve."

"Don't say that," Frieda admonished, her voice breaking. "You don't deserve to suffer."

He opened his eyes, gazing at the ceiling. "You don't understand. The things I've done… the orders I've given. There's a weight to such actions, a price to be paid."

Marta knelt beside him. "We all carry regrets, but punishing yourself won't change the past."

"Let us help you find peace," Frieda urged softly.

He turned his head away. "Leave me."

They exchanged a worried glance but recognised the futility of pressing further in that moment. As they exited the room, Klaus listened to their footsteps fading down the hall. The silence that followed was suffocating.

The days after his collapse passed in a blur. Klaus remained confined to his bed, drifting in and out of a restless sleep. Marta tended to him diligently, bringing warm broth and sitting by his side, humming old lullabies from their youth. Yet he consumed a little, his strength waning.

On 20 December 1949, a heavy snowfall blanketed Hamburg. The city seemed muffled under the weight of it, sounds dampened by the thick layer of white. Frieda trudged through the snow to buy additional coal for the stove, her determination fuelled by concern for her father's failing health.

At the market, she encountered Greta Schmidt, her friend and confidante. "Frieda, you look exhausted," Greta observed, her brow furrowed.

"It's *Vater*," Frieda explained. "He's unwell and refuses to see a doctor."

"That's not good," Greta replied sympathetically. "Perhaps I can recommend someone who could visit discreetly."

Frieda considered this. "He might be more receptive if it's not an official visit."

"I'll arrange it," Greta promised. "In the meantime, take care of yourself as well."

"Thank you," Frieda said gratefully. "Your support means a great deal."

Back home, Marta was organising the meagre supplies they had left. The harsh winter had strained their resources, and with Klaus incapacitated, the burden fell heavier on her shoulders. She steeled herself, recalling the resilience that had carried them through the war years.

The Engelhardt home became enveloped in a quiet melancholy as evening settled on 24 December 1949. Traditionally a night of celebration, Christmas Eve felt hollow without the warmth of family unity. Marta lit candles on the mantelpiece, their soft glow offering a semblance of festivity. She placed a small Weihnachtspyramide—a wooden Christmas pyramid— on the table, its delicate figures casting shadows as the candles' heat set it in motion.

Frieda entered the room, carrying a tray with three mugs of steaming Glühwein. "I thought we could at least share a drink," she suggested.

"Perhaps we can persuade Klaus to join us," Marta mused, though her tone lacked conviction.

"I'll try," Frieda offered, heading towards his room.

She knocked gently before entering. Klaus lay propped up against the pillows, eyes closed. *"Vater,"* she called softly.

He stirred slightly. "Yes?"

"It's Christmas Eve," she reminded him. "Will you join us downstairs?"

He opened his eyes, the weariness in them profound. "I don't think I can manage."

"Even for a short while?" she implored. "It would mean a lot to *Mutter.*"

He sighed. "Very well."

With Frieda's help, he dressed warmly and made his way downstairs, each step a visible effort. Settling into his armchair by the stove, he gazed at the modest decorations adorning the room.

Marta handed him a mug. "It's good to have you with us," she said softly.

He took a sip, the spiced wine warming him from the inside. For a moment, a flicker of contentment crossed his features.

They sat in companionable silence, the crackle of the fire filling the room. Outside, snowflakes drifted lazily, blanketing the city in a serene hush.

"Do you remember when the children were young?" Marta reminisced. "How Hans would sneak downstairs to peek at the presents?"

A faint smile tugged at Klaus's lips. "And Frieda would scold him for spoiling the surprise."

Frieda chuckled softly. "I was always the responsible one."

"You both brought us such joy," Marta continued, her eyes misty.

Klaus's gaze grew distant. "I wish I could have done better by you all."

"You did your best," Frieda assured him. "That's all any of us can do."

He shook his head slightly. "There are regrets that haunt me."

Marta reached over, clasping his hand. "We can't change the past, but we can embrace the time we have now."

He squeezed her hand weakly. "Perhaps you're right."

As the clock chimed midnight, signalling Christmas Day, they raised their mugs in a quiet toast.

"To family," Frieda said softly.

"To hope," Marta added.

Klaus nodded, his voice barely above a whisper. "To forgiveness."

The days that followed saw a slight improvement in Klaus's condition. The visit from the discreet doctor arranged by Greta provided some relief, though his recovery remained uncertain. Marta and Frieda continued to care for him, their dedication unwavering.

On 31 December 1949, as the year drew to a close, Hamburg prepared to welcome a new decade. Fireworks burst in the night sky, their colours reflecting off the snow-covered rooftops. The city pulsed with a cautious optimism, citizens eager to leave the hardships behind.

From his bedroom window, Klaus watched the displays, the explosions illuminating his gaunt features. Frieda joined him, standing quietly by his side.

"A new year," she remarked. "A chance for new beginnings."

He nodded slowly. "Perhaps for you."

"For all of us," she insisted gently. "Will you try to embrace it?"

He met her gaze, a hint of resolution in his eyes. "I will try."

As the final fireworks faded, leaving the sky a canvas of stars, Klaus felt a tentative stirring of hope. The journey ahead remained daunting, but the steadfast support of his family offered a beacon in the darkness.

The cold of winter still gripped the city, but within the Engelhardt home, the thaw had begun. Together, they faced the uncertainties of the new year, bound by shared history and the enduring strength of their bonds.

ooo

The first snow the New Year, 1950 blanketed Hamburg in a pristine layer of white, muffling the city's usual clamour. Frieda Engelhardt sat at the small wooden desk in her bedroom, the faint glow of a lamp casting a warm circle of light amidst the cold that seeped through the old walls. The date, 1 January 1950, marked yet another month without seeing her brother. She dipped her pen into the inkwell, tapping off the excess before setting nib to paper.

Lieber Hans,

Winter has settled upon us with a chill that seems to reach into one's very bones. Vater's health remains fragile, and Mutter and I do what we can to keep the household warm and spirits lifted.

She paused, gazing out of the frost-framed window at the quiet street below. A couple hurried past, their breath forming clouds in the crisp air. Children, bundled in layers, dragged sledges behind them, leaving trails in the fresh snow.

I think often of our childhood winters, the snowball fights in the park, building snowmen until our fingers were numb. Those days seem so distant now, but the memories bring warmth.

Frieda hesitated before broaching the subject that weighed heavily on her mind.

Hans, I wish to understand your views better. Here in the West, we are making strides towards democracy and rebuilding our nation on principles of freedom and accountability. I believe that acknowledging our past mistakes is crucial for moving forward. I hope you might consider this perspective.

She signed off with affection, sealing the envelope and setting it aside. The candle flickered as a draft slipped through the windowpane, reminding her of the need to fix the insulation—a task for another day.

Days later, on 8 January 1950, a letter bearing an East Berlin postmark arrived. Frieda recognised Hans's handwriting and felt a mix of anticipation and apprehension. She retreated to her room, unsealing the envelope carefully.

Liebe Frieda,

> *The winter here is harsh, but it brings a sense of renewal—a blank slate upon which we can build a just society. I appreciate your concerns about Vater's health; I wish I could be there to assist.*

He shifted to the ideological divide swiftly.

> *You speak of democracy and accountability, but I see a West influenced by capitalist interests that exploit the working class. Here in the GDR, we are constructing a society where everyone contributes and benefits equally. The socialist principles we uphold offer genuine hope for our nation's future.*

Frieda read his words with a furrowed brow, feeling the familiar tug of frustration. Hans's unwavering commitment to socialism seemed unshakable, and his criticisms of the West cut deep.

On 12 January 1950, she penned her response:

> *Hans,*
>
> *I respect your dedication to your beliefs, but I fear that your path ignores the oppressive measures being implemented in the East. Freedom of speech and thought are essential, and I worry the GDR suppresses these in the name of unity.*

She folded the letter, her thoughts heavy. The exchange continued over the weeks, each letter crossing paths over a divided Germany. The postal service, strained yet functioning, became their lifeline.

By 20 January 1950, the tone of their correspondence had shifted from affectionate to strained debates. Hans wrote,

> *Frieda,*
>
> *The so-called freedoms you champion in the West are illusions. The capitalist system breeds inequality and selfishness. Here, we prioritise the collective good over individual desires. I urge you to see beyond the propaganda.*

Frieda felt a surge of indignation. She penned her reply, her words firm yet laced with concern.

Hans,

Open your eyes to the surrounding realities. Hans, you cannot ignore the reports of censorship and the silencing of dissent in the GDR. A society that demands conformity at the expense of personal liberty is not just.

Frieda entered the room, a letter clutched in her hand. "Mutter, I've heard from Hans again," she announced softly.

Marta looked up from her knitting, a hopeful gleam in her eyes. "Is he well?"

"He says he's fine," Frieda replied, taking a seat beside her. "But our letters have become… contentious."

Klaus's gaze remained fixed on the fire, but his ears perked at the mention of Hans.

"Perhaps it's best to focus on what unites you rather than divides," Marta suggested gently.

"I try," Frieda sighed. "But he is so entrenched in his views."

Klaus finally spoke, his voice barely above a whisper. "We have lost him," Klaus finally spoke, his voice barely above a whisper.

"Don't say that," Frieda implored. "We must keep trying."

Klaus stood abruptly, the chair scraping against the wooden floor. "Attempts at reconciliation are futile when one's mind is closed."

He left the room, leaving Frieda and Marta in heavy silence. Marta reached over, squeezing Frieda's hand. "Your father struggles with his own regrets. Don't lose hope."

As a new month approached, the city buzzed with subdued anticipation. On 31 January 1950, the Engelhardt household prepared for a modest meal. Frieda helped Marta into the kitchen, the aroma of freshly baked *stollen* filling the air.

Upstairs, Klaus rummaged through an old trunk, searching for a photograph album. Amidst the clutter, he came across a bundle of letters tied with twine. Curiosity piqued, he untied the bundle, realising they were the letters between Frieda and Hans.

He knew he shouldn't invade their privacy, but a desperate need to understand his children compelled him. Sitting on the edge of the bed, he read. As he progressed through the exchanges, his hands trembled, the pages rustling in the quiet room.

Hans's words echoed his own disillusionment with the West, yet the enthusiasm of his son's commitment to socialism unsettled him. Frieda's pleas for openness and reconciliation mirrored Marta's gentle urgings towards himself.

A heavy sigh escaped Klaus's lips, filling the silent room. The cold draft from the window caressed his face, starkly contrasting the warmth he felt slipping away from his family ties. The flickering candlelight cast shadows that danced mockingly, emphasising his isolation.

He folded the letters carefully, returning them to the bundle. Guilt pricked at his conscience for intruding, but the insight into his children's minds left him more conflicted than before. The realisation that the ideological divide mirrored the chasm within his own family weighed heavily upon him.

Meanwhile, downstairs, Frieda suggested, "Shall we call *Vater* to join us?"

There was a pause before he responded. "I'm not feeling up to it."

"Please," Marta entreated. "It would mean a great deal to us."

The door opened slowly, revealing Klaus's weary face. He looked at them, the weight of unspoken thoughts clear in his eyes. "Very well," he agreed.

They gathered in the parlour, the warmth from the fireplace offering comfort against the winter chill. Marta poured a small measure of schnapps for each of them, raising her glass. "To health, to hope, and to family."

"To new beginnings," Frieda added, her gaze lingering on her father.

Klaus hesitated before joining the toast. "To finding our way," he murmured.

They sipped in silence, the crackling of the fire the only sound. Frieda mustered the courage to broach the subject. "*Vater,* I know you found our letters."

He looked up sharply. "How did you—"

"I noticed that someone had moved them," she gently explained. "It's alright."

He set his glass down, the amber liquid swaying slightly. "I shouldn't have read them. It was not my place."

"Perhaps it's for the best," she offered. "Now you understand what we've been grappling with."

He ran a hand over his face, the stubble rough against his palm. "I see now how deep the divide has become."

"It doesn't have to remain that way," Marta interjected softly. "We can choose to bridge it."

Klaus shook his head slowly. "Hans is convinced of his path, and Frieda, you are convinced of it as well. I fear I have lost both my children to forces beyond my control."

"You haven't lost us," Frieda insisted, reaching out to touch his arm. "We are still here, still family. Our beliefs may differ, but that doesn't diminish our bond."

He met her eyes, a glimmer of vulnerability breaking through his stoic façade. "I don't know how to navigate this new world."

"None of us do," she admitted. "But we can figure it out together."

He considered her words, the tension in his shoulders easing slightly. "Perhaps... perhaps I have been too rigid."

Marta smiled softly. "Acknowledging that is a start."

They sat together, the silence now companionable rather than strained. The flames danced in the hearth, casting a warm glow over them.

"Tell me about your work, Frieda," Klaus prompted hesitantly.

She brightened at the invitation. "We're focusing on housing initiatives, ensuring that those displaced by the war have proper shelter. It's challenging but rewarding."

He nodded thoughtfully. "And you believe this democratic approach will succeed?"

"I do," she affirmed. "But it requires patience and cooperation."

He sighed. "Qualities that are often in short supply."

"True," she conceded. "But I have hope."

"Hope is a precious commodity," he mused.

Marta glanced between them, grateful for the tentative connection re-emerging. "And Hans," she ventured. "Perhaps we can reach him."

Klaus's expression clouded. "His letters… he is so entrenched."

"Stubbornness runs in the family," Frieda remarked with a gentle smile.

He huffed a quiet laugh. "I suppose you're right."

As the early hours of 1 February 1950 approached, exhaustion settled in. Klaus stood, stretching his limbs. "I think I shall retire for the night."

Frieda and Marta rose as well. "Thank you for joining us," Marta said sincerely.

He offered a faint smile. "Perhaps this year will bring clarity."

"Perhaps," Frieda echoed.

They bid each other goodnight, the atmosphere lighter than it had been in months.

In his bedroom, Klaus sat once more by the window. The street below was quiet, the snow reflecting the pale light of the moon. He pondered the evening's conversations, the letters, and the choices that had led them here.

Reaching into his pocket, he retrieved a small photograph—their family portrait taken years ago, before the war had torn their lives asunder. The faces smiling back at the weight of ideology unburdened him and regret.

He traced a finger over Hans's youthful face. *"Mein Sohn,"* he whispered. "Where did we lose our way?"

The cold draft slipped through the window, but he scarcely felt it. His thoughts drifted between past and present, hope and despair.

As dawn broke, Klaus made a silent vow to try—to mend the fractures, to find common ground. The path ahead was uncertain, but perhaps with effort, they could navigate it together.

In the quiet of the new year, the Engelhardt family stood at the crossroads of reconciliation. The letters between Frieda and Hans remained a testament to their enduring connection, despite the walls that divided them.

Outside, the city of Hamburg stirred to life, embracing the possibilities of a new decade. And within the walls of their home, the Engelhardts dared to hope that the ruins of their past might give way to a foundation for a unified future.

ooo

The dawn of 1 February 1950 broke over Hamburg with a brilliance that seemed to mirror the city's burgeoning optimism. The first rays of sunlight glinted off the newly erected scaffolding that dotted the skyline, casting long shadows over streets that buzzed with renewed energy. Frieda Engelhardt stood at the window of her modest flat. She sipped her coffee, the rich aroma mingling with the crisp winter air that seeped through the slightly ajar window.

Frieda had much to reflect upon. The success of the Marshall Plan was becoming increasingly tangible; factories roared back to life, shops reopened, and unemployment rates were steadily declining. Her role within the local government had expanded significantly. Last week, on 27 January 1950, they promoted her to Deputy Director of Reconstruction Projects. The responsibility was immense, but so was the potential to effect meaningful change.

She glanced at the stack of files on her desk—blueprints for housing developments, proposals for community centres, and reports on infrastructure improvements. Each document represented a step towards rebuilding physical structures and the social fabric of a nation torn apart by war and ideology.

As she prepared to leave for the Rathaus, Frieda wrapped a woollen scarf around her neck, the vibrant red contrasting with her grey overcoat. The streets were alive with the sounds of hammers and the chatter of vendors setting up their stalls. The scent of freshly baked pretzels wafted through the air, mingling with the earthy aroma of coal fires and warming the early risers.

At the corner of Mönckebergstraße, she purchased a newspaper. The headline proclaimed: "West German Economy Shows Record Growth—Marshall Plan Credited." Frieda allowed herself a moment of satisfaction before folding the paper under her arm and continuing towards the imposing sandstone façade of the Rathaus.

Inside, the corridors bustled with activity. Colleagues greeted her with nods and brief smiles, their arms laden with documents and charts. In the conference room, a large map of Hamburg dominated one wall, and pins marked the sites of ongoing and proposed projects.

"Good morning, *Frau Engelhardt,*" said *Herr Fischer,* the Director of Economic Affairs, as she entered. "Congratulations on your new position."

"Thank you, *Herr Fischer,*" she replied, taking her seat at the long oak table.

"We have much to discuss," he continued, adjusting his spectacles. "The funding from the Marshall Plan has exceeded our projections. We must prioritise our initiatives accordingly."

As the meeting progressed, Frieda contributed confidently, and her ideas were well-received. Plans for a new harbour expansion set in motion, and she received the task of overseeing the development of affordable housing units in the Altona district.

Meanwhile, back at the Engelhardt home on 15 January 1950, Marta tended to the household chores with a quiet diligence. The old house creaked with familiar sounds—the ticking of the grandfather clock, the distant hum of the radio broadcasting news of economic recovery. Yet, despite the external signs of progress, an undercurrent of tension lingered within the walls.

Klaus remained confined to his room, his health deteriorating alongside his spirit. He sat by the window, gazing blankly at the world outside. The once-bustling street now symbolised a future from which he felt increasingly disconnected. Children played hopscotch on the pavement, their laughter a stark contrast to the silence that enveloped him.

On 2 March 1950, Marta brought him a tray with a bowl of steaming *kartoffelsuppe* and a slice of rye bread. "You must eat something," she urged gently.

He looked up, his eyes clouded. "I'm not hungry," he muttered.

"You've barely touched food in days," she insisted. "At least have a few spoonfuls."

He sighed, picking up the spoon but only stirring the soup absently. "What's the point?" he whispered.

"The point is to live," Marta replied, her voice firm yet tender. "To be here with your family."

"Family," he scoffed lightly. "Hans is gone, and Frieda is off chasing dreams I don't understand."

"She is helping rebuild our country," Marta countered. "You should be proud."

He set the spoon down, pushing the tray away. "I don't recognise this country anymore."

Marta felt a pang of sadness but chose not to press further. She collected the tray, pausing at the door. "Frieda will join us for dinner tonight," she mentioned. "It would mean a lot if you came downstairs."

He did not respond, his gaze returning to the window.

Throughout March, the gap between Klaus and the world outside seemed to widen. On 14 March 1950, Frieda visited home with updates about her work, hoping to engage her father. "*Vater,* the new housing project is ahead of schedule," she shared enthusiastically. "We've secured additional resources to ensure proper insulation and heating."

"That's good," he replied tersely, not meeting her eyes.

She took a deep breath. "Perhaps you could visit the site with me. Your experience could provide valuable insights."

He shook his head. "My experiences are relics of a bygone era. They hold no relevance now."

"That's not true," she insisted. "Your knowledge is timeless."

He finally looked at her, a mixture of exhaustion and resignation in his eyes. "Frieda, I appreciate your efforts but have nothing left to offer."

She fought back tears, realising that reaching him might be impossible.

By 20 March 1950, the signs of spring emerged. Small buds appeared on the trees lining the avenues, and the air carried a hint of warmth. The city seemed to breathe easier, the weight of winter lifting.

Frieda attended a reception hosted by Mayor Max Brauer on 19 March 1950, celebrating the economic milestones achieved. Banners and the flags of the occupying Allies adorned the grand hall, serving as a reminder of the complex political landscape. Music from a string quartet filled the room as dignitaries mingled.

"Frieda, congratulations on your promotion," Greta Schmidt said, approaching with a glass of wine in hand. "You've certainly made a name for yourself."

"Thank you, Greta," Frieda replied, smiling. "And how goes the world of journalism?"

Greta sighed. "Always a battle. Exposing the remnants of Nazi influence is not a task for the faint-hearted."

"I admire your tenacity," Frieda acknowledged.

"As I do yours," Greta returned. "By the way, any word from Hans?"

Frieda's expression dimmed. "No. His letters have ceased."

"I'm sorry," Greta whispered. "I know how much you hoped to maintain that connection."

Frieda nodded, taking a sip of her wine. "Perhaps one day."

On 31 March 1950, the Engelhardt family gathered for dinner—a rare occurrence these days. Marta had prepared *rouladen,* hoping to recreate a sense of normalcy. They set the table with their best china, and a vase of freshly picked daffodils added a touch of cheer.

"Es ist schön, dass wir alle zusammen sind (It's nice that we are all together)," Marta said, placing the dishes on the table.

Frieda took her seat, glancing at her father as he settled slowly into his chair. His face showed signs of fatigue, with shadows under his eyes revealing sleepless nights.

"How was your day, *Vater?*" she asked cautiously.

He shrugged. "Uneventful."

Marta served the food, and for a few moments, the clinking of cutlery was the only sound.

"There's encouraging news about the economy," Frieda ventured. "Unemployment in Hamburg has dropped significantly. And experts expect that the new harbour facilities will boost trade."

Klaus remained silent, his gaze fixed on his plate.

"Isn't that wonderful?" Marta prompted, looking between them.

"Progress is being made," Frieda continued, her tone hopeful. "We are truly rebuilding."

Klaus finally spoke, his voice barely audible. "At what cost?"

Frieda frowned. "I'm not sure I understand."

He looked up, meeting her eyes. "We rebuild the city, but our nation loses its soul. We align ourselves with foreign powers and submit to their agendas."

"*Vater,* the Marshall Plan has been instrumental in our recovery," she reasoned. "Without it, we would still struggle to meet basic needs."

"And in exchange, we sacrifice our sovereignty," he countered. "We become puppets in the hands of others."

"That's not fair," she argued. "We are taking control of our destiny, forging a fresh path."

"A path dictated by those who defeated us," he retorted.

Marta intervened gently. "Perhaps we can focus on the positives tonight."

Klaus pushed his chair back abruptly. "I've lost my appetite."

He left the table, his footsteps heavy on the wooden floorboards. Frieda's shoulders sagged, frustration and sorrow intertwining.

"I'm sorry, *Mutter,*" she said softly.

"It's not your fault," Marta assured her, reaching across to squeeze her hand. "A past that no longer exists is trapping him,"

"I don't know how to help him," Frieda admitted.

"Perhaps all we can do is be patient," Marta suggested. "And hope that he finds his way."

As April approached, the city continued to flourish. On 5 April 1950, Frieda attended the opening ceremony of the new community centre in Altona. Children laughed as they played on the freshly built playground, and families gathered to celebrate the new facilities.

Standing at the podium, Frieda addressed the crowd. "Today is not just about a building; it's about rebuilding trust, community, and our shared future. Together, we have transformed the ruins of war into foundations upon which we can all stand proud."

The applause was heartfelt, and for a moment, Frieda felt the weight of her efforts validated.

Later that evening, she returned home to find Klaus sitting in the parlour, a rare occurrence. He stared into the fireplace, though no fire burned.

"Vater," she greeted cautiously. "It's good to see you downstairs."

He glanced at her briefly. "I thought I'd change the scenery."

She took a seat opposite him. "I attended the opening of the community centre today."

"So I heard," he replied.

"It was a success," she continued. "The people are grateful."

He nodded slowly. "You are doing well."

"Thank you," she said, surprised by the acknowledgement. "It means a lot to hear you say that."

He sighed. "I may not agree with everything, but I can see your dedication."

She leaned forward. "*Vater,* I wish we could find common ground."

"Perhaps," he mused, "we can start by listening."

"I'm willing," she affirmed.

He met her gaze, a hint of the man he once was shining through. "Tell me more about your work."

She smiled, launching into descriptions of the projects, the challenges, and the triumphs. As she spoke, he listened attentively, occasionally asking questions. The conversation flowed more naturally than it had in years.

Marta watched from the doorway, a soft smile on her lips. Hope flickered within her—a fragile but persistent light.

Over the following weeks, Klaus made small but significant efforts to re-engage. On 18 April 1950, he accompanied Frieda to one of the housing sites. Workers greeted them with respect and a straightforward demeanour.

"*Frau Engelhardt* speaks highly of you," one of the foremen said to Klaus. "It's an honour to meet her father."

Klaus offered a modest nod. "She is the one accomplishing great things."

As they walked through the site, Frieda explained the architectural choices, the sustainable materials being used, and the importance of creating spaces that fostered community.

"It's impressive," Klaus admitted. "You've thought of everything."

"Not everything," she laughed lightly. "But we're trying."

He paused, looking out over the partially constructed buildings. "Perhaps there is merit in building anew."

She placed a hand on his arm. "There is always room for redemption, *Vater.*"

He gave her a faint smile. "You sound like your mother."

"She is a wise woman," Frieda remarked.

As spring blossomed, so too did the tentative reconciliation between father and daughter. While Klaus still grappled with his internal struggles, he accepted that the world was changing and that perhaps he could find a place within it.

On 30 April 1950, the family gathered once more for dinner. This time, the atmosphere was warmer. Klaus recounted stories from his youth, anecdotes that brought laughter and lightness to the table.

"Did I ever tell you about the time I nearly fell into the Elbe while trying to impress your mother?" he chuckled.

Marta blushed lightly. "Oh, that was quite the spectacle."

Frieda grinned. "I haven't heard this one."

Klaus leaned back, a sparkle in his eye. "I thought balancing on the railing of a bridge would show my daring spirit. Instead, I showed my clumsiness."

They laughed together, the sound filling the house with a joy that had long been absent.

As the evening drew to a close, Frieda felt a sense of contentment. The ruins of their family bonds were being rebuilt, much like the surrounding city.

Later that night, Klaus returned to his room, but this time, the darkness felt less oppressive. He sat by the window, the cool breeze carrying the scents of blooming flowers and the distant murmur of a city in motion.

He whispered into the night, "Perhaps there is hope after all."

In the months that followed, the Engelhardt family continued to navigate the complexities of their relationships amidst a nation undergoing transformation. The success of the Marshall Plan had set West Germany on a path to recovery, and within their home, the foundations of understanding and acceptance were being laid.

Frieda knew there was still much work to be done—both in her professional endeavours and in healing the fractures within her family. But as she stood on the balcony one evening, watching the sun set over a city that was rising from its own ashes, she allowed herself a moment of quiet optimism.

"Tomorrow is a new day," she whispered, the words carrying a promise she was determined to keep.

SIX:

COLD WAR TENSIONS RISE

The chill of 1 January 1951 lingered in the air, but Hamburg pulsed with a warmth that defied the winter cold. Once scarred by war, streets now bustled with life; new buildings reached skyward, their glass façades reflecting a city in resurgence. Frieda Engelhardt stepped out of the Rathaus, the crisp wind tugging at her navy coat. She clutched a folder brimming with plans for the HafenCity redevelopment—a bold project aiming to transform the harbour district into a modern commercial hub.

"Frohes neues Jahr, Frau Engelhardt!" called out *Herr Müller*, a colleague laden with blueprints.

"Happy New Year to you, too," she replied, her breath forming delicate clouds that dissipated into the bright morning.

The scent of freshly baked *brötchen* wafted from a nearby bakery, mingling with the sharp tang of coal smoke from chimneys. Children in woollen scarves chased one another along the pavements, their laughter echoing against the backdrop of construction sites. The rhythmic clang of hammers and the hum of machinery created a symphony of progress.

Frieda made her way to a meeting with the city council, her heels clicking purposefully against the cobblestones. Inside the council chamber, voices buzzed with optimism.

"The latest figures show a significant decrease in unemployment," announced Herr Fischer, tapping a graph with his pen on 15 March 1951. "Our initiatives are bearing fruit."

Frieda nodded, adding, "We must continue to support small businesses. They are the backbone of our economy."

As the meeting adjourned, she felt a surge of pride. The Marshall Plan's impact was undeniable, and she was at the heart of this transformation.

Meanwhile, at the Engelhardt home on 2 April 1951, Klaus sat by the window, the afternoon sun casting a gentle glow across his lined face. He watched as a group of young men unloaded crates from a lorry, their movements swift and coordinated. The distant strains of a radio playing upbeat tunes drifted through the open window—a melody unfamiliar to his ears.

Marta entered the room quietly, placing a cup of chamomile tea on the small table beside him. "It's a lovely day," she offered.

He grunted in response, his gaze never leaving the scene outside.

"Frieda is doing remarkable work," she continued, hoping to elicit a reaction. "The city is changing so quickly."

"Changing beyond recognition," he muttered.

She sighed softly. "Change can be good, Klaus."

He turned to look at her, the weight of years clear in his eyes. "For whom?"

"For all of us," she replied gently. "We cannot live in the past."

He shook his head, returning his attention to the window. "The past is all I have left."

As spring blossomed, so did the city's vibrancy. On 15 June 1951, banners adorned the Hauptmarkt in anticipation of the political rally. The sun hung high in a cloudless sky, its warmth tempered by a light breeze that carried the mingled scents of street vendors' sausages and freshly cut flowers. The crowd gathered early, a sea of faces alight with expectation.

Frieda stood backstage, reviewing her notes. Her heart pounded—not with fear, but with the exhilaration of the moment. She adjusted the microphone pinned to her lapel and smoothed the creases of her emerald dress.

"You're going to be brilliant," Greta Schmidt whispered, squeezing her hand.

"Thank you," Frieda smiled. "It's time."

As she stepped onto the stage, applause swelled. She paused, letting her gaze sweep over the crowd—a tapestry of hope woven from the faces of workers, families, and students.

"*Liebe Mitbürgerinnen und Mitbürger* (Dear fellow citizens)," she began, her voice clear and resonant. "Today, we stand at the threshold of a new era. Our city, once in ruins, rises anew—not just in bricks and mortar, but in spirit and purpose."

The crowd erupted in cheers. Flags bearing the black, red, and gold of West Germany fluttered in the breeze, a visual chorus to the people's enthusiasm.

Klaus stood at the square's periphery, leaning heavily on his cane. The journey from home had exhausted him, but an inexplicable urge had compelled him to attend. Marta had suggested it might do him good.

"You needn't stay long," she had assured him that morning. "Just see what Frieda has accomplished."

Now, amidst the throng, he felt adrift. The warmth of the sun pressed against his skin, yet a chill settled deep within. Frieda's voice echoed through the loudspeakers, passionate and confident—a stranger wearing his daughter's face.

"We don't just measure our economic recovery in numbers," she declared. "We feel it in the opportunities that bloom in every corner of our city, in the dignity restored to our people."

More applause. Klaus watched as she gestured gracefully, her hands painting visions of the future he could not grasp.

"We must continue to embrace democracy and collaboration," she urged. "Together, we will ensure that the shadows of our past do not define the horizons of our future."

The crowd's response was thunderous. Tears pricked at the corners of Klaus's eyes—not from pride, but from a profound sense of loss. The daughter he once knew had become a beacon for a world that had left him behind.

He turned away, the din of the rally fading as he navigated through the maze of spectators. His breath came in laboured gasps, each step a Herculean effort. The rough texture of his overcoat chafed against his neck, and he tightened his grip on the cane, knuckles whitening.

"Are you alright, sir?" a young man asked, steadying him as he stumbled.

"I'm fine," Klaus replied curtly, shrugging off the assistance.

He sought refuge in a quiet side street, the cacophony of the square replaced by the distant clatter of a tram and the chirping of sparrows perched on telephone wires. He sank onto a bench beneath a linden tree, its leaves rustling softly overhead.

Closing his eyes, Klaus allowed memories to surface—the camaraderie of his fellow soldiers, the weight of his uniform, the clarity of purpose he once felt. The world had been a different place then, or perhaps he had been a different man.

The laughter of children playing nearby intruded upon his reverie. He watched as they chased a ball, their carefree joy a stark contrast to the turmoil within him. One boy, noticing his gaze, waved cheerfully.

Klaus managed a faint smile, raising a trembling hand in return. The innocence of youth—untouched by the scars of war—was something he both cherished and envied.

Returning home later that afternoon, he found Marta in the kitchen, kneading dough for *abendbrot.* The comforting aroma of yeast filled the air.

"How was it?" she asked without turning around.

He hung his coat on the worn peg by the door. "Crowded," he replied.

"And Frieda's speech?"

"Well-received," he admitted begrudgingly.

Marta glanced over her shoulder, her hands dusted with flour. "You must be tired. Sit, I'll bring you some tea."

He obliged, settling into his usual chair by the hearth. The familiar surroundings offered a semblance of solace—the ticking clock, the faded photographs on the mantelpiece, and the soft glow of the lamp illuminating the room as evening encroached.

"She is doing important work," Marta ventured, setting a steaming cup before him.

"Important to whom?" he challenged, though his tone lacked conviction.

"To many," she answered gently. "Including us."

He wrapped his hands around the cup, savouring the warmth. "I don't belong in this new world," he confessed.

Marta pulled up a chair beside him. "The world changes, Klaus. It always has. But that doesn't mean there isn't a place for you."

He stared into the tea, watching the swirl of leaves settle at the bottom. "I feel… obsolete."

She reached out, placing her hand over his. "You're still needed. By me, by Frieda."

He looked up, meeting her gaze. The depth of understanding in her eyes both comforted and unsettled him. "I don't know how to be part of this future."

"Then let us help you," she offered. "One step at a time."

Outside, the sky deepened into hues of amber and violet. The fluttering of wings drew Klaus's attention to the window, where a sparrow perched on the sill before darting away.

In the weeks that followed, the city continued its relentless march towards progress. On 1 September 1951, people celebrated the opening of the new Elbe Tunnel with great fanfare. Frieda stood among dignitaries, cutting the ribbon that signified not just a feat of engineering, but a bridge between past destruction and future promise.

Klaus observed these developments from a distance, both physically and emotionally. The clatter of construction had become the soundtrack of his days, a constant reminder of a world rebuilding itself without his input.

One afternoon, on 12 October 1951, he ventured into the city centre, drawn by a restlessness he couldn't quell. The streets bustled with shoppers and businessmen, trams rattled along their tracks, and cafés spilt over with patrons enjoying coffee and conversation.

He paused before a bookstore display, the titles boasting of economic theories and political discourse. Among them, a book titled *"Der deutsche Wiederaufbau"* (The German Reconstruction) caught his eye. He entered the shop, the bell above the door chiming softly.

The scent of paper and ink enveloped him. He traced a finger along the spines, stopping at a collection of war memoirs. Pulling one from the shelf, he leafed through its pages—accounts of battles he'd fought, places he'd been. Yet the words felt distant, as though belonging to someone else's life.

"Interested in history?" the shopkeeper asked kindly.

Klaus regarded the man—a bespectacled figure with an inquisitive smile. "I lived it," he replied.

"Then perhaps you have stories to tell," the shopkeeper suggested.

"Stories best left untold," Klaus murmured, replacing the book.

As he exited the shop, the sound of church bells rang out—reminders of time's inexorable passage. He wandered aimlessly until he found himself at the banks of the Elbe. The river flowed steadily, indifferent to the changes on its shores.

He sat on a bench, the cool breeze carrying the faint scent of brine. Seagulls swooped and called overhead. Reaching into his pocket, he retrieved a worn photograph—his family, taken years before the war. Hans and Frieda as children, their faces alight with mischief; Marta, radiant and carefree; and himself, standing tall with a confidence he no longer possessed.

"Where did we go wrong?" he whispered, tracing the outline of their faces.

The months slipped by, and winter approached once more. On 20 December 1951, the Engelhardt family adorned their home with modest decorations—sprigs of pine and red ribbons. Frieda arrived bearing gifts and stories of the city's latest achievements.

"We've secured funding for the new hospital wing," she announced over dinner. "It will provide much-needed care for those still suffering from the war's aftermath."

"That's wonderful news," Marta exclaimed, her eyes shining.

Klaus remained silent, picking at his meal.

"*Vater,* what do you think?" Frieda prompted.

He looked up, meeting her expectant gaze. "It's commendable," he conceded.

A flicker of surprise crossed her features. "Perhaps you could visit the site with me after the holidays."

He considered her offer. "Perhaps," he echoed noncommittally.

On Christmas Eve, 24 December 1951, they attended the midnight service at St. Michael's Church. Candlelight filled the nave, and the scent of incense was heavy in the air. Hymns echoed against the vaulted ceilings, and voices united in solemn reflection.

Klaus stood between Marta and Frieda, the warmth of their presence both comforting and disconcerting. As the congregation sang "Stille Nacht," he felt a stirring within—a longing for connection, for redemption.

Back at home, they exchanged small gifts by the glow of the hearth. Klaus presented Frieda with a leather-bound journal.

"For your thoughts," he said simply.

She smiled, touched by the gesture. "Thank you, Vater. It's perfect."

As the clock chimed midnight, they raised glasses of spiced wine.

"To family," Marta toasted.

"To new beginnings," Frieda added.

Klaus hesitated before raising his glass. "To understanding," he said softly.

The year drew to a close, with a quiet acceptance settling over Klaus. On 31 December 1951, he sat once more by the window, watching fireworks bloom across the night sky. Each burst of colour reflected in his eyes, mirroring the tumult of emotions within.

Frieda joined him, wrapping a shawl around her shoulders. "It's beautiful, isn't it?"

"Yes," he agreed. "A reminder of possibilities."

She glanced at him, noting the contemplative expression. "*Vater,* I know these changes have been difficult."

He sighed. "The world moves forward, whether or not we're ready."

"We can move with it," she suggested gently.

"Perhaps," he allowed. "Tell me more about your plans for the new year."

Her face lit up as she described upcoming projects, such as the expansion of educational programmes, initiatives for veterans, and cultural exchanges.

He listened attentively, asking questions and offering insights. The conversation flowed easier than it had in years.

As the last seconds of 1951 slipped away, they counted down together, voices mingling with the distant celebrations.

"Happy New Year, *Vater,*" Frieda said, embracing him.

"Happy New Year, my dear," he replied, holding her close.

At that moment, Klaus felt a glimmer of hope—a tentative bridge spanning the chasm between his past and the uncertain future. The journey ahead remained daunting, but perhaps, with his family's support, he could find his place in this new Germany after all.

ooo

The first rays of sunlight on 1 June 1952 filtered through the lace curtains of the Engelhardt home, casting delicate patterns on the worn wooden floorboards. Frieda stood by the open window, inhaling the crisp morning air scented with the promise of summer. The distant chime of St. Michael's Church bells marked the hour, and she felt a flutter of anticipation. Today, they began preparing for their family's reunion, and she felt hopeful that they could bridge the chasm dividing them.

"*Frühstück* is ready (Breakfast is ready)," Marta called from the kitchen, her voice warm yet tinged with the weariness of years past.

Frieda joined her mother at the table, where freshly baked *brötchen* awaited alongside pots of jam and slices of cheese. "*Mutti,* I've finalised the arrangements for Hans's visit," she announced, spreading raspberry jam over her roll.

Marta smiled softly. "It's been too long since we've all been together under one roof."

"Seven years," Frieda noted, her gaze drifting to a faded photograph on the mantelpiece—a snapshot of simpler times when laughter came easily.

As the days of June unfolded, the house bustled with activity. Frieda and Marta cleaned and decorated, infusing the rooms with touches of life— a vase of wildflowers here, freshly laundered linens there. Klaus observed from his armchair that his once-imposing frame now diminished, but his presence was still commanding.

"You're going to exhaust yourselves," he remarked on 15 June 1952, watching as Frieda dusted the bookshelves.

She paused, brushing a stray lock of hair from her forehead. "It's worth it, *Vater.* This reunion is important."

He sighed, his eyes clouded with memories. "I hope it brings the peace you seek."

On 1 July 1952, the day of Hans's arrival, Hamburg basked in the sun's warmth. The city had transformed since the war's end—new buildings rose amidst remnants of ruins, and the harbour buzzed with the activity of trade ships. Frieda waited at the Hauptbahnhof, her heart pounding with a mix of excitement and trepidation.

The train pulled in with a screech of metal on metal, releasing a flurry of passengers onto the platform. Amidst the crowd, she spotted Hans—taller, leaner, his features sharper than she remembered. He neatly combed his dark hair and carried himself with an air of quiet confidence.

"Hans!" she called, waving.

He turned, and a genuine smile broke across his face. "Frieda!"

They embraced tightly. "It's so good to see you," she whispered.

"And you," he replied, stepping back to study her. "You look well."

As they made their way home, the city unfolded around them. Hans took in the sights—the restored façades, the lively cafés spilling onto sidewalks, the trams clattering along their routes. "Hamburg has changed," he observed.

"Rebuilt and revitalised," Frieda affirmed. "There's a sense of hope here."

He nodded thoughtfully. "Perhaps."

At home, Marta greeted Hans with open arms. *"Mein Sohn,"* she said softly, her eyes glistening. "Welcome home."

Klaus rose unsteadily from his chair, extending a hand. "Hans."

"Vater," Hans replied, shaking his father's hand firmly.

The initial days passed in a blur of shared meals and leisurely strolls along the Elbe River. On 5 July 1952, they visited Planten un Blomen park, where vibrant blooms painted the landscape in red, yellow, and violet strokes. Children flew kites against the backdrop of a cerulean sky; their laughter carried on the gentle breeze.

"It's peaceful here," Hans remarked as they sat by the pond, watching the swans glide gracefully across the water.

"It wasn't always," Frieda replied. "But we've worked hard to restore what was lost."

Hans glanced at her. "We all have our ways of rebuilding."

She smiled faintly. "Yes, we do."

As July waned into August, subtle tensions surfaced. Over dinner on 10 August 1952, the conversation turned to politics.

"The economic growth in the West is impressive," Frieda noted, passing the *kartoffelsalat* to Hans. "Unemployment is down, and living standards are improving."

Hans took a bite before responding. "At what cost? Capitalism breeds inequality. Not everyone benefits."

Klaus stirred his soup, his expression impassive. Marta interjected gently, "Perhaps we can focus on enjoying our meal."

Frieda conceded with a nod, but the undercurrents of disagreement lingered.

On 15 August 1952, they hosted a summer barbecue in the garden. The air was thick with the aroma of grilled *würstchen* and marinated meats, mingling with the sweet scent of blooming roses. Neighbours and old friends joined them, the garden alive with chatter and clinking glasses of sparkling *apfelschorle.*

Frieda stood to address the gathering. "*Vielen Dank,* for joining us today. This reunion reminds me of the strength found in unity. As our city thrives, so too can we as a community and as a family."

Applause rippled through the crowd. Hans watched her, a mix of admiration and scepticism in his eyes.

Later, as twilight painted the sky in hues of pink and gold, Klaus approached Hans, who stood alone at the edge of the garden.

"It's a beautiful evening," Klaus remarked.

"Indeed," Hans agreed, gazing at the silhouettes of rooftops against the fading light.

Klaus hesitated before speaking. "Your sister has achieved much here."

"She's passionate about her work," Hans acknowledged.

"She's building a future," Klaus continued. "One that perhaps we can all be part of."

Hans turned to face his father. "Our visions of the future differ."

"Do they have to?" Klaus asked quietly.

Hans sighed. "*Vater,* the West rebuilds with aid from those who once sought our destruction. The East seeks to forge a new path, free from capitalist influence."

Klaus's shoulders slumped slightly. "I fear the path may lead to further division."

"Perhaps," Hans conceded. "But I believe in the ideals we strive for."

As August drew to a close, the atmosphere grew strained. On 28 August 1952, Hans received a letter from a comrade in the East, urging his return and hinting at increased scrutiny for those who lingered in the West.

That evening, he approached Frieda. "I must depart soon."

She looked up sharply from her paperwork. "So soon? I thought you might stay longer."

"Responsibilities call," he replied.

"Or is it you feel uncomfortable here?" she challenged.

He met her gaze steadily. "There is truth in that."

She set her papers aside. "Hans, can't you see the progress we've made? The opportunities available?"

"Opportunities for some," he countered. "But the capitalist system inherently creates disparity."

"That's not true," she argued. "We're implementing social programmes, education reforms—"

He interrupted. "Under the guise of democracy, but who truly holds the power? The wealthy, the industrialists."

Frustration flashed across her face. "And in the East, is everyone truly equal? Or do the Party elites dictate every aspect of life?"

Hans bristled. "At least we strive for collective good, not individual greed."

On 31 August 1952, the day of his departure, the family gathered for a last meal. The mood was heavy, words cautious.

"I wish you didn't have to leave," Marta said softly, placing a hand over Hans's.

"I wish things were different," he replied gently.

Frieda remained quiet, her thoughts tumultuous.

After the meal, Hans and Frieda retreated to the parlour. The ticking of the grandfather clock filled the silence between them.

"Before you go, there's something I want to say," Frieda began, her tone measured.

He inclined his head. "I'm listening."

"I understand that we have different perspectives," she said. "But I had hoped that seeing the progress here might open your eyes to the possibilities outside of socialism."

He sighed. "Frieda, I appreciate your intentions, but you cannot easily sway my convictions."

"Even when faced with evidence to the contrary?" she pressed.

"What evidence?" he retorted. "Is it true material wealth measures that success? That individualism trumps community?"

She insisted that people have the freedom to choose their own paths.

"Freedom?" he scoffed lightly. "For whom? Those who can afford it?"

She stood abruptly, frustration spilling over. "You're blind to the reality of the East! The oppression, the lack of basic rights."

He rose to meet her gaze. "And you're blind to the flaws of the West. The exploitation, the superficial prosperity."

Their voices had risen, drawing the attention of Klaus and Marta, who lingered uncertainly in the doorway.

"Enough," Klaus interjected firmly. "This is not how siblings should part."

Frieda's eyes glistened with unshed tears. "I just want him to see reason."

Hans shook his head. "I could say the same."

Marta stepped forward, her voice soothing. "Please, both of you. Let us not allow politics to destroy our family."

Hans gathered his belongings, the weight of the unspoken pressing heavily upon him. "Perhaps it's best if I leave now."

Frieda's resolve wavered. "Hans, wait."

He paused at the door, turning back. "Take care of yourselves."

Klaus approached him, placing a hand on his shoulder. "Be safe, *mein Sohn.*"

"Thank you, *Vater,*" Hans replied softly.

Marta embraced him tightly. "Write to us."

"I will," he promised, though uncertainty lingered.

The late summer sun cast long shadows along the cobblestone streets as he walked away from the house. The bittersweet scent of lilacs hung in the air.

Back inside, Frieda sank into a chair, covering her face with her hands. "I've failed," she whispered.

Klaus sat beside her. "You haven't failed. You've tried to bridge a divide that is not of your making."

She looked up, anguish etched across her features. "But what if we've lost him?"

Marta joined them; her expression was resolute. "We must hold on to hope. The world is transforming. Perhaps time will bring clarity."

In the following days, the house felt emptier. On 5 September 1952, Frieda threw herself into her work with renewed vigour, channelling her emotions into the projects that had once filled her with pride.

During a meeting on 10 September 1952, her colleague Greta Schmidt noticed her distraction. "Is everything alright?" Greta inquired gently.

Frieda managed a weak smile. "Family matters. Nothing to trouble you with."

Greta squeezed her hand reassuringly. "Sometimes, focusing on making a difference helps."

"That's what I'm trying to do," Frieda replied. "But it's hard when those closest to you don't share your vision."

Greta nodded knowingly. "Change is never easy, especially when it challenges deeply held beliefs."

As autumn approached, Frieda found solace in the rhythms of her work. Yet, the memory of Hans's visit lingered as a persistent ache.

On 20 September 1952, she received a letter bearing the GDR's insignia. Her heart quickened as she opened it, only to find a terse note from Hans.

Frieda,

I arrived safely. I hope you understand that I have a predetermined path, just like you do. Perhaps one day, our roads will converge.

Hans

She traced the lines of his handwriting, a mixture of relief and sorrow washing over her.

That evening, she joined her parents for dinner. The meal was simple—*rinderrouladen* with potatoes and familiar and comforting flavours.

"I heard from Hans," she announced quietly.

Klaus looked up sharply. "Is he well?"

"He says so," she replied, handing the letter to him.

He read it silently before passing it to Marta. "At least he's safe."

"Yes," Frieda agreed, though uncertainty gnawed at her.

Marta reached across the table to squeeze Frieda's hand. "We must keep faith that things will improve."

Frieda nodded, mustering a small smile. "I suppose so."

As the leaves turned, the Engelhardt family settled into a new normalcy. The reunion had not healed the rifts as Frieda had hoped, but it had at least confirmed that the bonds of family, though strained, still existed.

On 31 October 1952, Frieda stood on the steps of the Rathaus, watching as the wind carried leaves in swirling patterns across the plaza. The air was crisp, carrying the scent of impending winter.

She thought of Hans, wondering if he felt the same chill in the East. Pulling her coat tighter, she resolved to continue her efforts—not just for her city and country, but for her family.

"Perhaps one day," she whispered into the wind, "we'll find our way back to each other."

The church bells tolled in the distance, their solemn notes echoing through the streets. As Frieda turned to re-enter the building, the sun broke through a cluster of clouds, casting a fleeting warmth upon her face.

It was a small sign, but for now, it was enough.

ooo

The leaves of East Berlin turned on 1 September 1952, their edges tinged with amber and russet, mirroring the subtle decay of Hans Engelhardt's conviction. The chill of autumn seeped into the city, carried on winds that whispered through the streets lined with austere concrete buildings. Hans pulled his coat tighter as he navigated the labyrinth of alleys, each step echoing the unease that had settled within him.

He arrived at the back entrance of an unassuming tenement, the façade cracked and unremarkable. A discreet knock—a rhythm learned in hushed exchanges—granted him entry. Inside, the dim glow of a single bulb illuminated a cramped room where shadows danced on peeling wallpaper. A handful of young men and women huddled together, their faces taut with apprehension.

"You're late," whispered Stefan, a wiry man with sharp features and eyes that flickered with cautious intelligence.

"Apologies," Hans replied, removing his hat. "The patrols are increasing."

As he settled into a rickety chair, the conversation resumed in muted tones. They spoke of the Stasi's tightening grip, of friends disappearing without a trace, of the oppressive weight of fear that now permeated every aspect of their lives.

"On 15 September 1952, they took Markus," Lena murmured, her fingers nervously twisting a handkerchief. "For a misplaced book—can you imagine?"

Stefan leaned forward. "It's not just about books or words anymore. It's about control. Absolute control."

Hans listened, his gaze fixed on a crack in the floorboards where a sprout of green dared to emerge. "What can we do?" he asked quietly. "We are but whispers against a storm."

"Whispers can become a roar," Stefan replied. "But only if we stand together."

The meeting dispersed as the clock struck midnight, each member slipping back into the shadows of the city. Hans walked home alone, the cobblestones slick with a recent rain that reflected the waning moon. The scent of damp earth mingled with the distant aroma of coal smoke, a reminder of the approaching winter.

On 1 October 1952, a letter arrived from his father. The envelope bore the familiar handwriting, but Hans hesitated before opening it, aware of the censors who might have already perused its contents. Seated at his small kitchen table, he unfolded the paper.

Mein Sohn,

Your mother and I think of you often. The days grow shorter, and with them, our hopes for a reunited family seem to fade. Your sister sends her love.

Vater

Hans traced the ink with a finger, the brevity speaking volumes. He longed to respond, to pour out his doubts and fears, but the ever-watchful eyes of the state stayed his hand.

In the subsequent weeks, they introduced a never-ending workload. The Jugendweihe office called him to their office on 1 November 1951. The corridors of the building were stark, lit by harsh fluorescent lights that cast an unforgiving glare.

"Comrade Engelhardt," greeted Herr Vogel, a stout man with a permanent scowl etched into his features. "We have an important project that requires your utmost dedication."

Hans nodded and questioned, "Of course, Herr Vogel, what is required?"

"You are to oversee the ideological education programme for the new recruits. Ensure they understand the principles of Marxism-Leninism thoroughly. There is no room for error."

"Understood," Hans replied, suppressing a sigh.

The days blurred into nights as he immersed himself in the task. Yet, the more he propagated the Party's doctrines, the more hollow the words felt. On 10 November 1952, during a lecture on collective responsibility, he caught sight of a young recruit's sceptical gaze—a mirror of his own burgeoning doubts.

After the session, Hans approached the recruit. "Is something troubling you?"

Before whispering, the youth hesitated and said, "I don't understand how they expect us to suppress our own thoughts for the supposed good of all."

Hans glanced around nervously. "Careful," he cautioned. "Such questions can be dangerous."

"But isn't questioning essential to progress?" the recruit pressed.

Hans felt a pang of empathy. "In theory, yes. In practice…" He let the sentence trail off, the unspoken words heavy between them.

That evening, Hans attended another clandestine meeting. The group's numbers had grown, the atmosphere thick with a mix of hope and trepidation.

"News from the West," announced Katarina, unfolding a smuggled newspaper dated 15 November 1952. "They speak of prosperity, of freedoms we can scarcely imagine."

Murmurs rippled through the room. Hans leaned forward. "But at what cost? They have their own inequalities, their own injustices."

"Perhaps," Stefan conceded. "But they do not live in fear of their own thoughts."

The conversation turned to action—what could they do to effect change? Suggestions ranged from passive resistance to more radical measures. Hans remained silent, his mind a tumult of conflicting loyalties.

On 1 December 1952, winter settled over the city, blanketing the streets with a thin layer of snow that muffled footsteps and softened the harsh lines of the architecture. Hans stood at his window, watching flakes drift lazily under the glow of street lamps. The stillness was deceptive; beneath it simmered unrest.

The next day, during a routine office meeting at the office, an incident shook him profoundly. The Stasi publicly reprimanded Herr Müller, a colleague known for his diligence, for failing to report a misplaced leaflet found on his desk.

"This negligence borders on treason," declared the Stasi officer, his voice echoing in the stunned silence of the assembly hall on 2 December 1952. "We cannot tolerate even the slightest deviation from our standards."

Someone escorted Müller away while Hans watched. He was pale and trembling. The assembled staff exchanged uneasy glances, and the atmosphere was thick with fear.

That evening, Hans sought solace in the dim recesses of a local tavern. The establishment was modest, its wooden beams darkened by years of smoke. He cradled a glass of schnapps, the fiery liquid offering scant comfort.

"Mind if I join you?" a voice asked.

He looked up to see Katarina, her brown hair tucked beneath a woollen cap. "Please," he gestured to the empty seat.

"It's becoming unbearable," she said, her gaze distant. "They're turning us against each other."

Hans nodded slowly. "Trust is a scarce commodity these days."

She leaned in, her voice barely above a whisper. "Some of us are considering leaving."

His heart quickened. "Leaving? How?"

"There's a route," she replied cautiously. "It's dangerous but possible."

He stared into his glass. "I don't know if I can."

"Think about it," she urged. "We can't continue like this."

The idea lingered in his mind, both alluring and terrifying. On 10 December 1952, he stood at the edge of the River Spree, the water's dark surface reflecting the overcast sky. The cold seeped through his boots, numbing his feet as he contemplated the choices before him.

A gust of wind carried the distant strains of a melody—a street musician playing an old folk song that stirred memories of childhood. He thought of his family, of Frieda's impassioned speeches, of his father's stoic presence. A longing for connection welled within him.

Back in Hamburg, Klaus sat by the hearth on 15 December 1952, the warmth of the fire doing little to ease the chill that had settled in his bones. He held Hans's most recent letter, its words cryptic yet tinged with an undercurrent of despair.

Vater,

I question the path I have chosen. The methods employed to achieve them overshadow the ideals I once held dear. I hope you can understand.

Hans

Klaus clenched the letter, his knuckles whitening. "Marta," he called softly.

She appeared at his side, concern etched in her features. "What is it?"

"It's Hans. He's in trouble; I can feel it."

She placed a comforting hand on his shoulder. "Perhaps he is simply wrestling with his beliefs."

"He needs guidance," Klaus insisted. "And I'm powerless to help."

"Write to him," she suggested gently. "Let him know you're here for him."

He sighed heavily. "Words feel inadequate."

On 20 December 1952, Hans attended what would be his final clandestine meeting. The tension was palpable as Stefan addressed the group. "We believe someone has compromised us. The Stasi may know of our gatherings."

Anxiety rippled through the room. "What do we do?" someone asked.

"Disband, for now," Stefan advised. "lie low until it's safe."

As they dispersed, Hans caught Katarina's arm. "Is the route still available?"

She searched his eyes. "Yes, but time is running out."

"I'll consider it," he promised.

The days leading up to Christmas were sombre. On 24 December 1952, Hans wandered the festively decorated streets, the bright lights and garlands incongruous against the stark reality of their lives. He passed a group of carollers singing *"Stille Nacht,"* their voices laden with a yearning for peace.

He paused outside a shop window displaying a nativity scene. The craftsmen meticulously crafted the figurines, creating a scene that evoked a simplicity and innocence that felt worlds away. A child nearby tugged at his mother's hand. "*Mutti,* will Santa find us this year?"

"Of course, *Liebling,*" she assured him, though her eyes betrayed uncertainty.

That night, Hans sat alone in his apartment, the silence oppressive. He penned a letter to his father, each word a struggle.

Vater,

I fear I have strayed too far to find my way back. The world here is not what I believed it to be. I question everything now, including myself.

Your son,

Hans

He sealed the envelope, uncertain if he would ever send it.

On 31 December 1952, as the city prepared to usher in the new year, Hans stood on the rooftop of his building. Fireworks burst in the distance, their colours fleeting against the night sky. Cheers and laughter rose from the streets below, a collective hope for better days.

He closed his eyes, inhaling the crisp air. The weight of his doubts pressed heavily upon him, yet a small ember of resolve flickered beneath it.

Uncertainty shrouded the path ahead, but one truth crystallised—he could no longer remain complicit in a system that betrayed its own ideals.

Hans whispered into the darkness as the clock struck midnight, *"Für ein neues Anfang.* (For a new beginning)."

In Hamburg, Frieda watched the fireworks from her balcony, the vibrant displays reflecting in her eyes. She thought of Hans, a silent wish forming on her lips. "May you find your way," she murmured.

Klaus sat by the window, the distant celebrations a stark contrast to his introspection. "Happy New Year, Hans," he whispered, his breath fogging the glass.

The new year dawned with a fragile hope, the threads of fate weaving an uncertain tapestry. Hans descended from the rooftop, and a decision was made. The time for action had come, and with it, the possibility of redemption.

ooo

The dawn of 1 January 1953 crept into Hamburg with a muted glow; the sun's rays filtered through a heavy veil of grey clouds. Klaus Engelhardt lay awake in his bed, the cold seeping through the thin blankets pulled tightly around him. The distant chimes of church bells heralded the new year, each toll resonating like a solemn reminder of time slipping away. He stared at the cracked ceiling, tracing the jagged lines that seemed to mirror his life's fractures.

He swung his legs over the side of the bed, the wooden floorboards icy beneath his bare feet. A shiver coursed through him, not solely from the chill but from a deep-seated weariness that had settled into his bones. The air carried the faint scent of burning coal, mingled with the sharp tang of impending snow. Outside, muffled sounds of celebration drifted through the streets, but they felt distant, belonging to a world he no longer recognised.

In the kitchen, Marta moved quietly, her footsteps soft against the worn tiles. She was brewing a pot of coffee, the rich aroma filling the small space and offering a semblance of warmth. Klaus entered, his shoulders hunched, the lines on his face etched deeper by the pale morning light.

"Happy New Year," Marta offered gently, her eyes searching his.

He managed a weak smile, the effort barely reaching his eyes. "Is it?" he replied, his voice hoarse.

She poured him a cup, the steam swirling upwards like ghostly tendrils. "We can hope," she said, placing it before him.

He wrapped his hands around the mug, savouring the heat against his cold fingers. Silence enveloped them, heavy with unspoken worries. The ticking of the clock on the mantelpiece counted the seconds with relentless precision.

As the days of January unfolded, the winter tightened its grip on the city. On 10 January 1953, a biting wind swept through the streets, rattling windows and sending flurries of snow spiralling into the air. Klaus sat alone in the parlour, the fire in the hearth reduced to glowing embers. He gazed into the fading flames, their warmth insufficient to dispel the chill that had settled within him.

Uninvited, memories surged within him, creating a chaotic mix of sights and sounds that reminded him of a past he desperately wanted to forget. The echo of marching boots, the acrid smell of gunpowder, the haunting eyes of those lost under his command. Guilt gnawed at him, a relentless ache that sapped his strength. His hands trembled as he reached for a photograph on the mantelpiece: a younger Klaus in uniform, standing proudly beside a beaming Hans.

A sudden wave of despair crashed over him. The room seemed to tilt, the walls closing in. His breath quickened, and each inhale was sharp and shallow. He clutched at his chest, the fabric of his shirt damp beneath his fingers. The edges of his vision blurred, darkness encroaching.

Marta found him moments later, crumpled on the floor. "Klaus!" she exclaimed, rushing to his side. "What is it?"

He looked up, eyes glazed with pain. "I can't... I can't bear it," he whispered.

She knelt beside him, her hands gently on his shoulders. "Let me call for the doctor."

"No," he protested weakly. "There's nothing to be done."

"Please," she pleaded, her voice tinged with desperation. "You need help."

He shook his head, the motion sending a fresh surge of dizziness through him. "I deserve this," he murmured.

Tears welled in her eyes. "No one deserves to suffer like this."

He closed his eyes, exhaustion overtaking him. "Leave me," he whispered.

Reluctantly, Marta rose, her heart heavy. She retreated to the kitchen, the weight of helplessness pressing down on her.

Throughout the rest of January, Klaus withdrew further into himself. On 20 January 1953, the snow lay thick upon the ground, muffling the sounds of the city. Frieda arrived at the house, her cheeks flushed from the cold, a bright scarf wrapped snugly around her neck.

"Father," she greeted, attempting a cheerful tone. "I've brought some fresh bread from the bakery."

He glanced up from his seat by the window, his gaze distant. "Thank you," he replied curtly.

She set the loaf on the table, its crust still warm. "It's a beautiful day," she ventured. "Perhaps we could go for a walk later?"

He turned back to the window, watching the snowflakes drift lazily to the ground. "I don't think so."

"Fresh air might do you good," she suggested gently.

"I prefer to stay here," he said, his tone brooking no argument.

Frieda exchanged a concerned look with Marta, who stood nearby, her hands clasped tightly together. "Very well," Frieda conceded, forcing a smile. "Maybe another time."

On 1 February 1953, a deep freeze gripped the city. Ice clung to the edges of rooftops, and the Elbe River bore a thin crust of ice along its banks.

Klaus sat at his old wooden desk, papers strewn haphazardly before him. He picked up his pen, the nib scratching hesitantly against the page.

"Dear Hans," he wrote, the ink blotting slightly as his hand trembled. He paused, the words elusive. What could he say after all this time? How could he bridge the chasm that had grown between them?

"I hope this letter finds you well," he continued. The platitudes felt hollow, inadequate. He crumpled the paper, tossing it aside. A sigh escaped him, heavy with frustration.

He tried again. "My son, there is much I wish to tell you…" Again, he faltered. The enormity of his regrets loomed over him, an insurmountable barrier. Sheet after sheet met the same fate, discarded in a growing pile at his feet.

By 10 February 1953, these unsent missives had littered the study, serving as tangible evidence of his inability to reach out. The cold had seeped into the house, and the steady fire in the hearth was insufficient against the relentless winter. Klaus shivered, pulling his cardigan tighter around himself.

Marta entered quietly, a tray with a bowl of steaming soup balanced in her hands. "You should eat something," she urged softly.

"I'm not hungry," he replied without looking up.

"Please, Klaus. You've barely eaten today."

He met her gaze briefly, the shadows under his eyes stark against his pale skin. "Very well," he agreed, taking the bowl.

She watched as he sipped slowly, her worry deepening. "Perhaps we could visit the doctor," she suggested tentatively. "Just to make sure everything is alright."

He set the bowl down firmly. "I don't need a doctor," he snapped.

Marta recoiled slightly. "I only want to help."

He softened, a flicker of remorse crossing his face. "I know," he said quietly. "But there's nothing that can be done."

On 15 February 1953, a heavy snowfall blanketed Hamburg, the city transformed into a landscape of stark whites and greys. Klaus donned his coat and hat, determined to venture outside despite Marta's protests.

"At least let me come with you," she implored.

"I need to be alone," he insisted, the finality in his voice silencing further objections.

He stepped out into the crisp air, the cold biting at his cheeks. The streets were quiet, footsteps muffled by the fresh snow. As he walked, familiar sights took on an otherworldly quality—the lampposts adorned with icicles, the shop windows frosted over.

On 20 February 1953, he stood before St. Michael's Church. The grand baroque façade rose before him, its towers piercing the leaden sky. He hesitated at the entrance, his breath forming clouds in the frigid air.

Inside, the warmth was immediate, the scent of incense lingering. Candles flickered along the aisles, their flames casting soft glows upon the ornate carvings. He settled into a pew near the back, the wooden seat hard beneath him.

Silence enveloped him, broken only by the distant murmur of prayers. He bowed his head, eyes closing. Words failed him, but a silent plea formed in his heart—a yearning for peace, for absolution.

After some time, he rose to leave. As he made his way towards the door, Father Müller, a kindly man with a gentle demeanour, approached him.

"Mr Engelhardt," the priest greeted. "It's been some time since we've seen you here."

Klaus offered a faint smile. "Yes, it has."

"Is there anything I can assist you with?"

He hesitated, the weight of his burdens pressing down. "I'm not sure," he admitted.

"Sometimes, speaking of one's troubles can offer relief," Father Müller suggested.

Klaus considered this. "I fear my troubles are beyond help."

"No soul is beyond redemption," the priest assured him gently.

A flicker of something—hope, perhaps—sparked within Klaus. "Perhaps another time," he said, the words tentative.

"Of course. The doors are always open."

He stepped back into the cold, the wind sharper now. The sky had darkened, heavy clouds threatening more snow. As he walked home, the streets seemed emptier, the shadows deeper.

Upon his return, Marta greeted him with a mixture of relief and concern. "You're frozen," she exclaimed, helping him out of his coat.

"I'm fine," he assured her, though his hands shook.

"Come, sit by the fire."

He complied, settling into his chair. The warmth seeped into his limbs but did little to thaw the numbness within.

On 25 February 1953, Frieda visited again, bringing with her news of the city's ongoing reconstruction efforts. "They're planning to rebuild the old Rathaus," she shared, her enthusiasm clear.

"That's good," Marta replied, casting a hopeful glance at Klaus.

He remained silent, staring into the distance.

"Father," Frieda ventured, "perhaps you'd like to attend one of the town meetings with me? Your experience would be invaluable."

He shook his head slowly. "Those days are behind me."

"But you have so much to offer," she pressed gently.

He met her gaze, his eyes filled with a sorrow that took her aback. "I have nothing left to give."

Frieda's expression faltered. "That's not true," she insisted softly.

Marta placed a hand on her daughter's arm. "Perhaps we should let him rest."

Defeated, Frieda nodded. "Of course."

That evening, as darkness enveloped the city, Klaus retreated to his study. The unsent letter to Hans lay on the desk, a stark reminder of his failures. He picked it up, weighing it in his hand. The urge to reach out was strong, but fear held him back—fear of rejection, of causing further pain.

On 28 February 1953, he decided. Gathering the crumpled drafts, he smoothed out a fresh sheet of paper. With deliberate care, he wrote.

My dear Hans,

There are no words to express the depth of my regret. I have been a poor father, blinded by my pride and unable to see the harm I caused. I understand if you cannot forgive me, but I needed to tell you I am sorry.

Your father,

Klaus

He folded the letter carefully, placing it in an envelope. This time, he addressed it, his handwriting steady. Sealing it, he set it aside, a faint sense of relief washing over him.

That night, sleep came more easily. The house was quiet, and the soft creaks and groans of settling wood were the only sounds. The snow outside had ceased, a pale moon casting a silvery light across the landscape.

As March approached, there was a subtle shift in the air—a whisper of change, a hint of thaw. Whether this would herald a new beginning or simply another chapter in his ongoing struggle remained uncertain.

Klaus lay in bed, gazing out the window at the stars piercing the darkness. For the first time in a long while, he allowed himself a sliver of hope—perhaps he could reconcile and mend the strained family bonds that were not irrevocably broken.

In the night's stillness, he whispered a silent prayer; the words carrying into the quiet. "Let there be peace."

SEVEN:

THE EAST GERMAN UPRISING

The morning of 17 June 1953 dawned grey over Hamburg, a sullen sky casting a pall over the city. Klaus Engelhardt sat alone in the dimly lit living room of his apartment, the curtains drawn tight against the outside world. The soft crackle of the radio was the only sound, its glow casting a faint light that danced across the peeling wallpaper. A single candle flickered on the windowsill, its flame wavering in the draught that slipped through the cracks.

He leaned forward in his chair, fingers absently tracing the worn fabric of the armrest. The newsreader's voice crackled through static, each word tightening the knot in Klaus's chest. "Reports from East Berlin indicate that thousands of workers have taken to the streets, protesting against the government's policies…"

His breath caught. Hans was there during it all. The son he hadn't seen in years, separated not just by distance but by an ideological chasm that seemed impossible to bridge.

Outside, the city of Hamburg muted its usual bustle, as if holding its breath. The scent of rain hung in the air, mingling with the musty aroma of old books and the lingering traces of Marta's cooking. But the warmth that once filled this home had long since faded, leaving behind a cold emptiness.

The radio hissed, then continued. "They deployed Soviet tanks to suppress the uprising. Several districts are experiencing reported gunfire,"

Klaus gripped his cane tightly, his knuckles whitening. Images flooded his mind—streets filled with smoke, the rumble of tanks, the cries of the wounded. Memories he had tried to bury now surged to the surface, each one a dagger of guilt and fear.

He rose unsteadily, crossing to the window. Pulling back the curtain just enough to peer outside, he saw a world that seemed oblivious to his turmoil. A young couple strolled arm in arm along the pavement, their laughter carried faintly on the breeze. Children played a game of football in the street, their shouts piercing the quiet.

How could life continue so normally here while chaos reigned in the East?

He let the curtain fall back into place, returning to his seat. The candle's flame reflected in the glass of a framed photograph on the side table—a family portrait from happier times. Marta, her eyes bright with youth; Frieda, a child clutching her mother's hand; Hans, barely a teenager, his gaze full of determination.

Klaus reached out, his fingers brushing against the image of his son. "Hans," he whispered, the name heavy with unspoken fears.

The radio's relentless updates offered no solace. "Casualties are mounting as the authorities move to quell the demonstrations. According to estimates, authorities have killed dozens of people and injured many more while attempting to suppress the demonstrations."

He closed his eyes, the weight of helplessness pressing down upon him. Every fibre of his being longed to reach out, to do something—anything—to protect his child. But the reality was a chasm he could not cross, a wall both physical and ideological that kept them apart.

The clock on the mantel ticked steadily, each second a reminder of time slipping away. He thought of writing a letter, but what could he say? Words felt inadequate, incapable of conveying the depth of his concern or bridging the divide that had grown between them.

A sudden knock at the door startled him. He hesitated before rising, his joints protesting with each movement. Opening the door, he found Frieda standing there, her expression a mirror of his own worry.

"Father," she said softly, stepping inside without waiting for an invitation. "I came as soon as I heard."

He nodded, closing the door behind her. "It's bad," he murmured.

She removed her coat, draping it over a chair. "Do we have any way of contacting him?"

"No," Klaus admitted, his voice barely above a whisper. "I don't even know exactly where he is."

Frieda sighed, running a hand through her hair. "I've tried reaching out through some colleagues, but the lines of communication are… difficult."

They stood in silence for a moment, the gravity of the situation settling between them. The radio continued its grim report. "They have declared martial law. The Soviet military is firmly in control of the city"

"Why now?" Klaus wondered aloud, his gaze distant. "What pushed them to this point?"

Frieda sank into a chair. "The increased work quotas, the lack of freedoms… people can only endure so much."

He nodded slowly. "I fear for him. If he's involved,"

"He's smart," she reassured him, though her eyes betrayed her own doubts. "He'll keep himself safe."

Klaus returned to his seat, the cushion sighing under his weight. "I should have done more," he confessed. "To keep the family together."

"You can't blame yourself for the choices we've made," Frieda replied gently. "We each followed our own path."

He looked at her, a flicker of pain crossing his face. "But perhaps if I'd been a better father. "

She reached across, placing her hand over his. "Father, we all bear our own burdens. The past is heavy enough without adding more to it."

He squeezed her hand gratefully. "Thank you."

They sat together, the quiet broken only by the distant hum of traffic and the steady drone of the radio. The afternoon light waned, casting long shadows that crept across the floorboards.

"Do you remember," Klaus began hesitantly, "when we used to visit the lakes in summer? You and Hans would race each other to the water's edge."

A small smile touched Frieda's lips. "He always let me win, though I didn't realise it."

"He adored you," Klaus said softly. "You were inseparable."

Her gaze drifted to the photograph on the table. "We were children then. So much has changed."

"Too much," he agreed.

The radio crackled, drawing their attention. "They have suppressed the uprising, according to the latest reports. The government has issued a statement blaming foreign agitators for the unrest,"

Frieda shook her head in disbelief. "They refuse to see the truth, even now."

Klaus's shoulders sagged. "It's the people who suffer."

"Perhaps this will be a catalyst for change," she suggested, though her tone lacked conviction.

"Or it will lead to further repression," he countered.

She stood, restless. "I can't just sit here. There must be something we can do."

"What do you suggest?" he asked, a hint of desperation in his voice.

"I don't know," she admitted. "But I feel so powerless."

He understood all too well. The impotence of watching events unfold from afar, the gnawing anxiety that consumed every thought.

"Maybe reaching out through official channels?" she mused. "I have some contacts in the government. Perhaps they can assist."

"Would they help?" Klaus questioned.

"It's worth trying," she resolved. "I'll make some calls."

He watched as she moved purposefully towards the telephone, her determination a stark contrast to his own paralysis. As she dialled, speaking in low tones, he turned back to the radio.

"…. The authorities have made many arrests. The authorities are urging citizens to return to normalcy and report anything suspicious,"

The words blurred, melding into a haze of static and white noise. Klaus felt a heaviness settling over him, a suffocating weight that pressed down on his chest. He struggled to draw a full breath, his pulse quickening.

"Vater?" Frieda's voice cut through the fog. She was beside him in an instant, concern etched across her face. "Are you alright?"

He nodded weakly, as though he was anything but. "Just… lightheaded."

"Let me get you some water." She hurried to the kitchen, returning moments later with a glass. "Here."

He sipped slowly, the cool liquid easing his dry throat. "Thank you."

"You need to take care of yourself," she admonished gently. "Hans wouldn't want you making yourself ill over this."

He managed a faint smile. "I suppose not."

She sat beside him once more. "I spoke to a friend at the foreign office. They're monitoring the situation closely, but information is scarce."

"At least you're trying," he acknowledged.

They lapsed into silence again, each lost in their own thoughts. The candle on the windowsill had burned low, wax pooling at its base. The room grew colder as evening approached, the fading light casting a sombreness that matched their mood.

"Do you ever think about leaving?" Klaus asked suddenly.

Frieda looked at him, surprised. "Leaving?"

"Germany," he clarified. "Starting anew somewhere else."

She considered the question. "Sometimes. But this is my home. I believe in what we're building here, despite the challenges."

He nodded thoughtfully. "I envy your conviction."

"You could find purpose again," she suggested tentatively. "There are opportunities, ways to contribute."

He sighed. "I'm not sure where I fit into this new world."

"With us," she said firmly. "With your family."

He glanced at her, a mix of hope and resignation in his eyes. "I fear I've lost that chance."

"It's never too late," she insisted.

The radio's monotone continued, now reporting on international reactions. "Western leaders condemn the actions taken by the GDR and Soviet forces, calling for respect of human rights and freedoms,"

Klaus shook his head. "Words. They offer words while people suffer."

"Words have power," Frieda countered. "They can inspire action."

"Or they can ring hollow," he retorted.

She reached out once more, her hand warm against his cold skin. "We can't lose hope."

He closed his eyes, exhaustion washing over him. "Perhaps you're right."

The room grew darker, shadows merging until the details blurred. Frieda rose to turn on a lamp, the soft glow illuminating the space.

"I should stay with you tonight," she offered. "In case any news comes through."

He was too weary to protest. "Thank you."

As the night deepened, they settled into a fragile peace. Frieda busied herself with paperwork, ever diligent in her duties. Klaus remained by the radio, its steady hum a constant companion.

In the quiet moments, he allowed himself to remember happier times—the laughter of his children, the warmth of Marta's embrace, the simple joys that now seemed so distant.

"Vater," Frieda's voice broke the silence. "You should rest."

He nodded absently. "Perhaps you're right."

She helped him to his feet, guiding him towards his bedroom. The journey down the hallway felt longer than usual, his steps unsteady.

"Will you be alright?" she asked as he settled onto the bed.

"I'll manage," he assured her.

"Call me if you need anything."

He offered a small smile. "Goodnight, Frieda."

"Goodnight."

Left alone, Klaus stared up at the ceiling, the patterns of shadow and light shifting with the flicker of the candle on his bedside table. The events of the day weighed heavily upon him, a tumult of emotions he could scarcely contain.

Somewhere out there, Hans faced dangers he could not fathom. The world was changing rapidly, and he felt himself slipping further behind, unable to keep pace.

Closing his eyes, he whispered a silent plea into the darkness. "Stay safe, my son."

Sleep came fitfully, dreams haunted by echoes of the past and fears for the future. The lines between memory and reality blurred, leaving him adrift in a sea of uncertainty.

As dawn approached, a pale light seeped into the room, heralding a new day. Klaus awoke with a start, the remnants of uneasy dreams clinging to his consciousness.

He rose slowly, every movement an effort. In the living room, he found Frieda asleep in the armchair, a blanket draped over her. The radio murmured softly, the news now focused on other matters.

He stood watching her for a moment, gratitude and sorrow mingling within him. Gently, he adjusted the blanket, careful not to wake her.

Returning to his seat by the window, he gazed out at the city stirring to life. The clouds had parted slightly, allowing beams of sunlight to pierce through. Perhaps it was a sign—a glimmer of hope amid the darkness.

He knew the road ahead would not be easy. The fractures within his family and his own soul ran deep. But perhaps, with time and effort, they could heal.

As the first birds sang their melodies, lightening the heavy air, Klaus allowed himself a tentative smile.

There was still time. And where there was time, there was a possibility.

ooo

The warmth of the sun embraced Hamburg on 1 July 1953, casting a golden glow over the city that had risen from the ashes of war. Frieda Engelhardt stood at the window of her modest office overlooking the bustling streets below. The hum of progress filled the air—the trams clattered, pedestrians chattered, and the distant sound of construction echoed as new buildings reached towards the sky. She took a deep breath, the scent of fresh bread from a nearby bakery mingling with the delicate aroma of linden trees in bloom.

Her tireless work within the local government was evident in the clutter of papers—proposals, reports, letters—on her desk. Frieda had become a formidable presence in Hamburg's political landscape, her dedication to rebuilding not just structures but the very fabric of society earning her respect and admiration.

On 15 July 1953, the city was alive with anticipation. Banners in hues of red, gold, and black adorned the central square, and organisers had erected a stage for the day's rally. The German flag fluttered proudly in the gentle breeze, its colours vivid against the clear blue sky. Stalls lined the edges of the square, vendors selling bratwurst and pretzels, the rich smells wafting through the crowd.

Frieda stood backstage, technicians were adjusting the microphone the microphone levels on stage. She smoothed down her navy skirt, the crisp fabric rustling softly. Her heart pounded—not with nerves, but with a fervent passion for the words she was about to deliver. She glanced at her notes one last time, though she knew the speech by heart.

"You're up," a colleague whispered, nodding towards the stage.

She stepped forward, the wooden boards creaking slightly underfoot. As she emerged into view, a wave of applause greeted her. Faces upturned, eyes shining with expectation, the crowd of thousands waited in attentive silence.

"Meine Damen und Herren," she began, her voice strong and clear. "Ladies and gentlemen, today we stand together in a city reborn—a testament to our resilience and determination."

Her words flowed seamlessly, weaving a tapestry of hope and unity. She spoke of the economic achievements made possible by the Marshall Plan, of the importance of democracy, of the shared responsibility to ensure a prosperous future for all Germans.

"The events in the East remind us of the fragility of freedom," she declared, sweeping her gaze across the audience. "Let us not take for granted the liberties we hold dear."

Applause erupted, a swell of sound that echoed off the surrounding buildings. The sun glinted off the newly polished windows of the reconstructed offices, symbols of the progress she championed.

Meanwhile, not far away, Klaus watched from the shadowed interior of his apartment. The faint strains of Frieda's speech reached him, carried on the summer breeze through the open window. He could see the edge of the crowd, a sea of movement and colour. The energy was palpable, yet he felt none of it.

He turned away, retreating into the dimness. The walls seemed to close in around him, the air heavy with the scent of dust and old memories.

Photographs lined the mantelpiece—images of a family once whole. Hans as a boy, his mischievous grin captured in black and white. Marta, her smile serene. Frieda, a young girl clutching a bouquet of wildflowers.

Klaus sank into his worn armchair, the fabric threadbare beneath his fingers. He picked up the newspaper from the side table, scanning the headlines. Reports of the uprising in East Germany dominated the pages, each article a reminder of the turmoil engulfing his son.

He closed his eyes; the words blurring into a jumble of letters. Guilt gnawed at him—a constant companion. He had failed to keep his family together, to bridge the gap between ideologies that now seemed insurmountable.

Back at the rally, Frieda mingled with attendees, her handshake firm, her smile genuine. "Thank you for your support," she told an elderly man who praised her speech. "Together, we can achieve great things."

"Your optimism is contagious," he replied, his eyes crinkling at the corners.

She moved through the crowd, exchanging words with workers, business owners, students—each interaction reinforcing her belief in the path she had chosen. Yet beneath her confident exterior, a shadow lingered. Thoughts of Hans crept in, unbidden. She wondered where he was, what he was enduring.

On 31 July 1953, Frieda sat in a café overlooking the Alster Lake. The water shimmered under the midday sun, sailboats gliding gracefully across its surface. She stirred her coffee absently, lost in thought.

"Mind if I join you?" a familiar voice interrupted.

She looked up to see Greta Schmidt, her long-time friend and journalist, standing beside the table.

"Please," Frieda gestured to the empty chair.

Greta settled in, setting her notebook and pen on the table. "I heard your speech. It was inspiring."

"Thank you," Frieda replied, though her tone lacked enthusiasm.

"What's troubling you?" Greta probed gently.

Frieda sighed. "I can't shake the feeling that we're celebrating while others suffer. The reports from the East… it's hard to reconcile."

Greta nodded, her expression sombre. "I've been following the stories closely. The government's response was brutal."

"And Hans is there," Frieda added softly.

"Have you had any word from him?"

She shook her head. "Nothing. I fear the worst."

Greta reached across the table, her hand covering Frieda's. "He's strong. If anyone can navigate that environment, it's Hans."

"I hope you're right."

They sat in companionable silence for a moment, the sounds of the café enveloping them—the clink of cups, the murmur of conversation, the strains of a violinist playing nearby.

"Tell me," Greta began, changing the subject, "how do you feel about your upcoming promotion?"

Frieda looked up, surprised. "Promotion?"

Greta smiled knowingly. "Word travels fast. It's well-deserved."

"I hadn't heard officially," Frieda admitted. "But if it's true, it will give me more influence to push for the reforms we need."

"Just don't forget to take care of yourself," Greta cautioned. "You can't pour from an empty cup."

Frieda smiled appreciatively. "I'll try to remember that."

As August arrived, the city basked in the height of summer. On 15 August 1953, Frieda visited the rebuilt Elbphilharmonie concert hall, attending a performance of Beethoven's Ninth Symphony. The music soared, filling the grand auditorium with its powerful melodies. She closed her eyes, allowing the notes to wash over her, each crescendo stirring emotions she struggled to name.

The chorus erupted in the last movement… "Ode to Joy"—voices intertwining in a celebration of unity and brotherhood. Tears welled in her eyes, the weight of her hopes and fears pressing upon her.

After the concert, she wandered along the banks of the Elbe River. The water flowed steadily, reflecting the fading light of the setting sun. Children laughed as they chased one another, their carefree innocence a stark contrast to the complexities of the adult world.

She paused on a bridge, gazing out across the river. "Hans," she whispered, the name carried away on the evening breeze. "Where are you?"

At home, Klaus sat in silence, the radio turned off. The quiet was oppressive, broken only by the ticking of the clock on the wall. He stared blankly ahead, his mind a labyrinth of regrets.

On 20 August 1953, he received a letter—not from Hans, but from an old comrade, Jakob Fischer. The handwriting was familiar, the words terse.

Klaus,

I heard about your daughter's political pursuits. Be careful. The world is changing, and not always for the better.

Jakob

He crumpled the letter, a surge of anger rising within him. Jakob's refusal to accept responsibility, his clinging to outdated ideals—it was a mirror of Klaus's own past stubbornness.

He stood abruptly, the sudden movement causing a wave of dizziness. Gripping the edge of the table, he steadied himself. The room seemed to spin, shadows creeping at the edges of his vision.

"Marta," he called weakly, though he knew she was out visiting neighbours.

He sank back into his chair, the moment passing. Taking a deep breath, he resolved to make amends where he could.

On 25 August 1953, Klaus ventured out into the city. The sun shone brightly, the air filled with the sounds of life. He made his way to Frieda's office, determination in each step.

Upon arrival, her assistant greeted him. "Herr Engelhardt, what a surprise. Frieda is in a meeting at the moment."

"Could you let her know I'm here?" he asked politely.

"Of course. Please, have a seat."

He waited, observing the flurry of activity around him. Young men and women hurried past, clutching files, engaged in animated discussions. The energy was infectious, a stark contrast to the stagnation he felt at home.

After a short while, Frieda appeared, her expression a mix of surprise and concern. "Father, is everything alright?"

He stood, offering a tentative smile. "I wanted to see you. May we talk?"

"Of course." She led him to a small conference room, closing the door behind them.

They sat facing each other, an awkward silence settling between them.

"I've been thinking," Klaus began hesitantly. "About the work you're doing. About… everything."

Frieda waited patiently, sensing the weight of his words.

"I haven't been supportive," he continued. "I've been… lost in my own regrets. But seeing you here, witnessing the impact you're making—I'm proud of you."

Emotion flickered across her face. "Thank you, Father. That means a great deal to me."

He reached across the table, his hand covering hers. "I want to mend things between us. I can't change the past, but perhaps we can build a better future."

She squeezed his hand gently. "I'd like that."

They talked for hours, the barriers between them slowly crumbling. Klaus shared stories of his own youth, his hopes and dreams before the war. Frieda spoke of her vision for Germany, her belief in the power of unity and understanding.

As they parted, a newfound warmth enveloped them. "Will you join us for dinner on 31 August 1953?" Frieda invited. "Some colleagues and I are celebrating."

Klaus sincerely replied, "I would be honoured."

That evening, Frieda received official confirmation of her promotion. She was to become Deputy Minister for Urban Development—a position that would allow her to further influence the reconstruction efforts she was so passionate about.

On 31 August 1953, the celebration took place in a cosy restaurant overlooking the harbour. The room buzzed with conversation and laughter, the clinking of glasses punctuating toasts made in her honour.

Klaus sat beside her, his presence a source of quiet joy. He listened as her colleagues praised her dedication, their admiration clear.

"To Frieda," Greta declared, raising her glass. "A true leader and a beacon of hope for our city."

"To Frieda," the group echoed, glasses raised high.

She blushed modestly, gratitude shining in her eyes. "Thank you all. I couldn't have achieved this without your support."

As the evening progressed, Klaus engaged in discussions, his insights valued by those around him. The isolation he had felt began to fade, replaced by a sense of belonging he hadn't experienced in years.

Yet amid the festivities, thoughts of Hans lingered. Frieda caught her father's distant gaze. "He's on your mind too," she observed softly.

"Always," he admitted.

"We'll reach him," she assured him. "I won't give up."

He nodded, a flicker of hope igniting within. "Nor will I."

As they stepped out into the cool night air, the city lights shimmered across the water. The harbour was alive with activity—ships docked, their masts silhouetted against the star-studded sky.

Klaus took a deep breath, the crisp air filling his lungs. "Perhaps things are changing for the better," he mused.

"Perhaps," Frieda agreed, linking her arm through his. "We have to believe they can."

They walked together along the cobblestone streets, the sounds of the city a gentle backdrop to their conversation. The future remained uncertain, but for the first time in a long while, they faced it together.

ooo

The chill of 1 September 1953 seeped into East Berlin, a city cloaked in the muted hues of autumn. Leaves, once vibrant green, now painted the streets in shades of amber and crimson, crunching underfoot as Hans Engelhardt navigated the familiar labyrinth of grey buildings and shadowed alleyways. The air was sharp with the scent of coal smoke and impending rain, a constant reminder of the approaching winter.

Hans pulled his coat tighter against the biting wind, his breath forming fleeting clouds before dissipating into the heavy atmosphere. The streets were quieter these days, a tense silence hanging over the populace since the uprising in June. Eyes avoided contact, conversations were hushed, and the omnipresent gaze of the Stasi lingered in every corner.

He arrived at the unassuming doorway of a derelict building on Friedrichstraße. Paint peeled from the wooden frame, and a faded sign swung gently in the breeze, its lettering long worn away. Hans glanced over his shoulder before slipping inside, the door creaking softly as it closed behind him.

Descending a narrow staircase into the basement, the damp scent of mould and earth enveloped him. The single bulb overhead cast a feeble light, flickering intermittently as if struggling against the darkness. A handful of familiar faces occupied the circle of chairs arranged in the centre of the room. Cigarette smoke curled lazily towards the ceiling, the glowing embers momentarily illuminating weary expressions.

"You're late," whispered Markus, a gaunt man with sunken eyes and a perpetual furrow in his brow.

"Apologies," Hans replied quietly, taking a seat. "I had to avoid a patrol."

Klara, a young woman with fiery red hair and a resolute gaze, leaned forward. "We were just discussing the latest arrests. Three more comrades taken last night."

Hans felt a knot tighten in his stomach. "Who?"

"Paul, Anja, and Dieter," she listed solemnly. "Accused of spreading anti-state propaganda."

A heavy silence settled over the group. Hans rubbed his temples, the weight of their situation pressing down on him. "How much longer can this continue?" he murmured. "We speak of revolution, of change, but all we face is repression."

Erik, a schoolteacher with a penchant for idealism, met his eyes. "We can't lose hope. The people need us to stand firm."

"Do they?" Hans challenged, his voice tinged with bitterness. "Or are we simply voices lost in the wind?"

The bulb above flickered again, casting erratic shadows that danced across the damp walls. The scent of damp concrete mingled with the acrid smoke, creating a cloying atmosphere that seemed to stifle any flicker of optimism.

On 10 October 1953, the group convened once more, the urgency of their meetings increasing as the Stasi tightened its grip on dissent. Hans arrived earlier this time, the streets eerily quiet under a blanket of mist. The autumn leaves clung stubbornly to skeletal branches, rustling softly in the breeze.

"There's talk of a new directive," Klara informed them, her voice barely above a whisper. "Enhanced surveillance measures. They're installing more informants."

Hans clenched his fists. "We can't continue like this. Fear shadows us every step we take."

Markus nodded grimly. "We need to consider our options. Perhaps it's time to think about leaving."

"Leaving?" Erik scoffed. "And abandon everything we've worked for?"

"What's the alternative? Should we stay and let this machine swallow us?" Hans interjected. "Watch as they erase any semblance of freedom?"

A heavy pause followed, each member grappling with their own doubts. The reality of their situation was stark—ideals clashed with survival instincts, and the lines between right and wrong blurred under the weight of oppression.

As the meeting dispersed, Hans lingered behind. "Klara," he called softly.

She turned, her eyes reflecting the dim light. "Yes?"

"Have you considered it? Leaving, I mean."

She sighed, her breath visible in the cold air. "Every day. But it's not just about me. My family relies on me."

Hans understood all too well. "If an opportunity arose, would you take it?"

She looked past him, as if searching for an answer in the shadows. "Perhaps. If it meant a chance at a real future."

He nodded slowly. "We need to be prepared for whatever comes next."

That night, Hans returned to his modest apartment, the walls thin enough to hear the murmur of his neighbours. He sat by the small window overlooking the street, the glass fogging slightly as he exhaled. The city stretched out before him, a mosaic of lights and darkness, hope and despair.

On 15 October 1953, hundreds of kilometres away in Hamburg, Klaus Engelhardt sat at his cluttered desk. The lamp cast a warm glow over the scattered papers, illuminating his lined face and weary eyes. The scent of old books and pipe tobacco permeated the room, a comforting familiarity amidst the turmoil of his thoughts.

He picked up his pen, the weight of it heavy in his hand. A blank sheet of paper lay before him, the emptiness mirroring the chasm between him and his son. Taking a deep breath, he wrote.

My dear Hans,

It's been too long since we've spoken, and there are things I must say...

He paused, the words catching in his throat. How could he convey the depth of his concern, the regret that gnawed at him? He continued, the pen scratching softly against the paper.

...I worry about you daily. The news from the East fills me with dread. I know we've had our differences, but you're my son, and I cannot bear the thought of you in harm's way. Please consider returning to the West. There is a place for you here, a chance for a new beginning...

Klaus stopped again, his gaze distant. He thought of the last time he'd seen Hans—the tense goodbye, the unspoken words hanging heavily between them. Folding the letter carefully, he placed it in an envelope but hesitated to seal it. Instead, he tucked it into a drawer, the act of sending it seeming both futile and overwhelming.

Back in East Berlin, Hans navigated the increasingly oppressive atmosphere. The Stasi's presence was palpable; men in plain clothes loitered on street corners, their eyes sharp and assessing. Posters adorned the walls, slogans extolling the virtues of the socialist state while warning against the dangers of dissent.

On 30 October 1953, Hans witnessed an arrest firsthand. He was walking along Karl-Marx-Allee when a commotion drew his attention. A young man, scarcely older than twenty, was being dragged into a car by two agents. A swift blow quickly silenced his cries of protest. Bystanders hurried past, heads down, unwilling to attract attention.

Hans felt a surge of anger and fear. The reality of his situation crystallised at that moment. This was no longer the society he had believed in. Those in power had twisted the ideals of equality and justice into tools of control.

That evening, he sat alone in his apartment, a small radio emitting a low hum. He tuned it carefully, catching snippets of broadcasts from the West. Voices spoke of freedom, prosperity, and a Germany rebuilding itself anew.

The temptation to defect grew stronger, but so did the risks. He knew of those who had tried—some succeeded, many did not. The consequences extended beyond the individual; families left behind often faced harsh repercussions.

On 5 November 1953, Hans met with Markus in a secluded park. The trees were shedding the last of their leaves, and the ground was a patchwork of damp earth and fallen foliage.

"I can't stay here," Hans confessed, his voice barely audible.

Markus regarded him with a mix of understanding and caution. "You realise what that means?"

"I do. But I can't continue living a lie."

"There are ways," Markus said slowly. "But they're dangerous. The Stasi are vigilant."

Hans nodded. "I have to try."

They discussed potential routes and contacts who might assist. Each option was fraught with peril, each step a gamble.

As the days shortened and the first hints of winter crept in, Hans prepared quietly. He gathered what little he could carry—a few clothes, some cherished photographs, and a worn copy of Goethe's poems. The book had been a gift from his mother, a tangible connection to a time when life was simpler.

On 20 November 1953, he wrote a letter to his family, unsure if they would ever receive it.

Dear Mother and Father,

I don't know when or if this will reach you, but I need you to know that I am safe. I've sought a different path, one that aligns with the values I hold dear. Please don't worry…

He hesitated, unsure how to articulate the turmoil within him. Folding the letter, he placed it alongside the others he had written over the years, all unsent, tucked away in a small box beneath his bed.

The evening of 29 November 1953 was bitterly cold. Hans stood at the window, watching as snowflakes drifted lazily from the darkened sky. The city below was a tapestry of shadows and sparse lights, the silence punctuated by the distant rumble of a tram.

A knock at the door startled him. Heart pounding, he moved cautiously towards it. "Who is it?" he called softly.

"It's Klara."

Relief washed over him as he opened the door. She stepped inside quickly, her cheeks flushed from the cold.

"I have news," she said, her eyes bright with urgency. "There's an opportunity tomorrow night. A guide can take us across the border."

Hans felt a surge of adrenaline. "Are you certain?"

"As certain as we can be. It's risky, but it's our best chance."

He glanced around his sparse apartment. "I can be ready."

She placed a hand on his arm. "I need to know—is this truly what you want?"

He met her gaze steadily. "Yes. I can't stay here any longer."

The following day, 30 November 1953, was a blur of preparations. Hans moved through the motions with a sense of detachment, his mind focused on the task ahead. As dusk settled, he made his way to the designated meeting point—a dilapidated warehouse near the city's outskirts.

Klara was already there, along with a small group of others. Faces were taut with tension, eyes darting nervously. The guide, a stern man with a no-nonsense demeanour, outlined the plan.

"We move quickly and silently," he instructed. "No lights, no talking. If we encounter patrols, follow my lead."

Hans's heart hammered in his chest, each beat echoing like a drum. The weight of his decision pressed upon him—the dangers, the uncertainties, the possibility of freedom.

As they set off into the night, the air was thick with anticipation. The path led them through back alleys and abandoned buildings, each step bringing them closer to the border—and to the unknown.

But fate is a fickle companion. As they approached a crossing point, the sound of barking dogs shattered the silence. Flashlights pierced the darkness, voices shouted commands.

"Run!" the guide hissed.

Chaos erupted. Hans sprinted alongside Klara, their breaths ragged in the frigid air. The terrain was treacherous, the ground slippery beneath their feet. Behind them, the Stasi closed in.

A sharp pain seared through Hans's shoulder as a bullet grazed him. He stumbled but pushed forward, adrenaline overriding the shock. Klara grabbed his hand, urging him onward.

They reached a cluster of trees, the dense foliage providing scant cover. The group had scattered, and the sounds of pursuit faded slightly.

"We have to keep moving," Klara whispered urgently.

Hans nodded, gritting his teeth against the throbbing pain. They pressed on, the landscape a blur of shadows and shapes.

Hours seemed to pass, time distorted by fear and exhaustion. At last, they reached a quiet stretch away from the border, the faint lights of West Germany barely visible but now out of reach.

"Wait," the guide urged, his face obscured by darkness. "We can't proceed."

With a heavy heart, Hans felt the weight of their predicament pressing down on him. The oppressive atmosphere of East Germany had driven them to desperation, but the risks were too great to continue.

He glanced around at his companions, their faces etched with weariness and apprehension. "We can't make it tonight," he murmured, his voice barely audible over the rustling leaves.

The guide nodded solemnly. "It's too risky. Let's return."

With a sinking feeling, Hans led the group back along the narrow path, their footsteps muffled by the thickening snow. The cold night air bit at their exposed skin, but the promise of uncertain freedom had been replaced by the harsh reality of their situation.

As they approached the relative safety of their home area, Hans felt a mixture of relief and resignation. They had come so far, only to be thwarted by circumstances beyond their control.

Back in their modest dwelling, Hans sat quietly, the failed attempt weighing heavily on his mind. The night was silent, save for the distant hum of the city and the soft fall of snow outside. He looked around at the familiar surroundings, the faces of his family reflecting a shared sense of defeat and lingering hope.

"We'll try again," he whispered to himself, determination rekindling within him. "We have to."

Together, they navigated the complexities of life in East Germany, each day marked by careful planning and cautious optimism. The oppressive regime's surveillance loomed ever-present, but the collective's commitment to one another and their silent hope for a better future kept their spirits resilient.

Hans often found himself reflecting on the narrow margins between hope and despair, the delicate balance they maintained to survive. His relationship with Frieda, though strained by ideological divides, remained anchored by familial love and a shared vision of reconciliation and unity. The Engelhardt household became a symbol of quiet resistance, their perseverance embodying the enduring human spirit even in the darkest of times.

As the first signs of spring began to thaw the winter chill, Hans felt a renewed sense of purpose. The failed escape had not broken him; instead, it had strengthened his resolve to find other ways to bridge the divide and foster understanding. The Engelhardt family's unwavering support provided the foundation he needed to continue striving for a future where unity and peace could prevail.

On 5 December 1953, Hans sat down to write once more. Detailing that earlier that month, he had made a desperate attempt to flee to the West, driven by the oppressive conditions in East Germany. However, his escape had been thwarted by vigilant border patrols. Exhausted and shaken, he had managed to slip back into the relative safety of his home, though not without enduring significant fear and uncertainty.

Dear Mother and Father,

My attempt to reach the West was unsuccessful. I encountered considerable dangers and was forced to turn back under intense scrutiny by the border guards. I am relieved to be back and safe, though the experience has left me deeply shaken. Please do not worry too much; I am determined to find another way to contribute to our family's future here. I hope to see you soon under better circumstances.

In Hamburg, Klaus received the letter on 10 December 1953. His hands shook as he unfolded the paper, his eyes scanning the solemn words with a mixture of relief and lingering concern.

"Marta!" he called softly, his voice heavy with emotion. "Hans is safe."

They embraced cautiously, tears streaming down their faces. The chasm that had separated them now felt bridged by Hans' safe return, the possibility of reconciliation delicately rekindled.

As the year drew to a close, the Engelhardt family faced the future with a blend of relief and cautious optimism. The scars of the past remained, but the hope for healing flickered like a candle in the darkness.

Hans stood at the edge of the Elbe River, gazing across the water towards the city he still called home. The air was crisp; the sky painted with the soft hues of dawn. He took a deep breath, the cold air invigorating yet reminding him of the fragility of his newfound safety.

For the first time in a long while, he felt a sense of cautious possibility. The road ahead was uncertain, but he was determined to face it—one step at a time.

ooo

Winter descended upon Hamburg with a bitter chill as December 1953 began. The first of the month brought a frost that clung stubbornly to the cobblestones and blanketed the city in a thin veil of white. Klaus Engelhardt stood at his window on 1 December 1953, watching as delicate snowflakes danced under the dim glow of streetlamps. The cold seeped through the glass, but it was the emptiness inside him that made him shiver.

The weight of years pressed heavily upon him—memories of the war, the haunting faces of those lost, the widening chasm between him and his children. Hans was still out of reach, his fate uncertain, and Frieda's political ambitions consumed her. Marta did her best to bridge the gaps, but even her gentle presence could not warm the icy void that had formed within Klaus.

On Saturday morning, December 5, 1953, Klaus awoke before dawn. The sky was a canvas of grey, promising more snow. An unfamiliar restlessness stirred him to action. Dressing in his warmest coat and scarf, he stepped out into the crisp air, his breath forming clouds that dissipated into stillness. The streets were quiet, the usual bustle subdued by the cold.

Drawn by an impulse he couldn't name, Klaus walked towards St. Michael's Church, its baroque spire piercing the dull sky. The bells tolled softly as he approached, each chime resonating deep within him. He hesitated at the grand wooden doors, the intricately carved saints seeming to watch him with knowing eyes.

Stepping inside, a warmth that contrasted with the frigid world outside enveloped him. The scent of burning candles mingled with that of aged wood and incense, creating an atmosphere both solemn and comforting. Stained glass windows lined the walls, their vibrant colours casting kaleidoscopic patterns across the pews as the morning light filtered through.

Klaus chose a seat at the back, sinking into the polished wood. Around him, parishioners murmured greetings, their faces reflecting the soft glow of the candles. The organist played, the rich notes filling the cavernous space and stirring memories long buried.

As the congregation stood to sing the opening hymn, *"Grosser Gott, wir loben dich,"* Klaus joined in, his voice tentative at first but growing steadier with each verse. The familiar melody wrapped around him like a balm, easing the tension on his shoulders.

The pastor took the pulpit, his voice resonant yet gentle. "Today, we reflect on the themes of forgiveness and redemption," he began. "No matter the burdens we carry, there is a path to peace."

Klaus listened intently, each word striking a chord within him. He thought of the choices he had made, the actions he could not undo. Guilt had been his constant companion, a shadow he could not escape. Yet here, in this sacred space, a glimmer of hope flickered.

After the service concluded, Klaus lingered, watching as others filed out into the cold. The pastor approached him, a kind smile on his face. "It is good to see you again, *Herr Engelhardt,"* Pastor Müller said warmly.

"Thank you," Klaus said, his voice barely above a whisper.

Returning home, he felt a subtle shift within himself. The oppressive weight had lessened, if only slightly. Marta noticed the change in his demeanour. "You look different today," she observed, setting a cup of steaming tea before him.

"I went to mass this morning," he admitted.

She raised an eyebrow, a hint of surprise in her eyes. "It's been years since you've attended."

Showing his understanding, he let out a sigh and said, "I know." "But perhaps it's time to find a new way forward." Even though he couldn't fully believe it, he couldn't deny the truth of the situation.

She placed a gentle hand on his. "I'm glad," she said simply.

Over the following days, Klaus established a routine. Each morning, he ventured out to St. Michael's, attempting to find solace in the community's rituals and quiet strength. The daily mass became an anchor, grounding him amidst the tumult of his thoughts.

On 12 December 1953, as the city prepared for the festive season, the church organised a charity drive for those still struggling in the war's aftermath. Klaus volunteered to help, surprising even himself. He spent the day sorting donations—clothing, food, toys for children. The act of giving brought a warmth to his heart he hadn't felt in years.

That evening, the congregation gathered outside the church for a carol service. The air was crisp, their breaths forming misty halos as they sang *"Stille Nacht"* under a canopy of stars. The soft glow of lanterns illuminated faces filled with hope and gratitude. Klaus stood among them, his voice melding with theirs, the music weaving a tapestry of unity.

Marta joined him, wrapping her arm around his. "It's beautiful, isn't it?" she whispered.

"Yes," he agreed, his gaze fixed on the flickering candles that lined the steps. "Perhaps there's still light to be found, even in the darkest times."

On 20 December 1953, with Christmas approaching, Klaus felt a growing need to unburden himself. After the morning service, he approached Pastor Müller. "May I speak with you?" he asked hesitantly.

"Of course," the pastor replied, his eyes reflecting genuine concern. "Shall we sit?"

They settled in a quiet corner of the church, the ambient sounds fading into the background. Klaus took a deep breath, the words catching in his throat. "I have carried a heavy burden," he began. "Things I've done… things I regret deeply."

The pastor nodded encouragingly. "Sometimes, speaking of our sorrows is the first step towards healing."

Klaus's gaze dropped to his hands, fingers twisting nervously. "During the war, I was an officer. I followed orders without question, and in doing so, I became part of atrocities I can scarcely admit to myself."

Emotion welled within him, years of suppressed guilt surging to the surface. "Despite my attempts to justify it and convince myself that I had no other option, I know that this is not the truth. I should have acted differently. I should have been stronger."

Silence hung between them, the weight of his confession settling like dust in the air.

"Thank you for sharing this with me," Pastor Müller said gently. "Acknowledging our faults is a courageous act."

"Will anyone ever forgive me?" Klaus asked, his voice strained. Klaus asked, his voice strained.

"The path to forgiveness begins within," the pastor replied. "We must first forgive ourselves and then seek reconciliation where we can. Our faith teaches us that redemption is possible, that no soul is beyond saving."

"But how can I make amends for what I cannot undo?" Klaus looked up, a glimmer of hope in his eyes.

"By living each day with integrity, by seeking to do good in the world," the pastor advised. "And perhaps, by reaching out to those you've distanced yourself from."

He thought of Hans, of Frieda, of the unspoken words that had built walls between them. "I've failed as a father," he admitted.

"There's still time," the pastor assured him. "Healing takes patience and effort, but it's never too late to begin."

Leaving the church that day, Klaus felt a profound sense of relief. The confession had been difficult, but it was a necessary step towards confronting his past. The streets were alive with the bustle of holiday preparations— vendors selling *lebkuchen* and *glühwein,* children laughing as they admired the festive decorations.

At home, he found Marta in the kitchen, the aroma of freshly baked stollen filling the air. "It smells wonderful," he remarked, smiling genuinely.

She looked up, pleasantly surprised by his cheerful demeanour. "I thought we could share some with the neighbours," she said. "It's been a while since we've had company."

"That's a lovely idea," he agreed. "I'd like to help."

They spent the afternoon together, wrapping parcels and writing cards. The simple act of engaging in these traditions reignited a sense of normalcy and connection. Klaus realised how much he had missed these moments.

On 24 December 1953, Christmas Eve, the Engelhardt home glowed with warmth. A modest tree stood in the corner of the living room, adorned with hand-carved ornaments and twinkling lights. Marta had prepared a traditional meal—roast goose with red cabbage and potatoes, followed by a rich black forest cake.

Frieda arrived early in the evening, her arms laden with gifts. *"Frohe Weihnachten!"* she greeted, kissing her mother on the cheek.

"Frohe Weihnachten, Liebes," Marta replied, embracing her daughter.

Klaus emerged from the study, a tentative smile on his face. "Merry Christmas, Frieda."

She turned to him, momentarily taken aback by the softness in his expression. "Merry Christmas, *Vater.*"

They sat together at the table, the clink of silverware and soft conversation filling the room. For the first time in years, the atmosphere was free from tension.

"Have you heard any news of Hans?" Frieda asked gently.

Klaus exchanged a glance with Marta. "Not recently," he admitted. "But I have faith that he's safe."

Frieda nodded solemnly. "I received a letter yesterday," she revealed. "Hans is still in East Germany. But he is well."

A wave of relief washed over them. "Thank God," Marta whispered, tears welling in her eyes as she embraced Frieda tightly.

Klaus felt a surge of emotion, a mix of relief and lingering worry. "How is he holding up?"

"He's been keeping busy with his work," Frieda explained, her voice soft but steady. "He's involved in some community projects that are helping him stay focused and positive despite everything."

Overwhelmed by a sense of gratitude, Klaus rose from his seat. "Excuse me," he murmured, stepping out onto the balcony. The chilly night air greeted him, stars glinting against the velvet sky. He closed his eyes, offering a silent prayer of gratitude for Hans' safety.

Frieda joined him moments later, wrapping a shawl around her shoulders. "Are you alright?"

"Yes," he replied, his voice steady yet filled with emotion. "More than alright. Knowing Hans is safe… it's the best gift I could have hoped for."

As they stood together in the quiet night, the bonds of family felt stronger than ever, the shadow of separation lifted by the assurance of Hans' continued presence. The Engelhardt family faced the future with renewed hope, their hearts lightened by the knowledge that one of their own remained safe, anchoring their collective spirit.

She placed a hand on his arm. "Father, I've noticed a change in you lately."

He nodded slowly. "I've been attending church again. Trying to find my way back to… something meaningful."

"I'm glad," she said sincerely. "I've missed this side of you."

He turned to face her. The lines of worry softened. "I've made many mistakes, Frieda. But I want to mend our relationship if you'll allow it."

She smiled gently. "I would like that very much."

They stood together, the quiet night enveloping them. From a distance, the sound of church bells heralded the arrival of midnight mass.

"Shall we go?" he suggested.

"Now?" she asked, surprised.

"Yes. I think it would be fitting."

Marta agreed to join them, and the three made their way through the snow-dusted streets to St. Michael's. The church was aglow, candles illuminating the path to the entrance. Inside, the congregation gathered, their voices rising in unison as they sang *"O Tannenbaum."*

Klaus felt a deep sense of peace as they took their seats. The service celebrated hope and renewal, themes that resonated profoundly with him. As the pastor spoke of the light that shines in the darkness, Klaus glanced at his family—Marta's serene expression, Frieda's attentive gaze—and felt a stirring of gratitude.

After the service, they mingled with other parishioners. Klaus introduced Frieda to Pastor Müller. "This is my daughter," he said proudly.

"A pleasure to meet you," the pastor greeted her warmly. "Your father has spoken highly of you."

Frieda raised an eyebrow playfully. "Has he now?"

Klaus chuckled softly. "Only the best, of course."

As they returned home in the early hours of 25 December 1953, snow fell gently, blanketing the city in a fresh layer of white. The quiet crunch of their footsteps accompanied them, the world hushed in the night's stillness.

In the days that followed, Klaus continued his journey towards reconciliation. He penned a heartfelt letter to Hans, expressing his deep concern for his son's safety in East Germany and his unwavering desire to mend their fractured relationship despite the persistent barriers that kept them apart.

On 31 December 1953, as the year drew to a close, the Engelhardt family gathered once more. This time, Hans was not with them, but his absence was profoundly felt. Although Hans could not join them physically, their reunion was filled with emotion as they shed tears, shared embraces, and bridged the gaps of time and distance through their shared hopes and memories.

They celebrated *Silvesterabend* together, sharing a traditional meal of carp and potatoes. At midnight, they stepped outside to watch the fireworks burst over the harbour, vibrant colours reflecting on the water's surface.

Klaus stood beside his mother and sister, the estrangement of the past years giving way to a newfound understanding. "I'm proud of all of you," he said quietly.

Frieda looked at him, a mixture of relief and sorrow in her eyes. "We are proud of you too, Vater."

As the last echoes of the fireworks faded, Klaus felt a sense of closure and hope. The journey was far from over, but the path ahead seemed less daunting with his family by his side.

The bells of St. Michael's rang out, welcoming the dawn of 1 January 1954. Klaus took a deep breath, the crisp air filling his lungs. "Happy New Year," he said, turning to his family.

"Happy New Year," they echoed, smiles illuminating their faces.

In that moment, amidst the cold of winter and the warmth of family, Klaus found a measure of peace. The shadows of his past remained, but they no longer held dominion over him. With faith, family, and a renewed sense of purpose, he stepped into the new year ready to face whatever challenges lay ahead.

Meanwhile, in East Germany, Hans remained hidden and safe. His health was robust, and he had successfully managed to stay off the radar of the Stasi. Engaging in low-profile community projects, he maintained a semblance of normalcy, all while nurturing the hope of one day reuniting with his family under better circumstances.

°°°

The icy breath of winter settled over Berlin on 1 February 1954, frosting windowpanes and cloaking the city in a shroud of white. Frieda Engelhardt stood at the train station in Hamburg, her breath forming delicate clouds that vanished into the crisp morning air. Clutching a worn leather satchel, she gazed at the locomotive hissing before her, its steam mingling with the swirling snowflakes. Determination hardened her features; it was time to face her brother.

As the train pulled away, she settled into her compartment, the rhythmic clatter of wheels on tracks echoing her racing thoughts. Outside, the German countryside unfurled like a monochrome tapestry—fields blanketed in snow, skeletal trees reaching towards a leaden sky. Frieda pressed her forehead against the cold glass, recalling the last time she and Hans had spoken without rancour, a time before ideologies had chiselled a rift between them.

On 10 February 1954, she arrived in East Berlin, the city's starkness intensified by the winter gloom. The streets were subdued, the usual hum of activity dampened by the oppressive atmosphere that had settled since the uprising in June. Posters bearing stern faces and bold slogans clung to walls, their messages of socialist glory faded and peeling.

Frieda made her way to the café they had agreed upon—a modest establishment tucked away on a quiet side street. The sign above the door, *"Kaffeehaus Müller,"* swung gently in the icy breeze; its paint chipped, but the warmth within was palpable. As she stepped inside, the scent of freshly brewed coffee enveloped her, mingling with the rich aroma of baked pastries.

Hans was already there, seated at a corner table beneath a fogged window. He stared into a steaming cup, fingers wrapped tightly around it as if seeking solace in its warmth. The soft glow of a lamp cast shadows across his face, accentuating the lines etched by stress and disillusionment.

"Hallo, Hans," she greeted softly, removing her gloves and tucking them into her coat pocket.

He looked up, surprise flickering in his eyes before they settled into guarded recognition. "Frieda," he acknowledged, gesturing to the seat opposite. "You made it."

She sat down, placing her satchel by her feet. An awkward silence stretched between them, filled only by the distant clink of dishes and murmured conversations from other patrons.

"You look well," she offered tentatively.

He shrugged, a hint of a smile ghosting his lips. "As well as one can, given the circumstances."

A waitress approached, and Frieda ordered a coffee. The waitress placed the cup before her, and Frieda cradled it gratefully, allowing the heat to seep into her chilled hands.

Hans admitted his surprise at receiving her message while he fixed his gaze on the swirling patterns atop his coffee.

"I felt it was time—" she replied. "time we spoke face to face."

He glanced up, eyes searching hers. "About what?"

"About us, the family. About everything that's happened."

He sighed, leaning back in his chair. "I'm not sure where to begin."

"Perhaps with how you're feeling," she suggested gently. "I know the events of 17 June have been… difficult."

Hans's jaw tightened. "Difficult doesn't cover it. The uprising was a wake-up call—a stark reminder of the chasm between ideals and reality."

Frieda nodded. "I've heard stories. The repression was brutal."

He laughed bitterly. "Brutal is putting it mildly. Tanks in the streets, comrades turning on each other, the Stasi's shadow growing longer daily."

She reached across the table, her fingers brushing his. "Hans, you don't have to stay here. Come back to the West. We can help you start anew."

He pulled his hand away, folding his arms defensively. "It's not that simple."

"Why not?" she pressed. "You've seen what this regime is capable of. You deserve better."

He met her gaze, eyes hardened. "And what of the West? Is it so perfect? Capitalism exploiting the masses, corruption seeping into every institution?"

"At least we have freedom," she countered. "The freedom to speak, choose, live without constant fear."

"Freedom?" he scoffed. "Freedom for some, perhaps. But at what cost? I've seen the disparities, the inequality."

Frieda's patience waned. "Hans, you're clinging to ideals that no longer exist. The GDR is not the socialist utopia you once believed in."

He bristled. "And the FRG is not the bastion of democracy you make it out to be. Both sides have their flaws."

"Then why stay?" she implored. "If you recognise the faults, why remain in a place that suffocates you?"

He stared into his cup, the surface now cooled and still. "Because leaving feels like admitting defeat, and is no easy task. Like abandoning those who still believe change is possible."

She softened her tone. "Recognising when a battle cannot be won can be the bravest thing we can do."

He shook his head. "You don't understand."

"Help me understand," she pleaded.

Hans sighed deeply. "It's not just about me. There are people here—friends, colleagues—who rely on me. If I try to leave, what happens to them?"

"You can't carry the weight of others on your shoulders indefinitely," she reasoned. "Think of your own well-being."

He glanced around the café, noting the subtle glances from the other patrons. "We shouldn't be having this conversation here," he muttered. "It's not safe."

She lowered her voice. "Then come with me. We can find somewhere private."

He stood abruptly. "No, Frieda. I shouldn't have agreed to this meeting."

She rose to her feet, desperation edging her voice. "Hans, please. Don't shut me out."

He hesitated, conflict flashing across his features. "I appreciate your concern," he said quietly. "But my path is my own."

She felt a swell of frustration and sorrow. "You're being stubborn."

"Perhaps," he conceded. "But it's all I have left."

Before she could respond, he turned and walked towards the door. The bell tinkled softly as he exited, the cold air rushing in to fill the void he left behind.

Frieda sank back into her chair, a heaviness settling in her chest. The warmth of the café now felt stifling, the clatter of dishes grating on her nerves. She signalled for the bill, paying hastily before stepping out into the frigid street.

The wind bit at her cheeks as she wandered aimlessly, the city's austere architecture looming over her like silent sentinels. She passed by a group of children building a snowman, their laughter a stark contrast to the bleakness she felt. The sound tugged at her heart, a reminder of simpler times when she and Hans had played together without a care in the world.

On 15 February 1954, back in Hamburg, Frieda sat in her office, pouring over reports. The words blurred on the page, her mind drifting repeatedly to the failed meeting. She wondered if there was more she could have said or done to reach him.

A knock at the door jolted her from her thoughts. "Come in," she called.

Greta Schmidt entered, her expression concerned. "You look miles away," she observed, taking a seat opposite Frieda.

"Just tired," Frieda replied dismissively.

Greta eyed her sceptically. "I heard you went to East Berlin."

Frieda sighed. "Word travels fast."

"Did you see him?"

"Yes."

"And?"

"It didn't go well," she admitted. "He shows no signs of budging and remains firmly entrenched."

Greta leaned forward. "You can't blame yourself. Hans has to make his own choices."

"I know," Frieda murmured. "But it doesn't make it any easier."

Greta offered a sympathetic smile. "Perhaps, in time, he'll come around."

"Perhaps," she echoed, though doubt lingered.

On 18 December 1954, Klaus sat by the window of their home, watching as snow blanketed the street. The house was quiet, the only sound the ticking of the grandfather clock in the hallway. Marta entered, carrying a tray with two steaming mugs of hot chocolate.

"Here," she said softly, handing him a mug. "It'll warm you up."

"Thank you," he replied, his gaze still fixed outside.

She settled beside him. "Frieda told me about her meeting with Hans."

He sighed heavily. "I had hoped they could reconcile."

"As did I," Marta agreed. "But sometimes, wounds take longer to heal."

"Or perhaps they never do," he mused.

She placed a comforting hand on his arm. "We can't lose hope."

He turned to face her, lines of worry etched deeply on his face. "I'm afraid that our family has reached a point where we cannot repair it."

"Families are resilient," she assured him. "We've endured so much already."

He nodded slowly. "You're right. We must keep trying."

On 20 February 1954, the Engelhardt family settled in for a family dinner.

Klaus embraced his daughter, noting the weariness in her eyes. "You look tired," he observed.

"It's been a long month," she admitted.

They sat down to a simple meal—roast duck with red cabbage and dumplings, the comforting aromas filling the room. Conversation was polite but strained, each of them acutely aware of the empty chair at the table.

"Have you heard anything from Hans?" Klaus ventured cautiously.

Frieda shook her head. "No. I doubt I will."

Marta reached for her hand. "He knows we care for him."

"Does he?" Frieda countered, bitterness creeping into her tone. "He seemed determined to push us away."

Klaus cleared his throat. "Perhaps we need to give him time. Fear can also be a pervasive factor."

"Time may not be enough," she replied quietly.

They exchanged sombre glances, the weight of unspoken fears settling over them.

Frieda stood by the window, gazing out at the snow-covered street illuminated by lamplight. "I remember when Hans and I would build snow forts in the garden," she reminisced. "We'd stay out until our fingers were numb."

Klaus joined her, his reflection appearing beside hers in the glass. "Those were happier times."

She sighed. "I wish we could return to them."

He placed a hand on her shoulder. "All we can do is move forward."

On 24 February 1954, as the year drew to a close, the Engelhardts prepared for a quiet evening at home.

Frieda sat alone in her apartment, the glow of a single candle casting flickering shadows on the walls. She clutched a photograph of her and Hans as children, their faces alight with joy. Tears welled in her eyes, blurring the image.

A knock at the door startled her. Wiping her eyes, she stood and opened it to find Greta holding a bottle of champagne.

"I thought you could use some company," Greta said with a sympathetic smile.

Frieda stepped aside to let her in. "I suppose I could."

They settled on the sofa, glasses in hand. "To those not with us," Greta toasted. "May they find peace in their lives."

"To Hans," Frieda echoed, clinking her glass against Greta's.

They sipped in silence for a moment before Greta spoke. "Have you considered taking a break? You've been working tirelessly."

Frieda shook her head. "There's too much to be done."

"You can't pour from an empty cup."

She offered a faint smile. "You're sounding like my mother."

"Well, mothers often know best," Greta quipped.

Frieda gazed into the amber liquid swirling in her glass. "I just feel like I'm losing everything important."

"You're not alone," Greta assured her. "You have people who care about you."

"Thank you," she whispered, her voice barely audible.

As midnight approached, the two women stepped out onto the balcony. The cityscape stretched before them, a mosaic of lights and shadows.

Hans, standing by his own window in East Berlin, gazed up at the same stars that adorned the sky above Frieda, who resided on the other side of the city that was divided. He wondered what Frieda was doing at that moment, whether she thought of him as he did of her.

Regret gnawed at him, but pride kept him rooted. The path he had chosen was fraught with uncertainty, yet turning back seemed impossible.

Back in Hamburg, Klaus sat alone in his study, the faint strains of a waltz playing on the gramophone. A half-empty glass of schnapps rested on the desk beside him. He contemplated the recent events—the fleeting moments of hope, the crushing disappointments.

Marta entered quietly, wrapping a shawl around her shoulders. "It's late," she remarked gently.

He nodded absently. "I was just thinking."

"About Hans?"

"About all of them," he admitted. "The family, the country… everything seems so fractured."

She placed a comforting hand on his. "We must hold on to hope."

He looked at her, his eyes reflecting a deep weariness. "Sometimes, hope feels like a luxury we can't afford."

"Without it, what do we have?" she countered softly.

He sighed, squeezing her hand. "You're right, as always."

As the clock struck midnight, they joined Frieda in the living room. The three of them raised glasses in a subdued toast.

Offering a toast, Klaus said, "To family."

Marta added, "In order to achieve reconciliation."

"To a future where we can all be together," Frieda concluded.

They drank in silence, each lost in their own thoughts.

Outside, the clouds started to obscure the sky a canvas of stars. The city gradually quieted, giving way to the stillness of the night.

Frieda retired to her room, exhaustion pulling at her. As she lay in bed, she allowed herself a final thought of Hans, wishing him safety and peace.

In his own bed, miles away, Hans closed his eyes. He knew the road ahead would be difficult, but he clung to the belief that one day it would be possible to mend bridges.

The Engelhardt family, though separated by walls both physical and ideological, shared the same sky, the same hopes flickering like distant stars.

Winter tightened its grip as January loomed, but beneath the frozen surface, the first stirrings of change waited patiently. The scars of war and division ran deep, yet amidst the ruins, the possibility of healing remained— a fragile promise carried into the new year.

EIGHT:

A DIVIDED FUTURE

The first day of March 1954 arrived with a whisper of spring in Hamburg. The morning air carried a hint of warmth, and the Elbe River shimmered under a pale sun breaking through the winter clouds. Snowdrops and crocuses poked their heads through the thawing soil in Planten un Blomen Park, promising renewal after a long, harsh winter.

Frieda Engelhardt stood on the steps of the Rathaus, the grand town hall that bore the scars of war yet stood resilient amidst the city's rebirth. Clutching a folder brimming with plans for new housing developments, she gazed out over the bustling *Rathausmarkt*. Vendors were setting up stalls, their cheerful banter mingling with the distant sound of church bells tolling the hour. The scent of freshly baked *brötchen* wafted through the air, mingling with the crispness of early spring.

"Frau Engelhardt," called a voice from behind. She turned to see Peter Müller, a young architect with whom she had collaborated on the reconstruction projects.

"Ah, Herr Müller," she greeted warmly. "Are we ready for the meeting?"

"Indeed," he replied, adjusting his spectacles. "I believe our proposals will please the committee," he replied.

Frieda felt a surge of purpose as they entered the ornate halls of the Rathaus. The grand chambers echoed with footsteps and murmured conversations, the atmosphere charged with the energy of progress. Since the implementation of the Marshall Plan, the city had been transformed rapidly, and Frieda was determined to ensure that the growth benefitted all citizens.

Throughout March and April, Frieda threw herself into her work. On 15 March 1954, she attended a community forum in Altona, addressing concerns about affordable housing and employment opportunities. Standing before a crowd of attentive faces in a converted warehouse, she spoke passionately about the importance of inclusive development.

"Our city rises from the ashes," she declared, her voice resolute. "Let us build a Hamburg that offers hope and prosperity for every family."

The audience enthusiastically applauded her words, and as the meeting ended, several attendees approached her with gratitude.

"Thank you, *Frau Engelhardt*," said an elderly woman clutching a worn handbag. "You give us faith in the future."

Frieda smiled, her eyes reflecting the sincerity of her commitment. "Together, we will make it so."

Meanwhile, Klaus Engelhardt watched these developments from a distance. On 20 March 1954, he sat by the window of their modest apartment on Schanzenstraße, observing the world outside with a sense of detachment. Children played in the street, their laughter contrasting with the heavy silence that enveloped him. The scent of freshly turned earth drifted in from the gardens below, yet it did little to stir him from his melancholy.

Marta entered the room quietly with a tray of tea and biscuits. "It's a lovely day, Klaus," she ventured gently. "Perhaps we could take a walk along the harbour?"

He shook his head without turning. "I prefer to stay here."

She set the tray down on a small table beside him. "Frieda has been working tirelessly," she mentioned, hoping to elicit some response. "The city is changing so quickly."

"Yes," he replied curtly. "Changing beyond recognition." Klaus' spirits, which had been lifting with his involvement in the church, had taken a downward turn with the news of Hans and Frieda's chilly meeting.

Marta sighed softly, retreating to give him space. She knew the wounds he carried were deep, but she longed for him to find solace in the present rather than being haunted by the past.

As April turned to May, the city buzzed with anticipation. Rumours circulated about West Germany's imminent accession to the North Atlantic Treaty Organization. On 5 May 1954, newspapers announced the Bundestag, the German Federal Parliament, had approved the motion, sparking both celebration and controversy.

Frieda attended a series of meetings to prepare for the official ceremony. On 10 May 1954, she met with local officials in a conference room overlooking the river. Maps, charts, and a palpable sense of excitement filled the room.

"Joining NATO solidifies our place among the free nations," declared Mayor Heinrich Schreiber, his eyes gleaming with conviction. With conviction gleaming in his eyes, Mayor Heinrich Schreiber declared, "We make sure that Hamburg's voice is heard."

Frieda agreed. "It's an opportunity to show our commitment to peace and cooperation," she added. "But we must also be mindful of the tensions this may exacerbate."

The mayor nodded solemnly. "Indeed. The shadow of the East looms large."

On 15 May 1954, the day dawned bright and clear. Flags adorned the central square—Germany's black, red, and gold interspersed with NATO's blue and white. Banners proclaimed messages of unity and strength. The scent of blooming lilacs filled the air, carried on a gentle breeze that rustled the flags overhead.

They had erected a grand podium before the Rathaus. Citizens gathered in the thousands, their faces reflecting a mix of hope, pride, and cautious optimism. The sound of a military band resonated through the square, playing stirring melodies that evoked a sense of national pride.

Frieda stood among dignitaries, her heart pounding with a mix of nerves and determination. Dressed in a tailored navy suit, she embodied the poise and confidence of a leader. As her turn to speak approached, she took a deep breath, allowing the crowd's energy to bolster her resolve.

Stepping up to the podium, she surveyed the sea of faces before her. *"Liebe Mitbürgerinnen und Mitbürger* (Dear fellow citizens)," she began, her voice amplified across the square. "Today marks a pivotal moment in our nation's history."

She spoke of the trials they had endured, the resilience that had brought them to this point, and the collective responsibility they bore to ensure a peaceful future.

"By joining NATO, we affirm our commitment to democracy, to protecting freedom, and to the collaboration with nations that share these ideals," she proclaimed. "Let us move forward together, united in purpose and hope."

The crowd erupted in applause, the sound swelling like a wave. Frieda felt a surge of emotion—a blend of personal fulfilment and a profound connection to the people she served.

As the ceremony concluded, fireworks burst overhead despite the daylight, their echoes reverberating through the city. Children waved miniature flags, and vendors sold pretzels and sausages to the celebrants. The atmosphere was festive, filled with laughter and song.

But amid the jubilation, not all shared in the elation. Back in Schanzenstraße, Klaus sat alone in the dimness of his study, with the heavy drapes drawn, allowing only slivers of light to penetrate the gloom. The muffled sounds of celebration reached him faintly, a distant reminder of a world from which he felt estranged.

On his desk lay an old photograph, edges frayed and sepia tones faded. It depicted a younger Klaus in uniform, standing beside comrades whose faces had blurred with time. His fingers traced the contours of his own image, the fabric of the past tangible beneath his touch.

He closed his eyes, unwanted memories flooding back—the camaraderie of soldiers, the cacophony of battle, the weight of orders followed without question. The guilt he carried was a relentless burden, pressing upon him like an anchor tethered to a bygone era.

Marta knocked softly before entering, a tray of soup and bread in her hands. "You've hardly eaten today," she said gently.

"I'm not hungry," he replied, his gaze fixed on the photograph.

She set the tray down, her eyes filled with concern. "Perhaps some fresh air would do you good. The city is alive with celebration."

He scoffed lightly. "Celebration of what? Of further entangling ourselves in alliances that will only lead to more conflict?"

"Klaus," she implored, "this is a new beginning for our country. Frieda believes in it, and so do many others."

"Frieda is young," he retorted. "She sees only the veneer of progress, not the undercurrents that threaten to pull us under."

Marta sighed, a mix of sadness and frustration. "She's working tirelessly to build a better future. Can't you find it in your heart to support her?"

He turned to face her, his eyes weary. "I cannot support what I do not believe in."

She reached out to touch his shoulder, but he pulled away. Defeated, she gathered the untouched tray and left the room, the door closing softly behind her.

Outside, the streets of Hamburg thrummed with life. On 20 May 1954, cafés overflowed with patrons, discussing the day's events. At Café Fritz, a popular meeting spot near the harbour, Frieda met with Greta Schmidt, her long-time friend and confidante.

"Your speech was inspiring," Greta remarked, stirring a lump of sugar in her coffee. "The papers are singing your praises."

Frieda smiled modestly. "I'm just grateful for the opportunity to contribute."

Greta leaned in conspiratorially. "There's talk of you running for a higher office."

Frieda waved off the suggestion. "Idle gossip."

"Perhaps," Greta conceded, "but you've made an impression. People are hungry for leaders they can trust."

They sipped their coffees in comfortable silence, the clatter of cups and murmur of conversations creating a soothing backdrop.

"How is your father?" Greta inquired gently.

Frieda's expression clouded. "He's… unchanged. Withdrawn. Paranoid that NATO is going to draw us into a new war."

"I'm sorry," Greta offered. "It must be difficult."

"It is," Frieda admitted. "I wish he could see the possibilities before us, but he remains locked in the past."

"Give him time," Greta suggested. "Healing isn't linear."

Frieda nodded though a heaviness settled in her chest. She yearned for her father's approval, or at least his understanding, but each attempt to bridge the gap seemed to widen it further.

As June arrived, the city's momentum showed no signs of slowing. On 5 June 1954, construction began on a new cultural centre, a project that Frieda had championed to revitalise the arts scene. She stood at the groundbreaking ceremony, shovel in hand, surrounded by artists and community leaders.

"This centre will be a beacon of creativity," she announced, her smile radiant. "A place where art and expression can flourish, reminding us of the beauty that endures even in the face of adversity."

The crowd applauded enthusiastically, and as she turned the first spadefuls of earth, she felt a renewed sense of purpose.

Yet, amid these triumphs, Klaus's isolation deepened. On 15 June 1954, he received a letter from an old comrade, Jakob Fischer. The letter, penned in a shaky hand, spoke of shared memories and lamented the state of the nation.

"We were soldiers once," Jakob wrote. "Men of honour in a world that no longer values such things."

Klaus stared at the words, a mixture of nostalgia and bitterness welling within him. He crumpled the letter and tossed it aside, unwilling to rekindle connections that tethered him to a painful past.

That evening, as the sun cast long shadows across the city, Marta found Klaus sitting in the darkness.

"Please, let me open the curtains," she urged. "The light might lift your spirits."

He remained silent, his silhouette a stark outline against the fading light.

"Klaus," she whispered, tears threatening to spill, "I miss you."

He turned his head slightly, the glimmer of emotion flickering in his eyes. "I'm still here," he murmured.

"Are you?" she challenged softly. "Because it feels as though I've lost you."

He bowed his head, the weight of her words pressing upon him. "I don't know how to be part of this new world," he confessed. "Everything I knew is gone."

She moved closer, tentatively placing a hand on his arm. "Then let us find a way forward together. We cannot change the past, but we can shape the future."

He looked at her, the vulnerability in his gaze unguarded. "I'm tired, Marta. So exhausted."

She enveloped him in an embrace, holding him tightly as if to anchor him to the present. "Rest, then," she whispered. "And know that you are not alone."

Outside, the city lights twinkled as night descended on 30 June 1954. Hamburg's skyline was a testament to resilience—a tapestry of old and new shadows and illumination. The harbour bustled with activity, ships arriving from distant shores bearing goods and stories alike.

Frieda stood on a balcony overlooking the river, the cool evening air brushing against her skin. The glow of the city reflected in the water, a shimmering mirror of possibility.

"To progress," she toasted softly to herself, raising a glass of Riesling. Yet, a lingering sadness tempered her satisfaction. The success she had worked so hard to achieve felt incomplete without her family's unity.

In the quiet of his room, Klaus lay awake, the faint hum of the city's nightlife seeping through the walls. He stared at the ceiling, tracing patterns in the plaster as his mind wrestled with memories and regrets.

On this last night of June, the Engelhardts found themselves at a crossroads—Frieda embracing the future with cautious optimism, Klaus ensnared by the shadows of his past, and Marta striving to bridge the divide between them.

The first half of 1954 had brought change and challenge in equal measure. As the city of Hamburg thrived, so too did the complexities within the Engelhardt family deepen. The promise of summer loomed ahead, carrying with it the potential for both healing and further strife.

The rhythms of life continued—the steady pulse of progress, the undercurrents of discord, and the enduring hope that something and beautiful might emerge amidst the ruins.

ooo

The sun hung heavy over East Berlin on 1 July 1954, its relentless glare reflecting off the concrete façades of the austere buildings that lined Stalinallee. The air was thick and stifling, imbued with the acrid scent of coal dust and the faint undertones of perspiration from the crowds that moved sluggishly along the wide boulevard. Hans Engelhardt wiped a bead of sweat from his brow as he navigated through the throng, the oppressive heat amplifying the weight of his discontent.

The grand avenue, once a symbol of socialist triumph, now felt like a corridor of confinement. Towering apartment blocks loomed on either side, their uniform windows like a thousand unblinking eyes. Banners bearing Walter Ulbricht's stern visage fluttered limply in the stagnant air, slogans of unity and productivity emblazoned beneath. Yet, despite the propaganda's insistence, a pall of unease had settled over the city.

Hans made his way to his office, a cramped space nestled within the labyrinthine corridors of the Ministry of Transport. On entering the building, the harsh flicker of fluorescent lights greeted him, casting a pallid glow over the drab interior. The scent of stale paper mingled with the lingering odour of disinfectant, creating an atmosphere devoid of warmth.

"Good morning, *Genosse Engelhardt*," murmured a colleague as he passed, her eyes avoiding his. Cautious formality had replaced the customary camaraderie of the workplace; each interaction weighed with unspoken suspicion.

"Good morning," he replied curtly, his gaze fixed ahead.

Settling at his desk, Hans surveyed the stack of reports awaiting his attention. Maps detailing railway schedules, cargo manifests, and resource allocations formed an intricate mosaic of bureaucracy. He reached for a pencil, the simple act of sharpening it, offering a brief respite from the monotony.

As he worked, his thoughts drifted back to the past year's events. The workers' uprising on 17 June 1953 had been a turning point—a day when the façade of the regime's benevolence had cracked, revealing the steel beneath. Tanks rolling through the streets, comrades silenced, hopes crushed beneath treads. The memory lingered like a shadow, casting doubt on everything he had once believed.

On 10 July 1954, a memorandum circulated announcing a mandatory party meeting scheduled for 15 July. The notice was brief and devoid of detail, yet it carried an implicit gravity. Hans folded the paper thoughtfully, slipping it into his jacket pocket. A knot tightened in his stomach—a premonition of what was to come.

That evening, he returned to his modest flat in Prenzlauer Berg. The building was a relic from before the war, its worn brickwork and narrow stairwells bearing the scars of time. Inside, the air was marginally cooler, the thick walls providing scant relief from the sweltering heat.

He sat by the open window, the faint sounds of the city drifting upward—a distant siren, the murmur of voices, the clatter of a tram. He retrieved a letter from his pocket addressed to his father, dated 1 July 1954. The page bore smudges where his hand had rested, the ink slightly blurred.

Lieber Vater,

I hope this letter finds you and Mutter in good health. The summer here is unforgiving, but we manage as best we can.

He hesitated, the pen hovering over the paper. What could he say that would convey the turmoil within him without inviting scrutiny? In the end, he settled for vague pleasantries, hinting at his doubts with carefully chosen words.

Work continues to be challenging,

There are moments when I question if my chosen path is the right one.

Folding the letter, he sealed it and placed it alongside others he intended to post. Communication with the West was increasingly fraught, and each missive was subject to inspection. He could only hope that his sentiments would reach his father unaltered.

The day of the meeting, 15 July 1954, dawned oppressively hot. The sky was a bleached canvas devoid of clouds, and the sun was a relentless sentinel. Hans meticulously dressed himself, making sure his party badge was polished and prominently displayed.

The organisers held the meeting in a grand hall near Alexanderplatz, with its neoclassical architecture serving as an imposing backdrop for the gathering. As he entered, Hans felt a chill despite the heat—a tangible tension that permeated the room. Rows of chairs faced a raised dais, where the party leaders would soon address the assembly.

He took a seat beside his friend, Markus Weber, a fellow transport official. "Any idea what this is about?" Hans whispered.

Markus shook his head subtly. "No, but it can't be good. They've been cracking down lately."

Before Hans could reply, the lights dimmed, and a hush fell over the crowd. A single spotlight illuminated the podium as a senior official approached, his expression stern.

"Genossinnen und Genossen (Comrades)," the official began, his voice resonating through the hall. "We convene today to reaffirm our commitment to the Socialist Unity Party and the principles that guide our great nation."

As the speech progressed, Hans felt a creeping unease. The rhetoric was harsher than usual, laced with veiled threats against those who exhibited "counter-revolutionary tendencies" or failed to show unwavering loyalty. Hans suspected that many echoed the sentiments out of fear rather than conviction, even though there were murmurs of assent to references to the recent purges.

They discreetly positioned surveillance cameras around the hall, their lenses glinting like watchful eyes. Hans noticed several individuals taking notes—not for personal reference but to report any deviations from the expected displays of enthusiasm.

The audience erupted into obligatory applause when the official concluded with a rousing call to action. Hans joined in mechanically, his palms meeting with hollow claps. He exchanged a glance with Markus, whose face was inscrutable.

After the meeting, as attendees filtered out into the blinding sunlight, Hans lingered. "Care for a drink?" he suggested to Markus.

They found a small café tucked away on a side street, its shaded terrace offering a reprieve from the heat. The proprietor served them lukewarm beer, the best given the shortages.

"That was quite the performance," Markus remarked dryly, taking a sip.

Hans nodded. "Indeed. It seems the noose tightens further."

Markus leaned in, his voice barely above a whisper. "We have to be careful. You never know who's listening."

Hans glanced around discreetly. Two men in plain clothes appeared engrossed at a nearby table in their conversation, but their occasional glances suggested otherwise.

"You're right," Hans conceded. "It's just… this isn't what I signed up for."

Markus sighed heavily. "None of us did. But what choice do we have?"

The question hung in the air, unanswered.

Back in Hamburg, on 20 July 1954, Klaus sat by the window of their apartment, a stack of letters before him. The latest from Hans lay unopened, the familiar handwriting stirring a mix of anticipation and dread. Marta entered quietly, placing a cup of chamomile tea beside him.

"Another letter from Hans?" she asked softly.

He nodded. "Yes, dated 1 July 1954."

"Will you read it?"

"In time," he replied, his gaze distant.

She rested a hand on his shoulder. "Perhaps it will bring good news."

He offered a faint smile. "One can hope."

Later that evening, Klaus summoned the resolve to read the letter. As he unfolded the paper, he noted the slight tremor in his hands. Beneath the surface, Klaus felt his son's turmoil in the carefully constructed words.

> *…. There are moments when I question if the path I've chosen is the right one.*

Klaus's heart tightened. He recognised the subtle plea for guidance, the unspoken yearning for connection. Yet, he felt powerless, the distance between them not merely physical but ideological—a chasm widened by years of silence and unspoken grievances.

On 1 August 1954, Hans received a summons to the Ministry's upper offices. The corridors were wider, and the walls were adorned with portraits of party leaders and motivational slogans. The air was cooler, and the hum of air conditioning was a luxury not afforded elsewhere.

An official greeted him tersely. "*Genosse Engelhardt,* you are to assist with a special assignment."

"Of course," Hans replied, masking his apprehension.

They assigned him the task of reviewing transportation logistics for an upcoming state visit—a meticulous endeavour requiring precision and discretion. As he delved into the work, he found a semblance of purpose, the familiar routines momentarily easing his disquiet.

However, on 10 August 1954, rumours began circulating of increased Stasi activity. Colleagues whispered of late-night arrests, of disappearances cloaked in official secrecy. The atmosphere grew heavier, each day punctuated by furtive glances and guarded conversations.

Hans sought solace in the company of his friend Karl Meier, a fellow idealist he had known since his early days in the Party. They met at a secluded spot along the Spree River, the water's gentle flow providing a soothing backdrop.

"It's becoming unbearable," Karl confessed, skipping a stone across the surface. "I can't even speak my mind without fearing who might report me."

Hans nodded grimly. "I know. The very essence of what we believed in is being eroded."

Karl turned to face him, eyes earnest. "We have to do something. Perhaps if we join forces with others, who feel the same…"

"Careful," Hans cautioned, his gaze scanning the surroundings. "Such talk can lead to trouble."

"But if we remain silent, nothing will change."

Hans sighed. "I admire your courage, but we must tread lightly. The risks are too great."

On 25 August 1954, as the sun dipped low on the horizon, casting long shadows through the city streets, Hans received devastating news. The authorities had arrested Karl the previous night, accusing him of subversive activities. The official report was terse and offered no details.

Panic gripped Hans. He replayed their conversations, wondering if he, too, was now under scrutiny. The walls seemed to close in, the ever-present surveillance now a palpable threat.

That evening, he sat alone in his flat, the air thick with anxiety. From his desk drawer, he retrieved a small photograph of himself and Karl taken years prior—a moment captured in happier times, both smiling against the backdrop of a May Day parade.

The knock on his door startled him. His heart raced as he approached cautiously. "Who is it?" he called out.

"It's *Frau Müller* from downstairs," came the muffled reply. Relief washed over him as he opened the door to the elderly woman.

"Forgive the intrusion," she apologised. "I thought you might like some fresh bread. I baked too much."

"Thank you," he managed, accepting the offering.

She peered at him kindly. "You look troubled, Herr Engelhardt. Is everything alright?"

He forced a smile. "Just tired, that's all."

"Take care of yourself," she advised gently before departing.

Closing the door, Hans leaned against it, the weight of his fears pressing upon him. Karl's arrest was a stark reminder of his situation's precariousness. Any misstep could lead to a similar fate.

On 31 August 1954, the culmination of his disillusionment arrived. At the Ministry, whispers spread of a public denunciation. Under the guise of an emergency announcement, employees gathered in the central courtyard.

A high-ranking official took the podium, flanked by stern-faced guards. "Comrades," he began, "elements within our ranks have sought to undermine the integrity of our socialist state."

Hans stood amidst the crowd, a cold sweat forming on his brow. He spotted Karl, flanked by officers, his hands bound and face drawn but resolute.

"This man," the official continued, pointing to Karl, "has confessed to treasonous activities. Let this serve as a warning to all who might harbour similar intentions."

The organisers instructed the crowd to watch as they led Karl away. The unspoken message made it clear—they would not tolerate dissent.

Hans felt a surge of helplessness and anger. The ideals he had cherished were now twisted into instruments of oppression. The very system he had dedicated himself to was destroying the lives of those he cared about.

That night, he penned a letter to his father, dated 31 August 1954.

Lieber Vater,

I fear I have made grave errors in judgment. The world here is not as it seems, and I question everything I once held dear.

He paused, the enormity of his admission weighing upon him.

I wish I could see you and speak with you face to face. Perhaps one day…

The sentence trailed off, unfinished.

Sealing the letter, he knew there was a risk it would never reach its destination. But the act of writing was a small defiance against the silence imposed upon him.

As dawn approached, Hans stood by his window, gazing out over the rooftops of East Berlin. The city slept, unaware or unwilling to acknowledge the quiet despair that permeated its streets.

He contemplated escape, the possibility of defecting to the West. But the barriers—both physical and psychological—seemed insurmountable. Fear tethered him, the risks too great, the consequences too dire.

In Hamburg, Klaus received Hans's letter weeks later. The anguish in his son's words pierced through the page, igniting a desperate need to help. Yet, he was acutely aware of his limitations—the distance, the political divide, his own frailties.

"Perhaps it's not too late," he murmured to himself, clutching the letter tightly.

Marta found him thus, the lines of worry etched deeply into his face. "Klaus, what is it?"

He handed her the letter silently. As she read, tears welled in her eyes. "We must do something," she implored.

He nodded, determination hardening his features. "I'll write to him. We'll find a way."

Back in East Berlin, Hans resigned himself to the reality of his situation. The summer heat had waned, a hint of autumn in the evening air. Yet, the oppressive atmosphere remained, the weight of the regime's grip unrelenting.

On 31 August 1954, as the city settled into the night, Hans made a silent vow. If he could not change his circumstances, he would at least hold on to his integrity, refusing to become complicit in the machinery of oppression.

The path ahead was uncertain and fraught with peril. But amidst the darkness, a flicker of resilience persisted—a quiet defiance that, though small, refused to be extinguished.

The leaves would soon turn, the seasons shifting as inexorably as time itself. With each passing day, the threads of the Engelhardt family's lives wove an intricate tapestry of hope and despair, unity and division—a reflection of a nation torn yet striving for redemption.

ooo

The first of September 1954 arrived with a whisper of autumn in Hamburg. A crisp breeze rustled through the elm trees lining the avenue, scattering early fallen leaves across cobblestone streets slick from morning dew. The scent of damp earth and distant chimney smoke permeated the air, signalling the slow retreat of summer.

A muted atmosphere filled the Engelhardt residence of Schanzenstraße. Klaus lay in his dim bedroom, the heavy drapes drawn against the pale light filtering through the overcast sky. The room held a stagnant chill, the kind that seeped into bones and lingered. Dust motes floated lazily in the thin shafts of light that pierced the gloom, dancing silently above worn wooden floorboards.

Klaus fixed his gaze on the ceiling, his eyes tracing the cracks that meandered like rivers across the plaster. His chest rose and fell shallowly beneath a thin woollen blanket that provided scant warmth. The once robust frame of a Wehrmacht officer had withered, leaving behind a frail silhouette of the man he used to be.

From the adjoining room, muffled voices reached him—Frieda and Marta engaged in quiet conversation. Their words were indistinct like echoes reverberating from a distant cavern. He strained to catch snippets, but they slipped away, leaving only the hollow resonance of his own thoughts.

On 15 September 1954, the post arrived with a letter from Hans. Marta brought it to Klaus, her footsteps soft against the creaking floorboards.

"A letter from our son," she announced gently, holding out the envelope.

He turned his head slowly, eyes lingering on the familiar handwriting. "Thank you," he murmured, accepting it with trembling hands.

"Shall I leave you to read it?" she offered.

He nodded absently, already absorbed by opening the envelope. The paper rustled delicately as he unfolded the letter. Hans carefully chose his words, but the underlying tension was palpable.

Lieber Vater,

The leaves are turning here as well, a reminder of the passing time. I reflect on choices made and paths taken…

Klaus's eyes blurred as he continued reading. Hans' disillusionment was clear, each line laden with unspoken fears and regrets. The weight of his son's turmoil pressed upon him, compounding his own sense of helplessness.

As the days progressed into October, Klaus retreated further into himself. On 5 October 1954, a rare sunny day bathed the city in golden light. Outside, children played in the street, their laughter a fleeting melody carried on the breeze. The scent of freshly baked *apfelstrudel* wafted from a nearby bakery, mingling with the earthy aroma of fallen leaves.

But within the confines of Klaus's room, time stood still. The air was heavy with the scent of stale linens and the faint trace of pipe tobacco—a habit he had long since abandoned. The only sounds were the rhythmic ticking of a mantel clock and the occasional distant clang of a tram bell.

Marta entered with a tray bearing a bowl of soup and a slice of dark rye bread. "You've hardly eaten today," she observed, concern etching lines across her forehead.

He glanced at the offering but made no move to sit up. "I'm not hungry," he replied flatly.

"You need your strength," she insisted gently, placing the tray on a small table beside the bed.

He sighed, turning his gaze back to the window where the drapes stirred ever so slightly with a draft. "Strength for what?" he muttered.

Marta reached out to adjust his pillow, her hand brushing lightly against his shoulder. "For yourself—us—when Hans comes home."

A flicker of emotion crossed his features—hope mingled with resignation. "If he comes home," he whispered.

"He will," she asserted firmly. "We believe that."

On 15 October 1954, a persistent drizzle shrouded the city, the kind that seeped into the very fabric of life. Klaus awoke to the sound of rain tapping against the windowpane, a melancholic rhythm that matched the heaviness in his chest.

He reached for the old photograph that rested on the bedside table—a captured moment from years past. The family gathered beneath a blossoming cherry tree in their former garden. Hans and Frieda stood on either side of him, their youthful faces alight with joy. Marta's smile radiated warmth, her arm entwined with his.

His fingers traced the worn edges, the glossy surface dulled by time. The image blurred as tears welled in his eyes. Memories flooded back—echoes of laughter, the scent of lilacs in spring, the simple pleasures of a life unmarred by the shadows of war and division.

A profound sense of loss engulfed him—not just for the years gone by but for the choices that had led them to this fractured existence. Regrets coiled around his heart like a vice; each beat a reminder of opportunities missed, words unspoken, and forgiveness withheld.

The depressive episode tightened its grip, rendering him motionless. Hours passed unnoticed as he lay adrift in a sea of desolation. Marta's attempts to rouse him went unheeded, her pleas absorbed by the suffocating silence.

Outside, the autumn leaves fell in earnest, carpeting the streets in hues of amber and crimson. The city's pulse continued unabated—vendors huddled under awnings, peddling roasted chestnuts and bratwurst; trams clattered along their routes; church bells tolled the passing hours.

But within the walls of Klaus's room, the world had narrowed to the confines of his own tormented mind.

On 1 November 1954, All Saints' Day cast a solemn mood over Hamburg. Candles flickered in windows, and the faithful made pilgrimages to cemeteries, honouring the departed with flowers and prayers.

Frieda stood in the parlour reviewing documents for an upcoming council meeting. Her career had continued its ascent, yet each achievement felt hollow against the backdrop of her family's disarray.

She approached her father's door hesitantly, pausing before knocking softly. "*Vater,* may I come in?"

A faint rustling signalled his acknowledgement. She entered to find him propped up slightly, eyes distant.

"I wanted to see how you're feeling," she began, forcing a smile.

He regarded her for a moment before speaking. "As well as expected."

Positioned next to the bed, she moved to the armchair for a comfortable seat. "The city is beautiful today," she offered. "The leaves are vibrant, and there's a crispness in the air."

He nodded absently. "Autumn was always your mother's favourite season."

Frieda seized the opening. "Perhaps we could all go for a short walk together and get some fresh air."

He shook his head. "I'm afraid I don't have the strength."

Silence settled between them, heavy with unspoken sentiments.

"*Vater,*" she ventured cautiously, "I've been thinking about Hans."

His eyes flickered with pain. "As have I."

"Maybe we could bring him home," she suggested. "There are organisations that help with reunifications."

He sighed deeply. "It's not that simple. The borders, the politics… it's a different world over there."

"But we can't just give up," she insisted, her voice tinged with desperation.

He met her gaze, his own filled with regret. "I fear I've already failed him. Failed both of you."

She reached out to take his hand, the skin cool and fragile beneath her touch. "It's not too late, *Vater*. We can still make things right."

He withdrew his hand gently. "Some wounds run too deep."

On 15 November 1954, Klaus's condition worsened noticeably. His appetite diminished further, and he spent long hours in a fitful sleep, plagued by nightmares that left him agitated and disoriented.

Marta observed these changes with a mounting alarm. She consulted their family physician, Dr Werner, who advised for a thorough examination. "He needs proper care," the doctor emphasised. The doctor emphasised that we cannot ignore the psychological aspect, although his physical decline concerns us.

Marta broached the subject delicately that evening. "Klaus, I think it's time we had Dr Werner visit."

He bristled. "I don't need a doctor poking and prodding me."

"Please, for my sake," she implored. "I'm worried about you."

He closed his eyes, exhaustion clear in every line of his face. "Very well," he conceded quietly.

On 20 November 1954, Dr Werner arrived, his presence a blend of professional detachment and genuine concern. He conducted a thorough examination, noting Klaus' weakened state and symptoms of depression.

"I recommend a period of rest and observation," he advised. "Perhaps a change of scenery—a stay at a sanatorium might be beneficial."

Klaus reacted with vehemence. "I refuse to let anyone treat me like an invalid and cart me off!"

Marta attempted to soothe him. "It's only a suggestion, darling. We want what's best for you."

He fixed the doctor with a steely gaze. "I appreciate your concern, but I will remain in my home."

Dr Werner exchanged a meaningful glance with Marta before acquiescing. "Very well, but you must take care. Any further decline, and we may have no choice."

On 30 November 1954, the situation reached a crisis point. Marta awoke in the early hours to the sound of a thud. Rushing to Klaus's room, she found him collapsed on the floor beside the bed, his breathing shallow.

"Klaus!" she cried out, kneeling beside him. "Can you hear me?"

His eyes fluttered open briefly, confusion clouding his features. "Marta…" he whispered before slipping back into unconsciousness.

Panic surged through her as she called for Frieda. Together, they lifted him back onto the bed. "We need to get help," Frieda urged, already reaching for the telephone.

Within the hour, Dr Werner arrived, his expression grave as he assessed the situation. "He needs immediate care," he declared. "I'm arranging for him to be admitted to the hospital."

Klaus stirred weakly. "No hospitals," he protested feebly.

Marta brushed his hair back tenderly. "You must, for us. Please."

Defeated, he made no further resistance as they planned. The ambulance arrived swiftly, its siren cutting through the stillness of the night. They loaded Klaus onto the stretcher, and he cast a lingering look at his home—the worn brick façade, the familiar doorway, the window from which he had watched the world pass by.

At the hospital, the sterile environment was a stark contrast to the intimacy of his bedroom. The scent of antiseptic hung heavily in the air, and the soft beeping of machines underscored the clinical atmosphere.

Over the following days, medical professionals conducted tests and administered treatments. But despite the medical attention, Klaus remained withdrawn, his spirit seemingly untethered from his physical form.

On 5 December 1954, Marta sat by his bedside, her hands clasped tightly around his. "Do you remember the day we met?" she asked softly, hoping to rouse him.

A faint smile ghosted across his lips. "At the winter festival," he murmured.

"Yes," she affirmed, her eyes misting. "You offered me a cup of mulled wine to warm my hands."

He opened his eyes slowly; the blue faded but was still piercing. "You were the most beautiful woman I'd ever seen."

She chuckled lightly. "Flatterer."

A moment of silence passed before he spoke again. "I'm sorry, Marta. For everything… the distance I've placed between us… the pain I've caused."

She shook her head gently. "There's nothing to forgive. We've all carried our burdens."

He squeezed her hand weakly. "I wish I could have been stronger. For you, for the children."

"You've done your best," she reassured him. "That's all any of us can do."

On 10 December 1954, Frieda visited, bringing a small bouquet of winter jasmine. The delicate white flowers filled the room with a subtle fragrance, a hint of freshness amidst the sterile surroundings.

"Hello, *Vater*," she greeted, placing the blooms in a vase on the windowsill.

He regarded her with a mixture of affection and sorrow. "You've always been so strong," he observed.

She pulled a chair close to the bed. "I learned from you and *Mutter.*"

He shook his head slightly. "No, you surpassed us both."

She reached out to adjust his blanket. "Rest now. We'll talk more when you're feeling better."

He closed his eyes, a hint of a smile playing on his lips. "Perhaps."

As the days shortened and the chill of winter settled in, Klaus's condition remained precarious. The doctors spoke in cautious tones, their prognosis guarded.

On 20 December 1954, a light snowfall dusted the city, blanketing Hamburg in a serene whiteness. From his hospital window, Klaus watched the flakes drift lazily to the ground, each one unique yet part of a collective whole.

He thought of Hans—wondered if he too was witnessing the snowfall in East Berlin. The divide between them felt insurmountable, yet the shared experience of winter's first touch offered a fleeting connection in that moment.

"Vater?" Frieda's voice pulled him from his reverie.

"Yes, *Liebchen?*" he responded softly.

"There's someone here to see you."

She stepped aside to reveal Greta Schmidt, her expression tentative. *"Herr Engelhardt,"* she greeted, her tone respectful.

He raised an eyebrow. *"Fräulein Schmidt.* To what do I owe this visit?"

"I wanted to offer my regards," she explained. "And to thank you."

He looked puzzled. "Thank me?"

"For Frieda," she elaborated. "Her dedication and integrity are a testament to the values you've instilled."

He glanced at his daughter, a mixture of pride and humility washing over him. "She's her own person," he replied. "But I'm glad if I've had some small influence."

Greta smiled warmly. "I believe you have."

As the month drew to a close, Klaus found himself oscillating between moments of clarity and bouts of exhaustion. On 30 December 1954, he requested a pen and paper.

"I need to write to Hans," he declared with quiet determination.

Marta and Frieda exchanged a hopeful glance. "Would you like us to help?" Frieda offered.

He shook his head. "No, I must do this myself."

For hours, he laboured over the letter, each word chosen with care. The effort drained him, but a sense of purpose sustained his resolve.

"Lieber Hans,

There is much I wish to say, though words seem inadequate…

When he finally sealed the envelope, a weight lifted from his shoulders. "Please see that this reaches him," he entrusted to Marta.

"We will," she promised.

That night, as the city prepared to usher in the new year, Klaus lay in his hospital bed, the distant sounds of celebration muffled by the thick walls. Fireworks painted fleeting patterns across the sky; their brilliance reflected faintly in the windowpanes.

He closed his eyes, the din fading into a gentle hum. In the quiet of his mind, he revisited moments of joy and sorrow, triumph and regret. A life lived in shades of grey, now distilled into fragments of memory.

As midnight approached on 31 December 1954, Klaus felt a profound peace settle over him. The voices of his loved ones echoed softly in his thoughts—Marta's unwavering support, Frieda's indomitable spirit, Hans's earnest idealism.

"Perhaps it's not too late," he whispered into the stillness.

The clock struck twelve, chimes resonating through the halls. A new year dawned, bringing with it the faint promise of reconciliation and the enduring hope that amidst the ruins, something precious could still be salvaged.

Outside, the snow continued to fall, blanketing the world in a pristine silence. And within that quiet, Klaus drifted into a restful sleep, the lines of worry easing from his face as he embraced the uncertainty of tomorrow.

ooo

The morning of 4 January 1955 dawned with pale light filtering through a veil of grey clouds over Hamburg. The city streets, slick with a thin sheen of frost, reflected the muted glow of street lamps flickering in the early morning haze. Snowflakes drifted lazily from the sky, settling on the cobblestones and rooftops like delicate lace. The air was crisp, carrying the scent of pine and the distant echo of church bells tolling the hour.

Frieda Engelhardt stood on the platform of the Hamburg Hauptbahnhof, her breath forming small clouds that dissipated into the cold air. She clutched a worn leather suitcase in one hand; the other buried deep in the pocket of her woollen coat. The journey from Bonn had been long and filled with restless thoughts. As the train had wound its way north on 10 January 1955, she had watched the landscape transform into a winter tableau, the passing fields and villages cloaked in white.

Now, back in her childhood city, a mixture of nostalgia and trepidation settled over her. The familiar sights and sounds stirred memories of simpler times—before the war and the fractures that had split her family and country. She took a deep breath, the cold air filling her lungs, and approached the exit, where a taxi awaited.

"*Zum Schanzenstraße, bitte* (To Schanzenstraße, please)," she instructed the driver, her voice steady despite the flutter of nerves in her stomach.

As the taxi navigated the winding streets, Frieda gazed out the window at the bustling city preparing for Christmas. Twinkling lights and evergreen garlands adorned the shop windows. Children bundled in scarves and hats pressed their noses against the glass panes, eyes wide with wonder at the toys displayed within.

Yet, amid the atmosphere, an undercurrent of solemnity persisted. The scars of war were still clear—buildings bearing the marks of bombings, empty lots where homes once stood. The division of Germany loomed over the nation, a shadow that darkened even the brightest of celebrations.

Arriving at the Engelhardt residence, Frieda paid the driver and stood for a moment before the modest townhouse. The façade was the same, but time had weathered it—the paint peeling slightly, the garden untended. She climbed the steps and knocked softly.

Marta opened the door, her eyes lighting up at the sight of her daughter. "Frieda! You're here," she exclaimed, pulling her into a warm embrace.

"*Mutti,*" Frieda replied, the familiar scent of her mother's lavender soap bringing a rush of comfort.

"Come in, come in. It's freezing out there," Marta urged, ushering her inside. The warmth of the house enveloped Frieda, along with the mingled aromas of cinnamon and freshly baked stollen.

"How is *Vater?*" Frieda asked, shedding her coat and placing her suitcase by the door.

Marta's expression faltered. "He's resting. Some days are better than others."

"I should see him."

"Of course. But perhaps after you've had some tea and settled in."

Frieda acquiesced, following her mother into the kitchen. The room was cosy, illuminated by the soft glow of candles placed along the windowsill.

"I've missed this," Frieda admitted, wrapping her hands around a steaming cup of chamomile tea.

Marta smiled gently. "Home misses you too."

They sat in companionable silence for a moment, the ticking of the wall clock marking the passing seconds.

"Have you heard from Hans?" Frieda ventured cautiously.

Marta's eyes clouded. "Not recently. The letters have become less frequent."

Frieda sighed. "I wish he could be here."

"As do I," Marta agreed softly. "But circumstances…"

"I know," Frieda interrupted, her tone edged with frustration. "But perhaps we could find a way."

Marta reached across the table to squeeze her hand. "Let's focus on the time we have together now."

Over the next few days, Frieda settled into the rhythms of the household. On 15 January 1955, she ventured into the city to purchase necessities. The Weihnachtsmarkt at Rathausmarkt was in full swing. Stalls offered an array of handcrafted goods—wooden toys, intricate lacework, delicate glass ornaments.

Frieda selected a carved figurine for her father, reminiscent of the ones he had admired in years past. For her mother, she chose a finely embroidered handkerchief, its edges adorned with tiny bluebells. As she perused the stalls, she couldn't help but think of Hans—what might bring a smile to his face. Was he here?

She purchased a small leather-bound journal, the pages blank and waiting to be filled. Perhaps, she mused, he might return one day, and they could share stories again.

Returning home, she found Klaus awake and sitting by the window, a blanket draped over his lap. His gaze was distant, fixed on the snowflakes that drifted lazily outside.

"*Vater,*" she greeted softly.

He turned slowly, a faint smile tugging at the corners of his mouth. "Frieda. It's good to see you."

She sat beside him, the warmth of his presence a balm to her weary soul. "I brought you something," she said, presenting the figurine.

His eyes lit up with a spark of genuine delight. "Ah, just like the ones from the Black Forest."

She nodded. "I thought it might remind you of happier times."

He ran his fingers over the smooth wood, tracing the intricate details. "Thank you, *Liebchen.*"

They sat in silence for a while, the quiet punctuated by the mantel clock's soft ticking and the city's distant hum.

"Do you remember when we used to go ice skating on the Alster?" he asked suddenly.

Frieda smiled wistfully. "Of course. Hans always insisted he could skate faster than anyone."

Klaus chuckled, a deep sound that seemed to stir memories long buried. "He had such spirit."

"Still does, I imagine," she replied, her tone tinged with longing.

Klaus's expression grew sombre. "I wish things were different."

"As do I," she agreed. "Perhaps, in time, they can be."

He sighed heavily. "Time… it's slipping away from me."

"Don't say that," she admonished gently.

"It's the truth," he insisted. "There are things I've left undone, words unsaid."

"Then say them," she urged. "It's not too late."

He looked at her with a mixture of hope and despair. "Do you think Hans would forgive me?"

She placed a reassuring hand on his. "I believe he would want to. We all carry burdens, *Vater.* But forgiveness is the first step towards healing."

On 20 January 1955, the Engelhardt home was quiet, the usual bustle subdued. The day of the reunion had arrived, yet Hans was absent. His empty chair at the dining table was a stark reminder of the spaces that separated them—a chasm of distance and political ideology.

Marta had prepared a modest meal—a roast chicken, potatoes, and red cabbage—recipes passed down through generations. The aroma filled the house, but we felt less excited about sharing the meal as usual.

As they sat down to eat, Klaus raised a glass of wine shakily. "To family," he toasted weakly. "May we find our way back to one another."

"To family," Frieda and Marta echoed, clinking their glasses softly.

The conversation was stilted, each mindful of the unspoken tensions. Frieda cleared her throat. "I received a letter from the Bundestag," she began hesitantly. "They're considering my proposal for educational reform."

"That's wonderful news," Marta responded warmly. "You've worked so hard."

Klaus nodded appreciatively. "Education is the cornerstone of our future."

Frieda smiled modestly. "I hope it will make a difference."

Silence settled again, the clink of cutlery against plates the only sound.

"I wish Hans could be here," Frieda ventured. "Perhaps we could try contacting him again."

Marta glanced at Klaus before replying. "I've written to him, but there's been no response."

"Maybe if I reached out," Frieda suggested. "I could go to Berlin."

Klaus' eyes flashed with concern. "It's too dangerous. The Stasi…"

"I'm aware of the risks," she interrupted firmly. "But he's our family."

Marta placed a calming hand on her arm. "We must be cautious."

As Frieda questioned, frustration bubbled up, and she wondered, "Should we exercise caution while our family is trapped behind a wall of oppression?"

Klaus's voice was barely above a whisper. "We all made choices."

"Choices influenced by circumstances beyond our control," she countered. "We can't abandon him."

Marta's gaze softened. "We haven't abandoned him, Frieda. We're doing what we can."

Frieda pushed back her chair abruptly, the legs scraping against the wooden floor. "It's not enough."

She left the table, retreating to the sanctuary of her childhood bedroom. The familiar surroundings offered little comfort—posters of literary figures adorned the walls, and books lined the shelves, their spines worn from years of use. She sank onto the bed, emotions swirling.

A soft knock interrupted her thoughts. "May I come in?" Marta's voice was gentle.

"Yes," Frieda replied, her tone resigned.

Marta entered, closing the door quietly behind her. "I know this is difficult."

Frieda looked up, eyes glistening. "I feel so helpless."

"We all do," Marta admitted, sitting beside her. "But we mustn't let despair consume us."

"I just want us to be a family again," Frieda whispered.

Marta wrapped an arm around her shoulders. "So do I. More than anything."

They sat together in shared silence, the weight of unspoken fears heavy between them.

On the evening of 23 January 1955, Hamburg was cast in a serene glow. Snow blanketed the city, muffled the usual sounds and transformed the landscape into a scene from a fairy tale.

Klaus sat in his armchair by the fireplace, the warmth easing the chill that had settled into his bones.

As evening fell, they gathered around the tree. Marta lit the candles carefully, their flickering flames casting a gentle glow.

"Shall we sing?" she suggested.

Frieda nodded, her voice joining her mother's in a harmonious rendition of a popular jazz tune from America that had been a constant on the radio—the familiar melody wrapped around them, a momentary balm to their aching hearts.

They sat together, the silence comfortable for once. Outside, the snow continued to fall, the world beyond their walls hushed and still.

"Tell me about your work," Klaus prompted. "I want to hear more."

Frieda hesitated before describing her recent projects, which involved advocating for educational reform, promoting cultural initiatives, and striving to bridge societal divides.

Klaus listened attentively, nodding thoughtfully. "You're making a difference," he observed. "I'm proud of you."

Her heart swelled at the affirmation. "Thank you, *Vater.*"

Marta leaned forward. "And perhaps, one day, these efforts will help reunite our country."

"That's my hope," Frieda agreed. "That we can heal the wounds and move forward together."

Klaus's gaze drifted to the window, where snowflakes clung to the glass. "I fear I may not see that day."

"Don't say that," Marta chided gently.

He shook his head. "It's all right. I've made peace with it."

Frieda reached out to take his hand. "We're here now. That's what matters."

He squeezed her hand weakly. "Yes. And for that, I'm grateful."

On 31 January 1955, the family gathered once more. They all understood that these get-togethers, as they knew them, may be coming to an end, which tinged the atmosphere with melancholy.

They shared a simple meal, reminiscing about times past. Laughter mingled with tears as they recounted stories of childhood antics and cherished moments.

As midnight approached, they stood by the window, watching snow bluster over the city skyline. Its softening beauty in the night sky, their reflections shimmering in the harbour below.

At that moment, despite the shadows of division and the weight of unresolved conflicts, they found solace in each other's presence. The future remained uncertain, but the bonds of the family offered a beacon of hope amidst the darkness.

The city settled into quiet, Frieda helped her father back to his room. He paused at the doorway, turning to face her.

"Frieda," he began hesitantly. "I want you to know… I'm sorry. For everything."

She felt a lump rise in her throat. "You don't have to apologise."

"But I do," he insisted. "I allowed pride and bitterness to cloud my judgment. I pushed you and Hans away when I should have held you closer."

She swallowed hard. "We all made mistakes."

He reached out to touch her cheek gently. "You've become a remarkable woman. I couldn't ask for a better daughter."

Tears welled in her eyes. "Thank you, Vater."

He offered a faint smile. "Perhaps, one day, you'll forgive an old man's failings."

"I already have," she assured him, her voice breaking.

He nodded slowly. "That brings me peace."

She helped him into bed, pulling the blankets up to his chin. "Rest now. I'll be here in the morning."

He closed his eyes, his breathing steadying. *"Gute Nacht, Liebchen* (Good night, sweetheart)."

"Goodnight," she whispered, turning off the lamp.

As she returned to her own room, Frieda felt a mixture of sorrow and relief. Despite the challenges ahead, they had successfully sown the seeds of reconciliation.

In the quiet hours of the new year, the Engelhardt household settled into a fragile peace. The snow outside continued to fall softly, blanketing the city in a pristine layer of white.

Frieda stood by the window, gazing out at the tranquil scene. She thought of Hans, somewhere beyond the divide, and sent a silent wish into the night—that he might feel the warmth of their family's love, even across the distance that separated them.

The clock chimed softly, marking the passing of time. With a resolute breath, she turned away from the window, determined to carry forward the legacy of hope and unity that her family so desperately needed.

1955 had great potential, but the story of the Engelhardts—and of a nation seeking to heal—was far from over.

ooo

The chill of February settled over Hamburg like a thick blanket, muffling the city's usual hum. On 2 February 1955, frost etched the usual intricate patterns on the windowpanes of the Engelhardt home, delicate webs that caught the pale morning light caused by condensation and cold air. Inside, the air was heavy with a quiet expectancy, each family member acutely aware of the sands slipping through the hourglass of Klaus's life.

Klaus lay in his dimly lit bedroom, the once robust lines of his face softened by the shadows. The faint curtains rustling disturbed the stillness as a draught found its way through the old house. His breaths were shallow, each inhalation a visible effort that raised the thin blankets ever so slightly. The scent of beeswax and lavender lingered, remnants of Marta's diligent care.

On 6 February, Frieda, having taken some time off work to help care for her father, sat by his bedside, her fingers entwined with his. *"Vater,"* she whispered, "can I get you anything?"

He opened his eyes slowly; the once vivid blue now faded like a well-worn tapestry. "No, *Liebchen,*" he replied softly. "Your company is all I need."

She offered a faint smile though worry knitted her brow. The silence between them was both comforting and heavy, filled with unspoken words and lingering regrets.

On 16 February, Marta prepared a modest meal in the kitchen, the aroma of *kartoffelsuppe* filling the house. She moved with purpose, her hands steady despite the weight on her heart. The radio played softly in the background, a broadcast that echoed faintly through the corridors.

Frieda joined her, rolling up her sleeves. "Let me help, *Mutti,*" she offered.

Marta glanced at her daughter, a flicker of gratitude in her eyes. "Thank you, dear. Could you slice the bread?"

As they worked side by side, the familiar rhythms of domesticity provided a brief respite from their concerns. "Have you thought any more about contacting Hans?" Frieda ventured cautiously.

Marta sighed, her knife stilling on the cutting board. "Every day," she admitted. "But the letters… they go unanswered."

Frieda nodded solemnly. "Perhaps he's unable to respond."

"Perhaps," Marta echoed, though doubt lingered in her tone. "I pray that he's safe."

On 20 February 1955, a letter arrived, bearing the East German postmark. Frieda retrieved it from the mailbox, her heart quickening as she recognised Hans's handwriting. She hurried inside, calling out, *"Mutti!* A letter from Hans!"

Marta emerged from Klaus's room, hope lighting her features. "Let me see."

They unfolded the paper together, eyes scanning the carefully penned words.

Liebe Familie,

I hope this finds you well. I regret I cannot be with you during this time…

As they read, it became clear that Hans was unable—or perhaps unwilling—to return home. His words were cautious, veiled references to restrictions and obligations that prevented his departure from the GDR.

"He mentions *Vater*," Frieda noted, her voice tight. "He sends his love."

Marta pressed the letter to her chest. "At least we know he's alive."

Frieda's jaw clenched. "It's not enough."

Klaus requested to be moved to the living room, his frail form bundled in blankets as he reclined on the couch. The warmth of the fireplace bathed the room in a golden hue, shadows flickering across the walls.

Marta placed a tray of biscuits and spiced tea on the table.

Klaus reached for Frieda's hand. "I need to say something," he whispered, his gaze earnest.

She squeezed his hand lightly. "I'm listening, Vater."

He swallowed with difficulty. "I've carried the weight of my mistakes for so long. I fear it's too late to make amends."

"Don't say that," she urged softly. "It's never too late."

He shook his head slowly. "Pride and bitterness blinded me. I pushed you and Hans away when I should have held you close."

Tears brimmed in Frieda's eyes. "We all did what we thought was best."

He looked at her intently. "Can you forgive an old man for his failings?"

She leaned forward, pressing a gentle kiss to his forehead. "I forgave you long ago."

Emotion flickered across his face—relief, gratitude, a hint of peace. "Thank you," he murmured.

They shared a simple meal, the conversation interspersed with moments of quiet reflection. Hans's absence was a palpable void, yet his letter provided a thread of connection that they clung to.

As the afternoon waned into evening, Klaus grew increasingly fatigued. Marta helped him back to his room, settling him comfortably amidst the pillows.

"Rest now," she whispered, brushing a stray lock of hair from his forehead.

He caught her hand, his grip surprisingly firm. "Marta, you've been my anchor through it all. I don't deserve you."

She blinked back tears. "Hush. None of that."

"It's true," he insisted. "You've shown me grace beyond measure."

She pressed her lips together, emotion threatening to overwhelm her. "We made a vow—in sickness and in health."

He closed his eyes briefly. "I wish I could have been a better husband and father."

"You've done the best you could," she assured him.

On 28 February, the reality of daily life continued for many. For the Engelhardts, time seemed to slow, each day marked by Klaus's diminishing strength.

Frieda sat by the window, watching as neighbours went about their routines. Children built snowmen in the courtyard, their laughter a distant melody. She felt a profound sense of isolation, the weight of her responsibilities pressing heavily upon her.

Marta joined her, placing a comforting hand on her shoulder. "You should return to your work soon," she suggested gently.

Frieda shook her head. "Not yet. I need to be here."

"They'll understand," Marta conceded. "But don't neglect your own life."

Frieda turned to face her mother. "How can I think of anything else when *Vater* is like this?"

Marta's gaze was steady. "Because life continues, even amid sorrow."

On 2 March, a quiet settled over the Engelhardt home. The clock on the mantelpiece ticked steadily, its hands inching towards the unknown. Klaus lay in the living room, his breaths shallow but peaceful.

Marta and Frieda sat nearby, the glow of candlelight illuminating their faces. They spoke in hushed tones, reminiscing about happier times.

"Remember when we visited the Baltic Sea?" Frieda recalled softly. "Hans got so sunburnt, he could hardly move."

Marta chuckled lightly. "And your father insisted on teaching us all to sail."

"He capsized the boat," Frieda added with a smile.

Klaus stirred slightly, his eyes opening to slits. "I heard that," he murmured.

They leaned closer. "We thought you were asleep," Marta whispered.

He offered a faint grin. "Not yet."

Frieda took his hand. "How are you feeling?"

"Weary," he admitted. "But content."

They sat in companionable silence as the minutes ticked by.

Klaus's grip on Frieda's hand slackened. His eyes closed softly, a serene expression settling over his features.

Marta sensed the change, her breath catching in her throat. "Klaus?"

There was no response. His chest rose once more, then fell still.

Frieda felt a surge of emotion—grief, relief, love—all intertwining. "He's gone," she whispered.

Marta nodded slowly, tears slipping down her cheeks. "At peace now."

They remained by his side, the candles burning low as the world outside celebrated new beginnings.

On 5 March 1955, dawn broke with a muted light, and the sky was overcast. They quickly organised the funeral, ensuring it was an intimate gathering that matched Klaus's quiet departure.

A thin layer of snow blanketed the ground at the cemetery, crunching softly beneath their feet. A small group of close friends and relatives assembled, their breath visible in the cold air.

Frieda stood beside her mother, their black coats stark against the white landscape. She scanned the faces of those present, her heart skipping as she recognised a familiar figure standing apart from the crowd.

Hans.

He met her gaze, myriad emotions flickering across his features—sorrow, hesitation, a glimmer of longing.

She made her way towards him, each step feeling both heavy and urgent. "Hans," she breathed as she reached him.

"Frieda," he replied, his voice laden with weariness.

They stood facing each other, the years of separation clear in the lines etched upon their faces. "You came," she said, a statement infused with both surprise and gratitude.

"I had to," he replied simply. "Despite everything."

She glanced back at Marta, who watched them with a hopeful expression. "*Mutti* will be glad to see you."

Hans hesitated. "I can't stay long. It wasn't easy to get permission to cross over."

"I understand," she acknowledged, a pang of disappointment piercing her. "But thank you for coming."

They returned to the graveside as the service began. The minister spoke solemn words, his voice carrying over the silent crowd, as he honoured Klaus Engelhardt, a man of complexity and depth.

As the coffin descended into the ground, Marta clutched a handkerchief to her lips, stifling a sob. Frieda wrapped an arm around her, offering support.

Hans stood a few paces away, his posture rigid. When the ceremony concluded, he approached their mother cautiously. "Mutti," he greeted softly.

Marta turned to him, tears shimmering in her eyes. "Hans," she whispered, pulling him into an embrace.

He stiffened momentarily before relaxing into her arms. "I'm sorry," he murmured.

She drew back, studying his face. "Your father would be glad you're here."

He glanced at the freshly turned earth. "I hope so."

Frieda joined them, the three standing together in a fragile reunion. "Perhaps we can stay in touch," she suggested tentatively.

Hans shook his head regretfully. "It's complicated."

"It doesn't have to be," she insisted gently. "We're family."

He sighed. "The world makes it so."

Marta placed a hand on his cheek. "Promise you'll try."

He nodded slowly. "I will."

As the gathering dispersed, Hans prepared to depart. "I have to go," he said, reluctance clear in his tone.

Frieda reached into her pocket, producing the leather-bound journal she had purchased months before. "Take this," she offered. "Write to us when you can."

He accepted it, a hint of a smile touching his lips. "Thank you."

They watched him walk away, his figure receding into the grey morning light. The weight of his absence settled upon them once more.

Back at the house, the silence was profound. Klaus's space felt vast and empty. Marta busied herself with tidying, her movements deliberate.

Frieda stood by the window, gazing out at the snow-covered street. The world continued, indifferent to their personal sorrows.

"Mutti," she called softly.

Marta looked up. "Yes, dear?"

"I think it's time I returned to Bonn."

Marta paused, considering. "I guess it is."

Frieda reassured her she would come back soon. "I don't want you to be alone."

Marta offered a faint smile. "I'll be all right. This house holds many memories. It's comforting, in a way."

Frieda crossed the room to embrace her. "We'll get through this," she promised.

"Yes," Marta agreed. "We will."

On 5 January 1955, Frieda boarded the train back to Bonn. As the landscape unfolded outside the window—fields blanketed in snow, villages nestled among frost-laden trees—she reflected on the events of the past weeks.

Klaus's death marked the end of a chapter, both personally and for the family. The divisions that plagued them mirrored those of their country—a nation split by ideology and history yet bound by shared heritage.

She resolved to continue her work with renewed vigour, striving for reconciliation and understanding. The path ahead was uncertain, but the foundations laid by confronting the past offered a glimmer of hope.

Frieda closed her eyes as the train chugged steadily southward, the rhythmic motion lulling her into a contemplative state. She thought of Hans, of the brief but meaningful connection they had forged at the funeral.

Perhaps, in time, someone could bridge the distances.

Back in Hamburg, Marta sat alone in the quiet house. The clock's ticking was a familiar companion, its steady rhythm a reminder that life moved forward.

She glanced at the photograph on the mantelpiece—a family portrait taken years before, all four of them smiling in the summer sun. Running a finger over the glass, she allowed herself a moment of melancholy before squaring her shoulders.

There was much to be done, and she intended to honour Klaus's memory by embracing the future with grace.

The Engelhardt family's journey was far from over. Though marked by loss and division, the seeds of healing had been sowed. In a country striving to rebuild from the ruins, they embodied the struggles and the resilience of a generation seeking to redefine itself.

As spring gradually took hold, the promise of renewal lingered in the air—a subtle whisper that, amidst the echoes of the past, new beginnings were possible.

NINE:

A NEW GERMANY

A brisk wind swept through the streets of Hamburg on 1 May 1955, carrying with it the fresh scent of the Elbe River mingled with the earthy aroma of blooming linden trees. The city was alive with anticipation, its people bustling like bees in a hive as preparations for West Germany's accession to NATO reached a fever pitch. Black, red, and gold banners fluttered from windows and lampposts, their colours vivid against the clear azure sky.

Frieda Engelhardt stood at the edge of Hamburg's central square, observing the organised chaos unfolding before her. Stalls were erected along the cobblestone paths, vendors arranging displays of bratwurst, pretzels, and steaming mugs of *glühwein*. Wooden beams clattered, voices murmured, and occasional bursts of laughter filled the air.

"*Frau Engelhardt,* the podium is ready for inspection," a junior assistant informed her, adjusting his spectacles nervously.

"*Vielen Dank, Peter,*" Frieda replied, offering a reassuring smile. Clad in a tailored navy suit, she exuded an air of quiet confidence. She neatly pinned back her auburn hair, with a few wisps escaping to frame her face. The excitement of the upcoming ceremony shimmered in her green eyes, though a shadow of weariness lingered—residue from weeks of relentless planning.

As she crossed the square, her heels clicking softly against the stones, she couldn't help but feel a swell of pride. This moment symbolised not just a political alliance but a definitive step towards stability and recognition on the world stage. West Germany was emerging from the ruins, reclaiming its place with dignity and democratic resolve.

On 10 May 1955, the last rehearsals were underway. Children from local schools practised songs, their high voices rising in harmony. Soldiers in crisp uniforms conducted drills, the rhythmic stamping of boots echoing through the square. Frieda oversaw each detail with meticulous care, her notepad filled with checklists and last-minute adjustments.

"Are the translators prepared for the international delegates?" she inquired of her colleague, Stefan Weber.

"*Jawohl,* everything is in order," he assured her, his moustache twitching as he spoke. "We have French, English, and Russian interpreters on standby."

"Excellent," she nodded. "And the security measures?"

"Heightened, as per protocol. The *Bundespolizei* are coordinating with military officials."

Frieda allowed herself a moment of satisfaction. Years of dedication to public service were culminating in this historic event. Yet beneath her professional poise, an undercurrent of melancholy persisted. The recent loss of her father, Klaus, weighed heavily upon her. His absence was a silent void, a shadow cast over the brightness of the occasion.

On 15 May 1955, the day of the ceremony, a golden sunrise bathed Hamburg in warm hues. The city seemed to hold its breath in anticipation. Frieda arrived at the square early, the crisp morning air invigorating her senses. She watched as the seats filled, dignitaries mingling with citizens, the atmosphere charged with optimism.

Taking her place on the podium, she surveyed the crowd. Faces were upturned, and eyes shined with hope. The German flag billowed gently behind her, its colours vivid against the backdrop of the Rathaus. She adjusted the microphone, her fingers brushing against the cold metal.

"*Meine Damen und Herren,*" she began, her voice clear and resonant. "Today, we stand at the threshold of a new chapter in our nation's history."

She spoke of resilience and renewal, weaving her words into a tapestry of shared struggle and collective aspiration. As she addressed the importance of unity and cooperation, her gaze drifted momentarily towards the horizon, where the spires of old churches pierced the sky—a reminder of the past's enduring presence.

"Our membership in NATO signifies not only an alliance but a commitment to peace and democratic values," she continued. "Let us move forward together, forging a future that honours the lessons of our history while embracing the possibilities ahead."

Applause erupted as she concluded; a wave of sound washed over the square. Frieda stepped back, allowing the next speaker to take the stage. She felt a mixture of exhilaration and relief, her heart pounding with the realisation of what they had achieved.

Throughout the day, the celebrations unfolded with vibrant energy. Bands played lively tunes, their melodies weaving through the air. Traditional dancers in colourful costumes performed folk routines, their movements graceful and spirited. The scent of grilled sausages and sweet pastries enticed passersby while artisans displayed handcrafted wares—intricate wood carvings, delicate lacework, and gleaming ceramics.

Frieda wandered among the stalls, accepting a warm pretzel from an elderly vendor who winked conspiratorially. "A little sustenance for our hardworking organiser," he chuckled.

"Danke schön, " she replied, tearing off a piece and savouring the buttery flavour. The simple pleasure brought a smile to her lips.

As evening descended on 15 May 1955, the square transformed under the glow of lanterns and fairy lights. Fireworks burst overhead, painting the night sky with brilliant colours. Frieda stood with her colleagues, their faces illuminated by the cascading sparks.

"It's quite a sight," Stefan remarked, his gaze fixed upwards.

"Indeed," she agreed softly. Yet, even amidst the splendour, she felt a pang of emptiness. She wished her father could have witnessed this moment and shared in the pride of their nation's progress.

On 20 May 1955, Frieda returned to the family home, a modest brick house nestled on a quiet street. The garden was in full bloom, lilacs and roses perfuming the air. She found her mother, Marta, tending to the flowerbeds, her hands clad in soil-stained gloves.

"Mutti," Frieda called, approaching with a wave.

Marta looked up, her face lighting up. "Frieda! What a lovely surprise." She wiped her brow, leaving a smudge of dirt.

"You have a green thumb as always," Frieda observed, admiring the vibrant blossoms.

"It keeps me busy," Marta shrugged. "Come inside. I'll make us some tea."

In the cosy kitchen, the kettle whistled merrily on the stove. The walls displayed framed photographs, which captured snapshots of family vacations and candid moments frozen in time. Frieda's gaze lingered on a picture of Klaus, his stern features softened by a rare smile as he held a young Hans on his shoulders.

"He would be proud of you," Marta said gently, following her daughter's line of sight.

Frieda sighed, her shoulders slumping slightly. "I hope so. I wish he could have been there."

"He is there, in a way," Marta assured her, placing a comforting hand over hers. "In your dedication, your passion. You carry his legacy forward."

They sipped their tea in companionable silence. The ticking of the cuckoo clock punctuated the quiet, its rhythmic cadence soothing.

"Have you heard from Hans?" Marta ventured cautiously.

Frieda shook her head. "No. Communication is… difficult." She hesitated. "Sometimes I wonder if he even receives my letters."

Marta acknowledged the complications of the situation over there, and concern and resignation were reflected in her eyes.

"I worry about him," Frieda confessed. "About the choices he's had to make."

"We all carry our burdens," Marta mused. "But we must have faith that he will find his way."

On 25 May 1955, Frieda visited her father's grave. The cemetery lay on the city's outskirts, a peaceful expanse where the hustle of urban life faded into a serene backdrop of whispering trees and weathered stone.

The trees cast a shadow as she walked along the winding path, with the gravel crunching softly underfoot. Wildflowers dotted the grass, their petals swaying gently in the breeze. She reached Klaus's headstone—a simple marker etched with his name and dates, a modest tribute to a complex man.

Kneeling, she traced the engraved letters with her fingertips. The cold granite sent a shiver through her, the physical sensation grounding her swirling thoughts. *"Hallo, Vater,"* she whispered, her voice barely audible.

The wind rustled the leaves overhead, a soft susurration that seemed to echo her unspoken words. She closed her eyes, allowing memories to wash over her—snippets of laughter, stern lectures, moments of unexpected tenderness.

"I wish you could see what we've accomplished," she murmured. "West Germany is rebuilding, stronger than before. But there's still so much work to do."

A distant church bell chimed the hour, the sound carrying across the quiet landscape. Frieda pulled her coat tighter against the chill, the fabric rough against her skin.

"I miss you," she admitted, her gaze fixed on the horizon where grey clouds gathered. "Despite everything, I hope you found peace."

As she stood to leave, a movement caught her eye—a figure approaching along the path. Squinting, she recognised Greta Schmidt, her old friend and steadfast journalist. Greta Schmidt had her blonde hair tucked under a woollen hat, and the cold had caused her cheeks to become flushed.

"Frieda," Greta greeted warmly. "I thought I might find you here."

"Greta! What brings you to Hamburg?" Frieda asked, surprised but pleased.

"I'm covering the NATO accession, of course," Greta replied with a wry smile. "Couldn't miss such a significant event."

"Of course," Frieda laughed lightly. "How have you been?"

They walked together, leaving the cemetery behind as they headed towards the city centre. Greta regaled her with tales of investigative reporting, her eyes alight with passion. "There's still so much to uncover," she insisted. "So many stories that need to be told."

"I admire your tenacity," Frieda remarked sincerely. "Your work is vital."

"And yours," Greta countered. "You've become quite the influential figure."

Frieda waved off the compliment modestly. "I'm just one piece of a larger puzzle."

"Don't underestimate your impact," Greta chided gently. "You have a voice that people listen to."

As they parted ways, Frieda felt a renewed sense of purpose. The conversations with Marta and Greta had reinforced her resolve. There were challenges ahead, but also opportunities to effect meaningful change.

On 31 May 1955, the month drew to a close with a brilliant sunset that painted the sky in hues of amber and rose. Frieda stood on the balcony of her apartment overlooking the bustling streets below. The city was alive—cafés filled with patrons, musicians playing on street corners, families strolling arm in arm.

She thought of Hans, wondering where he was at that moment. Was he safe? Did he think of home? The division between East and West seemed an insurmountable chasm, yet she refused to relinquish hope.

Re-entering her living room, she sat at her desk and pulled out a sheet of stationery. Dipping her pen into the inkwell, she wrote.

Lieber Hans,

I hope this letter finds you well. So much has happened here in Hamburg…

She detailed the NATO celebrations, the city's vibrant resurgence, and shared personal reflections. Folding the letter carefully, she placed it in an envelope, addressing it with meticulous script.

"Perhaps this time," she mused aloud, "it will reach him."

As she prepared for bed, Frieda glanced at the photograph on her bedside table—a snapshot of her and Hans as children, grinning mischievously at the camera. She traced their faces with her fingertip, a tender smile touching her lips.

"Goodnight, little brother," she whispered.

The gentle hum of the city lulled her into a restful sleep—dreams filled with visions of unity and reconciliation.

The dawn of 1 June 1955 brought a renewed sense of determination. Frieda rose early, the first light of day casting a soft glow through the curtains. The air was fresh, carrying the scent of possibility.

She dressed swiftly, donning a crisp blouse and skirt. There was much to be done—meetings to attend, initiatives to plan. As she stepped out into the morning sun, she lifted her chin, embracing the challenges ahead.

"Für eine bessere Zukunft (For a better future)," she murmured to herself. For a better future.

Hamburg bustled around her, a city in motion, its people moving forward despite the scars of the past. Frieda joined the flow, one individual among many, each contributing to the mosaic of their shared destiny.

The path was hard, and the wounds were deep. But with every step, Frieda carried her family's legacy—the lessons of love, loss, and resilience— guiding her towards a horizon tinged with hope.

ooo

The first of June 1955 dawned on East Berlin with a hazy sun struggling to pierce through the blanket of smog that hung low over the city. Hans Engelhardt stood by his apartment window, the glass fogged by his breath as he gazed out onto the grey streets below. The distant clatter of a tram echoed through the oppressive silence, and the scent of coal smoke mingled with the faint aroma of freshly baked *schwarzbrot* from the bakery across the street.

Hans rubbed his temples, the weight of exhaustion pressing heavily upon him. Despite the early hour, the summer heat was already seeping into his small apartment, turning it into a stifling box. He loosened his tie, the fabric rough against his skin, and prepared himself for another day entrenched within the socialist government's labyrinth.

By 10 June 1955, the city was sweltering under an unrelenting sun. The tall, austere buildings of East Berlin seemed to absorb and radiate the heat, amplifying the discomfort of those who walked beneath their shadows. Hans navigated the crowded pavements, the murmurs of the people blending into a monotonous hum. Posters adorned the walls, and bold proclamations of the GDR's achievements were emblazoned in stark reds and blacks. "Der Sozialismus siegt!" they declared. Socialism prevails.

Entering the government building where he worked, Hans was greeted by the familiar sterility of its corridors. The floors gleamed unnaturally under harsh fluorescent lights, and the air was thick with the scent of disinfectant. His office was a cramped space shared with two other officials; each desk was piled high with paperwork demanding attention.

"Morning, Hans," muttered Karl, barely glancing up from his typewriter.

"Morning," Hans replied, sliding into his chair. The keys of his own typewriter clacked rhythmically as he began transcribing the latest party directives. The words flowed mechanically—quotas to meet, behaviours to monitor, loyalties to affirm.

On 20 June 1955, a memo was circulated announcing a mandatory party meeting scheduled for 10 July. Whispers rippled through the office, colleagues exchanging wary glances.

"Another lecture on ideological purity, no doubt," sighed Ingrid, her fingers nervously twisting a loose thread on her sleeve.

Hans nodded absently. "They seem to think repetition breeds conviction."

That evening, Hans returned to his apartment, the oppressive heat lingering even as the sun dipped below the horizon. He peeled off his damp shirt, the fabric clinging stubbornly to his back. The radio crackled in the corner, broadcasting a monotonous speech by Walter Ulbricht. Hans tuned it out, his thoughts drifting to memories of his father.

Klaus had been a man of firm convictions, though they had often clashed with Hans's own.

On 1 July 1955, Hans received a letter from Frieda. Her handwriting was elegant yet urgent; the ink smudged slightly as though written in haste.

Lieber Hans,

I hope this letter finds you well. West Germany has joined NATO, which is a significant step for our country. I wish we could discuss these changes together…

He folded the letter carefully, a knot tightening in his chest. The chasm between them seemed wider than ever, their worlds drifting further apart with each passing day.

The organisers held the mandatory party meeting on 10 July 1955 in a cavernous hall, where the attendees felt a collective unease in the thick air. Rows of wooden chairs faced a raised platform draped in crimson banners bearing the hammer and compass emblem of the GDR. Hans sat towards the back, the hard seat digging into his spine.

A senior official took the podium, his voice sharp and commanding. "Comrades, our vigilance against subversion must be unwavering. The imperialist forces of the West grow bolder, and we must fortify our ideological defences."

Applause punctuated his statements at prescribed intervals. Hans joined in mechanically, his palms meeting without enthusiasm. The rhetoric washed over him, a familiar tide of grandiose claims and veiled threats.

As the meeting progressed, a young man was called to the front. "Comrade Fischer," the official intoned, "has shown exemplary dedication to our cause. Let his commitment serve as a model for all."

Hans recognised the man—an eager and earnest addition to their department. The applause swelled, yet Hans felt a pang of discomfort. The overt praise felt orchestrated, a display designed to mask underlying insecurities within the regime.

After the meeting adjourned, Hans lingered outside the hall. The evening air offered little relief from the day's heat, but he welcomed the open sky above. Ernst approached, lighting a cigarette with a practised flick.

"Another performance for the masses," Ernst remarked, exhaling a plume of smoke.

Hans glanced at him warily. "Careful with such talk."

Ernst shrugged. "We're all thinking it. Doesn't make a difference."

Hans fell silent, the weight of unspoken dissent heavy between them.

By 25 July 1955, the oppressive atmosphere in East Berlin had intensified. Reports of increased Stasi activity circulated quietly, citizens casting furtive glances over their shoulders. The ever-present sense of surveillance gnawed at Hans's nerves.

On 1 August 1955, a colleague and friend, Dieter Wagner, failed to arrive at work. Whispers suggested authorities detained him for "questioning." Hans felt a chill run down his spine. Dieter was a mild-mannered man; his only fault was perhaps being too outspoken in private conversations.

On 5 August 1955, the official news broadcast announced that Dieter had been found guilty of "anti-state activities." The charges were vague, and the punishment severe. Hans stared at the grainy photograph displayed on the television screen, Dieter's eyes lifeless, and resigned.

The following day, 6 August 1955, Hans sat alone in his apartment, the curtains drawn against the harsh sunlight. He poured himself a measure of schnapps, the sharp liquor burning his throat—memories of Dieter's laughter, their shared jokes, now tainted by fear.

On 10 August 1955, he attended a gathering at a colleague's home—a modest affair, the conversation stilted. The topic of Dieter's fate hung unspoken in the air. Ingrid broke the silence. "We must be cautious," she whispered, her eyes darting nervously. "They are watching us all."

Hans felt a surge of anger. "Is this what we've become? Afraid to even speak?"

"Lower your voice," Ernst hissed. "Do you want to end up like Dieter?"

Hans clenched his fists, the reality of their situation pressing on. The ideals that had once inspired him now felt hollow, betrayed by the very system that professed them.

On 15 August 1955, the Stasi orchestrated a public reprimand of Dieter, broadcasting a forced confession nationwide. Hans watched in horror as his friend's image flickered on the screen, eyes vacant, words devoid of spirit.

"This is a warning to all who would oppose our socialist paradise," the announcer declared sternly.

Hans turned off the television, his hands trembling. The façade had crumbled entirely. The regime's brutality exposed, causing any remnants of Hans' faith in their cause to disintegrate.

That night, the oppressive heat gave way to a sudden thunderstorm. Rain battered against the windows, and the sound was a relentless drumbeat. Hans stood on his balcony, the cool droplets soaking his clothes. Lightning illuminated the stark cityscape, the shadows of watchtowers and barbed wire momentarily stark against the sky.

On 20 August 1955, Hans received another letter from Frieda. In her words, Frieda expressed concern and a longing for connection.

Dear Hans,

I think of you often. Although our lives have taken such different paths, I hope that we might find common ground…

He traced the lines of her script, a sense of isolation enveloping him. The possibility of defection took root—a seed of thought that both frightened and enticed him.

On 25 August 1955, he scheduled a meeting with Markus, an old university friend whom people rumoured had connections to the West. They met in a discreet café on the outskirts of the city. The establishment was dimly lit, the air thick with the scent of strong coffee and the murmur of hushed conversations.

"You're taking a significant risk contacting me," Markus cautioned, his gaze steady.

"I have no choice," Hans replied earnestly. "I can't stay here any longer."

Markus leaned in, his voice barely above a whisper. "They tightly control the borders," Markus whispered, his voice barely above a whisper. "Any attempt to leave is perilous—not just for you, but for your family."

Hans swallowed hard. "I understand the risks."

"Do you?" Markus challenged. "You could disappear, like so many others."

Hans sat back, the weight of the truth pressing upon him. "What else can I do?"

"Survive," Markus offered grimly. "Wait for the right moment."

On 30 August 1955, Hans returned to his apartment, the hope that had briefly flickered now extinguished. The fear of endangering his mother and sister paralysed him. The Stasi's reach was vast, their retribution unforgiving.

He sat at his desk, the blank page before him mocking his indecision. Picking up his pen, he wrote to Frieda.

Liebe Schwester,

I received your letters and carry them close to my heart. The days here are long, and the nights longer still…

He hesitated, contemplating how much to reveal. The walls felt as though they had ears, the shadows concealing unseen eyes.

I hope one day we can meet and speak freely, as we once did. Until then, know that I think of you often.

Sealing the letter, he knew there was a chance it would never reach her, intercepted by the ever-watchful authorities.

On 31 August 1955, Hans walked along the Spree River, the water's surface rippling gently under the setting sun. The surrounding city was a mosaic of contradictions—the grandeur of historic buildings juxtaposed against stark socialist architecture.

He paused on a bridge, leaning against the railing. The air was cooler, and a hint of autumn was creeping in. A group of children played nearby, their laughter incongruous with the tension in the atmosphere.

Hans closed his eyes, allowing the sounds to wash over him. He recalled summers spent in Hamburg, the salty breeze of the North Sea, and the warmth of family gatherings before the war had torn their world apart.

The memory of his father's stern yet caring gaze surfaced unbidden. Klaus had been a conflicted man, his ideals clashing with harsh realities. Hans wondered if he was now walking a similar path—trapped between conviction and disillusionment.

As twilight descended, he turned away from the river, the weight of resignation settling upon him. The path ahead was uncertain, but the risks of defiance were too great.

Returning to his apartment, he prepared a simple meal—dark bread, slices of cheese, and a small glass of beer. The routine was comforting in its familiarity, a brief respite from the turmoil within.

He sat by the window, the city lights twinkling faintly against the darkening sky. In the distance, the Fernsehturm towered, a looming sentinel over East Berlin.

Hans lifted his glass in a silent toast. "To hope," he murmured, though the word felt hollow.

As the final day of August 1955 came to a close, Hans accepted that, for now, he would remain where he was. The dream of escape faded into the background, overshadowed by the immediate necessity of survival.

In Hamburg, Frieda sensed the unspoken despair in his letters. She, too, felt the sting of helplessness, her attempts to bridge the divide thwarted by forces beyond her control.

The summer of 1955 revealed harsh truths about their country, their leaders, and themselves. Family bonds strained under the weight of ideology and fear, yet a fragile thread of connection persisted.

Hans gazed out into the night, the distant sounds of the city a melancholic symphony. The future was a vast unknown, but in that moment, he clung to the remnants of his convictions, however fractured they had become.

"Perhaps one day," he whispered into the silence, "things will be different."

But as the shadows deepened, he knew that for now, he was bound to this place—a silent witness to a world that had promised so much yet delivered so little.

ooo

The first day of September 1955 arrived with a crispness in the air that hinted at the approaching autumn. Leaves in shades of amber and crimson fringed the trees lining Hamburg's avenues, their colours mirrored in the reflective waters of the Alster Lake. Frieda Engelhardt stood at her office window, gazing out over the bustling cityscape. The distant sounds of trams clattering and the murmur of voices drifted up to her, a symphony of progress that comforted and stirred her restless mind.

Her office, nestled within the newly renovated town hall, was a testament to West Germany's resurgence. Photographs of reconstruction efforts adorned the walls, and policy documents and correspondence cluttered her desk. Yet, despite the tangible signs of success surrounding her, a lingering sense of incompleteness gnawed at Frieda.

On 5 September 1955, she attended a meeting with local business leaders to discuss initiatives to bolster economic growth. Attendees shuffled agendas and notes, filling the room with the scent of fresh coffee and the rustle of papers.

"Fraulein Engelhardt," began Herr Bauer, a prominent industrialist, "your proposals for infrastructure development are ambitious. Do you believe we have the resources to implement them?"

Frieda met his gaze steadily. "With strategic allocation and international cooperation, I am confident we can achieve these goals. The Marshall Plan has provided us with a foundation—we must build upon it wisely."

Nods of agreement circled the table. As the meeting progressed, Frieda articulated her vision with clarity and passion, her words painting a picture of a Germany that could rise above its past through unity and innovation.

After the meeting, she walked along the harbour, the cool breeze carrying the salty tang of the North Sea. Ships bobbed gently against their moorings, sailors calling out to one another in a chorus of different dialects. Frieda found solace in the harbour's activity; it reminded her of her connection to the wider world.

On 15 September 1955, she received a letter from Greta Schmidt, her old friend and dedicated journalist. The envelope bore stamps from across the country, its edges slightly frayed from handling.

Liebe Frieda,

I have been following your progress with great admiration. Your dedication to our nation's recovery is inspiring. I wonder, though, how you are faring personally amidst all this. Do you find time to reflect on yourself and on your family?

Frieda folded the letter thoughtfully. Greta's words struck a chord, stirring emotions she often kept at bay. The memory of standing at her father's grave resurfaced—the icy wind biting at her cheeks, the rough granite of the headstone beneath her fingertips.

On 20 September 1955, unable to shake the weight of her thoughts, Frieda visited the cemetery once more. As Frieda made her way to the outskirts of Hamburg, she noticed heavy clouds covered the sky, showing that rain was likely. The path between the graves was uneven, overgrown with weeds and wildflowers that swayed in the breeze.

She paused before Klaus Engelhardt's grave, the engraved letters of his name darkened by moisture. Tracing them gently, Frieda felt a chill that had little to do with the weather. The scent of damp earth enveloped her, grounding her in the present even as her mind wandered through memories.

"Vater," she whispered, her voice barely audible above the rustling leaves. "I wish we could have found peace."

The wind picked up, tousling her hair and carrying the distant sounds of the city—a faint siren and the muffled hum of traffic. She pulled her coat tighter around herself, the fabric offering scant protection against the elements.

Standing there, she contemplated the choices that had led her and Hans to such divergent paths. The divide between East and West Germany mirrored the fissures within her own family—a chasm widened by ideology, pride, and unspoken grievances.

On 1 October 1955, back in her office, Frieda threw herself into her work with renewed vigour. The upcoming local elections were fast approaching, and her candidacy for a higher political office was garnering significant attention. Colleagues admired her tenacity and clear vision, often seeking her counsel on complex issues.

"Your leadership has been instrumental in our progress," remarked Stefan Weber during a strategy meeting. "The people see you as a beacon of hope."

Frieda smiled modestly. "I am but one part of a larger movement. It is our collective effort that drives change."

As the days counted down to 15 October 1955, anticipation built throughout Hamburg. Campaign posters bearing Frieda's image appeared on street corners and notice boards, her name spoken with respect in both political circles and among ordinary citizens.

On the evening of the election, the town hall buzzed with energy. Banners and West German flags adorned the grand hall, their vibrant colours shining under the glow of the chandeliers. The scent of polished wood and fresh flowers filled the air.

Frieda stood among her supporters, the murmurs of conversation surrounding her like a warm tide. As the results were announced, the crowd grew silent.

"With an overwhelming majority," the announcer declared, "we are pleased to confirm that *Fraulein Frieda Engelhardt* has won the election for the position of Deputy Mayor."

Applause erupted, a wave of sound that seemed to shake the very foundations of the building. Frieda felt a surge of emotion—pride, gratitude, a flicker of disbelief. Colleagues clapped her on the back, voices congratulating her on all sides.

Stefan raised a glass. "To Frieda! May your leadership continue to guide us towards a brighter future."

"Vielen Dank," she replied, her voice steady despite the whirlwind around her. "I am honoured by your trust and will strive to serve our community with dedication and integrity."

As celebrations continued, Frieda slipped away to a quiet balcony overlooking the city that night. The lights of Hamburg stretched out before her, a tapestry of life and activity. Yet amidst the glow, shadows lingered.

She pulled a folded letter from her pocket—one of many she had written to Hans but never sent. Unfolding it, she read the familiar words:

Lieber Hans,

Today, I have decided to run for Deputy Mayor. It's a significant step, and I wish you could be here to share this moment…

Her handwriting wavered in places where emotion had threatened to overcome her. Folding the letter once more, she exhaled.

On 25 October 1955, Frieda met with Chancellor Konrad Adenauer in Bonn. The Chancellor's office was austere yet dignified, reflecting the man's pragmatic approach.

"Fraulein Engelhardt," he greeted her warmly. "Congratulations on your recent election."

"Thank you, Herr Chancellor," she replied, shaking his offered hand firmly.

They discussed national policies, the ongoing challenges of reunification, and West Germany's role on the international stage. Frieda found herself both impressed by Adenauer's acumen and aware of the complexities that lay ahead.

"Our integration into the Western alliance is crucial," Adenauer emphasised. "But we must also consider the cultural and historical ties that bind us to the East."

"Indeed," Frieda agreed. "Economic prosperity is vital, but so is the healing of divisions within our own families and communities."

Adenauer regarded her thoughtfully. "You speak from personal experience, I gather."

She nodded subtly. "Yes. The separation has touched many of us deeply."

On 30 November 1955, Frieda stood at the podium of a grand hall in Berlin, the site of an international political conference. Delegates from across Europe filled the seats, their faces attentive as she prepared to address them.

The hall was a marvel of architecture—high ceilings adorned with intricate mouldings, chandeliers casting a soft glow over the assembled crowd, and the air hummed with anticipation.

"Ladies and gentlemen," Frieda began, her voice clear and resonant. "We stand at a pivotal moment in history. West Germany has risen from the ashes of war, not through isolation, but through collaboration and a steadfast commitment to democratic principles."

She spoke of the importance of international alliances, the role of NATO in securing peace, and the need for continued cooperation to prevent the mistakes of the past. As she spoke, images of her father and Hans flickered in her mind—reminders of personal stakes intertwined with political responsibilities.

She asserted, "We must measure our prosperity not only in economic terms but also in the strength of our shared values. We must strive to bridge divides, to heal wounds that linger beneath the surface of progress."

Applause filled the hall as she concluded, delegates rising to their feet in acknowledgement of her powerful message. Frieda felt a mixture of satisfaction and an undercurrent of melancholy—a recognition that while she could influence policy and inspire others, there were battles within her own heart that remained unresolved.

After the conference, she mingled with other officials. A French delegate approached her, his expression appreciative.

"Madame Engelhardt, your speech was most inspiring," he remarked. "You are a leader of grand vision."

"Merci beaucoup," she replied graciously. "I believe deeply in the path we are forging together."

As the evening wore on, Frieda found herself on the terrace, gazing out over Berlin. The city's skyline was a juxtaposition of historic edifices and modern constructions, a physical representation of Germany's complex journey.

The chill of the night air nipped at her cheeks, and she wrapped her shawl tighter around her shoulders. Footsteps behind her signalled someone's approach.

"Quite the view, isn't it?" came a familiar voice.

Turning, she saw Greta smiling softly. "Greta! I didn't realise you were here."

"I wouldn't miss it," Greta replied, joining her at the railing. "Your speech was remarkable."

"Thank you," Frieda said, her gaze returning to the city lights. "Though sometimes I wonder if words are enough."

Greta regarded her thoughtfully. "They are a start. But I sense there's more on your mind."

Frieda hesitated before confiding, "Despite everything—the achievements, the progress—I can't shake the feeling of something missing. Hans is still out there, and I do not know how he is or whether he's safe. Whether he resents me."

Greta placed a reassuring hand on her arm. "It's natural to feel that way. It's difficult to mend the divisions we've endured."

"I've tried reaching out," Frieda continued, her voice tinged with frustration. "But it's as if there's an invisible wall between us."

"Perhaps in time, circumstances will change," Greta offered. "Until then, all you can do is continue to lead by example."

On 5 December 1955, back in Hamburg, Frieda received a parcel from an unknown sender. Opening it cautiously, she discovered a book—an old volume of poetry that she and Hans had cherished as children. Inside, a note in Hans's handwriting:

> *Frieda,*
>
> *I came across this and thought you might like to have it. I hope you are well.*
>
> *Hans*

Her heart leapt at the sight of his familiar script. Though the message was brief, it was a connection—a thread spanning the divide. Clutching the book to her chest, she felt a glimmer of hope.

In the weeks that followed, Frieda immersed herself in her new role. She implemented programmes to support education and cultural exchange, believing that understanding and shared experiences could lay the groundwork for reconciliation.

On 20 December 1955, she attended a community event where children performed a *Weihnachtskonzert* (Christmas concert). The sweet strains of carols filled the air, their voices innocent and pure. As Frieda listened, the children's singing reminded her of simpler times and the unifying power of human connections beyond politics and borders. The warmth of the moment stirred something within her, a sense of hope that transcended the years of struggle.

As the year drew to a close, she reflected on all that had transpired. The successes were significant, yet the challenges ahead remained daunting. The inextricable link between her personal and political life influenced her path.

On 30 December 1955, Frieda visited her mother's home. The familiar scent of baking greeted her as she entered, the warmth of the kitchen a comforting embrace.

"Frieda! Just in time," Marta exclaimed, flour dusting her apron. "I'm making *stollen* for the New Year."

"It smells wonderful," Frieda replied, shedding her coat and joining her at the counter.

They worked side by side, kneading dough and reminiscing about past holidays. "I received a note from Hans," Frieda mentioned casually.

Marta paused, hope flickering in her eyes. "You did? How is he?"

"He's… well, I think. He sent me our old poetry book."

"That's a good sign," Marta mused. "Perhaps he's reaching out."

"Perhaps," Frieda agreed softly.

As they sat down to tea, Marta regarded her daughter thoughtfully. "You've accomplished so much, Frieda. Your father would be proud."

"I hope so," Frieda replied, stirring sugar into her cup. "But I can't help feeling that there's still so much to do."

"There always will be," Marta smiled gently. "But you've made a difference, and that's what matters."

On the eve of the new year, Frieda stood once more at her office window. Snowflakes drifted lazily from the sky, dusting the city in a blanket of white. The streets below were quiet, a peaceful hush settling over Hamburg.

She couldn't stop thinking about Hans, her father, and the countless others whose lives were intertwined with the fabric of Germany's history. The road ahead was uncertain, but she was resolved to continue her journey with courage and compassion.

"To new beginnings," she whispered into the silent night.

As the clock struck midnight, church bells tolled in the distance, their chimes echoing through the frosty air. Frieda raised her glass in a solitary toast, her reflection in the window superimposed against the city's lights.

In that moment, she felt a sense of peace—a fragile, tentative feeling, yet real. The past had shaped her, but it did not define her. The future beckoned, and she was ready to embrace it.

ooo

The first breath of December 1955 brought a biting cold that swept through East Berlin, seeping into the city's very bones. Hans Engelhardt pulled his threadbare coat tighter around himself as he navigated the icy cobblestones. The sky hung low and grey, a vast sheet of steel pressing down upon the world. Snowflakes drifted lazily, settling on the rooftops and dulling the harsh edges of the buildings.

Reaching his apartment, a stark block of concrete mirrored countless others; Hans fumbled with the key, his fingers numb from the chill. The door creaked open to reveal a sparsely furnished room—an iron bed, a wooden table scarred with age, and a solitary chair. Faded posters adorned the walls, their once vibrant slogans now ghostly whispers of socialist zeal.

He lit a small stove, the flame sputtering before casting a feeble glow. The warmth was minimal but better than the unforgiving cold outside. Hans sat at the table, the dim light illuminating a crumpled photograph of his family. Klaus and Marta stood side by side, their expressions solemn. Beside them, a younger Frieda smiled tentatively, and Hans himself stared back with a defiant glint in his eyes.

On 5 December 1955, as the wind howled outside, Hans stared at the photograph, visually tracing the outline of his father's face. Memories flooded back—Klaus's stern lectures, the weight of his expectations, the unspoken tension that had always simmered between them.

"Was it all worth it?" Hans muttered to the empty room. The silence was his only reply.

He reached into a drawer and pulled out a letter he had written months ago but never sent. It was addressed to Frieda; the words smudged where the ink had met hesitant tears.

Liebe Schwester,

I wonder if you think of me as I think of you…

He folded the letter once more, sending it seeming more impossible with each passing day. The ever-watchful eyes of the Stasi made any unauthorised communication a perilous endeavour.

On 10 December 1955, the city was blanketed in snow, muffling the sounds of daily life. Hans trudged through the streets to his workplace, a government office where the air was thick with bureaucracy and thinly veiled mistrust. Colleagues exchanged curt nods, their conversations guarded.

That afternoon, a mandatory meeting was called. The staff gathered in a stark conference room, the walls adorned with portraits of Walter Ulbricht and Soviet leaders. The smell of stale coffee mingled with the scent of damp wool coats.

"Comrades," began Herr Vogel, a party official with a sharp gaze. "As we approach the end of the year, it is vital that we reaffirm our commitment to the principles of socialism and the GDR."

Hans listened as Vogel droned on about productivity targets and the threat of Western influence. The words washed over him, hollow and repetitive. He glanced around the room—faces devoid of enthusiasm, eyes dulled by resignation.

On 15 December 1955, the GDR hosted a grand celebration to showcase its supposed achievements. Hans had to attend, the invitation more a command than a courtesy. They held the event in a grand hall, where the opulence starkly contrasted the austerity faced by the populace.

Crystal chandeliers cast a harsh light over the proceedings. Modest offerings—black bread, pickled vegetables, and watery soup—filled the long tables. Music played, a strained attempt at festivity.

Hans stood at the edge of the room, a glass of weak punch in hand. Conversations buzzed around him; voices strained with forced gaiety.

"Isn't it marvellous how far we've come?" a woman nearby exclaimed, her laughter brittle.

"Indeed," her companion replied. "Our production numbers have surpassed all expectations."

Hans resisted the urge to scoff. The façade was thin, and the cracks were clear to anyone. He felt a surge of frustration—a longing for authenticity in a world painted with lies.

Stepping outside for a moment's respite, a gust of frigid wind greeted him. The night air was sharp, the stars obscured by a veil of clouds. He inhaled deeply; the cold burning his lungs, a sensation that reminded him he was still alive.

On 20 December 1955, Hans received a parcel from an old acquaintance, a book of poetry by Rainer Maria Rilke. Tucked between the pages was a note: "May these words bring you solace in these times." There was no signature, but he recognised the handwriting—Ilse, a woman he had known before the war.

He spent the evening immersed in the verses, the elegant lines stirring emotions he had long suppressed. The words spoke of longing, beauty amidst despair, and the eternal struggle between hope and resignation.

"Perhaps there is still something worth holding onto," he mused aloud.

On 24 December 1955, Christmas Eve, the weight of oppression subdued the usual hum of activity, dampening the festive spirit. Hans ventured to the local market, hoping for a token gesture to mark the occasion.

The stalls offered meagre selections—wilted vegetables, stale bread, and a few tarnished ornaments. He purchased a small wooden carving of a bird; its wings outstretched as if yearning to fly. It was simple, yet it resonated with him.

Returning home, he placed the carving on the windowsill. Streetlamps illuminated pools of light onto the snow while darkness cloaked the world outside.

"Frohe Weihnachten," he whispered to no one in particular.

On 25 December 1955, Hans awoke to a muted world. The snowfall had intensified overnight, muffling sounds and creating a pristine landscape untouched by footsteps. He prepared a modest breakfast—black bread and a thin slice of cheese—savouring each bite.

He thought of Frieda, imagining her in Hamburg amidst warmth and celebration. Perhaps laughter filled the air as friends surrounded her. The divide between them felt insurmountable. A chasm widened with time and circumstance.

As the day wore on, he allowed himself a rare indulgence—writing. Pulling out a notebook, he penned his thoughts, the words flowing more freely than they had in years.

"The silence here is profound," he wrote. "Not just in sound, but in spirit. People surround me, yet I have never felt more alone."

He paused, tapping the pen against the paper. "Is this what *Vater* felt? A loneliness borne not of solitude but of disconnect?"

The hours slipped by unnoticed. When he finally set the pen down, a soft glow of candlelight illuminated the room. He read over his words, a mirror reflecting the depths of his soul.

On 28 December 1955, a rare piece of mail arrived—a letter bearing his sister's familiar script.

> *Lieber Hans,*
>
> *I hope this letter finds you well. I received the book you sent— it brought back many cherished memories. So much has changed since we last spoke, yet I hope we can one day bridge the distance between us…*

Hans's hands trembled as he read. Frieda's words were filled with warmth, and a longing which mirrored his own. She spoke of her work, her efforts to rebuild and heal, and subtly extended an invitation for reconnection.

He considered responding, and he had the urge to reach out strongly. But fear coiled within him—the ever-present threat of surveillance loomed large. Any unauthorised communication with the West was fraught with danger.

On 31 December 1955, New Year's Eve, Hans stood by his window, watching as the city prepared to usher in another year. Fireworks were scarce, but occasional bursts of light punctuated the night sky. The regime's tight grip muted the celebrations, constraining them.

He held Frieda's letter, his thumb rubbing gently over the ink. "What would happen if I replied?" he pondered. The risk was significant—not just for himself but potentially for her as well.

The clock on the wall ticked steadily, each second a reminder of time slipping away. Midnight approached, and with it, a swell of emotions he could no longer contain.

"To hell with it," he muttered, grabbing a pen and paper.

Liebe Frieda,

Your letter was a balm to my weary soul. I cannot express how much it means to know you think of me...

He wrote quickly, pouring his heart onto the page. He spoke of his doubts, his regrets, and the suffocating atmosphere of the GDR. Yet, he was careful—vague enough to avoid incrimination yet honest enough to convey his true feelings.

As he signed his name, a sudden knock at the door startled him. His heart raced, fear gripping him. He hid the letter beneath a stack of papers before opening the door a crack.

"Comrade Engelhardt," a stern voice greeted him. It was Herr Vogel, his superior. "May I come in?"

"Of course," Hans replied, stepping aside.

Vogel entered, his eyes scanning the room with calculated interest. "I noticed you left the gathering early tonight."

"I wasn't feeling well," Hans lied smoothly.

Vogel nodded slowly. "These are important times, Engelhardt. Unity and participation are essential."

"Understood," Hans affirmed, his expression neutral.

"See that you remember that." Vogel's gaze lingered a moment longer before he turned to leave. "Happy New Year."

"Happy New Year," Hans echoed, closing the door firmly behind him.

His hands shook as he retrieved the letter. The encounter had shattered his resolve. Sending the letter now seemed an impossible risk. He crumpled it in frustration, tossing it into the stove, where it caught fire and burned swiftly.

Outside, the distant sound of church bells heralded the start of the new year. Hans sank into the chair, the weight of isolation pressing heavily upon him.

"Another year," he murmured. "Will anything change?"

He gazed at the wooden bird on the windowsill, its wings poised for flight. A symbol of freedom tantalisingly out of reach. The room grew colder as the fire died down, the shadows lengthening.

On 1 January 1956, dawn broke with a pale light filtering through the frosted glass. Hans remained seated, eyes red from lack of sleep. The new day brought little comfort.

He rose mechanically, preparing for another day indistinguishable from the last. As he stepped outside, the icy air stung his cheeks. The streets were empty, a few souls trudging along with heads bowed.

Passing a newspaper stand, he glanced at the headlines—boasting of the GDR's successes, denouncing the West's decadence. It all felt hollow, a charade he could no longer partake in.

At work, the atmosphere was subdued. Colleagues offered obligatory greetings, their eyes avoiding direct contact. Hans buried himself in mundane tasks, each one a minor distraction from the emptiness he felt.

During his lunch break, he ventured to a nearby park. The trees stood bare, their branches reaching towards the sky like skeletal fingers. He sat on a bench, the cold seeping through his coat.

An elderly man approached, his face weathered but kind. "May I sit?" he asked.

"Please," Hans gestured.

They sat in silence for a while before the man spoke. "Strange times we live in."

Uncertain of where the conversation was headed, Hans nodded.

"I remember when this city was full of life," the man continued. "Before the walls—both seen and unseen—divided us."

Hans glanced at him cautiously. "You speak boldly."

The man chuckled softly. "At my age, what have I to lose? During the quiet moments, we can share truths."

Hans felt a flicker of connection. "Do you ever think it will change?"

"Perhaps. Perhaps not in my lifetime, but one must hold on to hope."

"Hope…" Hans repeated, the word foreign on his tongue.

The man stood, his movements slow. "Take care, young man. And remember, even in the darkest winters, spring eventually comes."

As the man walked away, Hans contemplated his words. Was it naïve to hope for change? To believe that the frost enveloping his world could thaw?

Returning home that evening, he stared once more at the wooden bird. He impulsively picked it up and slipped it into his pocket.

"Maybe," he thought, "it's time to fly."

He planned a plan—a tentative, risky notion of escape. The very thought quickened his pulse, fear and exhilaration intertwining.

But as he weighed the possibilities, the reality of the dangers loomed large. The Stasi's reach was extensive, and failure could mean imprisonment or worse.

He exhaled, the momentary spark dimming. "Not yet," he conceded. "But perhaps someday."

On 31 January 1956, as the month drew to a close, Hans resolved to keep the ember of hope alive, no matter how faint. He tucked a letter to Frieda into a hidden compartment beneath the floorboards—a silent promise to himself that he would not let go entirely.

The winter remained harsh, the world around him unforgiving. Yet, somewhere deep within, a seed of resilience took root.

"Für die Zukunft," he whispered into the night, for the future.

The wind howled outside, but Hans did not feel so alone this time.

ooo

The chill of February 1956 settled over Hamburg like a heavy blanket, each day colder than the last. On 12 February, Frieda Engelhardt made her way along the narrow path that led to the cemetery on the outskirts of the city. The sky was a canvas of muted greys, clouds hanging low as if weighed down by the collective sorrows of those beneath them.

She clutched a small bouquet of winter heather, its purple blossoms a stark contrast against the monochrome landscape. The wind whispered through the bare branches of the oaks lining the path, carrying with it the faint scent of the nearby Elbe River and the distant hum of city life—a reminder of the world continuing beyond this place of stillness.

As she entered the cemetery gates, wrought iron and rusted with age, Frieda felt a familiar ache settle in her chest. The overgrown gravestones stood like silent sentinels, their inscriptions weathered and worn. Weeds tangled around their bases, and patches of moss clung stubbornly to the cold stone.

She navigated the uneven ground; her footsteps muffled by a thin layer of snow that had fallen the night before. Reaching her father's grave, she paused, taking in the sight of the simple headstone etched with the name "Klaus Engelhardt" and the dates of his life. Kneeling, she brushed away the snow that had gathered, her gloved fingers tracing the carved letters with a tenderness that belied the tumult of emotions within her.

"*Vater,*" she whispered, her breath forming delicate clouds in the frigid air. "Another year has started, and still so much remains unresolved."

The wind picked up, tugging at the strands of her auburn hair that escaped beneath her woollen hat. She pulled her coat tighter, the fabric doing little to ward off the penetrating cold. The heather in her hands trembled slightly as she laid it gently at the base of the headstone.

"I wish you could have found your peace," she continued, her voice barely audible over the rustle of leaves. "I wish Hans could be here."

Her thoughts drifted to her brother, the physical and ideological distance between them. She wondered where he was on this cold December day, whether he felt the same emptiness that gnawed at her. The letters she had sent remained unanswered, each a message in a bottle cast into a sea of silence.

Frieda returned to her modest flat in the heart of Hamburg. The city sparkled with the prosperity of reconstruction. Children laughed; their voices were bright against the backdrop of a city reborn from the ruins of war.

Inside her home, however, the atmosphere was subdued. Marta had joined her for the evening, and together, they prepared a simple meal—roast goose, red cabbage, and potato dumplings, a traditional meal that harkened back to happier times.

"Frieda, pass me the gravy boat, please," Marta requested, her hands deftly arranging the table settings.

"Of course, Mutter," Frieda replied, retrieving the porcelain vessel painted with delicate blue flowers.

They sat opposite each other, and the clink of cutlery was the only sound for a few moments. Marta glanced up, her eyes reflecting the warm glow of the candles.

"It's a lovely meal," she offered. "You did well."

"Thank you," Frieda smiled faintly. "It's nice to have a bit of tradition."

They ate in companionable silence before Marta broached the unspoken subject between them.

"Have you heard anything from Hans?"

Frieda shook her head, her gaze dropping to her plate. "No. I sent him a letter at the beginning of the month, but there's been no reply."

Marta sighed softly. "I worry about him. The news from the East is… troubling."

"I know," Frieda agreed. "The reports of increased surveillance, the restrictions—it's as if they're trying to snuff out any remaining spirit."

"Do you think he'll ever come back?" Marta's voice wavered slightly.

"I hope so," Frieda replied, her tone firm despite her doubts. "We believe that for his sake and ours."

A couple of days later, Frieda visited Greta Schmidt at her apartment overlooking Alster Lake. The two friends sat by the window, cups of steaming tea in their hands, as they watched swans glide gracefully across the icy waters.

"Your speech last month was exceptional," Greta remarked, referring to Frieda's keynote address in Berlin. "It's been the talk of the political circles."

"Thank you," Frieda said modestly. "I only hope it can make some difference."

"You're too humble," Greta chided gently. "Your voice carries weight, Frieda. People listen to you."

Frieda gazed at the lake, her reflection merging with the frosted panes. "Sometimes I wonder if it's enough. The divisions seem deeper than ever and with *Vater* gone…"

Greta reached out, placing a reassuring hand on Frieda's arm. "You're carrying a heavy burden. It's natural to feel overwhelmed."

"It's more than that," Frieda confessed. "I feel… adrift. The more progress we make here, the more I feel the absence of my family—of Hans."

Greta nodded empathetically. "Perhaps the new year will bring new opportunities. Change is possible, even when it seems unlikely."

On February 28, 1956, Frieda again found herself at the cemetery. She sought solace among the quiet stones while the city, alive with anticipation, had fireworks ready to burst into the night sky.

As dusk settled, the sky turned into a tapestry of deep blues and greys as stars began to pierce through. The air was crisp, each breath sharp in her lungs. She stood before her father's grave, the silence enveloping her like a shroud.

Personal grief overshadowed the sense of accomplishment as she thought of the policies she had helped implement and the lives improved.

The weight of her father's unresolved legacy pressed upon her, the guilt and bitterness that had tainted their final years together.

A sudden gust of wind whipped around her, carrying the faint strains of music from the city—a waltz played in a distant ballroom, laughter echoing through the streets. The world moved on, but here, time seemed suspended.

She knelt, the cold seeping through her trousers, and laid a hand on the headstone. "I miss you, *Vater*," she admitted softly. "Despite everything."

Memories flooded her—the stern lectures, the rare moments of tenderness, the unspoken expectations. She recalled the last conversation they had before his health declined, a tense exchange about her political aspirations.

"You should focus on building a family, not chasing political dreams," he had insisted.

"And what about rebuilding our nation?" she had countered. "Should we not strive to create a better future?"

He had looked away then, the lines on his face deepening. "Policies and speeches can not heal some wounds."

Now, as she traced the rough edges of his name, she wondered if he had found peace in his final moments. Had he forgiven himself? Had he understood her choices?

On the same night, back in East Berlin, Hans sat by his window, the wooden bird still perched on the sill. The city was subdued.

He thought of Frieda, imagining her amidst the prosperity of the West, surrounded by friends and colleagues. A pang of longing pierced him—a desire not just for family but for freedom.

Reaching into his pocket, he pulled out a small piece of paper—a fragment torn from a larger sheet. On it, he had scribbled a single line: *"Ist as möglich, neu anzufangen?"* (Is it possible to start anew?)"

He sighed, folding the paper and tucking it away. More than physical walls, the barriers between them existed.

As midnight approached, church bells rang out across both cities, their tones overlapping in a dissonant harmony. In Hamburg, Frieda walked slowly back towards the city centre, the streets illuminated by lanterns.

She paused on a bridge overlooking the river, the water reflecting the city's kaleidoscope of lights. Leaning on the railing, she allowed herself a moment of vulnerability, tears welling in her eyes.

"Where do we go from here?" she wondered aloud.

A passerby glanced her way, offering a polite nod before continuing. She straightened, composing herself, and resumed her walk. Duty called—there were meetings to prepare for and initiatives to launch. Yet the emptiness lingered, a shadow that trailed her every step.

Hans extinguished the candle that had burned low in the East, plunging his room into darkness. The sounds of the city faded, leaving only the persistent ticking of a clock. Time moved forward, indifferent to his plight.

He lay down, staring at the ceiling, thoughts of escape intertwining with memories of childhood—running through fields with Frieda, their laughter unburdened by the complexities of adulthood.

"Perhaps one day," he whispered into the void.

On 1 March 1956, dawn broke with a pale light that filtered through the clouds. Frieda stood at her office window, the city slowly stirring to life below. She sipped her coffee, the bitterness grounding her.

A knock at the door drew her attention. "Come in," she called.

Stefan Weber entered, his usual jovial demeanour tempered by the early hour. "*Guten Morgen,* Frieda. I didn't expect to find you here today."

"I could say the same for you," she replied with a hint of a smile.

He shrugged. "Couldn't sleep. Thought I'd get a head start on the day."

She nodded appreciatively. "Dedication suits you."

"Likewise," he returned.

As he left, she turned back to the window. The streets were bustling, trams clattering along their tracks, vendors setting up stalls. Life persisted, undeterred by individual sorrows.

She resolved then to channel her grief into purpose. If she could not mend the fractures within her own family, she could help heal the wounds of her nation. It was a lofty goal but one she felt compelled to pursue.

In East Berlin, Hans ventured out into the crisp morning air. The city was subdued, yet the routine of daily life unfolded—workers heading to factories, children bundled against the cold making their way to school.

He passed a newsstand; the headlines proclaiming the GDR's latest achievements. He barely glanced at them, his mind occupied with thoughts of change. The encounter with the old man in the park lingered with him—a reminder that hope, however faint, still existed.

Approaching a bridge over the Spree River, he paused, leaning on the railing much as Frieda had done hours before in Hamburg. The water flowed steadily beneath him, constantly amidst the turbulence of human affairs.

"Für die Zukunft," he repeated to himself, for the future.

As the sun rose higher, casting a golden hue over the cityscape, both siblings stood on opposite sides of a divided Germany, connected by blood yet separated by tangible and unseen walls.

The year ahead was uncertain, fraught with challenges and the lingering shadows of the past. But at that moment, there was a shared, unspoken yearning—a desire for reconciliation, for a bridge to span the chasm that had torn their family apart.

The bells of a nearby church chimed, their notes carrying through the cold air. In unison, Frieda and Hans turned away from the water and stepped back into their respective worlds, each determined to face whatever lay ahead with resilience and a glimmer of hope.